# MORE PRAISE
# FOR
# SUSANNAH LEIGH

*THE SILVER SWAN:*
"Ms. Leigh has created an absorbing adventure that is rife with jealousy, secrets and deceit . . . that holds the reader's attention to the very last page."

—*Romantic Times*

*CHEYENNE STAR:*
"Well-written, with authentically detailed Indian lore . . . High drama, deep emotions and a love that would not be denied are woven throughout the fabric of this story."

—*Affaire de Coeur*

*THE TURQUOISE TRAIL:*
"A powerful story . . . smoldering with sensuality."

—*Romantic Times*

# DAWN OF FIRE

by
## Susannah Leigh

AN ONYX BOOK

ONYX
Published by the Penguin Group
Penguin Books USA Inc., 375 Hudson Street,
New York, New York 10014, U.S.A.
Penguin Books Ltd, 27 Wrights Lane,
London W8 5TZ, England
Penguin Books Australia Ltd, Ringwood,
Victoria, Australia
Penguin Books Canada Ltd, 10 Alcorn Avenue,
Toronto, Ontario, Canada M4V 3B2
Penguin Books (N.Z.) Ltd, 182-190 Wairau Road,
Auckland 10, New Zealand

Penguin Books Ltd, Registered Offices:
Harmondsworth, Middlesex, England

First published by Onyx, an imprint of New American Library,
a division of Penguin Books USA Inc.

First Printing, June, 1992
10  9  8  7  6  5  4  3  2  1

# Into the Dawn . . .
## August 1840

# 1

HE REALIZED SUDDENLY that he was going to die.

The August sun beat down, hot on the bare, glistening arms of green-clad soldiers as they worked their way methodically up the hill, poking into tropical shrubbery and clumps of elephant grass with long bamboo rods. The man peered out from behind the glossy leaves, barely daring to breathe, though the searchers were still a quarter of a mile away.

He had always known, of course, that one day it would come to this. Man was born to die: it was in the nature of things. And he had known, with the life he had chosen, that death might—probably *would*—come sooner rather than later.

But he had not known how it would feel. How it would taste, rising with the bile, bitter and salty in his mouth, and shame mingled with fury that it should be so. That there should be fear at this moment when he should have felt only strength and exultation in the righteousness of his cause.

I am not worthy, he thought. He had been called, and he had answered . . . but, O Lord, he would *never* be worthy.

A new figure appeared on the road that capped a nearby hill, forming the third point of a triangle with the watcher in his nest of foliage and the black-haired, yellow-skinned soldiers. He was garbed as a peasant, long sleeveless tunic bunched over baggy pants that might once have been white, and the rough pushcart against which he paused to lean was laden with farm tools and sacking. But there was nothing of the peasant in his face or bearing. Jet-black hair blew in a gentle breeze back from a brow that was as tawny as the soldiers', but smoother, more aristocratic, and nostrils flared like a thoroughbred horse as he stared down with arrogance and disdain.

They will see, the man in the shrubbery thought helplessly. The breeze did not reach him, and sweat oozed out of every pore, plastering the long gown against his legs and streaming from red-gold hair into his eyes. They will see that you are not a peasant . . . and they will guess. And then you will die too.

A surge of anger ran through him at the chances the other man was taking. It was pointless. Stupid. Against all their plans and contingencies. And yet . . .

The man was aware that his anger was not untinged with envy. At least the other, if he was facing death, was facing it with honor. And courage.

The soldiers had spotted the newcomer, and they began calling to each other in the strange twittering noises that still sounded like a flock of birds, though the man had been in southeast Asia for several months now. He had spent years in his native Paris, studying and preparing, but he had no ear for music; tonal languages came hard, and he could make out only bits and pieces.

*Is this it?* He hated himself for the way his heart seemed to stop and his stomach tensed. Had it come? Was this the day—at last?

But miraculously the soldiers did not appear alarmed. Sweat poured from them too, forming large dark spots on their chests and backs and under their arms. The man noticed for the first time that they looked exhausted as they leaned on their bamboo poles and gaped up at the peasant and his pushcart. One of them, obviously the leader, called out, asking what he was doing.

Moving some belongings, he seemed to call back, though the answer was not clear from that distance. Something about a sharp-tongued wife and going to live with his brother, a bachelor with the good sense not to mess with women—except, of course, for certain elemental functions. The tone was ribald and filthy, and the soldiers laughed as they moved closer, leaving several yards of shrubbery unsearched.

"And what are *you* doing?" the peasant asked, his voice noticeably coarse. His manner was totally different now, gruff and servile at the same time, a kind of bold cringing that was an even better disguise than the rags he wore, and the man could not help admiring his acting. "Are you beating the bushes to find a little animal for lunch? Or are you searching for some crazed assassin who dares threaten the supreme safety of the Son of Heaven?"

The officer seemed to enjoy the joke. "Nothing so exalted," he said as he strolled up the slope. A pair of mangy dogs that had been lolling in the dust sat up, their ears laid back, but the peasant muttered something under his breath and they slunk beneath the wagon. "The emperor has his own guards for that. We are merely looking for a lump of turtle dung. Worthless less-than-dogmeat. A French priest. There are rumors that one has been spotted nearby."

"A French priest? *Here?*" The peasant's face was a study of incredulity and scorn. "You have been listening to the gossip of women and old men. The blackrobes were driven out years ago. Our wise and illustrious emperor, Minh Mang, saw to that before his death. There are no French priests here."

"Maybe not." The other man shrugged. "But orders are orders. It is true we drove the contemptible dung-eating blackrobes out. We sent them home with their fingers chopped off as a warning. But the French are stupid. New ones have started coming back. Well, they won't get off so easily this time. The next one we catch will be taken to Hué in chains . . . and strangled!"

There was passion in those strange tonal phrases. The man in the deep green shadows felt the hair bristle on the back of his neck. But the peasant only grunted.

"Strangling's too good for the likes of that. Strangling is an honorable way to die." He pulled a jug of what appeared to be strong rice wine out of the cart, and popping the crude cork, put it to his lips and took a swig. "Bah!" he said, spitting the bitter aftertaste on the ground. "You *have* been listening to the old ones. The French are stupid, yes . . . but they are cowards! There are no French priests here. You have nothing to fear from the French. Native priests, now . . ."

He swung around slowly, hoisting the jug to his mouth again. Just for a second his eyes met the eyes of the man cowering in the shrubbery, and he seemed to be laughing.

Then he was turning back to the soldier, amiably holding out the jug. "Native priests are another matter. Or had you forgotten about them? They say those first long-skirts—what were they called? . . . the Jesuits—were so afraid to risk their necks they decided to train local men instead. The fathers who followed, the ones of the *missions étrangères*, especially that bishop—Pigneau de Béhaine—made many new priests in their seminary on Phu Quoc island. Priests of this land. And *we* are not cowards."

Too much, the man in the shadows thought. He was saying too much. Things a peasant wouldn't know. As if deliberately challenging the soldier, daring him . . . But then, of course, he was.

"What's that you say?" The officer gave a sharp look, then relaxed as he saw the jug coming toward him. "Us? Cowards? Not likely. Not like those whore-sniffing dog-meat French!" A thin stream of liquid ran down his chin, onto the front of his tunic, as he took a greedy gulp. Wiping his mouth on his forearm, he handed it reluctantly back. "What's all this nonsense you're spouting? I don't know about such things. Native priests? And *what* kind of fathers? I think it's you who've been listening to foolish gossip."

"Gossip, yes . . . but foolish?" He grinned slyly as he pushed the jug away, gesturing for the officer to take another drink. "Fathers of the *missions étrangères*—the foreign missions—that is what they are called. It is said that many young men went to them in their place on Phu Quoc island. . . . It is said that there are many priests among us, even now. Priests who look just like you . . . and me."

"You?" The man sputtered with laughter as he helped himself to another swig. The heat seemed to be getting to him, or maybe it was the alcohol, for he was reeling slightly. "Or *me?* That's a good one. Me a priest! No, take it from me, friend, there are no native priests among us."

"Probably not," the peasant agreed, taking the jug this time and holding it for a moment balanced in both hands. "Probably not . . . but isn't it an interesting idea?"

Interesting, indeed. The man in the shrubbery could

feel every muscle tighten as he squinted out at them. He was perspiring profusely now—if they came closer, surely they would smell him. What would he say, this soldier with the barrel body and blunt features, if he knew that the French dogmeat he was hunting was cringing not fifty yards away?

And that the peasant facing him in coarse black tunic and cropped-off trousers was a native priest himself!

# 2

"HE CAN'T BE DEAD. I won't *let* him be dead!" Green eyes snapped with spirit as Dominie d'Arielle spun around to face the man who was seated behind her in a secluded corner of the garden. "I'd die myself if anything happened to him! You're lying. I know you are!"

"I don't lie, my dear." The Bishop of Paris sighed as he readjusted his plump form on the uncomfortable stone bench. He had known this was going to be unpleasant—he had dreaded it all morning—but she was making it even more difficult than it had to be. "At least not when it serves no purpose. And you are not going to die, Dominique, just because you have lost your brother. Your life is only beginning. In a few months you will be married and—"

"Don't call me that! I hate it. *Dominique!*" She fairly spat the word out of her mouth. "It's the name my parents picked for the son they expected. They were very disappointed when I turned out to be a girl. Denis always calls me Dominie."

"Dominique is a perfectly suitable name for a girl as well," the bishop replied patiently. "Of course your parents wanted a boy. They had just lost your brother Hugo—their elder son. With Denis set for the priesthood, it was only natural they should long for another heir. It doesn't mean they cared any the less for you. And you are changing the subject, my child. You think if you don't talk about this terrible thing, somehow you can make it go away."

"And if this 'terrible thing' hasn't actually happened?" Dominie challenged.

The bishop sighed again. "It has," he said firmly. The sun was hot, but the breeze was cool and the sweet perfume of roses wafted temptingly over the garden. Even in August, Paris had its lovely days, and this should have been one of them, but somehow he had lost his taste for the beauty of nature. "The report from the Orient was very explicit. A priest was captured and publicly executed. Of course there might have been some Portuguese Jesuits in the area—perhaps a Lazarist or two—but they are wily fellows, with years of experience eluding the soldiers. I think you must face it, Dominique. The priest who died was almost certainly Denis."

"No!" There was still spirit in the girl's eyes as she came and knelt in front of him, but there were tears too, and the old bishop felt a stab of pity.

"I am sorry. Truly sorry." Blast those Jesuits anyway, and that arrogant assistant who had been appointed to oversee affairs in France! Why couldn't they do their own dirty work instead of leaving it to him because he was an old friend and had known the child since birth? "I wish I did not have to say these things—"

"No, it was *not* Denis! You think I am clutching at straws in the wind, Monsignor, but I am not. You know how close we are. Ever since our parents died—I was barely five years old—Denis had been everything to me. I feel what he feels. That time he broke his leg when the horse threw him . . . wasn't I waiting at the door when they brought him in the carriage? I knew even without being told that something had happened. If anything had happened now, I would feel it—*here*." She laid a melodramatic hand on the shimmering bluish-red silk that covered a firmly rounded young bosom. "And I don't. He is alive. I'm sure of that."

"You *are* close," the bishop conceded reluctantly. "God knows, I've worried about it often enough. A man should not have to be both brother and father to a child. The bond is too strong. . . . Perhaps you are right. Perhaps you *would* know if Denis were truly gone. I have heard of stranger things. But even if it has not yet occurred, it will come. Tomorrow or next week . . . or next month. Your brother has chosen a martyr's lot. He knew when he left that the situation in Cochinchine was extremely volatile. I'm sure you don't realize—"

"Oh, I realize more than you think." Dominie rose abruptly, her voice a littler sharper than she had intended. She had been telling the truth when she had said that she was confident her brother was alive. Every instinct in her heart told her that. But she was nowhere near as confident about the future, and she spoke quickly to cover her fears. "I'm very well educated. Denis doesn't believe that baby sisters are silly creatures to be taught music and social graces—and nothing beyond. He thinks a woman's mind needs cultivating every bit as much as a man's."

"I am very well aware of that," the bishop replied dryly. "It is a point on which we never agreed. Though he didn't express it quite that way. He said your mind was much too quick to be satisfied with childish pastimes. If you weren't kept occupied, you'd get into trouble. And on that, no doubt, he *was* right. Though how he managed to find a convent where they would instruct you in Latin and Greek, I have no idea."

Dominie laughed in spite of herself. The fact that her own dear, indulgent Sister Jean-Luc, who had nursed her since she was a baby, had spoken to the surprisingly liberal mother superior might have had something to do with it.

"Actually, I taught them almost as much as they taught me. Denis tutored me himself until I was twelve. I was thoroughly grounded in the classics by the time I went to the convent." She did not add that she had hated Latin and Greek, and especially philosophy, and had memorized countless long pages only to please her much-adored older brother. "I also learned about the land that you call Cochinchine—and I speak the language tolerably well. Poor Denis. It's a tonal language, you know, and he is tone deaf. He used to practice with me on vacations."

"Did he?" The silent sarcasm in his tone was lost on her.

"Yes . . . and incidentally, you have the name wrong. That's what the Portuguese called it. Cochin China. From the Malay word *Kuchi*, Denis thinks. The people who live there refer to it as Nam-Viet, or Vietnam. It has been an independent country for a long time—the Chinese were driven out nine hundred years ago—but it was just recently unified. For nearly three centuries the power was divided between the Trinh family in Tongking—the

North—and the Nguyens in Annam, which is how we know the South.''

''Indeed? It seems you *are* quite knowledgeable.'' In fact, the bishop was uncomfortably aware that she was considerably more knowledgeable than he. And she knew it, the minx!

''It is owing to the French,'' Dominie went on, ''or more exactly to a French priest, Pigneau de Béhaine, that the country is one now. He added the 'de Béhaine'—did you know that? I think he must have been a snob. Denis dropped the 'de' from his name. He is just Arielle now. . . . Anyway, this Pigneau was a friend of the southern Nguyens. He brought the little crown prince, Canh, all the way to France—they say he created quite a sensation at court. Songs were made up about him, and Marie-Antoinette's own hairdresser created a fashionable *chignon à la cochinchinoise.* But I suppose you recall all this.''

''I am not quite as old as that.'' The bishop could not resist a small chuckle. ''We have been through a revolution since then, the empire of Napoleon, the restoration of the monarchy, and renewed agitation for a new republic. I do admit to being alive at the time, but I was too young to be aware of what was going on at court.''

''Well, at any rate, it didn't do him any good. The boy prince, I mean. He was wildly *à la mode,* and King Louis promised support, but at the last minute he backed down. It was Pigneau himself who raised the army that helped the emperor, Gia Long, reunify the country under the banner of the South.''

Her voice rang with excitement, and the old bishop realized that this exotic, faraway land was very real to her. ''That was a long time ago, *petite fille,*'' he reminded her gently.

''I know that, and I am not a little girl! Gia Long felt no loyalty to the French—nor should he have, Denis says—but he owed a debt to Pigneau, so he allowed him to bring the true faith to the people. Denis says the next emperor, Minh Mang, turned treacherous and persecuted the priests because he was afraid of their influence, and the new emperor, Thieu Tri, looks to be no better. But many of the people are Christians now. Denis says we cannot abandon them just because we are afraid.''

Denis says. Denis says. Every other word out of her mouth was her brother's name. It broke the bishop's heart to look at her, she was trying so hard to bolster her courage.

It struck him at that moment how like her mother she was. Denise's aristocratic features, dominated by luminous green eyes, innocence and sensuality mingling in a way he had seen in no other woman. Denise's mouth, full and slightly curving, even in repose hinting at secrets that could only be whispered in a man's ear. Denise's body, too, not quite so full-breasted perhaps, but taller, more in proportion, and excruciatingly eye-catching, reminding him uneasily of temptations he thought had been left long in the past.

God help her if she had Denise's weaknesses as well.

"Do you remember your parents at all, Dominique?" he asked impulsively.

The question caught her off-guard. "A little. My mother was very sad. I remember her lying on a couch, in the east salon, I think. The draperies were drawn, and she had a rosary in her hand. I had to be very still and not jump or shout when they brought me in to see her. My father was big and loud. I don't think he liked me. I was afraid of him."

"Of course he liked you," the bishop said, guiltily conscious that this time he *was* lying. "He just didn't know how to behave with little girls. Your parents didn't have an easy life. At least your mother didn't," he amended, not wishing to compound the sin. "After Hugo died, they were never the same. They doted on him. They shouldn't have, of course—it's not fair, playing favorites—but they did, and they never recovered from his death. Perhaps it's just as well that they died themselves a few years later—together."

"I do remember that. Everything else is fuzzy, but I remember exactly how it was when they died. The servants kept whispering all the time, and people were there . . . and whenever I came near they'd stop talking. I didn't find out until years later that the horses had run away and the carriage been dragged over a cliff. I only knew that something dreadful had happened. . . . Then Denis was running up the drive, and suddenly I wasn't afraid anymore and everything was all right. He had been in the seminary for four years—he had said his simple vows and was already a scholastic—but he came back to take care of me. He had always wanted to be a priest. *Always*. It was very important to him.''

"Yes, yes, I know," the bishop said. "Other boys dream of sailing the high seas, or fighting duels for the honor of a lovely lady. But Denis always dreamed of being a priest. And a Jesuit at that." The ruby on his hand, the symbol of his authority, flashed in the sunlight as he reached out to smooth the folds of his long black skirt. "A most unsuitable choice, of course. The Jesuits are a proud order, set apart from the others, answerable only to Rome, and not always then. They wear the plainest robes and somehow manage to look more arrogant than the wealthiest nobleman in all his finery.''

Dominie half-smiled, thinking that he had described one or two of her brother's colleagues superbly. "You think Denis has no reason to be proud?''

"Reason has nothing to do with it. Denis is a simple man. Naturally humble. There is not a hint of pride in his bearing. Ah, well, they have always had a kind of glamour. . . . The Society of Jesus. Even the name has a certain ring. All those years when they were suppressed, except for the Russians, of course, who somehow managed to continue. Your mother's own confessor— the father who was with her when she died—had to go all the way to Pothotsk to take his vows, a fact about which he talked incessantly. I suppose that's where Denis got the idea.''

"But he gave it up. For seven *years,* Monsignor! For me. He continued studying, of course, and dreaming his dreams, but I was a little girl and I needed someone. Here.'' She swept out her arm, taking in the vast estate, the exquisitely manicured gardens, the reflecting ponds, the carriage house, the *bois* looming green and cool in the distance. "He gave up seven years of his hopes—and the longings of his heart—to take care of me. That's why I can't let anything happen to him!''

The bishop studied her sadly for a moment. "That is not for you to decide, my child. It is for God . . . and I fear the decision has already been made.''

"No! I will not let him die. I love him too much. Not

God, not the Vietnamese emperor—not *anyone*—is going to take him from me!''

"Don't blaspheme!" he said sharply. "The will of the Almighty is not to be questioned—or denied." Then, somewhat more kindly, he added: "I understand you are hurt, Dominique. And frightened. I see the fear behind that very touching bravado. But you must learn to bend with the wind or you will break. If God has chosen to take your brother from you—and if he has not, then he soon will—you must find the strength to accept."

"You have all the answers," Dominie's chin went up, her eyes boldly challenging. "What do you do, have a private chat with God each morning? How do you *know* it is his will that I stand back and let my brother be lost?"

"I have very few answers," the bishop replied, not rising to the bait. "The older I get, the less it seems I know. I am feeling my age. . . . But be reasonable, *petite*. Your brother is in this place you call Vietnam, many thousands of miles away. Even if you wanted to help him—even if God wanted you to help—there is nothing you could do from here."

Green eyes flashed defiance, but she did not speak. He sensed that the validity of his words had touched even her youthful exuberance. Turning away, she walked to the edge of the sheltered rose garden and stared out at the more formal symmetry of the paths and shrubs and fountains beyond.

How young she is, the bishop thought sadly. People went on and on about the delights of youth. Those wonderful, carefree years. It had always been his experience that youth was a time of vulnerability and the most excruciating pain.

He noticed again the resemblance to her mother, but this time it was elusive. There *was* much of Denise in her, but there was much of Hubert, the father, too, a man whom the bishop had not liked, but had sometimes grudgingly admired. Apart from those exceptional eyes, her coloring was almost exclusively his: ivory skin that tanned rather than burned in the sun; dark auburn hair blazing red sometimes, like now, as it caught in the light and shimmered down her back. Her face, in profile, showed a strength that might almost have seemed sharp had she not been so lovely, and her height, unusual in a woman, gave an air of poise and self-confidence the mother had never possessed.

Denise's sensitivity and Hubert's vitality. An interesting combination. Perhaps, after all, he fretted too much.

He got up and walked slowly over to the place where she was standing, his eyes following hers along the expanse of the grounds. Like this extraordinary child, the estate was a peculiar blend of the couple who had created it, Hubert's need for an ostentatious show of wealth tempered by his wife's superb good taste. Dominie had kept things much the same, doing little more than maintenance—a dying hedge replaced, a statue regilded when the glitter started to peel. Only the little rose garden, set off in a private corner, bore the impact of her personality.

He glanced back at the pattern of light and shadow that fell across the vibrantly colored rosebushes. It did his heart good to look at them. Always had. Even as a little girl, Dominie had been fascinated by roses, trailing after the gardeners, pestering them with questions, gradually taking over the planting and pruning. And Denis, doting as always, had indulged her.

Nothing rigid here, he thought. No pretentious formal arrangements. Roses grew half-wild, tumbling onto paths and benches, whole branches spared where a perfect bud had formed and she couldn't bear to cut it off. They were all colored red—she had no others—but it was amazing what a profusion of shades that one hue could show.

And standing at the edge, utterly unconscious of all the beauty around her, the girl herself, in a dazzling red dress, like one of her own blossoms come to life.

"What a lovely gown," he said sincerely. "That rose color becomes you. But then, I suspect you already know, since you frequently wear it."

"Red is Denis' favorite," she said, turning her head just slightly to glance at him. "He always looked over the fabrics the dressmaker brought and coaxed me to choose it. Oh, not gaudy red, of course . . . like the dancing girls who entertain at private parties. A deep rich red, with just a touch of blue. The color of shadows in the roses before the sun goes down."

Good heavens! The bishop willed his features not to look shocked. What did she know about dancing girls and private parties? A great deal more than she ought to, he'd warrant.

"Really? I would not have thought Denis had an eye for fashion."

Dominie smiled in spite of herself. "He didn't, poor thing. He knew nothing about style—he was hopelessly out-of-date—but he did know colors. 'Redheads aren't supposed to wear red,' I used to tell him. But he would only laugh and say, 'You aren't a redhead, you have auburn hair . . . and anyhow, it looks pretty, and who cares what you are *supposed* to do?' "

Her lower lip had started to tremble, and the bishop hastily changed the subject. Time enough to think of her brother later, when the hurt was not quite so fresh and she could deal with it better. "How are the plans for your wedding coming along? Here I am, one of your sponsors at baptism, and I don't know the first thing about it. What is it, six months now?"

"Four and a half," she replied dutifully, but without the excitement he might have hoped for. Undaunted, he pressed on.

"I must confess I was less than enthusiastic when Denis told me he was making arrangements for you to marry Honoré Ravaud. Of course he's one of the only men in France whose fortune matches yours, even after providing for the sons of his first marriage. But he is so much older. And he has always been something of a, um . . ."

He hesitated. The word "rake" came to mind, but that was hardly the sort of thing one said to an impressionable young lady.

"Well . . . he has always had a way with women. But perhaps he is past that now, and you are certainly a beauty. I suspect you have the spirit to keep him in line . . . and he has the strength of will to do the same with you. Yes, all in all, I think your brother has chosen wisely."

"Honoré is very charming." Dominie's face softened slightly as, just for a moment, the distraction worked. "And he is kind. At least he has been kind to me. It's not a love match, naturally—as you said, he is considerably older—but Denis says that is not important. Love is like the roses in my garden. Very pretty, but it soon fades . . . and nothing is left but dried petals to blow on the wind.''

"Indeed?'' The bishop had not missed the faint flush on her cheeks, and he eyed her suspiciously. In his experience, "charming" meant only one thing to young girls. He was relieved to see innocence in the eyes that rose freely to meet his. Apparently Honoré Ravaud was behaving with uncharacteristic restraint. Still, he wished her brother had not insisted that the wedding wait until after her nineteenth birthday. "So much wisdom in one so young. I wonder at it.''

"It is Denis' wisdom, Monsignor. And because I trust him, I believe he is right.''

"Yes, well . . . perhaps he is.'' He paused thoughtfully. "But it may be a love match after all. Not on your side, of course . . .''

"You think . . . Honoré loves me?'' Dominie looked startled for an instant. "But he's a very worldly man, Monsignor. And I am very . . . unsophisticated. Oh, I know he's *fond* of me.'' The flush came again, deeper, unmistakable this time. "But love? No, that is impossible. It is a good, sensible match, that's all. On *both* sides.''

"Nothing is impossible, child . . . especially when it comes to beautiful women. The older a man is, the more fool he seems to make of himself. Even the worldliest are not immune. Yes, my dear . . . I do not think he loves you.'' He laid a hand briefly on her forearm, patting it lightly. "Be kind to him, Dominique. Poor man. You hold his heart in your careless young hands.''

With that he took his leave, knowing there was nothing more to be said. He had distracted her for a moment from the grief over her brother, but it would return, and he had lived long enough to realize he could do nothing to help her. She had to come to terms with it herself.

How hard to be young, he thought again as his feet crunched on the gravel path that led around the wing of the house. The young took everything so seriously. The years had not yet taught them that pain was an inevitable part of life and must be accepted to be borne.

His carriage was waiting on the broad drive that swept in a wide semicircle up from the road some distance away. She had been young too, the mother—Denise. How old when they chose that handsome scoundrel for her? Sixteen? No, fifteen—barely more than a child, but already showing signs of the passion that would torment her life.

The footman helped him into the carriage, which seemed to be getting a little higher off the ground with each passing year. It had been, in many ways, a perfect union. Denise, the daughter of old nobility, fled from the horrors of the Revolution to exile in England—but not, like so many of the others, impoverished, for her father had had the good sense to convert his holdings into gemstones. And Hubert, the only son of opportunists, had thrived and grown rich in the years of chaos and bloodshed, hungry for the title that had become fashionable again.

What could be more fitting than that he should marry her and take her name—and the designation of *comte*—after her brothers died? It seemed there was a tradition forming. Only daughters to carry on.

He grunted as the carriage started, throwing him gently back into the padded seat. Sweet, sad Denise. Such an impressionable age. She had adored her older, much more vibrant husband. But then, she had hardly been alone in that. Many had adored the dashing new count.

She might have forgiven him his infidelities. The carriage turned from the oak-lined drive onto the road, leafy green giving way to brilliant blue splashes of sky. Probably she would have. Denise was a child of the times, and straying husbands were a fact of life. A wise wife learned to look the other way.

But Hubert had adored her too—at least in the beginning. He had wanted to be everything to her, share everything with her—even some of the less-conventional aspects of his life. The old bishop could still remember the look of shock and fear on that pretty face when she had sought him out in a private corner of the church—he had been only a humble priest then—and whispered haltingly the things her husband required of her.

She had been appalled, not because the acts he forced on her were repulsive, but because the vital, healthy young passions of her body had responded.

"What am I to do, *mon père?*" He could still see those fantastic eyes gazing up at him, brimming with tears.

"They are wrong, these things he asks of me. I know they are wrong. But he is my husband. If I refuse, he will not love me anymore."

And how had he answered her, this unhappy girl who had come to him for help? Had he said, "Your marriage is your first responsibility; obey your husband and do not feel guilty—God will look into the purity of your heart and understand." Or, "You cannot allow yourself to be coaxed into sin, no matter what the justification—give up these evil ways, even if it costs your marriage."

No, he had equivocated. He had hidden behind the solemnity of his robes. "I cannot tell you what to do, my child," he had said. Lord, how pompous. He had not been that much older than she. "You must find the answers within your own heart. Only you can decide what is right."

Well, there was nothing he could do about it now. She had needed him, and he had failed her. But he would not fail her daughter.

His thoughts drifted back to that solitary figure in the garden, so strikingly lovely in her rose-colored gown amidst the profusion of roses. She was still rebellious, still aching to fight what couldn't be changed, but he sensed she was beginning to accept. The fact that she had ceased to argue told him that.

Time was what she needed now. Time and the new marriage her brother had wisely planned for her.

The bishop would not have rested as easily on the over-stuffed cushions of his carriage if he could have seen Dominie at that moment. Whatever submission he had imagined in her manner was gone now. She was still, but alert, her head tilted slightly back, like a cat that has just spotted a bird, eyes snapping and full of fire.

The will of God, indeed! That was one of those silly things priests always said when what they really meant was that *they* wanted you to behave in thus-and-such way.

He might as well have claimed it was the will of God for the poor to suffer because that's the way they were born, even though Denis, and Maman on her good days—and the bishop himself!—always stressed that it was an obligation for the rich to help those less fortunate than themselves. Or that a sick man should lie around and wait for the will of God to make itself known instead of seeing what a physician could do with his herbs and leeches!

It seemed to her it was the will of God that people do what they could for themselves. And for those they loved.

She started toward the house, then hesitated, knowing there were things showing in her face that she did not want even the servants to see. It would have been different if her darling Jean-Luc were here. Jean-Luc had worried and fussed—she was a natural-born fusser—but Dominie had always been able to twist her around her little finger. If Jean-Luc were here, they could have talked this over, figured out between them what to do.

But Jean-Luc was not here. Jean-Luc had gone back to the convent when Dominie was old enough for school, and there was no point wishing for what she couldn't have.

*Even if you wanted to help him—even if God wanted you to help—your brother is many thousands of miles away. There is nothing you could do from here.*

No, there *was* nothing she could do from here. Dominie started down the path, half-walking, half-running, too restless to remain where she was, still afraid to go back to the house. But there was no reason why she had to *stay* here!

The bishop was not going to help her. She paused at the end of the path, past the large fountain that cast a glittering spray into the morning sunlight. She had stopped arguing not because she was ready to give in, but because she knew she was wasting her breath.

Well, the Bishop of Paris was not the only person in the world! She was just going to have to find someone else to help her. If not, she would do it by herself!

Somehow—she did not know how, but *somehow*—she was going to save her brother.

# 3

A REEK OF FISH paste and rancid pork fat rose from the
tamped-earthen floor, mingling with the livestock odors
that seemed to ooze through the woven palm-frond walls.
The sun would be setting soon; shadows darkened the
interior of the small hut almost to evening, but there was
no relief from the heat that had lingered throughout the
day. The priest's gown was saturated, his stomach
churned from the dirt and stench as he lowered himself
to a coarse straw mat and attempted without success to
arrange his long legs in a dignified manner.

"You are tired, Père Denis," a voice came from behind.

He looked around to see the man who had been disguised as a peasant standing in the space between two
rough partitions that sectioned off one end of the hut. He
was appropriately gowned now, in long-sleeved black
with a cross on a cord around his neck, but Denis Arielle
knew that underneath would be baggy knee-length trousers. And somewhere near at hand was a homespun shirt,
ready to be thrown on at a moment's notice.

"I *am* tired," he admitted. "I don't believe I have ever
been so tired in my life."

"It's the heat," the younger priest said, not unkindly.
They were speaking French, as always when alone together. "You are not accustomed to it. It saps the strength
from your body and leaves you too exhausted to move at
the end of the day."

"The heat is brutal, and you are right, Duong . . . I
am not accustomed. But it is not the heat that leaves me
so utterly drained."

Le Van Duong lowered himself easily to the floor. Like
many of his countrymen, he was short and slight of build,
with high cheekbones and delicately pretty features. But

fragility was only a brief illusion, for there was about him an almost feline aura, the sleek, sinewy grace of a jungle cat stretching out in the sun. He took no note of the mispronunciation of his name, a kind of Frenchified "Dong" rather than the more melodic "Zhung" that rolled off the Vietnamese tongue.

"If not the heat," he said curiously, "what then?"

"The fear. I cannot imagine anything more terrifying than cowering in that suffocating shrubbery . . . watching the soldiers come nearer and nearer." He grimaced wryly. "It is humiliating, being so debilitated by fear you cannot even move."

Duong let a faint smile touch his lips. So—he was not afraid to admit his fear, this strange European. A Vietnamese would have taken the opportunity that had been offered to save face. "Under the circumstances, it is not unnatural. If the rumors are true, a foreign priest has already been executed. And the soldiers were closing in. They would have caught you for sure if I hadn't come when I did."

"Which was dangerous—and very foolish!" Denis half-rose to his knees, then sank back, too weary even to protest effectively. The air was so close, he felt nauseous. "We talked this over again and again, and we agreed. You were not to jeopardize your safety if I got into trouble. Two lives lost serves no purpose . . . especially when there are so few of us."

"But two lives were not lost. Or one. And *I* was never in jeopardy." The younger man's face lit up, laughter sparkling in his eyes, ready at any second to come spilling out. "I know these soldiers the Emperor of Heaven sends into the countryside. Great brainless oafs who could not find their way through a stand of bamboo—much less take on a clever fellow like me! You see, we have none of your European modesty, we people of the hills and delta. And I *was* clever, wasn't I?" The laughter erupted, unquenchable. Black eyes danced with mischief, like a small boy who has just pulled off a prank. "Did you see the way I lured that captain with cheap wine? He was even denser than I expected. Closer and closer to the road . . . past the place where you were hiding. And then I pulled out the brandy!"

"It was clever," Denis conceded. "But much too

risky. He might have suspected. Where on earth is a peasant supposed to get hold of a bottle of decent brandy?''

A woman had come into the room, not young anymore, but probably not as old as she looked. Denis turned to watch her. She was dressed like the farmers in their fields and rice paddies, in loose trousers that left her shins bare, and a long soiled tunic. Following her, a boy of seven or eight carried two low tables, which he placed, first in front of the foreigner, then the young Vietnamese.

Denis knew that the meal they were about to be served was all the family had; they would go to bed hungry themselves to feed their guests, but he could not gracefully refuse. Not without implying that his stomach churned with revulsion at the thought of what they were setting before him.

''Not risky at all,'' Duong was saying as the woman shooed the curiously gaping boy out of the room and followed him. ''The brandy was not decent. It was awful stuff, smuggled in by Arab boatmen from Singapore. And I told the poor fool it belonged to my father-in-law—so naturally he assumed I had been thrown out by my shrew of a wife and had taken it for consolation. He was more than willing to commiserate with me.''

''Which, of course, left the jug of rice wine for the rest of the soldiers.'' In spite of himself, a note of admiration crept into Denis' voice.

''Of course. It would have been most ungracious to leave them out. And most foolish, naturally, to drink in the hot sun when there is such a pleasant grove of trees just a short way down the road. By the time I came back for you, they were all snoring loudly . . . and dreaming bawdy dreams.'' He laughed. ''They will wake up in the morning with huge heads feeling as if they are about to burst . . . and they will swear they will never touch the vile stuff again. But, of course, they will.''

He switched to Vietnamese as the woman returned, balancing on her hands and arms a number of small dishes, which she placed on the tables, the choicest portions clearly reserved for the French and elder priest. Denis wished he could manage something as sincere as the lavish praise that flowed out of Duong's lips, and for once he was grateful for the linguistic inadequacies that kept his compliments from sounding too lame.

The woman beamed and bowed as she went back and forth, putting a bewildering array of dishes in front of them. Denis had long since learned that the evening meal was usually served this way, a number of little saucers which might be filled with almost anything: some sort of fowl perhaps, or vegetables he could not always identify, chopped into tiny pieces; thin slices of buffalo meat; fish boiled in soy and onion; finely minced raw pork, over-spiced and ready to be wrapped in lettuce leaves.

And over everything the ubiquitous *nuoc mam,* a sauce made of fermented fish with an odor Denis had once been told was like ''tiger's urine,'' which, although he could not speak from experience, he was inclined to believe was true.

Tonight's meal seemed especially scanty, despite the profusion of dishes. Tough chicken in one—probably an old rooster, Denis thought, and judging by the aroma, none too freshly slaughtered. *Banh gio,* indescribably disgusting cake made of meat and bean paste, no doubt intended as a great treat, in another. The others held rice in various guises, wilted greens, and something that looked rather like eggplant, though with all that season-ing it was hard to tell. And, naturally, the *nuoc mam.*

Denis steeled himself not to recoil as the woman reached out and set one last saucer on the table. There was barely any light, but he could see the dirt under her fingernails. The smell of her body was as rank as the smell of the house.

''Very good, Father. Very nourishing,'' she said, pressing the vile sauce on him. ''You eat plenty. Make you strong, like Vietnamese man. Healthy.''

''Yes, yes,'' he agreed. ''It is very healthy, I know . . . but the day is so hot. I have no appetite.''

''I am sure Père Denis will find a *little* appetite,'' Duong admonished quietly, ''when he sees how tasty the food is. It is very kind of you to go to all this work for him. And for me, of course.''

''Of course,'' Denis echoed, hastily setting his face so nothing would show as he picked up the *banh gio* and bit into it. It shamed him to realize Duong was right. The heat was no excuse. He was a priest. He was supposed to love these people he was serving, not think about how dirty they were and how their food made him want to retch. "You are kind. Most kind. This is very delicious."

The woman seemed mollified, or perhaps she had not noticed his hesitation after all. "You will hear my confession?" she asked. "Tonight?"

Tomorrow, he longed to reply. He was so tired, he could not bear to think about it. But tomorrow he might be dead. Tomorrow they might *all* be dead—because of him.

"I will hear your confession tonight."

"And my husband's?"

"If he wishes." The man was not a Christian, but he liked confession because it gave him a chance to boast about his exploits in town. It was another time Denis was just as glad he was not fluent in the language, though the snorts and smacking sounds left little to the imagination.

"And the children?"

"They are too young," he started, then hesitated as he saw the look on her face. "Yes, yes, certainly. If they want to confess, I will hear them."

Denis laid the rest of the meat cake back on the dish as the woman left, apparently satisfied now that she had received the assurances she wanted. He could have sworn he had not sighed out loud, but he must have, for he looked up to see Duong watching him, amused.

"You are not enjoying your dinner?"

"I have not yet developed a taste for Oriental food," he said, slipping with relief back into French. "I never had much of an appetite. I've always been lean as a rail and picked at my food."

"Me, I have a marvelous appetite. And I love the food of the Orient. But I'm having as much trouble swallowing this slop as you are."

Denis gaped at him. He had been so sure the younger priest was shoveling in each dish with great relish.

"She is not a very good cook," Duong said with a surprisingly gentle smile. "I fear she is also not a good woman. There is too much spite in her. But life has not been kind. Her husband drinks the meager profits of their paddies, wastes his money on harlots in town, and smokes opium when he can get his hands on it. And her father's new wife is young and pretty—and has many beautiful dresses. This foreign religion is the only small pleasure she has. It sets her apart from the others. And vile as it is, I don't believe her cooking will actually kill us.''

He was laughing, but behind those dark, inscrutable eyes Denis caught a glimpse of something he had not seen before.

''You are more generous than I, Duong. I thought when I came that it was I who had much to teach the native priests. It seems I was too arrogant.''

The other man shrugged. ''Perhaps we have much to teach each other.'' Leaving the last scraps of food on the table, he headed toward the doorway, now deep in shadow, with the pale pink of approaching sunset barely beginning to show. Just as he reached it, a dog began to howl.

Denis froze, all the fear returning, sudden and gut-wrenching. Everything had been so normal—the squalid little hut, the sounds of life outside—he had almost forgotten the danger.

He watched anxiously, his mouth almost painfully dry, as Duong scanned the landscape. But the slim Vietnamese appeared relaxed as he came back and sat behind the little table again.

''Just the coming of night,'' he said reassuringly. ''And the moon. It's going to be full. The dogs always howl when there's a full moon. They make a very different sound when strangers are about. Don't worry, I've trained them well.''

''You are so calm,'' Denis said enviously.

''It is a waste of energy, worrying about things that cannot be helped. Here, I will take that *nuoc mam* off your hands—some foreigners get used to it after a while, others never do—but you are going to have to manage the rest yourself. You have a family too? A mother of your own, whose cooking perhaps gives as much difficulty as this one's?''

A mother of his own? Just for an instant a fleeting image tantalized his thoughts. Beautiful Denise d'Arielle, elegant in her sheer silk gowns. He could not imagine her serving a meal, much less actually cooking one. He had never seen her do anything but laugh and tease and look pretty . . . until that night he came downstairs . . .

He pushed the thought aside.

"No family at all, to speak of," he said gruffly. "Just a little sister. Well, not so little anymore. She's going to be nineteen in a few months. She will be married then."

"You love her very much?" Duong probed, catching something in his older colleague's tone. "This not-so-little sister?"

"*Very* much. You might say I dote on her. It is my greatest weakness."

"I do not see how this can be a weakness. It seems to me a good thing, that a man should love his sister."

Denis shook his head. "For others, yes . . . but I am a Jesuit. I am not supposed to be attached to anything—or anyone—except God."

"To love God most, that perhaps is right," Duong agreed. "But to love him exclusively . . . ?"

"You do not understand about the Society of Jesus. It is not an easy order. Our founder, the great Saint Ignatius of Loyola, has said in the *Spiritual Exercises* that all things on the face of the earth are created to help man praise, reverence, and serve the Lord. Insofar as they distract him from that end, a good priest must learn to distance himself from them. My sister has always been a distraction. I am not yet, I'm afraid, a very good priest."

Duong studied him curiously. He had sisters of his own, silly, giggling creatures whom he tolerated with a moderate amount of affection. But there was a younger brother for whom he would have laid down his life.

"It seems a strange choice," he said finally. "This Jesuit Order that will not allow a man even to love his own family. There are many other ways to be a priest."

Denis shook his head again, this time with a faint smile. "It is not a matter of choice. I never said to myself: This is what I want—or do not want. It was simply the way things were."

"But surely . . ." The other man hesitated, uncharacteristically groping for words. "You were not born a Jesuit. It is not a thing like an arm or a leg . . . or an extra finger on the left hand. There must have been some time when the idea entered your head."

"If so, I was never aware of it." He wrapped a last

bit of chopped vegetables and stringy rooster in a limp lettuce leaf and struggled to chew it. At least he had been spared the raw pork, which he particularly detested. "Oh, there was an old family confessor, a firebrand in his youth, to hear him tell of it, who defied everyone and suffered great hardships to journey all the way to Pothotsk in Russia to be ordained into the Society. I suppose, in a way, the idea—if there was such a thing—came from him. But even then, it was less something new than a confirmation of what I had always known but never been able to express in words. Almost as if he were not a man at all—not a mere mortal with significance in himself—but a light sent to show me the way."

He paused, laughing lightly, a thing he rarely did.

"But you don't understand a word I am saying. We Jesuits have a tendency to analyze everything in the vaguest philosophical terms. Some might call it pompous . . . But what about you, my friend? There was a moment when the 'idea' first came to you? When you said to yourself: I want to don the long black robes of the foreigners and give up everything—perhaps even my life—for God?"

"I didn't have to," Duong replied, a slight edge to his voice that had not been there before. "Others said it for me. The fathers of the *missions étrangères* are very persuasive. They saw a likely lad, and cultivated him with kindness and flattery, and before I knew it, I was in their seminary on Phu Quoc island. I was not at all sure at the time I was doing the right thing. Sometimes I am not sure now."

A crisis in faith? Denis looked up warily. He was always so bad at these things, never comfortable with other people's deepest feelings. Never even comfortable with his own.

But to his relief, the other priest did not seem to be looking for counsel. The sparkle was back in his eyes as he reached out and switched an empty saucer for the stuff that looked like eggplant on Denis' table.

"Here—just this once—I will help you out again. And I will take the rest of that sticky rice cake as well, with those little things in it that look like flies. Probably are, too. You have done quite valiantly."

"You are a gentleman and a hero, Duong." Denis gave

a wan smile as he awkwardly uncoiled his legs and stood up. Both his feet had fallen asleep and he stamped on the floor to get the blood back into them. "I thank you. My stomach thanks you. We are forever in your debt."

He was aware of a soft chuckle behind him as he strolled over to the door where Duong had stood moments before. It had darkened appreciably just in that short span of time. The sun was setting, a great glowing ball half-sunk beneath the horizon, and long, deep shadows alternated with glorious streaks of gold and saffron and crimson.

It almost seemed a different world. Denis stood and stared in wonder. Rice paddies stretched across the earth like a massive crazy quilt, mirror-bright patches of sun-reflecting water held together with a tangle of dark-green dikes, turned almost black by encroaching night. In the distance, stands of bamboo stood in jagged silhouette against the sky, while farther still, a feathery line of coconut palms followed a meandering stream out of sight.

Everything was still, no movement visible, but Denis was intensely aware of the life teeming beneath that placid surface. He could hear it in the twilight sounds around him. The gentle splash of water buffalo cooling in the irrigation channel that fed the paddies . . . the faint rustling of leaves in sandalwood trees as the breeze picked up, just subtly . . . the wallowing of an old sow in her mudhole outside the door . . . a burst of boyish laughter skipping across the shimmering water, echoing in the distance, softer and softer as it died away.

And somewhere near at hand, a flutter of wings. A false egret rising with startling grace, drifting into the night.

Denis stepped back abruptly, though he was already so deep in the shadowy interior he could not be seen from outside. So beautiful, he thought . . . so quiet and peaceful. It was hard to believe, in all that serenity, that men were searching for him, longing to deliver him to the executioner because of the color of his skin and the faith he carried in his heart.

Hard to believe . . . but God help him, they were. And he knew now they were going to get him.

# 4

GREAT BILLOWS OF FOG rolled up from the Boston waterfront, bringing the chill of approaching autumn to the large, sparsely furnished warehouse office. It was mid-morning, but smoky-shaded lamps were aglow, and little droplets of water glistened like specks of gold on the frosted windowpanes.

Even the most casual observer would have seen the tension in the three men who occupied the room. He would also have seen the resemblance. The craggy, aquiline features of the elderly man behind the massive mahogany desk, his white hair flying wildly around his face, were muted in the younger man who sat in a low-armed chair in front of him, but the same strong nose was there, the same high forehead, the same square, pronounced jaw. The third man, younger still, yet another generation, stood by the window, slightly turned away, his partial profile marking him as a member of the same extremely distinctive family.

Three tall men, powerfully built, all apparently strong-willed, but the observer would have noticed a strange air of expectancy about them, as if something were yet to happen. Someone yet to appear.

The old man with the tousled hair had been glowering at a paper in his hand. Now he slapped it down on the desk.

"We are all agreed, then," he said. "The situation is intolerable. It cannot be allowed to continue."

"I was not aware that you required our agreement, Father," replied the man in the chair, no rancor in his tone. "But since you ask—yes, certainly we are in agreement. At least I am. Something like this could jeopardize everything we've built up. It must be stopped at once."

"I don't suppose there's any chance we can keep it among ourselves. At least until we get things settled."

"Not likely. Unfortunately, the missive from your brokers in Macao was already here when I arrived this morning. At least four people had to have seen it. Given the efficiency of some of our clerks in everything except their work, I'd say the news was all over the warehouse in half an hour. By now they're buzzing about it in every bar on the waterfront."

The old man grunted. Veins stood out on his temples and neck like twisted strands of rope as his eyes flitted around the room, resting with possessive satisfaction on solid oak filing cases and gleaming mahogany map chests, made especially to his order half a century ago. The smell of wood and furniture oil blended comfortably with dust and age and the salt-dampness of the nearby harbor. Sea charts crowded three of the walls; the fourth was dominated by a large flag, white with two horizontal red stripes, the top one somewhat wider, signifying the Dawn that appeared in the name of each of the company's vessels.

This was the Barron Shipping Lines, a private empire that extended from the eastern seaboard, around both of the capes, to the other side of the world and back again. And he was Gareth Barron, a new kind of king in a land where royalty was measured not by ancient lineage, but by money and power, and he had plenty of both. The two men with him, his only surviving son, young Gareth—known from infancy as Garth to avoid confusion—and Garth's son Alexander, together with the two absent grandsons, formed the foundation of the dynasty he fully expected to carry on his name with the same fierce pride for generations to come.

"Damn the boy," he muttered under his breath, then repeated, louder: "*Damn* him! I gave him the best for his first command. The *China Dawn*. The biggest, the costliest, the *fastest* clipper we've ever built, and how does the ingrate repay me? Matthew has always been impetuous, but this is unconscionable. This time he has overreached himself."

"He has more than overreached himself," Garth replied calmly, knowing full well the old man would not listen. He had long since reconciled himself to the fact that his brother had been the favorite, and his brother's youngest son could never do anything irretrievably wrong. "Matthew deliberately flouted my orders. And yours, I might add. He knows very well that Barron Shipping has sworn never to touch opium—we've staked a good deal of our creditability on that honorable vow—yet the first time on his own, he dirties his hands with the stuff. You may call that unconscionable. I call it stupid."

"It couldn't have come at a worse time," his father admitted. "Olyphant's never handled opium, of course, the prissy Bible-spouters—they say their factory in Canton is nicknamed Zion's Corner—and J. P. Cushing quit twenty years ago. But Russell and Company is getting out too. Letters have already gone to the shareholders."

Garth gave a crisp nod. "Just in time. Things are reaching the boiling point. There'll be war soon, and war is always costly. The Chinese put up with the influx of opium for a while, mostly because there wasn't much they could do about it. But they were bound to take a stand sooner or later. The addiction's spreading like a plague—whole segments of the population have been decimated—and every bit of profit from the European trade is being drained out of the country. The warehouses that were destroyed in the last seizure were just the beginning. It's going to get worse."

"And better . . ." The old man chuckled unexpectedly. "*We* didn't have any opium to be sluiced down the river by indignant bureaucrats. But we did stand to pocket a penny or two when the British were banned from the China trade and needed neutral transport to get their tea and trinkets out of Canton. How much did we make on that?"

"Enough," Garth said quietly, recalling the enormous tariffs that had been collected, sometimes for the simple expedient of transferring the Barron flag along with the Stars and Stripes to British vessels. "More than enough for a thirty-mile trip down the Pearl River."

"Still . . . the ban won't go on forever. There's going to be war, as you say. Nasty business, but if it's the British against the Chinese, there's no question who's going to come out on top. . . . And even with the monopoly at Calcutta, a Yankee could make a nice profit in opium."

His son eyed him warily, catching a glimmer of what

he had been watching for. The rationalization for Matthew's behavior.

"In the short run, perhaps," he conceded. "But there are other ways to make the China trade pay. So far we've concentrated on trying to find more acceptable commodities that the Chinese might be willing to purchase. We did all right for a while on furs, until we got too greedy and the seal islands along the coast of South America were depleted." He cast a quick glance at the younger man at the window, but he seemed lost in thought, staring at beads of moisture dripping down the glass. "Now we're beginning to look at the possibility of new markets along the route, which seems to me the best idea. When Alex takes the *Shadow* out on Thursday, he'll be stopping at ports in Africa and Asia, particularly the Philippines. . . . And don't forget," he added shrewdly, "the opium trade is becoming increasingly unpopular. Never make the mistake of underestimating the impact of public opinion on the rest of our business. Our reputation is our lifeline to the future."

The old man's head jerked up. It was with considerable effort that he controlled the twitching of his mouth. It always surprised him, the way his son worked, getting what he wanted by the most devious means.

Gareth Barron's reputation was not just his lifeline to the future. It was his life's blood—and he would fight to keep it.

"I take it that means you're in favor of action," he said dryly. "Very well, then. One vote counted. What about you, Alex? We haven't yet heard from you. Or have you no opinion?"

Alex Barron turned slowly, not in a defiant manner, but showing himself as one who could not be hurried or ordered. He was the tallest of the three, perhaps six-foot-three in height, with the same distinctly chiseled features. But there was in his face a gentleness the others lacked. He was a kind-looking man, quiet, but not weak, with much of his father's good sense, though not altogether lacking his grandfather's iron will.

"I was just thinking," he said with a slight drawl that blurred the New England sharpness of his voice, "that in all the words I have heard flying back and forth, there was not a single qualm about the immorality of the opium trade.''

"Immorality? Bah!" Old Gareth spat out the word with contempt. That was what came of letting his son marry a woman from the South. All those visits "back home" with her bookish family had taken their toll. "What about the barrels of whiskey and rum you carry freely in the vessels you captain? *My* vessels, that *I* give you to command. Do you mean to tell me there won't be half a hold of spirits in the *Shadow Dawn* when you set out Thursday to search for new markets? Where is the morality in that, eh, boy?''

"Probably nowhere," Alex replied, faintly amused and not afraid to show it. "I am not a prude, Grandfather, which well you know . . . and there *is* a difference. A man can choose whether he wants whiskey or not, and most can handle it well. Once opium has taken hold, it is a compulsion. The choice is gone.''

"There is still a choice whether one wants to smoke the first pipe. The second pipe and the third, I think, are also choices.''

"Perhaps." The younger man's jaw tightened slightly, his face taking on more the look of his grandfather's for an instant. "But the fact is still that a market for whiskey existed long before the first barrel was loaded into any of my ships. The market for opium was deliberately *created* in China. The British got tired of sending out all their barks and brigs and fleet new clippers with nothing in the holds but sycee and ballast. All that money left behind in a foreign economy when they sailed home again with a full load! So they looked around to see what the Chinese might fancy—something with an easy profit attached, mind you—and created millions of addicts just to tip the balance of trade. You might not call that immoral, sir, but I do!''

"Yes, well . . . the Dutch are even worse," Garth cut in, determined to defuse the situation before it got out of hand. "They introduced the drug into Indonesia, not because they were worried about empty ships and a drain of silver, but because the population was unruly. Addicts make more docile slaves. . . . But all this is beside the point. We have definitely decided not to consider opium as a trading commodity.'' He looked pointedly at his father. ''Have we not?''

Whatever hesitation the old man might have felt, he did not have a chance to express it, for just at that moment the door flung open, slamming with a crash against the wall.

Three pairs of eyes turned, startled, but not surprised, to stare at the man who had just appeared on the threshold. There could be no doubt that he was one of them, just as there could be no doubt that his was the dominant personality in that room. Like the others, he was tall, his shoulders so broad they brushed the doorframe on either side, but there was in his size an almost visible power, a dynamic energy that made his body seem to burst out of the dark gray broadcloth jacket and smartly tailored tight-fitting trousers. Lamplight caught the sun streaks in dark blond hair, accenting the bronzed tone of his skin, and his eyes smoldered, more gray than blue. A strong man, arrogant in his confidence, but naturally so, as if he knew that men would always look to him for leadership. And knew that they knew it too.

In short, he was one of Gareth Barron's three grandsons, and clearly his heir apparent.

He took a step into the room, shutting the door behind him.

''Now, what the devil is this I hear about Matthew?'' he said.

# 5

CREASES OF AMUSEMENT deepened around Gareth Barron's dark gray eyes as he leaned back in his chair an hour later and replayed the scene in his mind. Jared had stirred things up, all right—but Jared was like that. No discussions or debates for Jared, no wishy-washy back and forth, this and that. Matthew was obviously wrong. Matthew had to be stopped, and he, Jared, was the one to do it. He would be on the *Shadow* when it sailed out of Boston Harbor at dawn on Thursday, heading for the Orient.

And he, of course, would be captain, with Alex as his mate.

Damn, that had gotten them going! The old man laughed under his breath, enjoying the memory. Angry words flying all over the place, and not a bit of good it had done a one of them. Might as well have tried to stand up against a boulder crashing down the hillside. There was no turning Jared aside once he made up his mind.

Like he himself when he had been young. Gareth Barron was vaguely aware as he swiveled toward the still-misted window that he was being eclipsed by this dynamic grandson of his, and the thought brought almost as many pangs of pleasure as distress. Jared was the better man in many ways. Wiser, when he stopped to think things through, more even-handed. But, by God, he was bullheaded too! There'd be plenty of the old Barron spirit left!

The fog was beginning to disperse, no longer a thick blanket that shut out the world, but elusive swirling tendrils with patches of brightness behind. If he got up and went over to the third-floor window, he would be able to make out traces of tall-masted Barron ships lying at anchor in the harbor. But there was no need to go to the window for that. He knew every inch of every vessel by heart.

And every one of them bore the name Dawn.

A grimace of satisfaction twisted his lips at the joke only he truly understood. A silly, frivolous name, Dawn—but then, she had been a silly, frivolous woman. He swiveled back from the window, forgetting the fog, the sun that was just beginning to break through. Silly . . . but ah, God, she had been pretty. All that strawberry-blond hair—no, almost red—floating around her face. He remembered that so much more clearly than her features. More clearly even than he remembered the devastating passion he had felt for her.

Strange, the way love faded over the years, bit by bit, so one didn't even note its passing. He had named his first ship for her, the *Scarlet Dawn,* an ugly old tub, but sturdy and swift, and set off with youthful optimism to win the fortune he had sworn to bring home to her. And she had stood on the dock and waved a white silk handkerchief until he was out of sight . . . and vowed that she would wait.

He had been no more scrupulous then than now. He had carried tea at first, and fine English fabrics in defiance of the colonists' boycott, and managed to make a modest profit. Then the Revolution had come, and he had blithely switched sides, running the British blockade with such spectacular success he had earned himself a daring reputation.

But the war had lasted too long. Dawn had not been able to wait, and he had come home to find the treacherous little witch married to a promising young banker. The dullest man on earth, mousy hair and no chin, but a man with a future.

Well, she had gotten exactly what she deserved. He reached for a heavy box at the side of the desk and, pulling it over, lifted the lid to release a pungent aroma of tobacco. Her promising young banker had grown to middle age with considerably less promise. No fancy estate for her, no glittering jewels, none of the wealth and social position she had so desperately craved.

He took out a fat cigar, rolled it lovingly between thumb and fingers, and lifted it to his nose.

And he had married Judith Asher, a tall, stately, somewhat intimidating woman from one of the proudest families in the area. It was Judith who had lived in the extravagant mansion he erected amidst all those fashionable old homes on Beacon Hill. Judith whose jewels had glittered on a long, perfect neck as she entertained the elite of Boston in her gracious, superbly appointed salon. Judith who had basked in the luxury and status that came with her husband's position.

And Dawn had had to watch and bite her tongue . . . and hate every minute of it!

He put the cigar back in the box and reached instead into the lower-left-hand drawer of his desk, where he kept a bottle of brandy and a glass. He could use a good stiff drink. They were always after him to give up the cigars, cut back on his brandy, the damn-fool doctors. Eighty-six, and his hand was as steady as ever. He'd seen three of them to the grave already and was looking to outlast a fourth, and they wanted *him* to give up his pleasures.

He did not know how Judith had felt about Dawn. They had never spoken of it, and it had not occurred to him then to wonder. He did not even know how she had felt about him. He supposed she had loved him; she had seemed contented enough, but she was not a demonstrative woman, and he had never cared to push. He supposed, too, that he had grown to love her, in his own way, though it was so long ago now, it hardly seemed to matter.

He took a deep gulp of the brandy—no dainty sips for him—and felt better. She had been a good woman, Judith, if somewhat bossy at times. He had felt the loss for many years after she died. Two strong sons she had given him, no weaklings in between, whining piteously for a few frail months, then giving up the ghost. Not like Dawn, who bore babe after babe and managed to raise only one. Vain, silly creature, like her mother.

Two sons . . . His mind drifted back to the years his boys had been growing up. He had never been close to Garth. Garth was too prudent, too sensible. An asset in the business, no doubt, but no fire there. No imagination. Asher, now . . .

A smile softened his lips, making his face almost tender as he thought of his younger son. A handsome, sunny lad, golden fair like his own sainted mother, and so sweet-tongued he could have charmed the birds out of the trees. He had been clever, young Asher. He had gotten everything he wanted . . . including the daughter of the beauty who had eluded his father.

God, how he had enjoyed that! Welcoming young Aurora to the family. Not because he had been fond of her. He hadn't. He had thought her a puling, weak-spined ninny of a girl. But he had loved showering on her the things that might have been her mother's, and watching Dawn seethe with envy and spite.

At least the girl had been good at producing sons. Six in all, though only two had lived, the first and the last. But Jared had come out healthy and kicking and ready to take on the world, and Matthew with his golden hair and dazzling blue eyes was the image of his father. Poor Asher. He'd probably kept his wife pregnant all the time so he'd have a good excuse not to hang around the house. She must have been a bitter disappointment to him.

Ah, well, they were all gone now. Asher, thrown from his horse more than twenty years ago. Aurora a few years later of diphtheria. And Dawn . . . He had gotten so out of touch, he hadn't even known when she died. He had heard about it later only by chance.

He finished his brandy, poured another, and put the bottle back in the drawer. They all thought that Dawn had been the love of his life; they thought he had been pining all these years, grieving for her, but they were wrong. They thought he had named his ships after her as a sad, romantic gesture, to keep the flame alive in his heart. But that wasn't it at all.

He had done it because she lived on a slope overlooking the harbor. Because every time she came out her front door and looked down at the waterfront, he wanted her to see all those tall, proud ships named after her—and know what she had lost.

Love had been sweet, but revenge was much, much sweeter.

He was still chuckling sometime later when a voice broke into his thoughts.

"You're very happy with yourself, Father. Does it give you so much pleasure, stirring up dissension in the family?"

The mirth vanished as he looked up to see his son frowning down at him. It always annoyed him, dealing with Garth when he was like this. Particularly when it looked like what he was about to say just might have a kernel of truth.

"What do you mean, stirring things up?" he blustered. "If anyone's doing the stirring, it seems to me it's young Matt. All I'm trying to do is set things right again. . . . And what are you doing, standing there like that? Sit down, boy. Sit. I'll get a crick in my neck looking up at you."

"I am not a boy, Father. I am fifty-nine years old. And I don't sit on command. Surely you've learned that by now."

"All right, all right," the old man grumbled. "But don't complain that I'm speaking to your belt buckle. God knows what things are coming to around here. Matthew first, then all this quarreling. I've done everything I could for those boys . . ."

"And made mistakes all along the way. You started Alex much too early, a cabin boy at barely twelve, and he ended up hating the sea. Jared you held back until he was sixteen, champing at the bit so badly he was a terror those first couple of years. Now Matthew at twenty-six—with exactly three voyages to his credit—has his own ship, and that the prize of the line. You gave him too much responsibility, Father, with too little experience, and now you're paying for it. . . . But that's not what I was referring to when I spoke of dissension. And you know it."

"You are referring," the old man said, forgetting his vow to speak only to his son's belt buckle, "to the fact that I gave Alex's ship to Jared. You're put out because you think he was treated unfairly."

"I'm referring to the dissension you are causing among your three grandsons. Alex may not be fond of the sea, but he's a damn fine captain, and it was galling to have his command taken away and given to a younger cousin. If there is bad blood between them on this voyage, it will be on your head. And there's going to be even more trouble when they get to the Orient and Jared pulls rank on his little brother."

The older Barron's bushy white brows lifted in faint surprise. Was this his self-controlled son, who rarely used strong language? "Well, what of it?" he said defensively. "Do 'em good to be shaken up a bit. Let 'em battle it out and see who wins. It will be interesting to watch."

"No, Father, it will not be interesting. We all know who the winner will be if those three battle it out. And the loser. Barron Shipping. The company is bigger than it was when you founded it, and the world is a lot more complicated. We need the talent—and cooperation—of all the younger generation."

He braced both hands on the desk and leaned forward.

"You set up this situation, just begging for trouble, Father," he said with a grim smile. "It wouldn't surprise me in the least if you got it."

# 6

"I thought you'd see it my way."

Dominie dropped her eyes demurely, letting long lashes flutter against her cheeks. A beguilingly innocent look, which she fervently hoped Honoré Ravaud would not be able to resist. Certainly he had never resisted before when she pulled out all her wiles.

"Did you?" he said noncommittally. Beckoning the hovering manservant off with a flick of his hand, he picked up the pot himself and poured out a cup of fragrant China tea. In fact, he was having considerable trouble resisting. He was even more conscious than usual, as he placed the cup in a delicate translucent saucer and carried it over to her, of the fascination her beauty always stirred in him, her vitality, her incredible youth . . . the supreme confidence with which she was so positive she could twist him around her little finger. "You are very sure of yourself, *cherie*. It is a pretty trait in one so young. Though not always, I fear, justified."

"But not always *un*justified," she reminded him, her lips, daringly touched with just a hint of rouge, twisting into a teasing smile. "And it would be perfect . . . you have to admit that, Honoré! Can you imagine anyplace lovelier for a honeymoon? They say autumn is the best time in the Orient. The breeze is sultry, the air perfumed with the honey of tropical flowers . . ." She looked up, giving him the full impact of her dazzling green eyes. "Of course we would have to be married sooner than we had planned, it would be necessary to leave right away . . . but somehow I don't have the feeling you would object to that."

Honoré stiffened. The little *diablesse*. She had not dressed in her usual red, which she knew he did not care for, but in a richly burnished gold silk gown, its deep glow set off by the burgundy velvet of the small settee in his exquisitely furnished salon. She could not have chosen anything more tantalizing. The sheer, sleek fabric clung rather than concealed, playing with the subtle outline of slender hips and deliciously long legs. And the rounded neckline . . . just high enough to accent youthful innocence, but not too high to catch—and hold—his eyes.

He let his gaze linger on the faint shadow of cleavage, the softness that rose and fell with each breath she took, and felt absurdly like a mule being lured by a carrot on a stick in front of its nose.

"I am tempted, Dominique," he replied honestly. "Very tempted . . . but I am afraid, in this case, all that pretty confidence *is* unjustified. I cannot possibly consent to this madcap scheme you have cooked up to rescue your brother."

"But . . ." Dominie faltered, feeling for an instant as if all the air had been knocked out of her. "I thought . . . I was so certain . . . Don't you *want* to push the wedding day up?"

"It's not that I don't want to." He set his own cup down, untouched, and came to sit beside her on the settee. "Sweet *cherie,* even young as you are, surely you can't be naive enough to believe that. I would like nothing better than to make you my wife as soon as possible. And if that were all there was to it, I might be persuaded. But that's *not* all there is. It would be a lie to lead you on. You would come out of the wedding chapel fully expecting to set sail for the jungles of the East. And I could not permit it."

"But why not?" There was a terrible finality in his voice; Dominie heard, but she could not bring herself to accept it. She had been so full of hope when she had ordered her coachman to drive her unannounced to his home. How could he refuse to help when it meant marrying—and bedding—her four months early? "What harm would it do? All I want to do is *look* for him. Just for a while. And if . . . if things didn't work out, we'd still have a fabulous honeymoon. Much more romantic than Italy, like we planned. And at least I would know I'd tried."

"Things couldn't possibly work out, Dominique," he

told her firmly. "You would be setting yourself up for the cruelest kind of disappointment. And it could be dangerous." He saw the look of defiance in her eyes, the way her chin jutted up suddenly, and exasperation mingled with the longing he felt for her. What kind of fool set his heart on someone so young? "Be fair, *cherie*. I am responsible for you. It is not just my feelings—I promised your brother. Denis signed the papers before he left that made me your guardian, along with the Bishop of Paris. I am sure, if you have broached this subject with the good monsignor, you found him every bit as intractable as I."

She pouted, unconsciously. "The bishop doesn't count. He's much too old to have any imagination . . . and you know what a fussbudget he is! Besides, he's only my guardian—my *co*-guardian—until we're married. After that, he won't have any say in the matter."

"Ah . . . so you did approach the old fussbudget. I thought as much. And he refused, naturally."

She had begun to tremble. The teacup clattered in its saucer, and taking it gently from her hand, Honoré leaned across to set it on the side table. As he did, his arm brushed against hers, just briefly, and she flushed. A reaction which experience told him was not altogether attributable to anger and disappointment.

"Dear, dear girl, we are not either of us being deliberately unkind. If there were any hope of success, both the bishop and I would have arranged things long ago. You are thinking with your heart, not your intelligence. What did you expect to do? Charge headlong into a country you've never even seen, where you don't know a soul, with customs that are totally alien, a virtually indecipherable language—"

"But I speak Vietnamese," she broke in eagerly. "You forget. I told you that!" Hope lit her face again. Honoré could almost feel it, a tangible physical presence, and he pitied her suddenly for the youth that had touched him so deeply before.

"You speak a few phrases, practiced with Denis—whose ineptitude in Oriental tongues is a joke, even to himself. That's a far cry from the diplomatic niceties needed to negotiate his freedom. Think about it, Dominique. The difficulties are insurmountable. You don't even know where he is. You don't know what part of the country to enter, assuming the authorities even let you land. You don't know if you need to bribe officials who have already captured your brother, or if you're going to have to hire guides to take you into the wilds to search for him. . . . And what do you plan to use for money? Drafts on your bank? In French francs?''

He was gratified to see that she at least look startled. ''Oh . . . I hadn't thought about that. Gold maybe. Or whatever the traders use when they buy all the tea and silk and things they bring back.''

''You haven't thought about anything, I'm afraid,'' he said stiffly. ''The traders use sycee. Silver ingots marked with brands, which they carry in great quantities in the holds of their vessels. A fine picture you'd make, wouldn't you?—setting out with trunkloads of sycee or gold. You'd be set upon by pirates or highwaymen long before you reached Cochinchine—Vietnam, as you call it. I'm sorry, my dear, but it is utterly impossible. I must forbid it.''

He had taken her hand as he spoke. Now he released it and bent closer, brushing back a wispy auburn curl that had slipped out of her coiffure. On impulse, he touched his lips to the curve where her neck met her shoulder, lightly enough not to be quite improper . . . but bold enough so they were both aware of the renewed trembling that ran through her.

A moment later, he crossed the room and, retrieving his cup from the tea table, poured the contents into a basin and refilled it from the still-steaming pot. Her eyes followed him to the window, where he stood for a moment, seemingly lost in thought as a flickering pattern of light and shadow from the trees outside played on his face.

It surprised her a little to see how handsome he was. No longer young, certainly—Dominie did not know exactly how old he was, though he was a contemporary of her parents' and they had both been well into their thirties when she was born—but his were the kind of looks that endured. He was slightly less than average height, barely taller than she, but with a lean figure shown to good advantage by the superbly tailored lines of a bottle-green broadcloth jacket and fawn-colored trousers, and his classically fine features still made women turn in the street to stare after him. Like the faces on statues in the garden, she thought, framed by thick dark curls only slightly tinged with gray.

Handsome, and yet . . . Her heart ached as she looked at him and she realized suddenly, for the first time, that she did not want to marry this man. She had not been lying to that old family friend, the bishop, when she said she found him charming. He was extremely charming, when he chose to be, and generally thoughtful. And there was no denying that he knew enough about women to set her blood racing, like that kiss on the neck a moment ago. But . . .

She turned to cover her confusion, though he was not looking her way. She had a dream sometimes—it had grown increasingly haunting lately. Always the same dream. A nebulous haze, fiery with the reflection of sunset or dawn . . . a sweet, moist smell in the air . . . warm wind whipping long hair out behind her. In her dream, there was a man in front of her. Turned away—she could not see his face—but with a compelling magnetism that drew her inexorably toward him. A tall, mysterious man, hair as black as jet, muscles that seemed to ripple through the thin fabric of his shirt . . . and she ached with longing to bring him into focus, to know who he was, to reach out and touch him with her fingertips.

Then, just as he was about to turn, she always woke up!

She did not know what it meant; she supposed she never would. But whoever he was, whatever he symbolized, that shadowy stranger who could take her breath away, even when she was awake, she knew instinctively she would not find it in this man across the room.

Something of what she was thinking must have shown in her face, for his expression as he turned back was thoughtful and vaguely troubled. For the second time he set his tea, barely tasted, on the table and came to sit beside her.

"Have you thought, Dominique," he said, quietly taking her hand, "that your brother might not want to be rescued?"

"Not want to be *rescued?*" Dominie pulled back abruptly, staring at him in amazement. "Of course he wants it. Do you think he wants to die in that place? For heaven's sake, Honoré, no one wants to die if he doesn't have to!''

"Even if he does . . .'' he said dryly. "But your brother is a very dedicated man. He has a kind of other-worldliness that's almost frightening sometimes. He is years my junior, but there are occasions when I have looked at him and felt that he was much, much older. If he believes in his cause—if he sincerely believes he is doing good in 'that place'—he may not wish to leave.''

"That's nonsense!'' She took the cup and saucer from where he had placed them and stared pointedly into the pale greenish-yellow liquid. "He could do every bit as much good somewhere else. And he could always go back later. When things have settled down.''

"Things might not settle down in his lifetime, *cherie*. And if he wanted to go somewhere else, he would have gone there.''

Honoré hesitated, forming arguments ahead in his mind and rejecting them. There was no point reminding her that Denis had been well aware of the situation when he left. She had already convinced herself that he had underestimated the danger. That once he got there and found things even worse than he expected, he would surely have come to his senses and wanted to leave. And perhaps, after all, she was right.

"This is so important to you?'' he said.

She looked him square in the eye, and he knew with a sudden cold foreboding that she would never forgive him if he denied her now.

"It is the most important thing in the world.''

"Very well . . . a compromise? Naturally I cannot permit you to undertake this foolhardy journey . . . No, no, it is much too perilous, and nothing would be accomplished. But I could arrange for an emissary. Someone who is at least familiar with the area. Perhaps something might be done. A draft on a bank in Singapore, if there is such a thing. Or one of the trading houses. Would that make you happy?''

She studied him piercingly, seeming to search for something in his face. "You would do that for me?''

He hesitated, but only for an instant. "I would do it.''

"I have your word?''

"You have my word.''

He waited a long moment for her to speak, aware suddenly that his future was in her hands. Not at all sure what he would do if she did not accept his proposition.

"Well, then," she said, her voice unexpectedly light, with something in it he could not identify, "I suppose it is Italy. The honeymoon, I mean."

"Italy, or anyplace else you want—except the East. That is much too rigorous a jaunt at my age. No, here," he protested as he saw her lift the cup to her lips. "It must be cold. Let me refresh it for you."

He was feeling giddy with the ease of his victory—experience still told over youth, after all!—as he brought another cup, not hot, but still pleasantly warm, and placed it in her hands.

"This will be a good marriage for you, Dominique, I promise," he said. "Not the romantic love match young girls have in their heads, I daresay, but good and solid . . . and secure. Your brother was very wise when he made the arrangements. And practical. I am hardly in the first flush of youth, or even middle age, and my health has never been strong. You will be a young widow, but not *too* young, with a good grounding in life—and the legal right to manage your own affairs."

"Honoré!" Dominie gasped, shocked at this frankness with which he had never spoken before. "You mustn't talk like that. Why, you'll probably live to be eighty!"

He refrained from pointing out that even if he did, which was unlikely, she would still be relatively young. "You are ignoring your tea again. How many times do I have to give it to you? Do you think I am your willing slave, to jump and fetch . . . and jump and fetch again?" He laughed dotingly, feeling somewhat easier now, though not quite off-guard. "Pretty, foolish Dominique . . . do you think I mind so much, the approach of the end? I might, I confess, had I not been given this one beautiful gift to brighten my final days."

"Don't say that—" she began, but he cut her off with the gentle touch of a hand on her arm.

"Shhh. Why must you be so sad? Silly girl, you should be thinking how lucky you are. Wealth, youth, beauty . . . everything in the world to look forward to."

"So everyone tells me." She made an effort to smile,

and just for an instant looked older, more sophisticated. "Especially about the wealth. How lucky I am my family isn't like all those other aristocrats, clinging to land they managed to get back but are too poor to do anything with. Lucky my grandfather saw the Revolution coming and converted everything into gemstones, which could be carried across the Channel."

"Ah, the famous jewels. Your *maman* told you all about them, I suppose."

Dominie shook her head. "She was ill from the time I was born. But she told Denis when he was a little boy, and he told me. They lived like paupers in England—my grandfather was too proud and too stubborn to spend a *sou* more than he had to in that heathen country, and they came back with nearly the whole collection intact. There are still some left, a bag of diamonds in a vault under the house. Denis said I must keep them, out of sentiment . . . unless of course I need them to live on."

She was laughing as she said it, not hilariously, but with some of her humor restored. Honoré thought of the offer she had made before, the early marriage and everything that went with it, and he was half-sorry now he had refused. It would not, after all, have been any more a lie than the other.

"Not likely," he said. "You have a considerable fortune in your own right, which I will manage very competently. And of course there will be more from my estate when the time comes. You will never want for anything. . . . Ah, Dominique . . ."

He eased his head forward, unable to resist any longer the warmth of this beautiful child beside him on the narrow settee. He did not pause to remove the teacup again, but let her cling to it, hoping she would not drop it when his mouth touched hers, not really caring if she did.

Dominie felt the sudden, only half-unexpected pressure of his lips, and she sat absolutely still, not moving toward him, but not pulling back either. His kiss was coaxing, soft. But there was something else too, greedy, demanding in a way he had never demanded before, and her whole body came alive, tingling with a sweet aching she could neither understand nor control.

She thought, just for a second, that he was going to slip his hand inside her dress . . . and just for a second she wanted him to . . . and all dreams of dark, mysterious strangers were lost in the promise his mouth seemed to offer.

"It will be a good marriage," he repeated as he drew back reluctantly. "I will make you happy. And you will make me very, *very* happy. . . . But, ah, God help me, I think it's going to be the death of me if I have to wait four months to make you mine."

# 7

THE FOG HAD nearly lifted. It lay several feet above the ground now, a low, swirling cloud that obscured but did not entirely block out the sun. Jared Barron stole a quick glance at his cousin's impassive profile as they hurried side by side down the nearly deserted street.

"A drink, Alex?" he suggested tentatively. "The Bull and Boar shouldn't be too rowdy at this hour. We have much to discuss and little time for it."

"The charts and cargo manifests are already on board the *Shadow*," his cousin replied in a voice that gave away nothing. "Whatever you need to know, you can learn from a perusal of them. As you said, we have little time. Thursday dawn is less than three days away. I don't know about you, but I have preparations to make and people to see."

Jared started to press, then hesitated. He was already beginning to regret that outburst in his grandfather's office a short time before. Blast his temper anyway! He did not regret the decision he had made. Matthew's blundering enthusiasm for the opium trade—so typical of his younger brother—could cost them dearly. Things had to be righted, and quickly. But he could have handled it more tactfully.

"I fear my mouth moves ahead of my brain sometimes," he admitted. "If I offended you, I am sorry. It was not my intent. I have no desire to fight with you over this."

Alex turned and gave him a piercing look. "I am a good captain," he said bluntly. "I run a tight ship, and I run it well. I deserve the respect I have earned. Did you seriously believe you could breeze in this morning, announce you were taking over *my* command, and I wouldn't be offended?"

In fact, Jared realized with some surprise, that was exactly what he had believed. He had a moment to study his cousin's features surreptitiously as a carriage clattered along the wet cobblestones and the two men stepped back to avoid the muddy spray. He didn't look angry, but then, you could never tell with Alex. As long as he could remember, Alex had always kept things inside, nothing to show what he was feeling or thinking.

"You never cared for the sea," he protested mildly. "You never made any bones about it. The only time I ever saw your eyes light up was when you came back from visiting your mother's people in Virginia. All you could talk about was the land. The rich red soil . . . the things that grew in it, the tobacco and grains . . . the way it felt when you picked it up and let it run through your fingers. I wouldn't have thought you'd give a damn if you ever captained a ship again."

"If it were another ship, I might not," Alex admitted. "But you forget, the *Shadow Dawn* was my first command. Others have captained her since, but not while I stood by and watched from an inferior position. I agreed because I have no choice. It is not my ship—or my line. But I do not give her willingly."

The wind picked up, blowing crumpled handbills down the empty street. Jared stooped absently to catch one in his hand. An advertisement for fine sandalwood furnishings and exquisite blue-and-white china vases brought in by a rival vessel, he noted ironically. It occurred to him that, if he did not somehow manage to smooth things over with his cousin, this was going to be an even rougher voyage than he had anticipated.

The mist was almost completely gone now. Crowded warehouses stood out sharply, every stain visible on sooty brick walls, and oil lamps could be seen flickering feebly behind grimy, curtainless windows. At the approaching intersection, traffic had begun to move. The echoing clatter of the cart that had just passed was joined by a rumble of heavy freight wagons from the nearby docks, and hooves clattered on the brittle pavement, harnesses jangled smartly, curses and cries and good-natured roars of laughter rose above the general din as the city came out from under its blanket of fog.

The moisture had intensified the smells. Wet stones,

wet brick, wet earth; the strong, familiar odor of dung; the reek of sewage running in open streams down the gutters; the distinctive mustiness of old buildings contrasting with an acrid bite of fresh grout from new warehouses under construction.

And always, Jared thought, the pungent salt tang of the sea, lingering in a man's nostrils, forming a thin crust on his lips.

He paused as they reached the corner. The city was throbbing again, people teeming in streets that only a moment before had been almost eerily still. Vendors were setting up their wares, flowing out of arched passageways to display the richly colored fruits of the autumn harvest on narrow brick sidewalks. The voices of the hawkers were hoarse and insistent, and an aroma of roasting nuts drifted temptingly from somewhere out of sight. Carpenters were busy in some of the shops, Jared could see them through the open doorways; blacksmiths and metalworkers toiled over red-glowing fires with ringing hammers in others.

The sun had brought out the sailors, and they swaggered down the street, rough-faced, leather-skinned men no longer in the first flush of youth, ready to part with a year's earnings for a day and a night of pleasure. Bar doors gaped, great black holes beckoning them inside, and garishly clad women with thick masks of paint covering pathetic extremes of age and youth grinned and waved from windows and stoops.

It was his city, for all its filth and crudity. He loved the vibrant, pulsating excitement, as he loved the great rhythmic, roaring waves that crashed against the hull of his ship at sea, and he knew he could never live any other way. Just as he knew, with a last sidelong glance, that the man beside him would never share either of his passions.

"Truce, Alex," he said quietly. "There's no other ship I can take. Newcombe will be steering the *Scarlet* toward Macao next week, but you know the *Scarlet*s." It was a family joke: there was always a *Scarlet Dawn* in the Barron fleet, but she was always an ugly old tub, as if to remind them of their humble beginnings. "She's much slower. And she'll be taking the long way, round Cape

Horn and up through the Sandwich Islands. I cannot afford the time."

"And you cannot consider traveling in the owner's suite instead of the captain's cabin?"

"You've seen the owner's suite on the *Shadow*. There's just about room for a very small person to turn around." He kept his voice light as they hesitated beside a rough wood plank that had been placed across the rivulet of sewage. "Be honest, Alex. You are a competent master, but I am better. I love the sea, and I love my ships. Could you imagine me casually strolling about the deck, a pipe clenched in my teeth, while you gave orders I disagreed with? . . . And could you imagine life being even remotely bearable if I tried?"

He was rewarded with the faintest hint of a smile. That was one thing about Alex, the humor that never lay far beneath the surface. The gentle ability to laugh, even when the joke was on him.

"A drink, cousin?" he said again. "I'm sure the lady, whoever she is, can wait a little longer."

"No ladies for me this time. . . . But you, if I don't miss my bet, are going to have a hard time squeezing your fond farewells into three short days."

Jared grinned ruefully. There were, in fact, several charming young women, one in particular whom he had even, fleetingly, considered marrying. But the impulse had passed, and he could hardly leave her dangling for the months or years he would be gone.

"I think I can put off the farewells for a while."

The smell of the ocean followed them into the tavern. The Bull and Boar was one of the oldest buildings on the waterfront, and dampness seemed to be everywhere, in the thick plastered walls, peeling and brown with age, and the filthy matted straw carelessly strewn across the wide-plank flooring. Dim light filtered through a cloud of stale smoke, barely illuminating a massive stone hearth charred by countless fires at one end of the room, a long bar tended by a surly-looking bearded barman at the other. Benches and settles flanked scarred wooden tables. On one, a mottled orange cat was stretched out, fat and lazy, mute testimony to the rife selection of vermin.

The ceiling was low, and the two men ducked their heads to keep from brushing against ancient blackened rafters. Several ships had just come in, and the bar was lively with raucous arguments and the threat of imminent song, but most of the tables were vacant. Jared jerked his thumb at the quietest corner.

"That looks as good as any. I'll grab a bottle at the bar. Or would you prefer a toby of ale?"

Alex shook his head. "You may take my ship, but I'll be damned if I'll let you buy me a drink. I'll get the bottle—you wait at the table."

A barmaid had just come in from someplace in the back. Not pretty, but buxom, with a good-natured grin. Jared eased himself onto one of the settles, conscious of the mildewy smell of the wall behind him as he watched his cousin slip an arm around the wench's waist and lean closer. As always, Jared marveled at his easy way with women. He himself would have given a pinch on those plump pink cheeks, perhaps a pat on the bottom, and the girl would have tossed back a bawdy retort, thoroughly enjoying the game. But it was Alex she would turn to if she needed a friend. Alex she would sit with in the quiet moments, spilling secrets she had never told anyone else.

Jared found himself wondering about his cousin. Alex, the quiet one, the most reticent of a volatile clan, but always able to laugh, if somewhat gently. Had the mirth ever been gayer? It seemed to him he could remember a difference, somewhere long in the past. But perhaps he was only imagining it. Perhaps they had drifted so apart in the years since they had gone to sea, he had forgotten what it was like.

"You must have been twelve or thirteen," he said as Alex returned to the table with a bottle and two surprisingly clean glasses. "That time you came back from your first berth as a cabin boy. I was just ten—and sick with envy. And furious with you because you wouldn't talk about it!"

He was venturing into dangerous waters. Alex was still disinclined to talk about those times, but he had to find some way to reestablish the rapport between them.

Fortunately, the other man did not seem to be taken aback as he popped the cork and poured out a steady stream of translucent amber liquid. "Perhaps," he said easily, "I had nothing to say that you wanted to hear."

Jared took a tentative sip of his whiskey. It went down

smoothly, with just a subtle edge of fire. Obviously the reason why the Bull and Boar, for all its roughness, attracted more than its share of traders and businessmen.

"It was not, I gather, the great adventure of your life."

"It was hell." Alex drained his glass uncharacteristically in a single gulp. "The ship was small—the fourth *Scarlet*, I think. One of them, anyway. The weather was foul all the way, especially abominable rounding the Horn, and I was seasick for months. I can still smell the rot and the bilge. And the blood."

He saw Jared's head jerk up in surprise and added grimly:

"You forget, she was a sealer. Do you know how seals are slaughtered? The men get in a long line, between the seals and the sea. Then they move in, swinging their clubs and shouting at the poor beasts, who are roaring with terror and confusion. The decks are solid red before the skinning is over, and so slippery it's impossible to walk. Hardly a pleasant experience for an impressionable young boy."

"Or for a boy who loves animals," Jared said, remembering the mangy curs with lame legs that always seemed to be trailing after his cousin. "Even Grandfather has to admit he's never seen anyone as good with horses." That explained a lot of things, he thought. It explained why Alex had turned in on himself, why he never developed the great Barron passion for the sea.

It also explained why Gareth Barron had held his second grandson back until he was so spitting mad he'd been ready to run off on a rival ship.

"Truce?" he said again, raising his glass. "Come, Alex, you know I'm right. There is no way I'm ever going to be an even remotely tolerable passenger on another captain's vessel. And for all that you seem to have some sneaking sentimental attachment to the *Shadow Dawn*, which I would never have suspected, I don't believe you truly mind. So . . . there must be some other objection."

His cousin hesitated, seeming to consider.

"I have two objections," he said finally.

"Which are . . . ?"

"The *Shadow* was to have made numerous stops on the way to the Orient. That was the main purpose of the voyage. We have to find new markets for our goods if we're going to be profitable enough to thumb our noses at the opium trade. You race out there, hell-bent on getting to the East in record time, and you're going to make a mess of months of careful planning.''

"I know that," Jared replied gruffly. "And I know it's important. The *Shadow* will make all scheduled stops. I won't like it—I don't say I'll be gracious about it—but I won't interfere. You have my word."

Alex nodded curtly. "We are agreed on that, at least."

Jared watched him warily.

"You said you had two objections," he prompted. "What is the other?"

"The other is . . . Matthew."

"Matthew?" Jared fairly bellowed the word, so loud even the rowdy celebrants at the bar turned to gape at him. It was with considerable effort that he lowered his voice. "What about Matthew?"

"I'm worried about him, Jared. He's been the baby too long—no one has ever taken him seriously. This venture is his one big chance. He desperately needs to succeed. If he messes it up, I don't know how he's going to handle it."

"*If* he messes it up? It seems to me he already has."

"Matt has a good head on his shoulders. He does the damnedest things sometimes, impulsively, but they always come out straight in the end. If he has time—if you don't go raging in like a mad bull and take over—I think he'll be able to work it out for himself. But you have to give him the chance."

Jared set his jaw in a straight line, bit down on an imaginary pipe stem, and choked back the hot retorts that rose to his lips. Matthew had nothing remotely resembling *any* kind of head on his shoulders. Matthew had just made a damn fool of himself, and coddling him now wasn't going to make up for all those years of babying. But he sensed that Alex was going to be adamant about this, and he needed his goodwill.

"Matthew will have three months at least to come to his senses and straighten things out. If he has managed by the time we arrive—or if it even looks likes he's made a start—I'll back off. I can't promise any more than that."

"No, I don't suppose you can. Well, then . . . the

truce you proposed?'' Alex held up his glass, touching it to his cousin's. ''To a safe and successful voyage.''

Jared took a cautious sip. ''To a safe and successful voyage,'' he echoed, but his mind was far from easy. The revels at the bar were bawdier now, spilling over to the tables, a mixture of merriment and latent hostility. He had made peace with his cousin, but it was a tentative peace, leaving both of them wary.

He had the feeling this was going to be a very long trip.

# 8

EVENING FELL SLOWLY in Paris in the summer. The room was bathed in shadow, but lamps had not yet been lit as the bishop settled his rotund body back in the same burgundy velvet settee where Dominie had sat earlier, and scowled down at a glass of very excellent cognac.

"I don't like it," he said slowly. "I don't like it at all. I gave the man my solemn word before he left."

"You gave him your word that his sister would not be married before her nineteenth birthday. But you also gave your word," Honoré Ravaud reminded him, "that you would protect her and keep her safe. Which of those two vows do you think young Denis would consider more important?"

The bishop sighed, a thing he seemed to be doing more and more of late. "I was so sure, " he said ruefully, "that I had talked her out of this nonsense about saving her brother. I explained, most carefully, that it was out of the question, that she could not possibly do anything to help him all the way off in that place—what is it called again? . . . ah, yes—Vietnam. She seemed to understand."

Honoré smiled indulgently. "Dominique has a wonderful way of understanding . . . when it serves her purpose. No doubt she turned big green eyes on you and looked sadly accepting—and all the while she was planning to come and try her hand with me! She did it very cleverly too. Oh, I managed to distract her, with false promises and a bit of flirtation. But that's all it was. A distraction. When she has time to think, she will begin brooding again. Of course, I can come up with other things to keep her occupied, but I hardly think you would, uh . . . approve."

His bawdy wink met with an answering shudder.

"Hardly," the bishop replied. "Such occupations are not likely to meet with priestly approval outside the institution of marriage." He tilted his glass back and drained it with a last satisfied swallow. A distraction, eh? But hadn't he himself thought, just that morning, that *he* had distracted her? "A most excellent cognac. This, I suppose, is *my* distraction. To addle my thoughts so I'll agree that the only way to save Dominique from her own impetuous temperament is to allow her to wed some months in advance."

"In that case," Honoré said smoothly, "permit me to offer you more." He brought over the bottle, calling as he did for a servant to bring them some light. The man must have been lingering just outside, for he came immediately with two lamps, which he placed, one on each side of the room. Later, chandeliers would be illuminated, and elaborate gilded sconces on the walls, but for now the pale glow was sufficient.

"You have found my weakness," the bishop admitted, holding out his glass with no further prompting. In his youth, temptation had taken the form of pretty, nubile girls, and he had spent many agonizing hours on his knees or in the confessional. Now it was fine food and, especially, fine brandy.

"Not really a bribe, Monsignor. This early marriage is what I want—I would not insult your intelligence by pretending it isn't—but I honestly believe it is right."

"I know, I know . . ." He took another sip and let the warmth spread through him as he sighed again. "I daresay I worry about her too much. She is a good girl—willful, but good—but sometimes she seems so like her mother. She has inherited much of Denise. Her looks, her mannerisms . . . the silvery sound of her voice when she laughs. I fear sometimes she has inherited her passion as well."

"Pray God she has," Honoré said with an amused look. "Passion is a good thing, even in a woman—*especially* in a woman, so long as she has an appreciative husband . . . I care very much for Dominique, Monsignor. But I think you know that, or we would be discussing that instead of the timing of the wedding. I would never abuse her. Every man is not a Hubert Magaux. Or

Hubert d'Arielle, as he called himself after he married into the aristocracy.''

"Ah.'' The bishop held the glass to his lips again, giving himself a moment before he spoke. "So you know about that. I wondered if you did.''

"The orgies at the d'Arielle estate were justly renowned. Even in an era of marvelously 'loose morals,' as you priests like to put it, the things that the count had his lusty wife do, and the men he had her do it with''— his nostrils flared with distaste—"caused considerable gossip. And, no, don't look at me like that. I never partook myself. I have not always been totally honorable in my relationships with the fair sex—I have not always been honorable at all—but I like my women one at a time.''

The bishop nodded heavily. "It was a bad thing, especially for the boy. The younger one. Denis. He was old enough to see what was going on, and sensitive enough to be disgusted by it. The other—Hugo—reveled in it. God help them, they doted on him. I sometimes think it was a terrible tragedy that he died. And sometimes I think it was a blessing.''

"There were no other children?'' Honoré asked curiously. "Just the two boys? No babies who died along the way?''

"There are ways to prevent babies from being conceived,'' the bishop reminded him with a sharp look. "And ways to prevent those who are conceived from being born. She had much on her soul, poor woman, those last tormented years of her life.''

"You speak of the years after Dominique was born? They decided to have her, I suppose, as a replacement for the son who died. But surely that was foolish. Denise must have been in her late thirties at the time.''

"Foolish—and fruitless. It was only a girl-child, not the heir they had longed for, and Denise's health was broken. They could not try again. Hubert took up with other women then, openly. There was one in particular, the last months . . . if he had not been killed himself in that carriage accident . . .''

He broke off, staring at one of the lamps. A moth was throwing itself against the glass, again and again, with a faint clicking sound. Going to its death, but it couldn't seem to help itself.

"I see what you mean," Honoré said quietly. "It gives one pause, does it not? But, as you say, Hubert was killed too, so there is no point speculating."

He, too, was staring at the moth, but he did not see it. He saw a little girl in a vast silent house, with a father who despised her, a mother whose guilty sins twisted like a knife every time she looked at her, and his heart swelled with compassion and protectiveness. No wonder she had grown so attached to her brother. He was the only one who had ever offered her love, security, laughter, acceptance.

"All the more reason," he said, flinging his glass aside so abruptly the contents splashed on an expensive Persian carpet, "that the marriage should take place at once. This bond with the brother is too intense. It could be dangerous. Even more dangerous than we feared. She needs to get on with her life, Monsignor. To find new interests, new duties . . . new devotions."

The bishop paused, hesitant, but not as hesitant as before.

"Yes," he said at last, "I expect you are right. I still have qualms, but . . . yes, I think Denis would agree if he were here. The wedding will take place as soon as it can be arranged."

The same sun that had just bidden farewell to France was beginning to rise over the lush coastal land half a world away. Denis Arielle stood alone in the same doorway where he had stood the night before and peered out at a faint line of pink hovering behind the jagged silhouette of palms on the horizon. It was deathly silent, the sounds of the night having faded, the day not yet begun, and in the staggering heat he found his thoughts drifting back to the coolness of dawn in Paris.

Dominie. . . . He allowed himself the faintest smile as he imagined his pretty sister greeting the morning in her rose garden. A thing she rarely did, for she was in the habit of sleeping late, the lazy little creature. His fault, he supposed. He had indulged her shamelessly. Loved her much too much.

His one weakness. He ran his finger under the already-damp collar of the cassock modesty had prompted him to put on. Or, if he was going to be honest about it, one of many weaknesses, but the one that would always defeat him. The one earthly attachment he could never quite give up.

A sound came from behind. Looking around, he saw Duong sprawled naked on a filthy mat, stirring slightly, but not yet awake. The others were all crowded together in the small partitioned-off section at one end of the hut.

Would she be all right? Doubt brought a chill for one agonizing moment. Lord knew, he had reservations about the marriage he had arranged for her, but it was the best he had been able to manage under the circumstances. Honoré Ravaud was not altogether scrupulous, but he was strong and generous, and he loved her almost to the point of obsession. He was also sensible. He knew he would not live forever; he would see that she learned to manage her own affairs . . . to understand her own heart . . .

Yes, she would be all right. He believed that. He *had* to believe it.

He turned back to see that the sun had brightened. A zigzag pattern of rice paddies sprawled from the isolated hut to the village some distance away. Still waters glistened like pieces of polished marble cut into whimsical angles by the dikes that ran this way and that, following haphazard boundaries of ownership. The faint pink glow had deepened to an almost unnaturally bright red, splashed like a streak of blood across the sky, and he felt himself shudder.

The blood of Christ and his martyrs. . . . He remembered going once, when he was still quite young, to the Lazarist mother house on the Rue de Sevrès and watching as the bloodstained gown of François Clet was displayed. The cord that had been used to strangle him in Wuchang. He had been filled with an overwhelming sense of awe and envy. What a noble death, how heroic it must feel, giving the only thing one truly possessed, one's life, for the glory of God. What a wonderful, satisfying, all-encompassing peace must come over a man at such a moment.

Now he knew there was no heroism. No nobility, no sweet, satisfying peace. Just fear, and a humiliating realization of his own unworthiness.

What am I doing here? he thought. He had come with

such elevating hopes. He had expected his heart to over-flow with love and compassion for these peasants whose souls he had come to save. Instead he found only filth and crudity and the most disgusting habits. They took their pagan idols out of the niches with the crucifix and the Virgin before he appeared, but he knew that, the min-ute he was gone, they would be back in their places again, all the gods together and equal, no one left out . . . just in case. He had not made any difference. Not one life had been changed, not a single soul touched by his pres-ence.

He was going to die here. He stared at the blood-red spreading across the sky, and he knew that as surely as he had ever known anything. Today—or tomorrow. Next week . . . next month . . .

He was going to die, and he didn't even know what he was doing here.

The dream came back that night. Dominie felt as if she were floating out of the wide soft bed in Paris, borne weightless on a current of air, carried off someplace she could only feel, not see. The wind was sultry, and the sweet brooding scent of tropical vegetation hung heavy and tantalizing in her nostrils.

*He* was there, as she had known he would be. Just beyond her reach, tall and powerful, and she stared with all her strength, boring into him with her eyes, willing him to turn. Then, just as she knew she had him—just as he finally started to move—the vision vanished, and she was left with the silent emptiness of her bedchamber.

She lay for a moment, disoriented, in that halfway state between sleep and wakefulness. The scent was still there, not sandalwood and magnolias, as she had imagined—she did not even know what magnolias smelled like—but the roses of her own garden beneath the open window. One day I will see a man like that, she thought, and she realized why the background had always been hazy, his features indefinable. Because he was not reality, not yet, but a mere yearning. An awakening of healthy young passions that cried out for youth and vitality . . . and romance.

She could never be happy with the strict, sensible, dot-ing old man her brother had picked out for her. Honoré

Ravaud might be a skillful suitor. Dominie shivered, not altogether with pleasure, as she recalled the way her body had responded, momentarily, to the skill of his lips the afternoon before. But a momentary physical response was not a substitute for true, deep love, and she knew instinctively that his face would never, *never* fill her dreams at night.

She slipped on a dressing gown and went over to the window. The sun had long since risen over the rice paddies of the East, passing over the jungles of Burma, the mountain ranges and great broad plains of India and Afghanistan, the hills and rivers and seas of Persia and Turkey, Greece and Hungary and Bavaria, to wake the dawn in Paris, and everything seemed sparkling and clean.

He had lied to her. She had known that even as he spoke. He had no intention of sending an emissary to Vietnam. For all his wealth, Honoré Ravaud was a prudent man. He would never waste money on a venture he was sure would not succeed.

She had looked him right in the eye. She had given him every chance . . . and he had lied. As far as she was concerned, all contracts between them were off.

She stared down into the garden. The roses looked dark and mysterious, bathed in the rich red glow of the rising sun. It was a relief, in a way, to know she wasn't going to have to marry him. But it created a whole new set of problems, for he had been her best hope of getting to her brother.

*Think about it, Dominique. . . . The difficulties are insurmountable. . . .*

Rebellion surged through her at the unfairness of that smugly superficial judgment. Except for the problems about money—which even she had to admit were valid—none of the objections he raised had any ground at all. Why did he simply *assume* she knew nothing of her brother's plans, or where to look for him? Because she was a woman, and it was all she could do to keep track of the latest fashions in her fluffy little head?

In fact, she knew exactly where her brother had planned on landing. He had posted a letter from Singapore, his last, telling her about the arrangements he had made with an Arab smuggler—she could almost hear the distaste in his voice as he described the odious man—to let him off near Tourane, from whence he would continue north on foot. She even knew the name of his Vietnamese contact, a native priest. Le Van Duong, whose family lived on the outskirts of the imperial capital of Hué.

And she most certainly did speak the language! She bristled at the mere idea that he thought she might be as inept as her hopelessly tone-deaf brother. Where on earth did he think Denis had learned it? From an old retired *père* of the *missions étrangères,* who had come many times to their home . . . and said she was really quite remarkably fluent!

Not fluent enough, naturally, to manage the delicate negotiations that might be necessary. But she could get to Duong and his family, and they would find someone to help her with the rest.

The only thing she had to worry about was the money, and unfortunately Honoré had been right about that. Dominie turned away from the window, smiling in spite of herself. She would indeed make quite a sight, traveling over windswept savannas and jungle trails with a long line of bearers staggering under the weight of huge trunks of gold or silver. What she needed was something small and light. Easily transportable.

Something easily . . . *transportable?*

She laughed aloud as the thought occurred to her. Of course! What a ninny not to have come up with it sooner. Why, they had been speaking that very afternoon of her grandfather's diamonds, safely tucked away in the vault under the house. There were at least a dozen, perhaps two, in a silk-lined black velvet bag—Dominie has seen them only once, but she had been told they were worth a king's ransom. Surely that would be sufficient to redeem one insignificant priest.

And the bag was small enough to be hidden in the full folds of a lady's skirt!

She began pulling dresses out of trunks and wardrobes, throwing them on the bed, choosing the three or four she would pack away with the necessary toilet articles in a small pigskin valise. The gown she had worn that afternoon was the newest and most fashionable—but, no, she reminded herself sternly. It was too flashy. Not at all appropriate. The dark green traveling dress with its matching flared-brim bonnet would be much better . . .

and where was that blue-striped Pekin silk she had had made up last year? Not exactly *au courant,* but that was just as well for what she had in mind. And maybe the gray-patterned afternoon dress with the deep rose collar and cuffs. Heaven knew when she was going to be able to get things cleaned. It wouldn't show the dirt.

Her eyes lingered for a moment on her favorite party gown. Such a pretty color . . . Denis' favorite shade of red. The deep V waist was wonderfully flattering, and little puffed sleeves accented a neckline which plunged just deep enough to be decidedly interesting. Wildly impractical . . . but Dominie was unable to resist. She needed one becoming outfit, after all, to wear when she found her brother. With a lace fichu to tuck into the neck, of course, so she wouldn't offend his modesty.

All the while she was sifting through the dresses, and putting the discards away with uncharacteristic tidiness so she wouldn't arouse suspicion, her mind was whirling. She had some cash in the house. Not much—most transactions were done on credit—but enough for gewgaws and fiddlefaddle, as the bishop liked to put it. And surely she could coax more out of the bankers who handled her affairs, approaching them separately, a little here . . . a little there. There were so many things a young bride needed as her wedding day approached.

It would not occur to them that traveling expenses to Vietnam might be among them.

# Mornings Clear
## and Misty

### Late October

## 9

CEYLON. Even the name had a magical sound. Dominie leaned as far as she dared over the wooden railing and took a long, deep breath. Tantalizing hints of cinnamon and turmeric and sweet-scented tropical blossoms wafted on a salt breeze from the shore. The sun was just rising, an almost colorless dawn, and frothy patches of white foam floated on a luminous green sea. Off on the horizon, a flock of flying fish skimmed across the water.

Ceylon. The wind picked up, streaming a long black veil out behind her. It was barely morning, but already it was warm: a sultry, languid warmth that made her wish she could stay awhile. She had never been anywhere exotic in her life, and she longed to hail one of the dirty little boats that had crowded around the gangplank yesterday, dark-skinned sampan-wallahs cursing and spitting as they fought over the disembarking passengers, and explore the thickly forested slopes and curving beaches that looked so tempting from the ship. That little pagoda all alone on the crest of a hill, its graceful upturned corners catching the sun—she would have loved to see what was inside. And could it be true, as the mate had told her when they arrived the afternoon before, that cinnamon really grew wild on the hillsides?

The sound of ships' bells echoed across the water from other vessels at anchor nearby. Three bells. Half-past five, though by the sun it seemed earlier. There was no point, Dominie reminded herself firmly, wishing for things that could not be. They had stopped just long enough to let some of the passengers off and take on supplies. More would embark this morning; then they would be on their way.

She shivered. Another ship was just to the east, no more than twenty or thirty yards away, and she almost felt as if they were lying in its shadow. The next stop was Calcutta, where she would pick up an East Indiaman bound for Singapore. The end of her journey . . . or the beginning, depending on how one looked at it.

The end of the nice, safe accommodations on nice, conventional vessels. And the beginning of a venture into the unknown.

She reached up automatically, brushing back the veil that had blown across her face. As her fingers encountered the starched wimple underneath, she started to laugh in spite of herself. What a goose she was, worrying about things that hadn't happened yet! She had gotten this far, hadn't she—with remarkably little trouble? Though not in quite the guise she had imagined.

She laughed again, enjoying the morning and the sudden remarkable freedom she felt despite the confining aspects of her garment. She had made it to Ceylon. She would make it to Calcutta and Singapore—and beyond. And home again, with her brother safe beside her.

She leaned against the railing again, her weight resting easily on her forearms, as she thought back over the journey that had brought her this far. She had been frightened out of her wits at first. The horrible ride in a public coach from Paris to Lyons . . . that dreadful gawking man who had actually had spittle running out of the corner of his mouth when he looked at her! She had nearly swooned in terror the first time he had managed to corner her outside one of the way stations.

Mercifully, a kind older woman had seen what was happening and had taken her under her wing. But the experience had impressed upon Dominie all too vividly the perils that even a modestly dressed young lady faced traveling alone, and for one brief, awful moment she had considered turning back.

Then she had gotten the brilliant idea of detouring to the small convent on the outskirts of Genève. . . .

Darling, darling Jean-Luc. Dominie smiled to herself as she recalled the expression on her beloved nursemaid's face in that dim, cramped antechamber where visitors from outside were received. Delight first, then surprise— then incredulity dissolving into sheer horror as Dominie had explained what she was planning to do.

"But, no, *chère* Dominique," she had protested,

shocked to the core. "Of what can you be thinking? It is too hazardous, this expedition that you describe. There are many dangers."

"Only if I don't plan carefully," Dominie had replied, feeling somehow better just being there. Jean-Luc was the only person in the world she had ever willingly allowed to call her Dominique. "That's why I came to you, sweet, sweet Sister. You are so much cleverer than I. You will figure a way to keep me safe."

"What way, if there is none?" the older woman had grumbled. "You have seen yourself already how difficult it is. What if next time there is no motherly *madame* to watch over you? No. You cannot undertake such a questionable journey. *Le bon Dieu* alone knows what you would find at the end."

"I will find my brother," she had reminded her gently. "And you know how I love him. I will not be dissuaded."

Jean-Luc had continued to protest. She had brought out every argument she could think of; then, when they failed, she had brought them out all over again. But in the end she had given in, as Dominie had known she would. She was a practical woman. If she could not keep this child she loved from taking risks, then at least she would do what she could to minimize them. She had put on her thinking cap—and come up with the perfect solution!

Dominie was filled with wonder all over again as she looked down at the black veil floating out over the railing. Truly, Jean-Luc was amazing! Pretty girls traveling by themselves were bound to attract unsavory attention—but a nun was treated with the greatest respect. The journey on the stage back to Lyons had been considerably pleasanter. And from Lyons to Marseilles, where she had caught the French mail to Alexandria.

From there it had been wonderfully easy. Overland first to Suez. No trouble arranging that when there were ample funds at her disposal, some of which she had cleverly converted to pounds so she would be prepared for any contingency. Then, with a bit of good fortune—which saved ten days' waiting for the Bombay mail—she had obtained passage on a surprisingly luxurious British brigantine carrying officers and their families to India.

Easy . . . but it had taken more than two months.
Dominie gripped the rail unconsciously. Even if the con-
nections were just right, she still had another couple of
weeks to Singapore, a week after that—at least—to Tourane or Hué. Three weeks minimum. And in three weeks
Denis might be dead. Or captured and scheduled for execution, which would make rescue more difficult.

Her throat grew tight, and just for a moment it was
hard to swallow. She had been so confident when she had
stepped back into the coach in Genève in her pious black-
and-white disguise. She had concentrated all her thoughts
on the journey, as if somehow all she had to do was get
there and everything else would follow. Now, for the first
time, she realized the enormity of what she had under-
taken, and she was terrified that she would fail.

The sun was rising rapidly, no longer pale, but a deep
yellow with faint touches of pink. The shadow of the
other ship had stretched across the water to caress the
hull of her own vessel, and Dominie turned to look at it,
grateful for the distraction.

It was what they called a clipper. A relatively new kind
of ship, lean and sharp-bowed, built for the China trade,
where competition was fierce and speed essential. Even
in repose, there was a singular beauty about its long,
sleek lines, a dynamic sense of power in the tall raked
masts that caught and held her attention. Dominie could
almost see the sails unfurled, a great cumulus of snowy
canvas, billowing and slapping in the rising wind. A simple banner, two red stripes on a white ground, was over-
shadowed by a bolder red-white-and-blue flag, which she
recognized instantly.

A Yankee vessel, then. The first she had seen. She
studied it curiously. Not a large ship, but full-rigged,
decks immaculately holystoned, every rope coiled in
place, the brass so thoroughly polished it gleamed in the
sun. Was the captain a cruel taskmaster who had his men
lashed if they dared to slack? she wondered. Or a popular
leader who inspired his crew to such devotion they could
not bear to let him down?

Probably the former, she thought with amused disdain.
Everyone knew Americans were barbarians.

It was a moment before she realized that there was a
man standing on the deck. A tall, powerfully built man,

half-turned away from her, absorbed in himself as he gazed at the immaculately pure line where the sea met the sky. Blue-black shadows blurred his form—that was why she had not noticed him before—but she could see enough to make out a general outline, distinct and strangely familiar.

*Like my dream,* she thought with a start. Her breath caught in her throat as she stared at him, so mesmerized she could not tear her eyes away. The wind gusted again, and she could feel the long, loose veil floating out behind her.

Like her dream . . . but not her dream at all. For in her dream, everything had been vague and hazy. Here the clarity was so sharp it was almost unnatural. The dazzling blue of a tropical sky, not a wisp of cloud in sight; shimmering green water so transparent she could make out the rocks on the bottom; breathtaking splashes of color in the trees and flowers and awakening life on-shore. But the air was the same, the warm sensuality she had imagined, the exotic scents on the breeze . . .

And *he* was the same.

Dominie could not stop staring at him. He was so exactly the man in her dreams. Even from a distance, she was conscious of his height, of the arrogant ease in his bearing, the slim-hipped, broad-shouldered torso, strong but lithe, like a stalking panther, still now, but tensed and ready to strike. His hair was panther dark, flaring slightly in the breeze, almost incredibly black—and utterly maddening because it hid his face!

"Turn," she willed him with every ounce of concentration she could muster. Disregarding the danger, she stretched as far over the rail as she could, longing somehow to get closer. "Turn around so I can see who you are!"

She knew she was being foolish. She was bound to be disappointed. He would probably turn out to be old, or ugly and hideously pockmarked. Or worse yet, pallidly bland! But the dream had been part of her life for so long—she had imagined this moment so often—she had to know.

Then suddenly, as if he heard, as if obeying the intensity of that whispered command, he turned and stepped into the light.

He was not ugly at all. Dominie saw that at once, and a shiver of excitement ran down her spine. He was quite a nice age, perhaps thirty, perhaps a little more, just old enough to be intriguing. And if he was not the handsomest man she had ever seen, he was certainly the most dynamic. And compelling.

He was not dark at all. It was only the shadows that had given that illusion. In fact, he was almost fair. His hair was a sort of neutral tone, streaked lighter by the sun, and shorter than it had appeared, curling with deceptive softness around the most fascinating face Dominie had ever seen.

It was not a perfect face—his brow was too wide for classical proportions, his jaw too square, his strong, slightly angular nose a bit too sharp—but it was the face of a man who clearly knew who he was, and was comfortable with it.

She had no doubt that this was the captain she had wondered about before, and she sensed instinctively that both her judgments had been right. Here was a man who could be cruel when the occasion demanded, but also a man who would inspire great loyalty.

His eyes met hers, curious for an instant, unflinching, and Dominie realized with a sudden stab of regret that her dream had come true in the bitterest way possible. She had sensed that she would never be satisfied with an arranged marriage. No sensible alliances for her, with suitable monied mates. She had sensed that one day she would find a man with the power to capture her heart— that all she would have to do was look at him once and she would know she belonged to him forever.

What she had not sensed was that he would be a man whose name she did not even know. A man she wouldn't have been likely to meet even if destiny and a desperate mission were not drawing her elsewhere.

Anguish swelled her heart as she continued to stare at him, memorizing his features, knowing it would have to last a lifetime. His eyes, were they blue or gray? How agonizing not to be able to tell for sure. His mouth, curving and sensuous, a surprise somehow in the austerity of his face. A boyish lock of hair that the wind had tumbled onto his forehead.

She knew how wanton she must look to him. Only the

brazenest hussy would gape at a man so openly. He had to have noticed, and no doubt was feeding his ego on it if that sheer male arrogance she had sensed before was real.

Well, let him, she thought with a flare of defiance. He could imagine all sorts of lewd things, it wouldn't do him any good. The gulf of green-glittering ocean between them, the even greater chasm of circumstance that had pained her so deeply before, was her protection now. He could think what he liked—he could think she was going to leap into the water and swim the space between them— she did not care! She had just found the one man she could ever truly love, the man who had filled her dreams for years, and it tore her heart apart to realize she would never see him again.

He seemed to sense what she was thinking. Or perhaps it did not matter: perhaps he had only recognized the longing she made no effort to conceal, and was responding to it. His eyes grew hooded, dropping insolently, running slowly, deliberately down her body.

Why, he's undressing me, she thought, shivering, but unable to draw away. He was ravishing her thoroughly, and very expertly, and she was letting him do it.

When at last he raised his eyes, she saw that he was laughing. A mocking, contemptuous laugh—as if he had just raped her and despised her for it! Dominie felt a surge of anger and horrible, irrational betrayal.

She *had* behaved shamelessly. But from a distance, where surely he knew she had to feel safe. And he had been shameless too! Was it all right for him because he was a man—and she, as a woman, was supposed to have no feelings?

"Oh, *mon Dieu!*" Dominie gasped as she recalled suddenly how she was dressed. In the prim white wimple and long black veil of a *religieuse*. He had looked across from the deck of his ship and seen a woman gazing at him with frank desire in her eyes—and thought she was a nun!

Her cheeks flushed crimson as she turned and stumbled toward the stairway that led to the cabins below. Ropes sprawled this way and that, carelessly left loose when the sails were hauled down, and she nearly fell more than once, but she didn't care how clumsy she looked. All she wanted was to get away from there.

No wonder he had been so contemptuous! The steps were steep and she slowed down now that she was safely out of sight. Americans were such disgusting heathens; they had no sense of piety or dedication. He probably thought a life in the service of Christ was pathetic and unnatural. To him, nuns would be poor sex-starved creatures who spent all their time panting after men.

And she had just proved him right!

She burst into the tiny cabin she shared with three other women and was relieved to find it empty. Everyone must have gotten up early and taken advantage of the brief interval before sailing to enjoy a stroll on the beach. How she wished she had done the same!

What on earth had gotten into her?

She could feel herself shaking as she sank down on the side of the bed. What was she thinking? Nun's habit or no, well-bred young ladies did not carry on blatant flirtations with impudent-eyed strangers. It had been wildly improper—and foolhardy! A few yards of water meant nothing when every ship carried at least one swift cutter.

And all because he bore a few vague similarities to the man in her dreams! The tension eased somewhat, perspective returning as she tucked her knees up to her chin and rested her wimpled cheek on them. And in truth, she had to admit, the similarities were precious few. His height, the fact that he had been turned away, albeit partially, that his hair looked black in the shadows. All the rest had been made out of whole cloth. She had been so captivated by her own dream, the first time a situation came along that even remotely resembled it, she had pounced like a cat on an unsuspecting mouse.

And then he turned out to be handsome. How could she resist?

A puckish sense of humor got the better of her, and she started laughing in spite of herself. How she had always hated it when people treated her like a featherbrained adolescent. I am not a little girl! she had insisted indignantly. I am a young woman with the maturity to make my own decisions.

Now here she was acting like the silliest kind of adolescent with her first wild infatuation!

Love, indeed! How could she possibly have imagined she was in love with a man she had seen for only a few seconds—from a good twenty yards' distance. A man she would never meet, and would probably despise if she did. An insolent, arrogant, depraved man who clearly did not have a courteous instinct in his body!

It occurred to her that she had just had a very fortunate escape. A different time, a different place, and her girlish fantasies might have entangled her in an extremely unpleasant situation. She was going to have to see to it that she was more sensible in the future.

Still, he *was* handsome, she thought with a sigh. And after all, from a distance, what harm had it done? She would never see him again anyway.

# 10

JARED BARRON was more disturbed than he would have
cared to admit as he stood at the rail of the *Shadow Dawn*
and watched the first morning sunlight stretch across the
now-empty deck of the British brigantine at anchor
nearby. Try as he would, he could not shake an unsettling
impression of seductive green eyes, daring, challenging,
filling him with unwanted desire.

Green? He half-smiled, a rueful twist of a mouth that
was otherwise taut. An illusion probably, from that distance. A reflection of the sea, he thought, and wondered
why it bothered him so much.

Because of the long black veil that blew teasingly
around pretty features and a nubile young body? But sacrilege was not a concept that had ever concerned him
overmuch. And at any rate, in this case the sacrilege, if
there was one, was hardly *his*. He turned abruptly from
the rail with the same expression of contempt that had
struck Dominie so bitterly before.

In fact, his thoughts at that moment were much as she
had imagined them. Not that he was a heathen. Far from
it; the faith of his forefathers and their passionate commitment to freedom of worship was a very real and tangible part of his life. But long boyhood Sundays on his
knees in the austerity of a New England chapel with harsh
white light streaming through unstained windows had
given him an inherent suspicion of anything that smacked
of softness or opulence in religion. The great Catholic
cathedrals, with their gilded altars and candles flickering
in statued niches, with the cloying smell of incense and
the eerily echoing wail of Latin incantations, had seemed
to him the few times he had wandered in almost blasphe-
mous, and he had been glad to get out into the air and
sunlight again.

He found his eyes flitting back to the other ship, and he was annoyed with himself as he realized that he had half-hoped to see her again. The Romish enthusiasm for celibacy was something he could understand, even admire, in a man. The dedicated parish priests and selfless missionaries who subjugated their own passions and pleasures to direct all their energy to the service of mankind at least accomplished something with their sacrifices.

But to cloister women away, to shut them off from everything that was normal and natural just so they could pass their days and nights in prayer, was more than incomprehensible. It was inhumane!

He felt an unreasoning surge of anger, as though somehow he himself had been personally affronted. The thought of rows and rows of little cells, each with a woman sleeping alone on a narrow wooden pallet calculated to enure her body against feminine weaknesses, filled him with the utmost disgust. He had heard that they flagellated themselves nightly, raking the tender skin on their backs until they bled, to drive away sexual desire. From what he had just seen, he could well believe it.

And yet . . .

Jared pushed back from the rail and began to stride along the deck, long, angry paces that echoed across the glittering water. Ordinarily the area would have been swarming with men, everyone up at first light to put in two or three hours before breakfast, but the crew had been given shore leave the night before, and the morning's work was slated to start later.

And yet . . . there had been something almost sweet and naive in the way she had let her eyes touch his for an instant. An awakening of innocence, such as he had seen sometimes in the eyes of a pretty girl at her first ball, or carrying on her first flirtation as carriages passed not quite by chance in the park, and Jared found himself wondering what it would be like to take her in his arms. To kiss her gently, teasingly . . . to show her what life was really about. . . .

"Dammit it, Barron," he muttered under his breath, "you've been at sea too long!" What he needed was a good woman—or better yet, a bad one!—and he would stop this adolescent mooning over willowy nuns who might or might not have melting sea-green eyes. And most certainly weren't the sort for the distractions he had in mind!

He ran his eyes along the deck, checking things out, looking for even the smallest infraction, and not finding any. Barron Shipping ran a tight operation: discipline was strict, and no letting up on maintenance. Every morning, except in the most inclement weather, the decks were swabbed and holystoned, first with a large soft stone, slid fore and aft by means of ropes at each end, then the smaller "prayerbook" stones that scraped the last bit of tar and salt out of crevices and corners. After that, there were brass fittings to be polished, rigging to be checked, sails mended, scuppers and cannon cleaned, until everything met the rigid standards of the line. It was the Barron boast, and every man from old Gareth himself to the greenest tar was proud to claim that their ships could be recognized with not a flag flying by the immaculate sheen of their decks and hulls and the glint of sun on their brasses.

Too damn long at sea, he thought as he paused at the bow, staring out at a flock of flying fish soaring across the water. And not much of a fond farewell in Boston either.

He grimaced uncomfortably. Blast women, anyway. Why did they have to turn all teary and recriminatory? He headed toward the starboard side, continuing his relentless round of inspection. He had been honest with her, God knew. She had not been the only lady in his life at the time, and he had not pretended she was—nor had he made any promises. He had not even told her when, just briefly, he had had a flicker of an idea that this might be it, that she might be the woman with whom he would finally settle down. But he realized now that she had sensed it; she had been hurt and disappointed when he said good-bye, and he regretted it deeply.

That seemed to be his lot lately, hurting and regretting. He stopped to check the chain cables, noting with less than his usual satisfaction that they were well-oiled and free of rust. There had been a time in his life when he had simply assumed he would get married, as his father and uncle and grandfather before him. That he would return after months at sea to find a gentle woman waiting, her eyes lighting with quiet enthusiasm when she spotted his ship from the widow's walk on the top of the house . . . that children would come running and shrieking down to the dock to greet him.

Now, for the first time, it occurred to him that the excuses were growing thinner and thinner. No woman was ever quite right, no situation exactly what he was looking for. Perhaps, after all, he did not have whatever it required to share one's life with another human being.

Or perhaps he had just put it off too long. Perhaps a man reached an age when he was too settled in his life, when routine, like an old garment, was too comfortable to be cast aside, and the joys of home and hearth no longer had the same appeal.

He glowered down at a rotten-looking water barrel, giving it a swift kick with his boot, but despite its appearance, it held sturdy. Why the devil was he so on edge? Because the journey was taking so long? Because port after port yielded no positive results, and every day they delayed was another day that Matthew could get in deeper? . . . Or because, for reasons he could not understand, he was still haunted by those bold, disturbing eyes?

Unaccountably, he found his thoughts drifting back to the past. To the first time his ship had floated into the exotic blue-green waters of Macao. Other eyes then. Black, sensual, laughing, provocative. Mei-ling . . . the one serious relationship in his life. He had been nineteen when he met her, she twenty-six; and while she was far from his first romance, she was the first—the only—woman he had loved in any sense of the word.

She had, Jared supposed, in the way of the Orient, belonged to him. He had paid for her keep. He had set her up in a small house with a high-walled garden not far from the Praya, and she had waited there, presumably faithfully, though he had not required it, for the infrequent times one Dawn or another brought him into the harbor.

There had never been any question of marriage. Such things were not done, nor would it have been practical even if they were. Much as Jared enjoyed his intervals in Macao, he could never have lived there, just as he could not have brought Mei-ling back to Boston. Her beauty was exquisitely Chinese; long black hair and graceful silken robes would have seemed absurdly out-of-place in the conventional rigidity of a Boston parlor.

And if he knew the conventional Boston matrons, they would have found a way to let her know it! It would have been like transporting a fragile tropical flower to a cold climate where it was certain to wither and die.

He tried to shrug off the feeling of discontent that clung with the humidity and rising heat. All that was in the past now. She had given him two sons, which he had never made any attempt to conceal. Ten and seven at their last birthdays, by European count, and Jared was not ashamed to take pride in them. He had never worried about their future. Half-caste sons were frequently acknowledged and places of responsibility set aside for them in the great trading houses. But he had been bitterly aware as he had waited, pacing anxiously, for the protracted birth of his second child, that it could as easily be a girl. And a girl with mixed blood could look forward to only one kind of life.

He had cared very much for the beautiful Mei-ling. He had loved her in his own way. But the relationship he had with her was not one he would want—not one he could *accept*—for his daughter.

He had broken with her after that. As was customary in that area, he had seen that she was well, even handsomely, provided for. She could have made an excellent marriage with one of the more substantial Chinese merchants had she so desired, but she had chosen to remain single, and Jared had the uncomfortable feeling sometimes, as with the pretty girl left behind in Boston, that she had hoped for more than she could reasonably have expected. Perhaps was hoping still.

"Damn!" he said, his eye lighting at last on what he had been looking for. A set of carpenter's tools, strewn carelessly just aft of the forecastle, was already coated with corrosive salt spray. "Carmichael!" He raised his voice to a bellow. "What the blasted hell are these doing here? Mackler! Get your ass on deck!"

The sound of scurrying footsteps came from all directions, every man rushing to attention as if the call had been: "All hands ahoy! Tumble up!" A thin, anxious face appeared first, eyes blinking in genuine surprise as a youngish man with a tuft of yellow hair gaped at the little droplets of morning mist glittering on the tools.

"Sorr?" he said, but Jared took one look at those bland, startled features and turned his attention to a large apelike man lumbering across the deck from the direction of the crew's quarters. He had a sullen expression and was just pulling on his shirt, as if he resented being asked to get dressed and turn out.

"Here, Mackler!" Jared waved him over and gestured at the tools. "What the devil's the meaning of this? I've warned you about leaving things out before. And don't try to blame your assistant this time—I know damn well you did it!"

"Well, and w'at of it?" the man mumbled in a surly, whining tone. "Bloody waste of time, 'ammerin' an' sawin' just ter fix an 'atch cover w'at looked fine ter me . . . an' all the rest of the 'ands long ashore. So I got a little 'urried an' forgot ter stow 'em aft. So w'at the bloody 'ell?"

"We haven't had a good flogging yet this trip, Mackler—maybe it's time we started. That would teach you to keep a civil tongue in your head!" Jared could feel eyes boring into him, and he knew that the rest of the men had gathered and were watching, deathly silent, wondering what had gotten into their captain. But the anger had a healing effect, almost cathartic as he took all his pent-up doubts and frustrations and channeled them into one intensely satisfying burst of fury. "Pull something like this again, and I'll have you stripped to your waist and bound to the rigging. Hands and ankles tied, and I'll wield the cat myself! Thirty lashes—and thirty the next day for good measure! Is that understood?"

"Sixty lashes? For an 'ammer an' chisel?" The man's lips curled. He was an insolent troublemaker, press-ganged in a tavern in Liverpool and roughened by years at sea, and Jared felt disgust mingle with the rage as he stood there and struggled to control his temper.

"And a saw," he said coldly. "Now, pick them up and get out of my sight or I'll have you flogged today. I've half a mind to take you into port and dump you there. And see that the other vessels are warned not to sign you on."

"Aye . . . an' w'at will ye do for a carpenter then,

*sorr!*'' The man's tone was openly mocking, much too cocky as he deliberately baited his captain. ''Carmichael 'ere can't 'it 'is finger, let alone a nail—an' 'e ain't figured out yet which side of the saw be for cuttin'. 'E's fine ter fix the chicken coops, but w'at 'appens w'en a spar need replacin'? Or the main mast come down in a storm?''

''I'm a pretty fair carpenter myself,'' a new voice cut in. Jared looked around to see Alex standing just behind him. His face was impassive, but his feet were apart, firmly planted on the deck, and his shoulders were squared back. ''I can manage a mast if I have to, or a spar . . . or a chicken coop. And if we're going to dump you somewhere, I vote we look for an isolated island where no ship passes, and leave you to rot on the sand.''

Mackler's face distorted. ''You wouldn't dare—'' he started to growl, but Jared cut him off.

''One more word, and it *is* thirty lashes. And it will give me great pleasure. Here, boy—you there! Fetch the cat-o'-nine-tails. On the double!''

A hand touched his arm, light, but firm.

''Easy, Jared,'' Alex said in an undertone, ''this is not a lashing offense. Besides,'' he added, raising his voice, ''as first mate, it's my duty to take care of petty problems with the crew. And I assure you, the pleasure will be mine.''

He strode over to where the man was leaning with impudent nonchalance against the gunwale.

''Stand up straight,'' he said quietly. ''Now, hear this. You are going to pick up those tools, clean them off, and put them where they belong. Then you are going to come back and help the others holystone the deck. And if I hear one word from you—*one*—from now to the end of the voyage, I will personally see to it that you are put off the ship wherever we happen to be. And I don't care if there's land in sight or not. You got that, swab?''

''Yes, sorr!''

''Sir.''

''Yes*sir!*''

Jared watched with grim amusement as the man gathered his tools and tried almost comically to put a swagger in the slink that propelled him down the deck and out of sight. Alex had handled the situation perfectly—and just in time, he had to admit. There was more laughter than apprehension as the crew dispersed, heading to their mops and "prayerbooks." But he saw the curious side-long looks they cast in his direction, and he knew that he had come within a few seconds of letting things get out of hand.

Discipline was important on a ship; flogging was sometimes necessary, and back talk never tolerated. But discipline had to be fair to be effective, and he had badly overreacted.

"I suppose I owe you thanks," he said with a wry grimace as the men settled to their chores and he was left with his cousin.

"No need for that," Alex replied evenly. "You might choke on it, and we're not carrying a surgeon this trip. I'm not sure I'm up to reviving you."

"I might at that," Jared admitted, almost laughing in spite of himself. He was aware that his cousin was watching him strangely, a kind of searching look that made him uncomfortable. "Grandmother Judith always used to tell me I should watch my temper. She said it would get the better of me one of these days. It looks like she was right." He paused, searching for the words he wanted. "It looks like you were right too. Lashing would have been excessive. This time."

Alex was silent for a moment, still watching him.

"You gave your word, cousin," he said at last

"Often . . . and on many things," Jared admitted. "And I always keep it."

"You gave your word that the *Shadow* would follow the route we had set. She would stop at every port . . . and stay as long as necessary. And you would not interfere."

"And I haven't, blast it!" Jared burst out, surprised at the one accusation he had not expected. "We've stopped at every damn port, large or small, on both coasts of Africa, and Madagascar to boot! We even stopped at Zanzibar, for Chrissake—for all the good it did us. But we stopped!"

"Yes, and your temper has gotten fouler every time. If this keeps up, we're going to have a mutiny on our hands before we reach Macao. The men respect a strict master, but not an erratic one. They don't know what's going to happen next, and it's beginning to stir up resentment. It has to stop, Jared. Now.''

Jared stiffened, anger clouding his face momentarily. ''This is my command. You make suggestions if you want—and I might agree with them. But you don't tell me what to do.''

''I do when you've given your word. And broken it.''

He did not wait for a reply, but turned and walked away, leaving Jared alone with thoughts that were more than a little disquieting. Technically, of course, he had not broken his word. He had kept it—to the letter. But actually he had been making it increasingly difficult to stop at port after port, especially when they had so little to show for it! Now they were going to waste precious weeks tacking up the East Indian coast to Calcutta, which was strictly British territory! How could he be expected not to chafe?

But it *was* having an effect on the crew. Jared turned his face up, catching the sun that had deepened his skin to bronze and put more streaks of gold in his hair. A ship took the mood of the captain. If there was tension on board—and he had no doubt Alex was right about that— then he was the primary cause. Most of the hands had been with them for some time; they knew and respected him, and even bragged about their captain's hot temper, the fact that no man ever put anything over on him. But a considerable portion were newcomers, the lascars and Malays and Manila men who came and went at regular intervals, and it would be asking for trouble to ignore the growing restlessness in their ranks.

He had cooled down enough by the time the men finished the deck and turned to their other tasks—with a frenzy, he noted wryly, calculated either to please or to appease him—to realize that he had two choices. He could renegotiate the route with his cousin, if Alex was willing, or he could accept the inevitable with good grace and keep his mouth shut. Anything else would be devastating for the ship and its crew.

''If you think I'd choke on a word of thanks,'' he said later as he leaned in the doorway of the chart room, hands resting on the sturdy oak beam across the top, ''imagine how apologies sit on my stomach. I'm sorry, Alex. You were right . . . again.''

His cousin looked up from the table where he was seated. A large map was spread out in front of him, and he had been poring over it.

"I think we can forget Calcutta," he said evenly. "The British have the market pretty well sewed up, and their vessels have plenty of cargo space to the point. But I would like to stop at Singapore." He jabbed with his finger at a dot on the map. Jared bent to look at it, though he already knew every inlet and island and harbor by heart. "It may be an English colony, but the East Indiamen are hauling opium by the time they get to Singapore, with little or no room in their holds for anything else. And here, along the Annamese coast—Cochin China—we might have a chance. A xenophobic place; it makes the Chinese look downright friendly, but it's worth a try. No one but a handful of Arab smugglers has looked at it for decades."

Jared nodded. "A fair compromise, and probably more than I deserve."

"Fair—and sensible," his cousin admitted. "You were right too. I've been pushing because I wanted things to work out. But all the pushing in the world isn't going to make markets where they don't exist. We'll have to hope Newcombe had better luck, coming round the other way. California should be opening to the Americans soon, and there's always the Sandwich Islands."

"We are agreed then?" Jared said. "Singapore, Cochin China, and, of course, Manila. And that's it?"

"We are agreed."

His cousin was looking at his strangely again, and Jared knew what he was thinking, though he knew that the most private of the Barron men would never put it into words. Alex would not intrude on his feelings, but he had to be wondering what had caused this sudden outburst today of all days. Why the tension that had been building slowly, visibly since the start of the voyage should have exploded now, without so much as a spark to ignite it.

He was wondering himself as he stood at the rail late that night and watched the moonlight on the water. An eerie, almost phosphorescent green . . . and he was reminded again, uncomfortably, of eyes that had seemed to be green as they met his for what could not have been more than a few brief seconds.

It was as if she had done something to him, he thought—that pretty little witch with her black veil and absurd white cloth wrapped around her head and neck. As if she reminded him of the time when he, too, had been heartbreakingly young and dreamed of love, of the one special person who would sweep everyone else away. And, in reminding, had made him feel suddenly alone.

Damn, he would be glad when this trip was over.

## 11

DOMINIE HAD NO IDEA what she had expected of Singapore—Singapura, in the language of its people. The city of the lion. Something glamorous perhaps. Sloe-eyed ladies in flowing silken robes peering out from behind the curtains of lacquered palanquins, narrow twisting lanes with gardened pagodas on either side . . . the silvery tinkle of temple bells in the distance. Certainly not the dust and heat and stench that swirled around her now as she stood at the corner of two raucous, bustling dirt roads and tried to get her bearings.

She glanced down at the paper in her hand. The directions, stark black against the crisp white of the hotel stationery, had seemed clear enough when she left. Two streets up, turn right, straight ahead for seven streets, then right again. But it was hard to tell what was a street in that sprawling jumble of stone structures and flimsy ramshackle wooden huts, and what was an alleyway leading into a filthy yard—swarming with garbage and screaming small children and dogs with oozing sores—into which the homes of several families seemed to empty.

How far had she come? She glanced back over her shoulder, but there was no sign of the river with its busy commercial development. It was late afternoon, and the sun had all but disappeared into a bank of menacing gray clouds. She had been told that when the monsoons began, any day now—it was already well into November—the streets would be flooded, overflowing with sewage and the festering carcasses of dead animals.

She did not even know, she realized with sinking heart, if she was searching for the right man. Denis had mentioned only one name in his letter—Aziz—and his description of the Arab smuggler had been sketchy at best.

But the kind dark-skinned man at the hotel, with a neat white turban wound round his head, had assured her that the person whose name he had written in English and Arabic on the paper in her hand was known for ferrying illicit goods and passengers up the Annamese coast. And even if by some strange chance this was not the right Aziz, she would surely find him somewhere in the area, for Arabs, like the Malays and Indians and Indonesians, clustered together, living and working among their own.

"But missee," he had said in his funny singsong tones, "this Aziz, he is not good man. He is not good at all. Much better missee-sahib not to go to him. There are many boatmen."

"Perhaps," Dominie had admitted, grateful for the thorough grounding in languages that allowed her to understand even heavily accented English. "But none of the other boatmen can take me where I need to go." Then, seeing the expression on his face, she had added, "I'll be all right. We've had dealings with this man before. He has taken my . . . a friend of mine, a priest, to this same place. He will remember where it is."

The man had continued to look distressed, but Dominie had insisted, and in the end he had conceded with an eloquent shrug. Now, looking down at the explicit instructions he had written, she felt the first twinges of doubt. He had seemed genuinely concerned . . . and she couldn't help remembering the distaste in her brother's letter.

But this Arab smuggler was her best hope for reaching Denis! Dominie tossed back her head with an abruptness that sent the black veil floating around her and caused several passersby to turn and stare. He knew where he had left Denis; he could take her to the exact spot. He could probably even tell her the direction her brother had gone from there.

Besides, if she didn't go to him, she was going to have to find someone else—and she had a feeling the smugglers were all much of a kind.

An old man in loose black pants and a ragged tunic was squatting in the dusty weeds along the edge of the road. He might have been any nationality. There was a Chinese cast to his features, but his skin was dark, and his eyes seemed glazed, as if he had seen as much as he wished of life and did not want to look any longer.

Dominie stopped beside him.

"Arab Street?" she asked slowly, taking care to enunciate each syllable. "I am trying to find Arab Street. Can you tell me where it is?"

He seemed to understand, for he raised a thin arm and gestured in the direction she had been heading, but he did not speak, and she couldn't be sure. She was surprised to see that it was getting dark. Afternoon turned to night almost without dusk this close to the equator, and it occurred to her that it might be wiser to turn back. She had not realized it was so late. Coconut-oil lamps flickered feebly at intervals along the street—someone must have lighted them, though in the jostle and confusion she had not noticed—but the illumination they gave was barely enough to soften the shadows.

She would just go to the next corner. Then if she still couldn't find the place, she would turn back. Tomorrow early would do as well.

She recognized the street even without a signpost. An eerie wailing drifted through the twilight, a man's voice, seeming to come from above, crying out words she could not understand in strange, elongated tones. The muezzin calling the faithful to prayer? Then suddenly it ended, and people seemed to be everywhere, coming out of doorways, materializing in little flickers of light that broke the almost total blackness.

Dominie stared in fascination. It was as if she had come around the corner and stepped into another world. The buildings were the same, two-story for the most part, stone interspersed with rotting, unpainted wood, but while some were fronted with the covered walkways that were standard in a city where the sun was brutal and shade a luxury, others had vivid squares of cotton or silk stretched out in front like the tops of desert tents. The people were different too—the strong, sharp features of the men in their many-colored robes, the dark, mysterious eyes of women peering through slits in graceful street-length veils—the sounds, the colors, the smells all combining to let her know that this was a corner of the Arab world transported to the distant East.

She started down the street, forgetting everything else

as she turned her head this way and that, wishing fervently that nuns didn't wear starched wimples that stuck out like blinders on both sides of their faces. In the heat of the tropics, everything came to a stop at midday, reviving late in the afternoon, and the open-fronted shops and cafés that lined both sides of the road were alive with people and laughter.

Music started somewhere nearby, the haunting sound of a single instrument, throbbing and vibrating over the boisterous rhythm of the night-awakening city. Men with turbaned heads and thick dark beards cleared spaces in the street, shouting and snapping their fingers, and barefoot boys in loose-fitting trousers and shirts hustled out to set up tables and stools. Oil lamps seemed to sputter and crackle everywhere, inviting pinpoints of light, and yellow tongues of flame lapped through the grilles of braziers that appeared beside the tables.

The smells of the city were there, the pervading decay of the surrounding swamps, the refuse and sweat, the wood rot and stagnant water and human waste. But there were other smells too—the pungent sharpness of fresh-roasted coffee, teasing the nostrils; the cloying sweetness of incense floating down from second-story windows; the rich masculine odor of strong tobacco, mingling with the smoke from the braziers; the complex perfume of exotic spices, displayed in great heaps and pyramids of gold and sienna and deep mahogany-red in some of the shops.

Dominie stopped at one, looking in to see what she could identify. Ground cloves, surely—there was no mistaking that smell—and cinnamon sticks and funny fat seeds of nutmeg, ready for the grater, and odd little star-shaped bits of brown with a faint aroma of anise when she bent her head and sniffed. In the next building, a barber had set up his basin, and a customer was already leaning back in the chair, a warm wet towel wrapped like a misplaced turban around his face. Beyond, baskets of brightly colored fruit spilled out of a small shop into the street, and the sound of haggling rose as women pinched and prodded, and sometimes tasted, to great exclamations of protest and dismay.

Across the way, the sharp clatter of a chisel against metal caught Dominie's ears, and she picked her way between the tables to watch as a skilled artisan patiently created intricate patterns on a large round brass tray. Other trays were piled on the floor or hanging on the walls, or sometimes were even made into tables with clever wooden tripods to form the legs. Next door, an old man whose hands were shaking so badly it looked as if he could barely hang on to the mallet was pounding sheets of silver and gold into the most exquisitely delicate jewelry she had ever seen.

She paused for a moment, feeling almost anonymous in her black veil as she stared down at the magic being created by those ancient trembling hands. With her head lowered, the wimple pushing the fabric forward over her face, she looked almost like the Arab women in their long dark garments with only the curiosity in their eyes showing.

The tables were beginning to fill as she turned back toward the street. Men were lounging on the stools, sending blue clouds of smoke into the lamplight as they laughed and chatted with each other, and women with flat round loaves of bread on boards on their heads and covered dishes in their hands paused beside the braziers and steaming pots. The meat was starting to spatter and hiss, fat dripping onto the coals, and Dominie's mouth watered as she caught sight of a heavenly-looking pilaf, rich and golden and studded with tiny dark raisins. How she wished she could sit with the others, communicating in English or French—or sign language, if she had to— and enjoy the savory food and lively camaraderie. And pretend she had not a care in the world.

The music stopped briefly, then began again, more frenzied this time, new instruments joining in, and Dominie forced her mind back to the task at hand. She felt safe here, with the profusion of lamps and the good-natured, bustling crowd, but she did not relish the long walk back to the riverfront, where the hotels and trading houses were located. She would do best to get her business over as quickly as possible.

She picked a shop at random, a small cluttered space crammed with baskets of brightly woven straw. No sooner had she stopped than a man in a dirty brown robe with a clean-shaven pockmarked face sidled over.

"I am looking for a man named Aziz," she said quickly, then repeated in French, *"Je cherche un homme*

*qui s'appelle Aziz.''* She glanced down at the paper she
was still clutching. "Seyid Azin bin Ali-Haroun."

The man gave her a long, strangely penetrating look,
then slowly started to grin. "You want Aziz?" he said
with a thick guttural accent.

Dominie shivered. A gold tooth caught the lamplight
and glittered at the side of his mouth, giving him an
oddly satanic look, and his breath reeked of garlic.

"You know him? You can tell me where to find him?"

The grin broadened, an extremely unpleasant expression. "There," he said, bobbing his head toward a building a short distance away. "But what you want with Aziz,
eh? He is old man. Better you come with me—yes?"

Dominie choked back her disgust as she turned away,
making no attempt to answer. She could feel those dark
lewd eyes boring into her back, laughing at her confusion, and suddenly she was frightened.

Should I have listened to the clerk at the hotel? she
thought. Should I listen to my own instincts now, when
everything is telling me to get away from here?

But if she gave up, if she turned tail and ran, how
would she ever find her brother?

The building the man had indicated was surprisingly
sturdy, constructed of huge blocks that looked like granite, with a carpet shop taking up the whole of the ground
floor. As Dominie approached, she saw a stairway on
one side, dark, but a glimpse of light showed at the top.

Without giving herself a chance to think, she hurried
up. The door on the landing was half-open, leading into
a shallow entry hall. She raised her hand and knocked.

The man who responded was not what she had expected, and just for a moment Dominie felt the tension
ease out of her body. He made a tall, striking figure,
expensively gowned in green-gold silk that flowed without a crease to the floor. Not thin, but there was more
solidity than flab in his bulk, and he seemed surprisingly
lithe for a man of his size. His hair was hidden beneath
a turban of a slightly darker color than his robe, but his
beard was ebony black, dramatically streaked with silver.

Then she saw his face. Dark eyes shifting slightly to
the side, studying her without seeming to, deep lines
sinking into the soft flesh around them—a full, sensuous,

self-indulgent mouth curving cruelly as he took her measure—and all the fear came back.

"Seyid Aziz bin Ali-Haroun?" she said.

"I am Aziz." His voice was guttural, like that of the man in the basket shop, but with a subtler accent. The amusement that showed in his eyes as he continued to look her over did not make him any more appealing. "What is it that I may do for you, Sister? . . . Ah, yes, I am familiar with the customs of your religion. I recognize the costume—the habit, you call it?—that is worn by the 'brides of Christ.' And may I say, it looks particularly charming on one who appears so young."

Dominie stiffened, as she sensed he had intended. "It is not meant to be charming," she replied, struggling to keep her anxiety from showing. "It is meant to disguise whatever charms the wearer may possess. And to discourage vanity. I am sorry if you see it otherwise."

"I am corrected." He bowed, more mocking than conciliatory, and gestured toward a brighter glow that showed at the end of the short hall. "But please . . . you must come into my humble abode. It would be an honor to receive you as my guest."

The room that appeared as Dominie rounded the corner and stopped abruptly was even more of a surprise than the man himself in his elegantly tailored robe. From the exterior of the building she had expected something modest, even dilapidated, crude furnishings backed up against peeling plaster, and an odor of filth and mildew. But here was opulence more suited to a sultan's palace than the residence of an Arab smuggler in Singapore. Walls and ceiling were like a giant tent, draped in heavy silk, almost iridescent in the light of several highly polished brass lamps, and the richly patterned carpets with their deep jewel tones covered not only the floor but also several long benches. The simplest furnishing she could see was an elaborate version of the three-legged tray-table she had noticed in the shop below.

"Oh!" she gasped. The smell of incense was sweet and exotic, the sense of otherworldliness even stronger. It would not have shocked her if dancing girls had appeared in skimpy harem pants—with nothing else but rows of bells on their ankles!

She was aware of a soft chuckle behind her.

"It strikes many people that way. The building is so plain, they think the man who lives inside must be very poor. But it is only a fool who displays his wealth ostentatiously for everyone who passes to see. And Aziz is not a fool. . . . Here, I suggest you take this bench. You will find it comfortable, I think. I was about to partake of a cup of coffee. You will naturally join me."

"No, thank you," Dominie said, sitting gingerly on the edge of the bench. He moved the table closer and settled himself opposite on a plump cushion on the floor. "I don't drink coffee."

"Ah, but you cannot refuse. It is considered rude in the Arab world to refuse a man's hospitality. You would not wish to be rude—now, would you?"

There was just an edge of sharpness to his tone, and Dominie felt her senses come alert. Every instinct warned her that this was not a man to be taken lightly. Or trusted.

"Very well, then. But just a sip, please. Remember, I am not accustomed to it."

"It will not offend your palate." He was pouring as he spoke, from a long-necked enameled pot with a graceful curving spout. "I am a great connoisseur . . . of many things. The coffee I serve you now is the best to be found anywhere in Singapura."

Dominie took the cup he offered, a small demitasse, barely bigger than a thimble, made of such exquisite porcelain she could see the light glowing through it.

"You are right," she said, taking a sip. "It's delicious." The rich flavor warmed her stomach, like a glass of fine champagne. Dark and bitter, but with a heavenly sweetness, sugared almost to the point of a confection.

"You have nothing like that in France, I think. I am right, yes? That is a touch of French I hear?—though your English is quite flawless. Come, Sister, take another sip—do not be afraid, it will not bite you—and then you must answer my question. What is it that I may do for you?"

Dominie felt her heart skip a beat, and she wondered if, after all, she ought not to thank him for the coffee and make some excuse and go away. She might have, for she sensed in him something more dangerous than the distaste in Denis' letter had indicated, had she not had the uncomfortable feeling that this was someone who could not be put off with excuses.

"A year ago, a little less perhaps," she plunged in, "you took a man, a French priest, to the Vietnamese coast. Annam, I suppose you call it. His name was Père Denis Arielle. You left him off somewhere near a town named Tourane. I want you to take me to the same place."

"It was a little more than a year, actually. Nearly two months earlier than this. And I am familiar with the name Vietnam. But you surprise me, Sister. I did not think the Catholics sent their women there. Only their men."

"It has not been customary in the past," Dominie admitted warily. It seemed he knew more about the church than she had expected. "But once the priests have blazed a trail, then the nuns follow. To bring the faith to the women. No religion can survive without the support of wives and mothers. And it takes one woman to know what will touch another."

"So . . . perhaps." He was eyeing her intently. "Or perhaps you are being very foolish. But . . . no matter. If you are to go, you must go quickly. The place I left the priest was nearer Hué than Tourane. Several days up the coast. He was perhaps seven weeks earlier, but even then there was risk. The monsoons begin sooner in the north. We would have to start tomorrow."

Dominie's hands had begun to tremble. She put the cup down and twisted them in her lap. "I can be ready at daybreak."

Aziz nodded. "You cannot go looking like that. The Vietnamese are ignorant. Most have never even heard of women priests—these 'brides of Christ'—but to wear such a garment is to court trouble. You will have to arrange something else."

"I am aware of that. There are dresses in my baggage."

"Good." He nodded again, more heartily this time, but still his eyes did not leave her face. "Then there is the matter of money. There will be some considerable peril, especially this late in the season . . . and in that area. The devil winds could rip my boat apart, or the soldiers of the emperor could see us land. The cost will not come cheap. You did bring money?"

"I have English pounds. I assume that will be satisfactory." Dominie's hand slipped into her pocket automatically, an instant before she realized what she was doing. She should have told him the money was back at her hotel, should have haggled over the price—now it was too late.

"Most satisfactory." His eyes were glinting with greed as they followed her hand to her pocket. "How much do you have?"

Dominie curled her fingers tentatively around the notes. She had paid for the hotel in advance, and already picked up bread and fruit for dinner. She would probably not need any more cash, but she couldn't be sure. Taking hold of what felt like about half, she pulled it out.

"This is all I have. Will it be enough?"

He startled her by catching her wrist with one hand. Then, quick as lightning, the other hand shot out, and both her wrists were clasped in a painful vise and he was dipping into her pocket.

His eyes were more amused than angry as he drew out a wad of bills.

"And I thought the good sisters never lied." He shook his head gently. "Another illusion shattered. How sad."

"I meant, of course," Dominie said with as much dignity as she could muster, "that that's all the money I have at my disposal. I will need the rest to pay for the hotel room—or they won't let me out with my valise."

"Ah, but you are a very clever young woman. I am sure you will find some way to arrange things. *If* you still want to go to the Vietnamese coast. . . . You do still want to go, don't you?"

Dominie hesitated. It was almost as if he could read her mind. She was not at all sure she wanted to go, but she knew she had to. And really, what did she have to fear? He was only a thief, after all. A thief who had stolen no more than she would have been willing to give if he had negotiated honestly.

"I want to go."

"I thought you would," he said, smiling the same horrible smile that had set her teeth on edge when she first saw him. "It is a fair bargain . . . everything you have for the risk of my boat. And perhaps my life. You could have done worse, Sister, uh . . . ?"

"Sister Marie," Dominie said, not knowing why, but feeling the need to lie. She could not bear the thought of giving this odious man her name. "Marie-Josephe."

"Sister Marie. A pretty name . . . for a pretty lady. But, ah, I forget. Nuns are not supposed to be pretty. That would be vanity."

His eyes were caressing her, proprietary in some strange way, as if it had been his money that just made a purchase, and not the other way around. For a moment Dominie was terrified that he was not going to let her go, and she realized belatedly that she had put herself completely at his mercy. All he had to do was step between her and the door. With the noise below, no one would be likely to hear her screams.

But he only raised his hands, clapping them above his head. A young man appeared, dressed like the boys in the street in their baggy trousers and shirts.

"This Abdul. He does not speak English or French, but that will not be necessary. I am going to give him orders to see you back to your hotel. It was very foolish of you, Sister Marie-Josephe, to come out by yourself so late in the day."

He turned to the young man, spoke a few terse sentences, waited for a nod of comprehension, and then turned back to her.

"I will see you tomorrow. Midmorning will do—it does not have to be daybreak. Unless, of course, you change your mind between now and then."

Dominie forced herself to meet his gaze. "I won't," she said.

"No," he replied softly, "you won't."

And she would not. Seyid Aziz bin Ali-Haroun turned back into the room he had created for himself, every piece chosen by his own eyes and hands, and thought how fortunate a man could be when he least expected it. If he had thought there was any chance at all that the girl might panic and not return, he would never have let her go. But she wanted something desperately from this journey up the coast.

Perhaps merely religious fervor, he thought—perhaps something else. He did not know, but it did not matter. She would be back.

And he could use the time to prepare.

Aziz moved soundlessly across the carpet on soft-soled slippers to a small plain chest half-hidden in the corner. Those eyes . . . he had never seen eyes like that before. A deep emerald color in the shadows, almost yellow when the lamplight struck them. He found himself wondering what her hair was like. Golden, he hoped—golden would be just right. Or perhaps red. He had heard that red hair often went with green eyes.

He was smiling to himself as he lifted the lid and peered into the trunk. It was a smile that would have sent shivers down Dominie's spine if she could have seen it. Eyes like that alone would double a woman's price—many men would pay a fortune for those eyes. And if the figure beneath that bulky gown and stiff white headcloth . . .

He spent a pleasant several minutes imagining perfect ivory-smooth skin and firm young curves freed to tease and tantalize a man's basic instincts. She was tall—that was good. Oriental men were fascinated by tall women. And delightfully slim of waist. The cord with the cross that dangled provocatively against her hips—the outfit designed to conceal her charms, he thought with a short, cruel laugh—formed an exquisitely small circle. But the breasts above were anything but small, straining almost indecently against the fabric that struggled to encase them.

Good, too. He took a few small objects out of the trunk and raised the heavy dark cloth that concealed the bottom. Oriental men, like men everywhere, liked what they could not readily have, and Oriental women were for the most part extremely slight on top. A man with certain inclinations would be driven nearly mad by the sight of pretty Sister Marie without her ugly costume.

One man in particular. . . . Nguyen Duc Linh was a thoroughly disreputable member of the royal family. It was said the emperor despised him, but he was an elder cousin, thus entitled to a certain degree of respect, and the Son of Heaven had no choice but to treat him with courtesy.

And, of course, see to it that he had the wealth to tend to his wants, which were many and diverse.

Aziz had had occasion to bring this Linh a few "baubles" before. He ran his tongue over his lips, thinking of the best of them. A boatload of fine French cognac, the purest English opium pirated off an East Indiaman bound for Canton, a pair of twin slave girls from the Phillippines with the most astonishing accomplishments, a lovely little Thai creature, twelve years old, never touched by a man before.

He had liked the little Thai the best.

He had a taste for virgins, old Linh. Aziz chuckled. Men of a certain type liked to be the first to possess a woman; it fed their aging egos. He had heard that the Catholics insisted on chastity in their holy sisters. He hoped it was true. If her hair was anywhere near as lovely as her eyes, if her breasts were as he had imagined, *and* if she was a virgin, he could ask any price for her. And he would get it.

He reached into the shadows at the bottom of the trunk. Yes, it was there . . . just where he had left it. But where else would it be? None of the servants would dare to touch his things.

"Perfect," he whispered as he opened the small paper packet and revealed a fine white powder. The smallest amount would make a person incredibly sleepy in a matter of minutes; a little more and he—or she—would be dreaming for hours.

It was fortunate that she seemed to like the coffee he had served. The flavor would disguise a faintly bitter taste.

No one would question when a roll of unusually bulky carpet was carried down the stairs and along the streets to the dock where his boat was moored. They might wonder, but they would not question. They valued their lives too much.

The other powder would come later. He removed a small brass vial from the trunk and, uncapping it, held it up to the light. Not much inside . . . but then, he didn't need much. Just a pinch in a glass of wine, it was said, would send flashes of heat searing through a woman's body. Two pinches, and the desire would be so intense she could not resist any man.

Even a man as ugly and despicable as Linh.

He did not know it if worked. He had never tried it, but he had paid a great deal of money to a Chinese herbalist whom he trusted as much as he ever trusted any man. He assumed it would accomplish the desired ends. Of course, he would have to try it out first, find the correct dosage. But there would be many days at sea before they reached the landing point near Hué.

It was a pity she had to remain a virgin. Still . . . there were other ways to make the time pass pleasantly.

Dominie lingered one last moment in front of the mirror that hung above the small dressing table in her hotel room. The sun was streaming through the window, warning her the morning was advancing, and she knew she would have to leave soon.

The young woman who stared back at her seemed almost a stranger after weeks of catching only glimpses of a primly garbed nun in the glass. Her hair was beginning to look pretty again. She had cropped it off to fit under the wimple, so short that little ringlets had sprung up like miniature sausages all over her head. But now that it had grown somewhat, the curl had loosened, and it fell in soft waves to her shoulders.

Her face had also changed. Tanned, to her utter dismay, from weeks of strolling back and forth on the decks of ships—though mercifully none of the dreaded freckles had shown up! But it was not her hair or skin that had made the difference. It was a strange new maturity she had never seen in her own features before.

Why, I've grown up, she thought, and wondered why that should surprise her so much. She had been a girl when she left home, laughing, carefree, full of irrepressible high spirits. Now she was a woman, not solemn exactly—she would never be solemn—but thoughtful, and filled for the first time in her life with a sense of dedication and purpose.

She backed away, assessing the total effect of her appearance. She had chosen the pearl-gray afternoon dress with its deep rose collar and cuffs, a lightweight cotton outfit that would best suit her needs in that torrid climate. It fitted a little more snugly than she remembered—not as modest as she might have hoped—but it was suitably long-sleeved and high-necked. If she was not a nun anymore, at least she looked like a proper young lady.

A stab of fear caught her off-guard, and she thrust it resolutely back. She had made her choice long ago, the day she set foot on the stage in Paris. No, even before that—the night she had crept by candlelight into the cellar under the house and retrieved the diamonds.

Her hand slipped to her skirt, feeling the reassuring bulge just beneath her waist that told her the velvet pouch was safe. She had made her choice, and she would abide by it.

She went over to the bed and picked up a small bundle. The red dress she had brought for the day she was reunited with her brother and a few toilet articles wrapped in a length of bright Indian fabric purchased at one of the stalls on Serangoon Road. The rest would be left behind. She did not need it, and the valise would attract the wrong kind of attention when she passed through the lobby. They might wonder about her, this strange woman with the shoulder-length hair whom they had never seen before, but if she did nothing to attract attention, they would be too polite to ask.

The red dress, a few toiletries—and one small item she had traded one of the precious diamonds to purchase that morning. Dominie paused, her hand on the doorknob. It had been an uneven trade, but not altogether unreasonable. A small revolver, several rounds of bullets, and a hasty lesson on how to use it might well save her life.

Let Aziz pull whatever tricks he wanted, she would be ready for him. She opened the door and started down the hall.

"What a very lovely surprise." Dark eyes widened slightly as Aziz stepped back to allow the woman in the gray cotton gown move past him into the large main room. A faint aroma of perfume followed her, as if caught in the folds of the garment. Not a surprise exactly—he had thought she would be pretty—but a most gratifying confirmation of his appraisal. He was already beginning to adjust the price upward.

"A surprise?" Dominie turned to face him with a sharper look than he had expected.

"I had dared to hope your hair was red, but still . . . it does take one's breath away. Since you are no longer dressed as a sister, perhaps I may say that it will give me great pleasure to have such a beautiful traveling companion."

Dominie ignored the remark as she headed toward the bench where she had sat the night before. "I hope I am not late," she said, trying to sound cooler than she felt. Thank heaven she had had the wit not to come unarmed.

"Not at all, not at all," the Arab replied, his wide sensuous mouth curving in an unpleasantly ingratiating smile. "In fact, you are some minutes early. We will have to wait. I hope you will not mind. I am arranging to have some carpets transported to the boat. But, here . . . allow me to take that awkward parcel from you."

"No," Dominie snapped, then added, somewhat more steadily: "I can manage, thank you. It's not heavy. Just a change of clothes and a few other necessities." She set the bundle beside her, half on her lap, half beneath her arm, so he could not reach out and surprise her as he had with the banknotes in her pocket the day before.

This time Aziz did not smile. Not because he did not want to, but because he did not wish her to know what he was thinking. So, she had arranged protection for herself. A gun probably. A most sensible move. Futile . . . but more sensible than he would have thought.

"You will take some coffee with me," he said. "A bigger cup this time. If I know the ladies, you have been so busy with your preparations, you have not taken time to break your fast."

Dominie started to protest, but he had already poured out a cup and was stirring a little extra sugar into it. Besides, he was right. She hadn't even thought about breakfast.

"Well . . . all right. It does smell tempting."

She took a sip and made a face. Not as good this time, bitterer somehow. But it was sweeter too, and the sugar would give her strength. She took another sip, and then another, and hardly noticed the bitter taste anymore.

## 12

IT WAS DARK when Dominie woke. The room seemed to be pitching violently, and nausea rose in great recurring waves from her stomach. Desperately she struggled to remember where she was. In her hotel room—where? In Singapore?

No, not a hotel. She remembered now. She had gone to see that man, that Arab smuggler in his surprisingly sumptuous residence. He had said they had to wait, for something odd—carpets, he had said—and he had given her a cup of coffee.

Coffee . . . ?

Slowly Dominie's head started to focus, though the nausea was still hideously intense. A sickening sense of horror swept over her as she realized what had happened. She had thought the coffee had a funny taste—

"So . . . you are awake."

Dominie looked up, startled to see that it was not night at all. That cramped, windowless room was deep in shadow, but a shaft of faint grayish light spilled through a hole in the ceiling. Beneath, at the base of a ladder that led down, the man Aziz was standing. He was wearing a short robe of dark gray-green, open in front, with loose-fitting white trousers gathered at the ankles and a shirt of the same color. No turban now; his hair was as black as his beard, and untouched by gray.

"What . . . what am I doing here?" she asked groggily. It was hard to make the words come out. Everything seemed to be swirling around, and she couldn't make herself concentrate. She was half-seated, half-reclining on a narrow bunk against the wall, and when she tried to move her arms, she realized they were restrained behind her. "Why have you tied me up? What are you doing? What do you want from me?"

"Here, here . . . be careful." The oily smoothness of his voice was more sinister than any threat he could have uttered. "Don't try to pull loose—you'll only hurt yourself. I deeply regret the bonds, but there were things I had to tend to on deck. I have only a crew of two, and most unfortunately, I could not know when the effects of the potion would wear off."

*Potion?* Dominie thought with anger and disgust. That was a delicate way to put it. He had drugged her!

And he had said "on deck." Her head was clearer now, but it was throbbing horribly, as if someone had gotten inside and were pounding with a hammer, and her stomach churned so badly, it was all she could do to keep from retching.

"We're on a boat!" she said. "That's what that awful lurching sensation is. I thought I was imagining it. We're on our way already. Up the coast? But how long have we been gone?"

"Twelve hours or so. It is just past dawn. And, yes, certainly up the coast. Where else? We should make good time, though the wind is picking up, and I don't like the looks of the clouds. But don't worry, my men know what they are doing. They can handle the vessel in a typhoon if they have to."

"Your . . . *men?*"

He heard the panic in her voice and smiled evilly.

"You need not be alarmed. They are eunuchs, both of them. I always think it wiser to use eunuchs when I am shipping certain 'cargo.' " His upper lip curled over long white teeth in an almost wolfish look. "And, of course, their tongues have been cut out . . . so they cannot offend you with rude comments. They were, you see, guards in a sultan's harem. A most prudent man. It is claimed that he had the tongues removed so they could not communicate with his favorites. But I wonder myself if he didn't do it to keep them from offering the bored ladies certain, uh . . . other pleasures."

Dominie shuddered. She had no idea what he was talking about, but there was no mistaking the lewd obscenity in his tone.

"You have gone to great trouble," she said, trying desperately not to let her terror show. "But it doesn't make sense. You drugged me and bound me and carried me by force to the boat—but I would have come willingly! I *paid* you to bring me.''

"Yes, but you see, it was not you about whom I was concerned. A pretty red-haired woman coming to my place at the dock—who would not notice such a happening? That is not something I would wish people to remember . . . and talk about. It is so much simpler when one prepares for things in advance and does them sensibly.''

"What things?'' Dominie started to say, but the words stuck in her throat. The room was stifling, even with the menacing weather that grew darker moment by moment, but suddenly she felt cold.

He seemed not to hear that half-uttered question, or if he did, he ignored it. A backless chair stood against the wall, rather like a stool with arms, and he pulled it over and sat so close Dominie could see every pore on his nose and cheekbones.

"There is a man named Linh,'' he said, so casually it might have been idle chitchat. "He is Vietnamese. One of the people you have been sent to save. It will perhaps amuse you to attempt to convert him, though I think not. I think he is beyond such things. He finds other . . . interests more distracting. Lovely ladies with exotic eyes, for instance, and silken soft young bodies that have never known the hard demands of a man. I have heard that the nuns of your church are virgins, Sister Marie. Please tell me this is so.''

You mean . . .'' Dominie stared in sheer horror as the reality of what he was saying sank in. "You're planning to give me to this man?''

"Give? *Give?*'' He looked surprised. "No, lovely lady. Aziz does not give. To a brother, a cousin, a trusted friend to whom a favor is owed—perhaps then. But to such an infidel as Linh? Never! I intend to present you to him, naturally. I would have thought that was extremely clear. But there is no question that you will be a present.''

"You're going to *sell* me? Like a slave?''

"No, no, no, no, no . . .'' he protested. "That is much too harsh. You would be . . . what shall we call it? A plaything? A toy? A bauble? Linh collects baubles.

You will be the prettiest in his collection, for a while. Until he tires of you.''

Until he *tired* of her? Dominie felt faint with terror and revulsion. She could just imagine the sort of torments this Linh would inflict on her before his gross lust had waned. And then what? The light in Aziz's eyes, the look of sadistic pleasure on his face, told her there was even worse to come.

I have to get out of here, she thought helplessly. Her mind was still too groggy to work properly. The effects of the drug he had given her? How many days would it take them to go up the coast? How near were they to shore? Even if somehow she managed to get her hands free, was there any escape?

She was so wrapped up in her thoughts, it was a moment before she noticed that his gaze had dropped and he was studying her body with a hideously knowing expression. Horrified, Dominie realized that the fabric was too sleek against her skin. Silk, not cotton. And much too loose, with no restraining stays or undergarments.

He had undressed her! Looking down, she saw that she was clad in some sort of robe, open down the front, with no buttons or fastenings, though it was pulled around and sashed now at the waist.

Her first sickening thought was that this vile, depraved man had seen her, touched her. Her second thought was for what she had been carrying beneath her skirt, and her eyes darted involuntarily toward that awful flat space where smooth silk stretched unbroken across her hip.

Soft laughter broke into her despair, a deep, gurgling, throaty chuckle.

"You look for the small velvet pouch," Aziz said. "But naturally it is not there. It was—may I say?—a most, *most* delightful surprise."

He was still chuckling as he thought of the many surprises she had brought him. The first had come when he examined the bundle she had been clutching so possessively and found not only the gun he had expected—quite good quality, actually; it would make a welcome addition to his personal arsenal—but also an extremely lovely red silk gown.

Not at all the dress one would expect a nun to choose, he thought, eyeing her speculatively. Hardly designed to discourage vanity. But who was he to question such a windfall? He had brought along several hastily selected gowns—he could hardly have presented her to a man of Linh's discerning taste in that drab gray outfit—but they were of Chinese origin and not as provocative as he would have liked.

Yes, the red gown would be perfect. Sensually cut, the waist nipped in, breasts pushed out—and, of course, Orientals were fond of red. They considered it the color of good fortune.

The fortune, it seemed, was to be his as well as Linh's.

Aziz let himself dwell briefly on the second surprise, which had occurred when he had drawn off the last petticoat and discovered the diamonds. Thirteen large flawless stones, an unlucky number in Western superstition. Unlucky for the girl, anyhow. She had lost them.

He looked for her for one long moment and thought perhaps the diamonds might be enough. Linh was not the only one who liked lovely young virgins. With her, he could fulfill his every fantasy, long enchanted nights of the most erotic excitement he had ever known if the powder in the small vial worked—pleasures of another, equally intense sort if it did not. His tongue flicked across his lips; he could taste the sweat at the corners of his mouth as he pushed the thought away.

He was weary of ferrying contraband up and down the coast, of risking devil winds and soldiers and other pirates for profits that never seemed to be enough. With the money from Linh and what he got for the diamonds, he could put all that behind him.

And, of course, Linh would not want her forever. He would be only too glad after a while to have her taken off his hands. She would not be a virgin anymore . . . but then, a man could not have everything.

"I find it most curious," he said evenly, "that you should be carrying a fortune in diamonds. You must want something very much. To establish a mission? But the Son of Heaven and his troops would never permit that. And there could be nothing in the country you wish to purchase."

"Nothing you would understand!" Dominie retorted hotly. The drug was wearing off, and her spirit had begun to return. She might have her hands tied behind her back, she might be a prisoner in the foul-smelling hold of his boat, but she was not about to give this evil vulture the satisfaction of seeing her quake! "The diamonds are for the priest. The man you left near Hué last year."

"The priest?" He leaned toward her curiously. "But what need would a priest have for beautiful gems?"

"None, personally. But priests are being persecuted in Vietnam. And killed! The diamonds are to buy his freedom, if need be. And to arrange his escape."

"So . . ." His breath came out in a low sibilant hiss. "You come alone, at great peril to yourself . . ." A new, extremely unpleasant thought was forming in his mind. She had not answered his question before, whether nuns were virgins. It occurred to him now that it had been only a rumor, one that had always seemed most unnatural. And then there was the dress . . . "He is your lover, this priest! That is why you risk so much to save him."

"My . . . *lover?*" Dominie gaped at him, too appalled to do anything but stammer. He is my brother! she longed to cry out, but she bit back the urge. The more he knew about her, the more of an advantage he had. "That's . . . that's disgusting! He's a priest! He's taken a vow of chastity. And I'm a nun."

Aziz shrugged. Her shock was too genuine not to be believed. The price would not have to be lowered after all.

Still, it was a pity in a way. If she had not been a virgin . . .

He reached out and, grasping the sash of her robe, jerked it open. Dominie shuddered. She tried to pull back, but there was no place she could go, no way she could fight with her wrists bound behind her, and she felt sick with terror and anger and humiliation.

"You are a pig," she hissed at him.

"I am," he agreed, and continued to gaze at her, bare shoulders, bare arms, bare chest glowing faintly bluish in the light that filtered through the hatch to the deck. That had been the third surprise, and the best. When his body had responded, as now, his manhood renewed, passion kindled to make him feel young again, he had known that the beauty he saw before him was more precious than the high price he would ask for her and all the perfect diamonds in the world.

And she *was* beautiful. Before Allah, he had never seen the likes of her before. He had imagined the way she would look now, stripped of her clothes, and in his considerable experience with women, he had come close to being right. But he had not imagined the smoothness of her skin, the pale milky quality, almost translucent, as if he could see the veins beneath it. He had not imagined the firmness of her breasts, full and deliciously round, like the ripe melons he used to love as a boy, so succulent to his taste. He had not imagined the sharp little nipples, peaking toward him, hard with chill and fear, but it could as well have been desire.

And would be . . . if the powder worked.

"I would like to take you in my mouth," he said coarsely. "I would like to suck your nipple and bite until you scream."

She gasped, and he laughed. Softly, slowly, enjoying her reaction.

"I would like to," he said, "but I won't. What a pity. Bites leave marks. Linh likes his women without flaws."

The winds continued strong throughout the morning, rising to gale force by afternoon, and rain buffeted the deck so fiercely that the hatches had to be battened down. The only light came from a single lamp bolted to the wall, and an inch of scummy water sloshed across the floor.

"We seem to have ridden into the weather," Aziz said during a brief respite as he came to check the oil lamp and change his saturated garments. "The northeast monsoon hits the Vietnamese coast around September or October—it turns especially nasty in November. It seems to have made its way south a little earlier than usual."

Yellow light spilled across his skin as he pulled off the loose white tunic, and grabbing a square of bulky nubbed cloth, began to rub his upper body. Dominie tried not look—his chest was soft and flabby and almost startlingly devoid of hair—but the room was small, and there was no place else to put her eyes.

"I had thought I would have more time to spend with you," he went on, "but alas, it is not to be. My men are good, but they have only four hands between them, and more are needed. I will have to do my share on deck."

His face twisted into a sly insinuating leer. "But never fear . . . I do not intend to neglect you altogether."

Dominie watched, sick with horror, as he removed the rest of his clothing. She could only close her eyes, but even then she could imagine, and every sound he made as he moved around the close space, never more than a few feet away, made her retch with fear and despair.

Fortunately, the rains began again, almost immediately, and with the renewed screeching of the wind, he was forced to return topside. Dominie was to have occasion in the days that followed to be grateful for the storm which kept him occupied most of the time. She was still tied, still cramped and uncomfortable, but he made no attempt to drug her again, mercifully, for whatever he had given her affected her stomach badly, and with the violent motion of the boat, she would not have been able to keep anything down.

Occasionally, when the rain let up, Aziz would take her on deck for a breath of air. She was still bound, stout cords not just on her wrists, but around her arms as well, and lashed to the mast whenever he was not there to hold on to her.

"We wouldn't want a wave to wash you overboard," he would say as he secured the rope around her. But Dominie knew it was not the sea he was afraid of. He was afraid she would fling herself over the rail, and given the opportunity, she might have considered it. The situation seemed so hopeless sometimes, so terrifying and humiliating, that she thought she would rather die than endure it another moment.

Only the hope of escape kept her going. Her eyes were in motion every second she was on deck. The boat was alarmingly small, built like the Chinese junks she had seen in Singapore, but nowhere near their size. Just right, she supposed, for a smuggler whose goal was slipping in and out of coves unseen, but terrifying in a raging wind. She scanned the horizon constantly, searching for a hint of land, a sign that something—*someone*—was there.

Once she caught a glimpse of another vessel, not far away, and her heart soared with hope. It was a tall rake-masted clipper, its sails furled like theirs as it rode out the storm, and just for an instant she thought it was the same ship she had spotted in the harbor at Ceylon. But then they veered course, taking dangerous chances to get away, and the hope was dashed as she realized it didn't make any difference one way or another.

Clearly Aziz was not going to let her come within hailing distance of anyone. If she was going to get away, she would have to do it by herself.

The nightmare continued for nearly two weeks. Dominie did not mind so much when they were moving, for the needs of the boat at least kept Aziz's mind and hands and foul, roving eyes busy. But several times they took shelter from the storm in small bays or what appeared to be the deltas of rivers. And there, while the rain battered the hull and the wind screamed its fury, Aziz, true to his word, found occasion not to "neglect" her.

It sent shudders through Dominie's body, even later, when she was alone again, to think of those terrible, humiliating hours. He would undress her completely, taking off the loose white harem-style pants he allowed her on deck, the silken robes that opened down the front, and sit there and stare at her. Not speaking, just looking . . . but his thoughts were eloquent in his eyes.

"I despise you!" she said one awful evening, unable to bear the silence any longer. "You're hateful and loathsome, and I cannot stand the sight of you! I will despise him too—this Linh you are going to sell me to. I will tell him so, and spit in his face . . . and then he will not pay you!"

"It is not necessary that you like the man," he replied, unruffled. "It would please him if you did . . . but it might please him even more if you don't. Linh is a man of most . . . primitive tastes. But no matter, all that is important is that you are a virgin. He will pay double for that."

Dominie felt a sudden urge to tell him that she was not. That he had been right before, that nuns only joined convents to enjoy wild, debauched affairs with the priests! That he would be lucky to get anything at all for her overused flesh!

But she held her tongue, knowing that virginity was her only protection against this grossly sensual man.

She was only putting off the inevitable. The same things—and worse—would happen when they finally reached their destination and he handed her over to Linh.

But putting off the inevitable at least bought time. And time was her best hope.

It was late on the morning of the fifteenth day when the boat angled into another cove, and Dominie knew at once that something was different. It was still raining; great sheets of water gushed out of the heavens, nearly blocking visibility, but she was brought on deck anyway and allowed for the first time to set foot on land.

While she watched, the rain streaming down her face, making it difficult even to breathe, Aziz and his men pushed the boat up onshore and chained it to nearby trees.

Had they arrived? Dominie felt a painful catch in her throat. Was this the place where the man Linh lived? She could see nothing that even remotely hinted at wealth. The vague outline of hills pushed in on three sides, forming a haven from the wind. A short distance away, rising on stilts from the ground, was what looked to be a bamboo hut.

Having finished with the boat, Aziz grabbed her bound arms and jerked her toward the elevated shack. The rains had flooded the land; water swirled around Dominie's calves, rising to her knees as they reached the short ladder that led to a shallow platform in front of the door. When she could not negotiate with her arms tied, he took out a knife and slashed the cords, giving her a momentary sense of almost giddy freedom.

The hut proved surprisingly sturdy. Wind beat against the sides and rain drummed on the roof, but the interior appeared to be dry and relatively free of drafts.

Dominie looked around the single large room, curious and vaguely relieved. It did not seem the kind of place that a man like Linh would favor. The walls were woven rattan, reinforced with mud; the floors a double thickness of rough boards, clean, but stark; the roof pitched high above a row of rafters.

A bare wood table stood almost exactly in the center, nothing on it, and a pair of stools, one on each side, shoved slightly underneath. Along one wall a pile of cushions had been arranged in a cozy grouping with a heavy chest of drawers, Chinese in style, several low tables, and an assortment of various dishes and utensils. The only other piece of furniture was a bed, an oddly crafted thing, with raw square posts like ends of leftover lumber at the corners. The surprisingly soft-looking mattress was covered with red silk on which the fantastic image of a dragon had been elaborately embroidered.

Dominie turned to see Aziz standing just inside the doorway. Water dripped off him, forming puddles on the floor.

He seemed to see the question in her eyes.

"We will be here for a few days," he said. "Perhaps a week or two. Until the rains stop and the land dries somewhat. The city of Hué is only a few hours upcoast by boat, but Linh's estate is inland, and the roads are impassable in the monsoon. And, no, I regret I cannot leave you unbound. I fear you are not yet reconciled to your destiny."

Dominie was to learn all too soon what the posts at the corners of the bed were for. Aziz removed her wet clothes, catching her arms in a terrifyingly strong grip when she tried to resist, then tied her, wrists and ankles, to the rough slabs. The cords were relatively long—she could move around and almost sit up—but the knots were secure, and she realized with a terrible sense of helplessness as she lay spread-eagled on the luxurious silk cover that there was no way she could get loose.

Aziz stood at the side of the bed, staring down at her, mesmerized as much by her fear as by the exquisite beauty of her naked body, sprawled out in an obscenely suggestive pose, and for the first time since he had taken her prisoner, he was seriously tempted to forget about the double price and bring her to Linh somewhat less than perfectly intact. He ran his tongue along his lips, tasting the salt of the sea which even the pelting rain had not washed away, and thought what it would be like to climb on top of her. To drive the hard rod of his manhood, already stiff, through the fragile resistance of that slender membrane.

But the thing once done would be over forever. Aziz let the temptation reluctantly slip away. A momentary exhilaration, and then she would be like all the others. Besides, he reminded himself, the greatest pleasure came not in the action but the anticipation. If he gave her to Linh first, he would have considerable time for the most excruciating anticipation imaginable.

He took off his own clothing, slowly, standing directly

beside the bed, knowing it disgusted her and enjoying her reaction. It would not disgust her for long if the herbalist was right. She would be panting for him, screaming, begging . . . and perhaps he would oblige her.

He reached into the pocket of his sodden trousers and ripped out the oilskin pouch that had been securely stitched inside. A quick glance at the bed showed him her eyes were tightly shut against the affront of his nudity. So much the better—it would be easier if she did not catch on too quickly.

He arranged himself on the cushions and measured a small amount of powder from the brass vial into a delicate crystal glass. Three grains. That would be enough the first time; he could adjust the dosage later. It would not do to waste it.

He hesitated, then added some of the sleeping powder as well. He hated to keep her groggy, but even with her hands tied, he dared not trust her alone. And until the storm abated, he would be spending most of his time with the men tending to the boat.

He slipped on a dry robe from among the store he kept in the chest—no sense frightening her too much now—and uncorked a bottle of wine. As a good Muslim, he did not indulge himself, but he always kept a supply on hand.

"Here," he said, thrusting the glass in her face. "Have a drink of this. It will do you good—you got drenched in the storm. I cannot bring you to Linh all shivers and bones."

Dominie opened her eyes warily to see a glass of amber liquid. He's trying to drug me again, she thought, and for an instant she considered resisting. But as he was strong enough to force it on her, she didn't see the point.

Anyway, if he hadn't been lying before—and she didn't think he had—they were going to be here for some time. It wasn't the drug he gave her now she had to worry about. It was the ones that would come later.

Aziz watched with intense curiosity as she took a sip, made a slight face, then obediently took another, and finally drained the glass. He did not know what he expected. Surely the drug would not act instantaneously, but he had expected *something*.

Perhaps, after all, he thought, disappointed, the Chi-

nese had cheated him. When some time had passed and
the other drug had worked, glazing her eyes and making
her head nod, but still nothing had happened, he was
sure of it.

He had always thought he was a good judge of character, and he had been positive the herbalist had been
telling the truth. But then, the perfidy of some men never
ceased to amaze him.

Dominie had drifted off almost willingly. She could
feel the drug seeping insidiously through her system, but
she could not bring herself to care any longer. She had
been so tired. And so afraid. If only her stomach were
not so horribly upset. It would be good to let herself go
and fall into a deep, dreamless sleep.

But the sleep was not dreamless. She was aware of
nothing for the first few hours; the narcotic was much
too potent. But somewhere toward evening, when the
wind had ceased wailing and lamps spilled their light,
rich and golden, over her naked limbs and torso, vague,
troubling images began to disturb her, calling her half
out of her slumber.

The man she had seen before . . . the nebulous figure
from her adolescent fantasies . . . the arrogant sea captain who had ravished her with his eyes . . . Only now,
there was no space between them. Now he was right
there, coming toward her, his lips parted, laughing, but
seductively . . . his arms stretched out, beckoning her to
come. . . .

Dominie groaned, writhing against the mattress, feeling the sweat prickling and pouring off her body as she
struggled against the bonds that kept her from reaching
back to him. Heat seemed to be everywhere, burning her
naked skin, radiating from somewhere deep inside, until
her arms, her legs, her lips, even her toes felt as if they
were on fire.

He was here, he was coming toward her—she had not
lost him, after all—and they were together at last.

His hands were on her breasts. How could he have
come so quickly? She could not see him anymore—her
eyes were tightly shut—but she could feel him, cupping
the soft, firm flesh in his fingers, teasing her nipples.
Desperately she tried to open her eyelids, but they seemed
to be glued shut.

Then it was not his hands anymore, but his mouth, and he was kissing her breasts, her stomach, her hips, and she had no will anymore. Only instincts and feelings . . . and every instinct in her body told her she loved this man and wanted to belong to him.

Her eyes opened at last, dreamily, hungrily, longing to feast on him. Funny, his hair was not fair after all, but jet black, as she had imaged at first. Not fine, but oddly coarse. She stared at it, wet and dark, streaming across her belly, and tried to force her mind to focus.

Then he raised his head, and she saw a thick black beard, streaked with silver, and dark eyes gleaming out of swarthy features.

Aziz!

Disgust surged through her, heaving up with the nausea from her stomach. It had been Aziz, touching her as no man had ever touched her before. And she had allowed it!

*Allowed* it? She had writhed with pleasure. She was dreaming, she had been drugged, but that did not make it any less degrading. He had had his hands all over her, his gross, slobbering mouth, and she had groaned for more!

She saw him coming at her again, and she knew instinctively that whatever he had planned now would be even more humiliating. All the queasiness she had been holding back rose in a wave of horror and helplessness and self-revulsion, and arching forward, she threw up all over the front of his robe.

# 13

AZIZ HAD ALWAYS been a fastidious man. His clothes were always compulsively clean; even at sea he changed into a fresh outfit at least twice a day, and his hair and fingernails were immaculate. The thought of the contents of someone else's stomach, however meager, drenching his robe, touching his skin, was so repugnant as to bring acute discomfort. Rushing out of the small hut, he tore off the expensive silk robe even as he hastened with a hoarse shriek down the ladder. He flung it into the mud—he would never wear it again!—and stood for some time, naked, letting the rain purify his body again.

He was somewhat calmer when he finally returned, but there was a dangerous glint in his eyes as he looked over at the woman who seemed lost in sleep again after her violent throe of passion. He had made two mistakes, he realized grimly. He had not given her enough of the love potion and he had badly overdosed her with the other.

Four times over the next several days he carried out his cruel experiment, each time adding a little more of the powder from the brass vial, and each time Dominie thought she would die with the horrible degradations he inflicted on her.

She learned much about her body during those short, excruciating trials. She learned that passion was a part of her nature, that the heat which seemed to sear through her centered after a while in the tender space between her legs, until she thought she would die if it were not relieved. She learned that her nipples were traitors, responding to sensory stimuli, hardening into little peaks that embarrassed and humiliated her. She learned that, with her inhibitions sedated away, even the touch of the grossest hand could evoke terrifying, bewildering sensations in her in unspeakably intimate ways.

But she also learned that, with strength and will, she could master her own feelings.

I will defeat you! she thought, staring at him again and again with hatred blazing out of her eyes. You can do what you want with your drugs—you can use your hands to force all kinds of physical reactions—but you will never make me groan with pleasure. And you will never, *never* make me look on you as anything but a disgusting swine!

After the fourth time, the experiments finally ceased, and Dominie realized with more dread than relief that he was coming to the end of his supply of powder. Clearly he was saving the last—no doubt considerably stronger—dose for her introduction to Linh. She had already learned that the potion required several hours to take effect; she would have that much warning anyway. He would probably drug her before they left. But by that time it might be too late, and she lived in constant terror of the moment she would see him sidle over to the cushions and take out the vial again.

At least he was not doping her as heavily with the sleeping preparation. She was still hazy sometimes, and so weak she could hardly move—it seemed to have the most debilitating effect—but her mind was lucid for long stretches and she could begin to make plans. Realizing why he had reduced the dosage, she feigned a spell of retching and was secretly exhilarated when he seemed to decrease it even more. If she could just feign drowsiness as well, perhaps he would let down his guard.

It seemed to work, for the cords around her wrists were nowhere near as taut now. Perhaps he noticed the ugly red marks that had begun to appear, perhaps he had simply gotten careless—it didn't matter. They were loose enough so Dominie was almost positive she could squeeze her hands through if only he didn't tighten them again. Just to make sure, she tugged at them once or twice when she knew he was looking, then gave up with a little whimpering sound and, curling up as best she could, pretended to go back to sleep.

It was only when Aziz went outside to take care of the boat or check on the men that she dared to be alert, and she used every second of that precious time to plot her escape. He had taken the clothing she wore on the boat—the harem pants and luxurious robes—together with her gray dress and toilet articles and stashed them high in the rafters where she knew she could never get at them. He had had to push the heavy chest over himself, and place a stool on top, and he was taller than she. In her weakened state, it would be folly even to try.

But the red dress was much lower, hanging from a nail on the wall. Doubtless to keep it from wrinkling, she thought. All she had to do was slide the table over a few feet. She would not have any undergarments, of course—she would feel dreadfully immodest—but it was better than cavorting naked like a monkey through a jungle.

And at least she would have the diamonds. Dominie had been terrified at first that she was going to have to leave them behind. It had taken over a week to figure out where Aziz had hidden them, and even then it had been purely luck. She had been playing at being more heavily drugged, her eyelids quivering closed, her breathing slow and heavy, and he, apparently unable to resist the temptation, had gone over to the corner and pried up one of the floorboards.

He had been so intent on his greedy perusal of the glittering gems that he had not noticed Dominie's eyes pop open, then shut abruptly. But that one brief glimpse had been enough. She had seen the sparkle on his palm, and she knew that at last she had everything she needed. She would make her move soon.

As it turned out, she was forced to act much sooner than she had expected. When she woke the next morning, she was startled to find herself blinking into unexpected brightness. Sunlight was streaming through the doorway and the single window from which shutters had been flung back, and a sudden chill ran down her spine. The rains had stopped. Even the smell was different, hot and sultry as moisture steamed out of the mud.

How long would it take the roads to dry? she wondered. And how dry did they have to be? How soon would Aziz want to start?

She got her answer a few minutes later when he came back into the hut and, making no effort to conceal his movements, went over to the chest, opened the top drawer, and pulled out the vial. He poured a larger glass of wine than usual, put in both the powders—more of each? she wondered in fright—and brought it over to the bed. She tried desperately to resist, tried to bite his hand, to spit the stuff out, but grabbing a handful of hair, he jerked her head back and forced it down her throat.

Today. She was choking and sputtering, but she barely noticed the discomfort. It was going to be today. She had a few hours, perhaps only minutes, and then the chance would be lost.

She forced herself to lie still until he had gone. To tend to the boat? she thought, and wondered how long he would be. She was terrified for a moment that she was going to fall asleep—her eyes felt heavy—but common sense told her he would not have upped the dose too much. He would never run the risk of her throwing up all over his wealthy client! She was only reacting to her own fears.

Willing herself to concentrate, she struggled to free her hands, finding it harder than she had expected. She twisted and tugged so fiercely, she nearly tore the skin off. She would tear the skin off is she had to, or worse—she had heard of foxes chewing off their feet to get out of a trap—but she finally managed to work loose.

Her ankles took longer. She had to undo the knots. They had been tied so tight, it was almost as if they were glued together, and she was sweating with fear and exhaustion by the time the last one succumbed to her efforts.

She had not even noticed that the red dress was no longer hanging on the wall, but had been spread with exaggerated neatness over the table. He must have taken it down while she was still asleep. Dominie's legs were wobbly as she stumbled over and slipped it on. She had lost weight, but it still fit well enough, if not altogether snugly, and she breathed a sigh of relief that she was at least adequately clad again.

Too bad about the rest. She threw a regretful glance at the rafters. The harem pants would have been much more convenient, and she longed for her comb and chemise. But it would have taken too much time to get them, even had she had the strength. All she could do was recover the diamonds and get out of there.

She fell to her knees at the place where she had seen Aziz before, scouring it with her eyes. The board was easy to pick out—there were tiny nicks along the edge—

and she gouged at it with her fingernails, trying frantically to pry it up, but nothing worked. No matter what she did, it held fast. She could not get it to budge.

Please, *please* move, she thought helplessly. She could not leave the diamonds. They might be her only means of rescuing her brother. But she dared not stay any longer. She had already pressed her luck.

She cast her eyes around desperately, searching for something—anything—that might give her leverage. Aziz had used a knife, but he must have taken it with him; she did not see it on any of the low tables or near the cushions where he usually lounged. Perhaps if she looked in the chest . . .

In her haste, she knocked over a table, and the sound of metal clanking against metal and shattering glass echoed through the room. Dominie stopped, terrified, and listened to the ominous silence that followed.

The ocean was so close. The hut was only a short distance in from the shallow beach. Even if they had already pushed the boat onto the water, surely they must have heard.

She raced over to the door, praying that the sound hadn't been as loud as she thought—that it hadn't carried so far.

But as soon as she stepped out on the narrow deck, she saw Aziz emerging from a small copse of scraggly trees along the shore. In another second he would be at the ladder.

"The trouble wi' the captain, he's nae had the benefit of tender companionship, ye get the drift of what I'm saying." Angus Dougal's kind red face crinkled with something between amusement and concern as he paused for a moment beside the gunwale to have a word with his first mate. "Looks like the lad needs a wee bit of help finding his way to the ladies."

Alex repressed a grin. Not another man on board would dare to call Jared Barron a "lad."

"If there's one thing my cousin has never had, it's difficulty finding the ladies. If anything, he has trouble staying away. Another sly devil might have a woman in every port—Jared considers it a personal failure if there are less than three or four."

"Aye, but we've nae seen much o' the ports this trip. A day here, a day there—I dinna see us stopping any longer. For us common swabbies, there's pleasure aplenty in some of the livelier houses. But a captain canna risk his reputation—or his manhood—with the waterfront tarts. Ye take my advice, lad. Stop awhile in Manila. See to it the captain finds himself a nice bonnie lassie. Ye too—ye're too quiet by half. 'Tis nae good for a man."

Alex was still shaking his head as he made his way to the chart room, where he was reasonably certain he would find his cousin. Angus Dougal was far from a common swab. He had been with the Barron Lines for some time, as second mate the last several years; he would have been first mate this time if Jared had not rearranged the order of command. His lack of deference was refreshing, coupled as it was with honest respect, and he had more than his share of good Scottish sense.

He also had an uncanny knack of hitting on the truth. Not that Alex actually believed his cousin was starved for a woman. But clearly there was something more to Jared's tension than just his impatience with Matthew and his need to get to Macao or Canton to straighten things out.

"I suppose that's what passes for self-control with you," he said as he peered into the chart room and saw the other man pacing back and forth. Two long strides to the end of the narrow space beside the table, two strides back, then around and down again.

"Better than treating the crew to a display of stalking on deck," Jared replied with an ironic lift of his brows.

Alex slipped easily into one of the chairs and stretched his legs in front of him. "Dougal thinks you're in dire need of a woman. Take his advice, he says, and you'll be a new man. Pardon—a new 'lad.' "

"Good idea." Jared perched half on, half off the edge of the table. "I like the way his mind works. Send him ashore, will you? Tell him to bring back a little cutie for me—and another for you while he's at it. Or didn't he offer you the same advice?"

Alex reddened. "He's a good sort, old Dougal. He takes a fatherly interest in all the Barron 'lads,' one of whom he's known since the age of twelve. He was on my first ship. I doubt I would have survived if it hadn't been for him.''

"I doubt half the cabin boys on any of the Barron vessels would have survived. Or the men who had to deal with all that youthful temperament. He was on my first ship too, and if ever any of the arrogance was knocked out of me, it was his doing. But for all the magic he's managed to work over the years, I don't think he can conjure up a sweet young thing onshore.''

"No,'' Alex agreed. "But it might not be a bad idea to send him out with some of the other men to do a little scouting. We're low on supplies, and it looks like we'll be here for a while. Lovely ladies of easy virtue might be beyond his ability, but he can probably come up with some fresh fruit and vegetables. And a pig or two would be welcome.''

Jared nodded. "Take care of it, then. The sun looks good for a couple of hours at least, and it will give the men a chance to work off some of their energy. Just don't send Mackler—I don't trust him. Or Bates or Hogan. The rest can go out in teams every couple of days.''

"Right.'' Alex paused in the doorway, grinning unexpectedly. "Too bad about the cutie,'' he said. "Dougal might have been onto something there.''

Might be? Jared was startled by the thought as he continued pacing, then stopped abruptly and took the chair his cousin had vacated. In dire need of a woman? Absurd! There had always been women in his life. He enjoyed women, sometimes worried about them, frequently tried to take care of them, but he had never needed them. It seemed a strange choice of words for a man like him.

He got up and started to pace again. He was restless, true—but that was only natural. The last part of the voyage had been even less productive, if that was possible. Singapore had offered some slight promise, but Vietnam was a total washout. They had pulled up the river into a city called Saigon, flags streaming in the wind, waiting for everyone to come and gape in wonder at the tall, proud clipper—and not a soul had even crept out in the night to peek at them.

Like the Chinese for centuries, these strange xenophobic people had no desire to trade with the Western barbarians. They had simply pulled down the blinds, refusing with elaborate politeness even to speak to the translators, and haughtily returned every elephant tusk and bolt of cotton and pretty chiming clock that had been presented as gifts.

Eight days they had cooled their heels, and not once had they even been allowed off the ship! Jared felt his Yankee impatience coming back, and he left the cramped cabin and strode out on deck. Eight days, and then when they reached the mouth of the Mekong, they had run into the worst damned monsoon he had ever seen. Every time he thought they were making headway, a new gale had come up and they'd been beaten back again, driven farther and farther off course, until there was nothing to do but lay anchor in the best place they could find and wait for it to be over.

The sun beat down with deceptive brightness as he leaned for a moment on the rail, but the wind seemed to be rising slightly and clouds showed on the horizon. Monsoons were never predictable; it might be over now, or there might be another bout or two yet to deal with. At any rate, it would be some time before repairs were finished. They had lost a mast in the last go-round and several spars, and much of the canvas was badly torn. Even if the weather held, they'd be stuck for days.

In dire need of a woman . . .

It was funny, the way those words kept echoing in his head. Nothing urgent, of course—he had always been self-sufficient—but it occurred to him that a little femininity *would* be nice. Not the easy sensuality of a harlot, with pert red lips and a way of making a man feel good all over, but the tenderness of a gentle companion who would sit and talk to him, laugh when he wanted to . . . look serious when he was sad . . .

Perhaps, after all, he did need a woman.

He was vaguely aware as he stared out at the sea that he had reached a crossroads in his life, and the thought was somehow strangely disconcerting. He could continue as he was going; his life was not bad—not bad at all—but it was never really quite good. Or he could stop, take stock of what he was doing, and look for something else.

Only he didn't know what else there was. Or whether he would even like it if he found it.

* * *

Dominie gasped with terror as Aziz loomed suddenly in the doorway. Without so much as a break in his stride, he was coming toward her, his face so livid it was nearly purple.

"Please . . ." She started to beg, but even as she did, she knew it was no use. His manhood had been affronted. She had thwarted his every attempt to make her long for him: she had gritted her teeth and loathed his foul advances, she had defiled his immaculate clothing with her vomit—and now she had nearly gotten away! He hated her too much to show any mercy.

Rough hands caught her arms and jerked her toward him. Dominie gave a little cry, terrified he was going to beat her. Then he pulled her against him, hard, unrelenting, and she realized that what he had in mind was even worse. She could smell his breath, feel the heat of it on her face as he bent her backward, forcing his mouth, cruel and punishing, on hers.

God help her, he had decided to forfeit the double price from Linh. Her passion would never be his, but her humiliation would . . . and he was going to glory in it.

She had defied him once too often. Now she would pay for it.

The path was sodden but passable; a man's feet sank no more than an inch or two before hitting solid ground. Angus Dougal paused and rubbed his forearm across his brow to wipe away the perspiration. The rains had stopped only a few hours before, but already it was sweltering, and insects buzzed annoyingly around his face and ears. He had never cared for the hot countries of Asia. He had traveled all over the world and enjoyed it, but he was never quite comfortable anyplace where a man couldn't see bare gray rocks and feel a bracing nip in the air at night.

He threw up his arm with a broad gesture, beckoning the men behind to come forward, but slowly. The small hut perched on its fragile-looking stilts appeared to be empty, but he didn't want to take any chances. The captain had warned him, just as they were leaving, that he didn't want any problems with the natives, and Angus was a man who took his responsibilities seriously.

He let his thoughts linger for a moment on the man

who had seen them off, just as his eyes lingered on the stilted shack, taking in every aspect of its silence. He liked young Jared Barron. Always had, since the lad had been sixteen and set off for the first time before the mast. A cocky, swaggering youngster; the memory made him chuckle. He'd wanted it all, and he'd wanted it right away! And damned near got it, too, if Angus Dougal hadn't been there to set things to rights.

He sucked in the hot air and blew it out through his cheeks. He'd been worried about the lad lately, didn't like the turn his life seemed to be taking. Jared Barron was not a man to spend all his days at sea, no home, no family, no ties beyond his ship. That did fine for some—he couldn't imagine anything else himself—but others turned hard and strange. It was like the sea took them over and wouldn't let go. He had seen it happen too often. He would not want it to happen to one of his lads.

It would bear some thinking when he got back to the *Shadow,* but right now he had other things on his mind. He checked the hut one last time, then slipped his gun out of his belt.

"All right, lads. Follow me. Up the ladder, and step to it—but hold your fire if there's someone inside. Remember the captain's orders."

He moved quietly, a big man, but stealthy, only faint squishing sounds in the mud betraying his progress. Up like a cat, swift and silent, then in through the open door—and he stopped dead in his tracks.

A large dark man with a turban wound around his head and a knee-length silk robe over some sort of white outfit was just straightening up. The woman in the red dress whom he had been embracing with passionate enthusiasm sank to her knees, hastily tugging her bodice over one round white, very exposed breast.

He would have laughed, it was so outrageously unexpected, had not the man reached just then for a long curving knife in the sash at his waist.

Angus raised his gun and leveled it at his head.

"Dinna try it," he said coolly. "I'm a fine shot at thirty paces, and ye're nae a spit away."

Aziz reacted with the instinctive caution that made him a natural survivor. He tucked the knife back in his sash, slowly, careful to make no overt moves, all the while his eyes shifting back and forth, taking in the situation. Two more men in the room now, at least another on deck. A minimum of four, all armed—and his guns were in the chest or on the boat.

He backed away, his mind working furiously. No way out through the door. That left the window behind him. He hesitated as he reached the wall and felt the large open space.

"My compliments, pretty Marie," he said lightly. "You were a wonder, but all things come to an end . . ."

Abruptly he flipped himself over the edge, dangling by his arms for one brief instant before dropping to the ground.

"Damme!" Angus resisted his first impulse, which was to race over to the window and see it he could get a bead on him. The man was clearly not Vietnamese, but he supposed the captain's admonition against trouble extended to him as well.

"Here, hold on," he called out as he spotted one of the men loping toward the door. "Let him go. We have nae use for the likes of him. You, Carmichael—see to the others below. I dinna want any fights."

He watched for a moment as the yellow-haired lad scurried for the ladder. No question his orders would be obeyed. The second mate was in a peculiar position—not an officer, nor ever quite accepted as one of the men—but the rank did have its advantages. No one would defy him openly.

He turned back to see that the woman was still where she had sunk to her knees on the floor. He studied her with gnawing uneasiness. If the man in the turban had truly absconded, something was going to have to be done about her, though what, for the life of him, he couldn't imagine. The captain would not thank him if they had to waste precious days taking her back to Singapore. But they could hardly tote her like so much extra cargo all the way to Macao.

He was still mulling over the equally unappealing options when she raised her head and he got a look at her eyes. The most remarkable eyes, he thought—green and yellow at the same time where the light from the doorway spilled over them. But they were strange, and not quite focused. As if she had taken some kind of drug . . . or perhaps was in shock.

Well, and what did he expect? Angus felt a throb of conscience. He was not an unkind man, and it occurred to him for the first time to look at the matter from her point of view. She had been alone in the room with the dark-skinned man, obviously enjoying what they were doing—or about to do—when in had burst half a dozen man, thrashing around, waving their pistols! Was it any wonder she was in shock?

"Dinna worry, lassie," he said as gently as a gruff-voiced man could manage. "We are nae here to hurt ye. Ye have nothing to fear from us."

She seemed to calm somewhat, though she did not answer, as if it were too much effort to speak. Or perhaps, Angus thought, she did not understand English. He looked at her more closely, taking in her dress, brazenly sensuous, clinging in some places—like she didn't have anything on underneath—gaping almost lewdly in others.

The dark man's mistress, he guessed. Or more likely, judging by the bawdy gown, his fancy lady. And from the way she looked, Angus would be willing to bet he'd paid a pretty penny for her. Women like that didn't come cheap.

The men tumbled up the ladder a few minutes later. Angus counted as they spilled into the room. Three in addition to himself; that meant two were still below. And it looked like they were spoiling for a fight.

"He got away?"

"Aye, sorr." It was Carmichael who answered. His pale eyes bulged with excitement, and the tuft of straw-colored hair on top of his head was bobbing up and down. "He had a boat—behind them little trees. That's why we didn't see it when we come up."

"Any hands on board?" Angus asked.

"Two. Maybe three. Broad and Benson are on lookout. He won't be back—not the way he run off—but you might want to keep a couple o' men posted. Looks to me like he's a smuggler. Probably opium. You know how the cap'n feels about opium."

Angus nodded. Carmichael had had about as much experience with smugglers as Queen Victoria, but he himself had seen a bit of the world. And the man had looked like a smuggler to him too.

You're sure he got away? he started to ask. But before the words were even out of his mouth, they were echoed almost exactly from behind.

"You're sure he's gone?" the woman said. "He won't be back?"

Angus turned to look at her. She did speak English, quite well, though with a slight, charming French accent. He could not see anything in her face to tell him if she was distressed that the man had left her. He supposed she must be. The sizzling ardor of their lovemaking had seemed in that one brief glimpse entirely mutual.

"He's gone, lass . . . for good. Ye'll nae be setting eyes on him again." He watched her carefully. No tears—at least she was not desperately unhappy. But then, if he had been right before, the arrangement between them was primarily financial. An idea began to tug at the corners of his mind.

They could not, after all, just go off and leave her. And a lady had to make a living . . .

"Our ship is nearby," he said. "A great Yankee clipper—the finest afloat. I will take ye there. I dinna think you will find it disagreeable."

She rose slowly, as if she heard what he said but had not quite taken it in. As he bent to help her, Angus got a vivid look down the front of her dress, and whatever doubts he may have had were put to rest once and for all. The bodice was just loose enough to reveal a considerable part of her very considerable charms, with absolutely nothing between them and the silk of her gown.

To a man like Angus Dougal, a French accent, a daringly provocative dress—and no underwear—meant only one thing. She was a fancy woman, all right. But such a one as old tars like himself were rarely privileged to see. A man could get a great deal of pleasure from a woman like that.

"Come, lads," he called out jovially. "Back to the ship. I think the captain's going to be in a better humor from now on."

# 14

DOMINIE HUDDLED in a corner of the small, dimly lit cabin and tried to sort through what had just happened, but her mind was hazy with fear and exhaustion and the effects of the sleeping powder Aziz had given her. At least there was no queasiness this time, she thought with a vague sense of relief. She seemed to be developing a tolerance for the drug.

She had only the sketchiest memories of that brief trip from shore: the hoarse, rhythmic breathing of the boatmen, the groan of the oars in their locks, the *splash-splash-splash* against the water. There had been something oddly familiar about the ship as they brought her up the ladder and onto the deck, but everything was so confusing, she couldn't focus on her impressions. The captain . . . they kept talking about someone they called the captain, as if he didn't have a name . . . talking and laughing and winking at each other . . . Then suddenly she had found herself alone, and a great weariness had come over her, like a fever that clouded the mind and made it impossible to think. She could feel the effects of the other drug now too—the love potion—and for just a moment, as the heat and yearning and strange, disturbing sensations tingled through her body, she felt a surge of fear. But then she remembered. Aziz was no longer there; she was safe. He would never hurt her again.

A faint flicker of gold from two lamps clamped to the walls played lushly on dark wood paneling. Dominie stared almost hypnotically, letting the warmth and desire flow with the weariness through her body. She could relax now; she could recognize the sweet aching passion that coaxed up waking dreams of strong male arms and full, kissable lips without shudders of aversion. The danger was over at last.

She was not sure when she became aware that someone was there. She sensed rather than saw the door open, felt a faint draft, cool against skin that was prickling from the potion. Rising slowly, too tired and groggy even to be alarmed, she struggled to make out the dark figure of a man standing on the threshold. She could not see his face in the shadows—she could tell only that he was tall and powerful of frame—but there was something inexplicably compelling about him.

Then he stepped into the light and Dominie recognized him.

The man she had seen in Ceylon!

Relief flooded through her, and gratitude—and the first tentative feelings of that love she had been so quick to deny before. Seen close, even through the fog that seemed to be swirling around her, his face appeared even stronger. Hard, but not cold, like rocky tors she had glimpsed on islands as they passed, hot with the tropical sun beating down on them. His eyes were smoky, halfway between blue and gray, his hair somewhat darker in the artificial light. His shirt, open at the neck, revealed tantalizing wisps of curl rising from his chest, and she felt a sudden idiotic urge to reach out and tangle her fingers in them.

Partly the effects of the potion, she knew . . . but she had felt these same wanton yearnings before, and there had been no drugs in her system then. . . .

This was her destiny. Her mind was still blurred, she was finding it hard to make things come together, but she knew that as surely as she had ever known anything in her life. He had filled her dreams for years . . . this hard, strong, sensual man. She had seen him once, and she had known instantly, but she had not trusted her instincts. Now the fates had brought them together again.

She stood for one brief moment, waiting for him to recognize her. Then she remembered that the starched white wimple had changed the shape of her face, the long black veil disguised her hair. He did not know. He would never know until that sweet, secret time someday in the future when she decided to tell him.

She took a step forward and smiled, a soft, unintentionally provocative smile, her lips parted slightly, her eyes seeming to melt in the misty light. She started to stretch out her hands, then realized just in time the inappropriateness of the gesture, and dropped them to her sides.

"Mademoiselle . . ." His voice was harsh, like the voices of all Americans, but deep-pitched, seductively resonant. "You are welcome on my ship. *Very* welcome."

Dominie was too confused, and too overwhelmed with the way things were turning out, to catch the subtle inflection in his tone. "I must thank you, Captain," she said, "you and your men. Your sailors. For, um . . ." She faltered. "Rescuing" was the word she was looking for, but her English seemed to be leaving her. The harder she struggled, the heavier her accent became. "For . . . for bringing me here. It was very . . ." "Timely" was what she wanted, but "timely" would not come. "Very . . . convenient."

Jared raised one eyebrow, just slightly, taking her words with unfortunate exactness. "The pleasure, I assure you, is all mine," he said. "Or perhaps I should say . . . it will be ours."

He stood just inside the threshold, studying her for a long moment in the lamplight, surprised and intrigued by the feelings he had not expected. He had been furious when he found out about the French tart Dougal had picked up. He had nothing against ladies of pleasure, heaven knows. The one constant passion of his life, the lovely Mei-ling, had made quite a reputation catering to the desires of men. But he liked to choose his own ladies, his own time—and he was damned if he was going to have one dropped off like a bawdy jest in his cabin! He had come fully intending to escort her, politely but firmly, to the owner's quarters. And leave her there. Alone.

Then he had stepped across the threshold—and seen her.

Dougal had said she was a beauty, and by God, he had been right. Everything about her was sheer perfection, from the glorious blaze of her hair to the outline of long slim legs showing through the sheer silk of her skirt. He had said that Jared would not be able to resist her, and it looked like he was right about that too. Jared reached back and closed the door, which he had deliberately left ajar behind him. The old salt had always been right about everything else, as long as he could remember. He should have known better than to question him now.

Green eyes . . . Fascinated, Jared drank in her face, the warmth of the light caressing faintly flushed cheeks, the intriguing changeable color of those devastating eyes. He had longed for a woman with green eyes since that disturbing dawn in Ceylon. . . . Come to think of it, there was a certain resemblance . . .

He laughed softly, surprised at the twists his mind was taking. Absurd, imagining that a poor little nun had anything in common with this beautiful woman of the world who had obviously learned to enjoy life to the fullest. And to see that the man she was with enjoyed it as well.

He laid a hand on her shoulder, feeling the incredible smoothness of her skin beneath his fingertips. When she did not pull back, he assumed the bargain had been made.

"I am not a very patient man," he said huskily. "And I am not very gentle. But I will be gentle with you, if you want . . . or rough, or wild . . . or playful. This is not going to be just for me."

He slipped the dress off her shoulders, so slowly she did not seem to notice what he was doing. It was almost as if she were in a trance as she stood there, absolutely still, while the fabric slid down, bunching around her waist, leaving her naked above. Jared sucked his breath in audibly. So slender—she was almost painfully thin—but her breasts were incredibly full. As if made to cradle a man's head when the lovemaking was over and he was too exhausted to move.

He was aware of a sudden unexpected sense of tenderness fusing with the desire that had already made him hard for her. Old Dougal had been right about that as well, it seemed. He was in dire need of a woman. . . . No, not a woman—not any woman—but this woman.

He drew her, unresisting, into his arms. God, how soft she felt, how good in his embrace. His mouth sought hers, almost humbly, like a pilgrim approaching a holy shrine.

The immediacy of her response surprised him, free and uninhibited, and obviously aroused. Longing throbbed through his body, more violent than anything he could remember, and it was all he could do to keep from dragging her to the ground, possessing her right there. But he had promised he would satisfy her too. Her wants . . . her needs. He would take the time to learn what they were.

Dominie sensed his restraint, as sweet as the great well of tenderness in his kiss, and she let herself drift with the emotions he evoked. Like a dream . . . it all seemed like one of her dreams . . . pretty and perfect, and she could not bring herself to draw back.

Somewhere in the dim recesses of her mind, she knew what she was doing was wrong. This was not a dream, it was real—she should not allow him to take such liberties. But the warmth of his mouth was so tantalizing, the rough feel of his shirt against her bare skin. Every sensation seemed to be heightened, every smell, every sound, every touch, by the drug that was coursing through her system, and she could not bear to let go. Not now. Not yet.

Just another second, she thought . . . just one more second. Then suddenly his hands were sliding down her back, pushing the crumpled fabric of her dress to the floor, finding her buttocks, pressing her against him. Dominie gasped as she felt the unmistakable bulge beneath his belt.

"Oh, *mon Dieu* . . ."

She pulled back hastily, horrified and ashamed. Everything seemed to be whirling dizzily—why couldn't she think straight? This was not a roguish kiss she had allowed. She was standing before him stark naked. And he was devouring her with his eyes.

"My sentiments exactly," he said with a rakish look that sent shivers not altogether of trepidation down her spine. His voice was cloudy, muffled with desire. "Only I would have said: My God, how beautiful you are. My God, how good you feel in my arms. My God, I want you. . . ."

"No!" Dominie cried. "Don't . . . don't touch me! How dare you!" She knew she was being wildly inconsistent. She could see the surprise on his face, the shock, but she didn't care. Somehow she had to stop him. She dared not let him come near her again.

She had thought the danger was over, but it was not. Heaven help her, it had just begun. Not danger from outside, but the danger that lay within. The danger of her own deep, untapped passions.

"What kind of man are you?" she railed on. "What gives you the right to take off my clothes and force your kisses on me—and tell me that you want me! Did it ever occur to you to ask if I was remotely interested in your lewd advances?"

His eyes hardened, his jaw set in a taut line, and Dominie was suddenly, irrationally terrified that he was going to turn away from her.

"You came here in a red dress that left nothing to the imagination, you smiled at me invitingly, you let me caress your shoulder without so much as a word of protest—then you wonder why I thought you might be 'interested'? Come, madam, I don't know what your game is, but you'll have to do better than that."

"I . . . I was confused," Dominie stammered, trying to make the words fit together. "It's just that I . . . I've been so tired . . . I couldn't think straight. You don't know what it was like when I was . . . *there* . . . with that man . . . that Arab . . ."

"Don't I?" he said coldly. Jared was surprised at the jealousy that stabbed like a knife through his gut. He knew only too well what it had been like in that shack. Dougal had described it vividly. They had been going at it hot and heavy, she and the Arab, when he burst into the room. She had already been half-undressed; they were locked in a passionate embrace.

The thought of her in that villain's arms, writhing with the same sweet eroticism he had just felt, made him sick with revulsion. Illogical, utterly unreasonable—he had never given a damn about a woman's past before—but he wanted somehow, if only illusively, to think for this brief time that she was his.

"I know you were lovers," he said roughly. "And if that little sample I just got was any indication, it must have been extremely wearying. But you don't seem to be pining away for him."

"Oh . . . no!" Dominie gasped. How could he think— how could *anyone* think—that she would ever willingly go with a wretch like that? "You don't understand . . . there wasn't any love . . ." She was tripping all over her tongue again, nothing coming out the way she intended.

"It wasn't like that at all. Not *love*. Just . . . lust. And money—"

"Ah," Jared broke in, aware of a bitter sense of disappointment. "That's what this is all about, is it? Money?" She was like the others after all. Why had he expected her to be any different? Because she had green eyes and an innocent quiver to her lips? "You want to up the ante? That's fine. I want you enough to pay. God knows why, but I do. Name your price, and I'll meet it."

Dominie shook her head, too stunned for a moment even to speak. He had moved closer; he was almost touching her again, a warm, pulsating, unbearable temptation. She had to keep her head. She had to try harder to think.

"I don't want to talk about money," she said miserably.

"Good," Jared replied, softening somewhat. There was just a trace of tears in her eyes, and he regretted his anger. She had a right, after all, to be concerned about money. It *was* her trade. "Because I don't want to talk about it either. You can trust me to be generous."

He was closer now, his finger just touching the tip of her chin, tilting it up, and waves of panic flooded through her. She had to keep this from happening.

"You think because I put on a red dress," she said, trying desperately not to get things muddled up again, "you think that means . . . because I dress like . . . like a harlot . . ."

She barely whispered the word; it was hard to bring herself to say it. "Because I dress like a harlot," she was trying to tell him, "because I have on a loose, gaping gown with nothing underneath—that doesn't mean I *am* a harlot."

Jared misunderstood, though the poignancy in that earnest plea touched a core of honesty deep within him. Because she put on a red dress, because she earned her keep selling her body to strangers, did not give a man any automatic claims on her. Every woman, even a prostitute, had the right to say no.

"I am not a monster," he said gruffly. "I will not force you, if you really do not want me. But you are going to have to prove it."

Dominie shivered as his head bent toward her. Both his hands were on her face now, one on each side, and his eyes seemed to darken, teasing, challenging.

"I am going to kiss you one more time," he said. "And if you do not kiss me back, if your lips tell me no, I will go away and leave you alone."

Only her lips would never say no, Dominie knew. Whatever will, whatever resistance she had had, was gone.

She had not known a man's mouth could feel like that. She had never even imagined it. Barely touching, the pressure little more than a light breath on her lips, but every corner of her body seemed to respond, aching, pulsating, needing him desperately.

His arms were around his neck suddenly. Was that really her, that brazen creature pulling him closer, gripping him taut against her? Confusion and longing mingled in her heart, the one inseparable from the other, and she knew that even if the drugs were not flowing through her bloodstream, sapping her strength, she would still be with him now, like this.

She felt strangely languid, as if she were floating on a cloud, as he lifted her in strong, enclosing arms and carried her to the narrow bunk. I don't even know your name, she thought, I don't know who you are—and then his mouth was seeking hers again and even that one brief flicker of doubt was gone. This was right. This was what her body wanted, her heart craved. This sweet, sweet agony that only he could assuage.

They were on the bed; he was beside her, on top of her, struggling to tear off his clothes, and somehow she was struggling to help him. She didn't know what she was supposed to do, what he expected her to do, what she expected of herself. She only knew that her body seemed to be bursting, aching all over.

His hands slid under her, hard, impudent, cupping her buttocks, thrusting her up, his mouth all the while scouring hers, hot and demanding. Dominie felt the intrusion of his tongue, felt him searching that warm, moist cavern, and suddenly her own tongue was searching for him.

Jared strained to hold back, excited by her response, but not wanting to press too quickly. The desire was so intense, he could feel the blood rushing through his veins, the sweat beading on his forehead.

God, he wanted her. He had never wanted a woman so much. Never *needed* a woman, never lost control so utterly and desperately. With a groan of surrender he drove himself into her.

He felt the resistance—that slight barrier her body put up against his savage assault—and instantly understood. Damn, he thought, but it was too late. Dominie gave a little cry and went rigid beneath him.

"You hurt me," she accused.

Jared lay motionless, still hard and painfully large inside her, hating himself for his clumsiness. He, who never felt clumsy or unsure with a woman.

"I'm sorry, sweet. I know." His lips were on her cheek, tracing a little course of kisses down to her neck, lulling away the fear and bewilderment. "But it only hurts for a minute. I promise. See . . . it's already going away."

He had begun to move again, very slowly, gently, easing his swollen manhood in and out of that soft flesh. He had not, Dominie discovered, been telling altogether the truth. It did still hurt, though nowhere near as devastatingly as that first stab of pain that had seemed to rip her body apart. And mingling with it was another bittersweet agony, rising from somewhere deep inside until she could not think of anything else.

Her hips seemed to have a will of their own, surging up to meet him, sinking back, up again, following the rhythm he had set, bold, hungry, aching for release. The agony was excruciating now. She longed to cry out, to beg him to stop, to tell him she could not bear it any longer—only she knew she would die if he did.

Then suddenly she *was* crying out, and her body seemed to explode, a thousand little quivering jolts of the most exquisite pain. Almost at the same instant, a deep, convulsive shudder ran through him, and with a low moan he collapsed, clinging, holding on to her as hard as she was holding him, so closely entwined they seemed for a sweet, perfect moment to be one.

A wave of tenderness overwhelmed her. She loved this man so much. Incredible, but somehow it had happened . . . her own private miracle. She had seen him from a distance, she had fallen madly, hopelessly, forever in love, and now they belonged to each other.

"Mmmm . . . that was nice," she said, amazed at the banalities of which she was capable, and not minding at all as she fell asleep in his arms.

Nice? Jared looked down at her, amused. "Nice" was not quite the word he would have chosen. "Sensational" . . . "earth-shaking" . . . "you are a magnificent lover"—those were more the words he would have expected.

But "nice" would do. He adjusted her weight in his arms, resting her head against his shoulder, and touched his lips to her hair. Gently, taking care not to wake her. It had indeed been "nice." Nicer than anything he had ever known.

He was surprised at the feelings of possessiveness that came over him as he held her in his arms and watched the shadows play on her sleeping face, accenting her youth, touching the fragility he had noticed with her slimness before. She was his. Only his. The horrible sickening specter of her quivering in some anonymous Arab's arms was finally laid to rest. Whatever had happened between those two, at least it had not come to this.

He did not know why it should matter so much. He had never cared before whether a woman was a virgin, never particularly wanted her to be. Her history with other men had been no concern of his, any more than his history was of concern to her. But somehow this woman was different. He wanted more with her.

Perhaps if things worked out . . .

He was aware that he was getting ahead of himself. He had assumed too much before, and she had been furious, and rightly so. They had made love beautifully and satisfyingly—very "nicely"—but that did not mean she wanted more than one sweet, magical night with him.

Still, it would be good to be with her again, and again and again. Jared let the fantasy take hold. He would set her up in a place of her own. Manila perhaps. There was a large foreign community in Manila, and such arrangements were winked at with open tolerance. A mistress was as good as a wife there. She would have a comfortable life.

It would be good for both of them. He would spend

more time on land, work it out so they could be together often. She would ease the discontent that had been gnawing at him lately. And surely what he was offering would be better than anything she had expected when she put on that absurd red dress and forced herself to go out and sell her body.

*Forced?*

His lips twisted into a wry grimace. There he went again, trying, illogically, to make her into something she wasn't. With her passionate nature, she had probably thought it would be fun! If he was going to be fair to her, and fair to himself, he had to be honest.

He leaned closer, kissing her gently awake. Her lips responded instinctively, parting even while she was still half-asleep, receiving his passion naturally, openly, as if they had been lovers for years. Her legs were parting too, and Jared realized, without even being aware of it, he had grown hard for her again. Unable to resist, he slipped between them.

"I don't know much about men," she murmured unnecessarily. "Can this happen again? So soon?"

"It can," he replied, equally unnecessarily, for she had to feel the pressure of his erection against that soft sweet space that was already moist and ready for him. "And it will. And in fact . . . it is."

He had promised himself he would take time with her, tease her, play with her, teach her what love was about. But as before, he was too eager, his need too urgent. He would tire of her, he knew—he always tired of a woman in time—but until then he could not imagine any greater ecstasy. He buried himself deep inside her, as conscious at that moment of her responses of his own ravenous hunger. To his delight, she was more than equal to his passion, and they found their culmination together again, sinking deliciously, totally satiated, into each other's arms.

The afternoon passed, and the evening. It was well into the night before Jared finally left the small cabin, having made love one more time with the same ardor and urgency which she seemed to receive with enthusiasm, though he couldn't help feeling somewhat guilty. A woman experiencing love for the first time was entitled to something more than an oaf who couldn't keep his hands off her. And the stiff rod of his manhood out of her!

He made a quick tour of the deck, ignoring the sly looks of the men on the lonely night watch. Luckily the storm seemed to be holding at bay, though the wind had kicked up once or twice. He doubted he would have been much good if they'd needed him for anything—even in that brief time, he couldn't keep his mind off her. He went to the galley, brewed a pot of tea, heated some chicken broth and rice, and carried it back to the cabin.

"I cheated you three times," he said as he set the tray on the small captain's desk beneath the porthole and brought over a cup of tea. "Which is twice more than I intended. At least I can be a good host and offer some sustenance."

"Cheating? Is that what you call it?" Her hair was tousled, tumbling every which way around her head as she rubbed her eyes sleepily, like a little girl, and accepted the cup. "My English must be very faulty. I had thought it was something else."

"That's not what I meant, minx—and you know it." Her English was, in fact, almost flawless, barely a trace of a delightfully soft accent now, as if it came and went with her mood. "How do you say 'minx' in French? *Coquette? Diablesse?*"

Dominie giggled. "You have the words right, but I will have to teach you how to pronounce them. Your accent is awful. You sound like an American."

"Perhaps that's because I *am* an American."

"That's no excuse." She finished the tea and placed it on a shallow night table beside the bed. "And what did you mean before? When you said you cheated me?"

Jared took the cup from the table, set it back on the tray, and returned to half-kneel, half-squat in front of her.

"I meant that I didn't *know,* sweet. Why in God's name didn't you tell me? I might have been gentler if I'd understood . . . given you a prettier introduction to love. It should have been less painful. Less frightening."

"Oh?" Dominie did not mention that he'd given her precious little time to tell him anything at all. "I don't think you frightened me. I frightened myself a little . . . but I wasn't frightened of you. But," she added with a mock pout, "you *could* have hurt me less." She was amazed at how natural it felt, being with him. She was absolutely naked, sitting on the rumpled bed—as if she were indeed the trollop he had imagined before—and she was not even slightly self-conscious. "I think I am being most improper. I ought to have something on. You are fully clothed, and I . . . well, I am not."

"I like you that way." He put a spoon in one of the heavy earthenware bowls and waved it temptingly under her nose. "I could always remove my trousers, of course—but that might have drastic consequences."

"And your shirt," she said, "if we are to be even." A heavenly smell rose from the broth and rice, reminding her that it was a long time since she had eaten, and her stomach was growling. She knew she should feel utterly, disgracefully wanton. She had just surrendered the prize she had been taught to value above all others, and under highly dubious circumstances.

But she had, after all, been drugged—the fault was not wholly her own. And as she could not get her virginity back anyway, she might as well make the best of it.

Besides, she loved this man, and love made everything all right. She took a spoonful of the thick, rich soup, then another, and another. It settled comfortably on her stomach, quelling the last of her queasiness, and she knew that both the drugs were finally out of her system. That her love was not altogether requited did not bother her overmuch. Men, she knew, were slower than women to give their hearts. And he had been treating her—looking at her—with the greatest tenderness all day.

"Do you realize," she said softly, "that I don't even know your name?"

He looked vaguely discomfited.

"Ah . . . no, I suppose you don't. I am, uh . . . Jared Barron." It felt strangely awkward, introducing himself to a woman with whom he had made love three times already. And soon would a fourth if the way he was feeling and the messages she was sending him were any indication. "Captain Jared Barron. From Massachusetts. This ship is my command. . . . And you, I know, are Marie."

"Marie? . . . Where on earth did you get that?" She stared at him, startled for a second, then suddenly remembered. "Oh! Of course. That's what he called me when he ran away. The Arab. Aziz."

"That's not your name?"

"He thought it was . . . but, no. It isn't. I lied to him." Her face clouded as memories came flooding back, too awful to talk about, even with him. "I couldn't bear to give him my real name. It's Dominie . . . Dominique, actually, but I like Dominie better."

"I don't wonder," he said gently. Sensing her change in mood, he came to sit beside her on the edge of the bunk. "It's much softer. Prettier. . . . But why did you lie to him, Dominie? Why didn't you want that man to have your name?"

"Because I loathed him!" she spat out passionately. "He was an awful, evil, disgusting *toad*. He tried to . . . to do terrible things to me. But I showed him. I threw up all over him!"

"You . . . what?" In spite of himself, Jared started to laugh. Obviously Dougal had misinterpreted that "passionate" clinch he had come upon in the shack. Perhaps if he had arrived a minute later . . . "No, never mind— I heard you quite clearly. I guess I should consider myself lucky you didn't loathe me. I had a few 'terrible' things in mind myself."

She looked up at him, her eyes so clear and beautiful it made his heart contract. "They weren't disgusting when you did them. And I *wanted* to be with you."

"You didn't want to be with him?" Jared rose abruptly, striding across the cabin, horror mounting—and, God help him, relief—as the implication of her words set in. "You mean he forced you to go with him? He *kidnapped* you? Out of where—Singapore? By God, they have laws against things like that. I'll track him down. I'll—"

"No," Dominie said miserably. She wanted to explain to him, she longed to explain, but just thinking about what had happened sent chills of terror through her, even now that she was safe. And to explain meant she would have to tell him about Denis, which, no matter how she adored him, she was not ready to do. "No, he didn't kidnap me. I went with him willingly—I wanted to go— only I . . . I didn't know what it would be like . . ."

Jared stood for a long moment on the far side of the room, fighting the conflicting feelings that both tormented and angered him. Blast it, who was he to judge? He was hardly without sin himself. Only just for an instant he had hoped . . .

"I see," he said quietly. Then, catching the look of confusion and unhappiness on her face, he went over and took her in his arms.

"It's all right, Dominie . . . I have no right to make demands on you." Or unrealistic expectations, he added mentally, though he did not utter the thought aloud. "I can only ask humbly . . . and I have never been very good at humility. You are a beautiful, passionate, very special woman, and I am very lucky that you want to be with me."

This time he found the patience he had been looking for previously. Their lovemaking was sweet, slow, tender, as he taught her about her body, and his, and why they fitted together so perfectly. There was no part of her left untouched, and very few parts of him, the exploration as important this time, the newness and discovery, as the culmination that seemed to catch her by surprise, taking her breath as if it were the first time it had ever happened and she was filled with awe and wonder. They lay absolutely still for a long time afterward, awake but not speaking, engulfed in a sea of contentment, like a soft blanket that covered them both.

It was morning when Dominie finally woke. A gray morning, the lamps were still lighted—or was it again?—and she could hear the wind howling, though the boat was relatively steady. Jared must have been out someplace, for he was fully dressed and had just finished placing something on the captain's table under the single tiny window.

"You left me." She pouted teasingly. "But now you are back."

Jared turned, startled to see her awake. "I am back," he admitted. Not for long, he wanted to add, though when he saw her lying there, looking fresh and remarkably untouched, he was not so sure.

"You brought something?" She was wriggling out of the covers, twisting them modestly around her breasts, enchanting him even more. "For me? What is it?"

"I thought you might like something to wear. I know, I know—I said I preferred you the way you are. But it occurred to me you might enjoy a stroll on deck, and that dress you were wearing yesterday . . . well, it would hardly be fair to the men to parade around in that.''

He was holding up a pair of white pants and a prettily checked blue-and-white shirt. Not exactly feminine, but Dominie had to admit they looked about her size.

"One of the cabin boys is going to be a little short on wardrobe," she hazarded.

"A couple, actually. And I found one with small feet and an extra pair of boots. There's a comb too. Carmichael's contribution. One damned tuft of hair sticking straight up from his head—the oddest thing you ever saw—and he's so vain about it, he had three combs to spare.''

Dominie knew instantly who Carmichael was. She had seen him only briefly, and then through a haze of drugs and fear, but the description fitted perfectly.

"That was kind of him," she said.

"There's, uh . . . one more thing.'' Jared shuffled awkwardly, hating what he was about to say, and hating himself even more for the qualms he felt. Dammit, Barron, he told himself angrily. She is what she is. Why can't you accept it? "I cheated you out of more than tenderness yesterday." He brought over a small bundle, something bulky wrapped in a clean white handkerchief. "You would have been paid a great deal of money for the, uh . . . innocence I took for free last night. I don't know how much of it that bastard would have let you keep, but you deserve all of this. And more."

Money! Dominie gaped in horror as he unfolded the cloth and a glitter of gold coins came into view. He wanted to give her money for what had passed between them! She had offered her heart, her soul—her love—and this was how he repaid her? Oh, *mon Dieu!* She was still nothing better than a prostitute to him! She had not explained very well, she had been too confused, the memories had been too ugly, but she had thought he understood.

And now he was giving her money!

"Is *this* what you think I am worth?" She took a handful of the coins, as many as she could grasp, and clenched until the edges dug into her palms.

"It's not enough?" Jared's eyes narrowed. The harshness in her tone was unpleasant and utterly unexpected. He had promised to be generous, and he thought he had. "It's all the cash I carry. We trade in sycee, or notes. I'll get you more—whatever you want—when we reach port."

"Not *enough?*" Dominie could hear the hysteria rising in her voice. She saw the puzzlement written all over his face, the mounting anger, and she despised herself as much as him for letting this man think he could buy her. "I hate you! Don't come near me! Don't ever come near me. Don't you ever, *ever* dare *touch* me again!"

"Dominie . . . ?" He took a step forward, then stopped as she raised her hand, threatening to hurl the heavy coins at him. "For God's sake—"

"Just get out," she cried. "Get out, get out, get *out!*" She held the coins in her hand one last second, then hurled them at the door as it closed behind his hastily retreating form. They smashed loudly against the wood, then clattered to the floor and began to roll around the room.

How could she have been such a fool? She had seen him once, and thought she loved him—and been naive enough to think she could make him love her too! Only it wasn't love at all. It was some base physical urge she was too depraved to resist!

She didn't even know him, and he didn't know her. Or care to. All he wanted to know was how much she would take for her "favors"!

She sank miserably back on the bed and tried desperately to keep from crying.

She would never, never, *never* trust a man again. And she would never let herself love. It hurt too much.

# 15

"WOMEN!" Jared leaned against the rail and stared out broodingly at whitecaps rising on the churning gray expanse of an angry sea. "As long as I live, I don't think I'll ever understand them!"

His cousin concealed an amused smile.

"Is this the infamous Jared Barron speaking? Love 'em and leave 'em, and half a dozen waiting in the wings if this doesn't work out? Plenty to choose from? I've never known a woman to get under your skin before."

Jared threw him a dark look.

"Who said one has now?"

Alex ignored the obvious. "I thought things were going well with the little mademoiselle. You disappeared for hours—right after you went stomping down to throw her out of your cabin. The men have been congratulating themselves and clapping each other on the shoulder. They thought they were going to have a nice even-tempered captain from now on."

"Things *were* going well," Jared said wryly. "Until the subject of money came up. Damn, I've never been naive about women before. I don't know why I thought this one was different. All she's interested in is cold hard cash."

Alex regarded him thoughtfully. "You've never been cheap with women either. If you liked her enough, I'd have thought she could have what she wanted."

"That's just it." Jared watched the sea change, the grays growing deeper, almost black, the white more violently raging. Like my own mood, he thought, and wondered why the devil it mattered so much. "I don't *know* what she wants. I let the discussion of money go a little long, I admit. I swore I'd be generous—and blast it, I was! But when I finally got around to giving it to her, she threw it back in my face.''

"Because it wasn't what she expected?" Alex asked shrewdly. "Or because you picked an inappropriate moment to play Lord Bountiful with your gold?"

"Oh, God," Jared groaned. "I don't know. Who can tell with women? She's in the thing for the money—she admitted she went with that damned Arab of her own free will. Why should she turn into a fire-breathing dragon when I try to give it to her?"

"Why indeed?" Alex was watching his cousin, laughter dancing suddenly and irrepressibly in his soft gray eyes. "You never met my mother's uncles, did you? A pair of old reprobates, but charming. I remember George, the elder—he was a gentle, dreamy sort—always used to say, 'Alex, you want to make a beautiful woman happy, tell her how smart she is. You want to make an intelligent woman happy, tell her she looks pretty.' "

Jared almost smiled in spite of himself. "I think I would have liked George."

"You'd have liked Eddie better, the younger. Eddie was more direct. 'Always treat a whore like a lady,' Eddie would say. 'And a lady like a whore.' Not bad advice, at least the half that's appropriate in this case. Respect is important. For everyone. You might like to think about that.''

Jared tried to keep his features composed as he watched his cousin saunter nonchalantly down the deck. Blasted impertinence, coming from a first mate. But Alex always seemed to know when it was time to inject a little gentle humor into an otherwise tense situation. And Alex did have a way of hitting the nail on the head.

But dammit, he thought irritably, he always treated women with respect! He had never looked down on whores. Never thought that cash payments gave any man the right to use or abuse a woman. And he had respected Dominie—except for those obvious moments when respect was not what either one of them had in mind. He had treated her with tenderness. Concern. Genuine caring.

Then she up and tossed his money back at him. And probably would have liked to slap his face in the fury of her disdain!

Damn, she did have spirit! He was grinning involuntarily as he started toward the narrow flight of steps that led to the deck below. He had always like a woman with spirit. Red hair and spirit were an unbeatable combination.

Maybe Alex had a point, he thought somewhat guiltily. Maybe he *had* been a little tactless. Tact had never been one of his strong suits, God knows. Maybe if he made a little effort, he could work things out with her.

And maybe, just maybe, for the first time in his life, he cared enough to want to.

Dominie had had time to cool down, and she was feeling more than a little foolish about the violence of her outburst. There was only one small cracked mirror in the cabin, barely enough to see half her face, but she managed to comb the tangles out of her hair, and the shirt and pants seemed to be a remarkably good fit.

He *had* hurt her . . . but he hadn't intended to. She stood on tiptoe and tried to get a good look in the mirror, but all she could tell was that the blue-and-white checks were not uncomplimentary. If she was going to be fair about it, she could hardly lay the whole of the blame on him. She had not exactly been forthright. She hadn't told him about her brother, she had cringed at the mere idea of discussing Aziz—and he had leapt to all the natural conclusions. Wouldn't any man have done the same?

It was her own unrealistic expectations that had given her grief, she reminded herself sadly. She had wanted so much from him. She had wanted him to take her in his arms and somehow, miraculously, understand everything that was in her heart. But how could he, when she hadn't even tried to tell him?

Still . . . she was glad she hadn't mentioned Denis.

She walked back and forth across the room, pacing, though she couldn't know it, much as Jared did when he was disturbed. Her instincts had been right about that. She was even more positive now. She wasn't sure why— it didn't altogether make sense when she stopped to reason it out—but she knew somehow that she had to keep her desperate mission in Vietnam a secret. She dared not let anyone, especially Jared, guess what she was doing.

Her heart ached when she thought of her brother. It

was almost as if somehow, in the days that had passed, she had forgotten his existence. With the fear of Aziz and her new conflicting feelings for Jared, she had been too preoccupied to think of anything else. He had been out of her mind for long periods of time.

Too long, she thought, and felt a sudden chill.

They had always been so close; she had known absolutely when he was safe, sensed when danger was near. Now she could no longer feel his presence, and she was terrified for the first time that he might be dead and she wouldn't even know it.

She had to concentrate on what was important. She stopped her pacing and stood still, trying to collect her thoughts. She had wasted too much time as it was; she had made so many mistakes. She could not let anything else distract her.

Denis was her first priority, her only priority. He needed her. She would not let him down.

Jared's face was so contrite a short time later as he lingered like a great awkward bear on the threshold of the small cabin that Dominie was almost tempted to forgive him. She wanted to be furious—and she knew she had to be cautious—but it was hard when he looked at her like that.

"You are about to hear my two least favorite words," he said dryly. "I'm sorry. . . . Or is it three? I . . . am . . . sorry. I didn't mean to offend you, Dominie. I still don't know what I did, but I honestly never intended to cause you pain."

He didn't know what he had done? Dominie stared at him in frustration and anguish. "You offered me money. You tried to *pay* me!"

"I thought you wanted it," he said, not unreasonably.

"But I told you . . ." There were tears in her voice suddenly. She heard them—they embarrassed her horribly—but she could not keep them away. "I told you I didn't want to talk about money. I wanted . . . I thought . . . you had feelings . . . and all you wanted was to buy me! You didn't even care!"

"Didn't *care?*" My God, he cared so much it hurt. He wouldn't call it love, not yet, perhaps not ever—love was not a word he bandied about lightly—but he felt more deeply for her than he ever had for any other woman. "I cared like hell! You said you didn't want to *talk* about money, not that you didn't *want* it. Be fair, Dominie. You told me you went with the Arab willingly. This was the kind of life you said you wanted to lead."

I know, but . . ." Dominie cast about in her mind, searching for something to reconcile what she had told him with her true feelings. She still could not talk about her brother without feeling somehow she was betraying him. And what other reason could she give for being there? "I . . . I realized I was wrong once I came. When I found out how . . . how horrible that man was. Did it ever occur to you that I might have changed my mind?"

"No," Jared said honestly. He knew it should, but it hadn't. Perhaps because he himself was inclined to be rigid—once he set a course, he followed through, no turning back—he never stopped to think that others might bend with the breeze.

But she was a woman. A beautiful, soft, whimsical woman. She had a right to change her mind as often as she wished.

"I'm sorry, Dominie. There it is—'sorry' again. I seem to be wallowing in the word. I should never have tried to trade cash for the very lovely things that happened between us. If you ever need anything—if you want anything—you have only to ask, and I will give it to you. I swear. But I will never mention money again."

"I won't ask!" She tilted her chin up, looking like a little girl again, as she had when he came into the room that morning. "I don't need anything from you. And I will never want your money!"

Jared suppressed the beginnings of a grin. All the fire was back, the fierce pride he suspected was all that was keeping her going right now. But he noticed that she had picked up the gold coins and stashed them away somewhere. Perhaps not quite as disdainful as she appeared?

"As you will," he said. "But naturally I'll see that you are provided for. We should be getting to Manila in a couple of weeks. If you like it there, we might—"

"Manila?" Dominie broke in, forgetting everything else as she gaped at him in shock and horror. In a couple of weeks? Somehow, she hadn't thought that far ahead.

But of course, with the monsoons ending, they would be leaving the area.

"Is there something there that troubles you?" he said sharply. "You know someone in Manila? There's something you're afraid of?" But she was shaking her head distractedly, and he went on: "Listen, Dominie . . . it doesn't have to be Manila. It can be anyplace you want. I'm not trying to be arbitrary. We're going on to Macao. You might prefer that, or the Sandwich Islands . . . or back to France. I can't take you to Boston. You wouldn't like Boston—it's too cold in the winter. But anywhere else in the world."

"And what," she said softly, "if where I want to go is . . . *here?* Back onshore where you picked me up?"

Jared tried not to notice the unpleasant thoughts that were creeping into his consciousness. She said she had changed her mind. But he couldn't help remembering that she had come here to ply an extremely profitable trade, which for some damn-fool reason he could not tolerate for her.

Unless, of course, he thought wryly, it was with him.

"That is out of the question," he said. "It's much too dangerous. Have you forgotten the difficulties you ran into with that Arab 'toad' who treated you so despicably? God knows what might happen if you tried to go back. I cannot allow it. You wouldn't be safe."

Dominie could have screamed with exasperation. You wouldn't be safe! It's too dangerous. *I* cannot allow it! Wasn't that exactly what she had heard from every man she had tried to talk to about her brother? Had begged to help her with her plans?

She knew now why she had not wanted to tell him about Denis. Because he would think she was foolish to try to rescue him. He would *forbid* her to do it—he would immediately begin taking steps to "keep her in line." And unlike the Bishop of Paris and Honoré Ravaud, he might be clever enough to succeed.

"You are a typical man," she said.

Jared relaxed enough to grin. "Why do I get the feeling that's not a compliment?"

He reached for her elbow, intending to guide her through the door and out onto the deck. But Dominie, misinterpreting the gesture, pulled back. Frightened, he sensed, not of him—as she had said before—but of herself. She held back only a second, then leaned toward him, lips puckering just slightly, and Jared knew she expected him to kiss her.

She looked so charmingly innocent at that moment, so sweet and defenseless, it was all he could do to keep from catching her up in his arms, with no doubt the same disastrous consequences as before.

"Trust is the most important thing between a man and a woman," he said, amused at the disappointment he saw when she opened her eyes, and suddenly wanting her even more. "You don't yet trust me not to hurt you again . . . and I'm not sure I trust myself. You will have the cabin to yourself tonight. I'll sleep in the owner's quarters. And if you ever see what a blasted cramped little place that is, you'll know what a sacrifice I'm making."

"You don't . . . want me?" Dominie was surprised at the way her heart seemed to stop beating, and annoyed with herself for the inconsistency of her reactions. She had told him in no uncertain terms never to come near her again. Now that he seemed to be doing just that, she was devastated.

Jared laughed gently.

"Think it over, Dominie. Be very, very sure. Come to me at any time, tell me you know what you want— and what you want is me—and I assure you I will not turn you away. Until then, I'll be sleeping in the owner's quarters. By myself. And if that doesn't convince you I care, I'll be damned it I know what will!"

The weather continued changeable. The storms held off long enough sometimes for land parties to go ashore, scouting both the mainland and a small uninhabited island a few miles to the south. But other times the wind would return with almost gale force, battering the already-damaged vessel, and waves swept across the deck, making any attempts at further repairs impossible.

Dominie could see that Jared was impatient with the delay. True to his word, he was spending his nights in the owner's quarters, but she could not have asked for a more attentive companion during the day, and she noticed that he made a visible effort to keep his temper whenever he was around her. He even relaxed enough to let all of the men, including one called Mackler, whom he seemed to dislike particularly, take a turn at going ashore.

"You are a good influence on me," he said one afternoon. The wind had been quiet for a brief time, and the sun peeked through the clouds long enough to glitter on the rippled water. "It seems that even a crusty Boston sea captain can be a civilized human being."

"Really?" she said tartly. She was leaning on the rail, her back to the ocean, her hair loose and buffeted by a soft breeze around her face. "I hadn't noticed."

In fact, she *had* noticed, much to her consternation. Jared had been extremely civilized, a perfect gentleman, and she was beginning to wonder if there had ever been anything between them, or if she had just imagined the sizzling passion that had engulfed them for a day and night. He was invariably kind; he was thoughtful; he was as generous with his time as he had once tried to be with his money, but she never caught him looking at her in ways that made her feel like a woman again.

*Come to me anytime,* he had said. *Tell me you know what you want . . .* Only she had the awful feeling that even if she did, even if she swallowed her pride and went to him, it would be too late. She had had her one brief chance, and she had let it slip away.

Not that he did not seem to enjoy her company. Quite the contrary. As he showed her around the *Shadow,* explaining the mysterious workings of the sails and rudder and helm, she could see that he took great pleasure in the quick, eager way her mind caught hold of things, and her genuine interest in the ship. They would sit and talk for hours sometimes when the wind came back and the ocean crashed against the hull, and she sensed that he liked those companionable times together almost as much as he liked the things that had passed between them before.

She learned much about the sea and ships from him. She learned that you never went to the front of the vessel, or sauntered back. You went "fore" and "aft"—and great gales of laughter broke out if you forget. She learned that the ropes were not ropes at all, but halyards and sheets and shrouds. And sails were not sails. They were jibs and lugs, sprits'ls and gaffs, with tacks and clews and peaks instead of corners.

The *Shadow Dawn* was a full-rigged clipper, meaning it carried square sails on all three raked masts: the main, in the center, soaring well over one hundred feet, the foremast, which was "fore," of course, and the mizzen, which was "aft." The lowest of the sails was called the "course"; above it came the "lower topsail," the "upper topsail," the "topgallant," and finally, the "royal." If there had been a sixth, it would have been a "skysail," a seventh a "moonraker." A pretty, romantic name, but one that Dominie quickly discovered was reserved for the newest and biggest of the Barron vessels, the *China Dawn,* which was apparently at that very moment resting at anchor in the harbor at Macao.

She heard the pride in Jared's voice as he spoke of his ships, and she knew that the *Shadow* and *Scarlet* and *China* and all the other Dawns were more than an assemblage of wood and brass and canvas to him. And Barron Shipping was more than just the family business. It was a passion that ran with the blood through his veins, like the innate arrogance she had sensed the first time she saw him, and his deep, intense love of the sea.

"That's why you're in such a hurry to get to Macao?" she said, curious at the urgency that impelled him. "Because your brother—Matthew—is carrying opium on one of the Barron ships? But even if you disapprove, can it really be that important? You make it sound as if he's defiled your own personal honor."

"In a way, he has," Jared replied grimly. "My reputation is tied up with the company's—and, yes, my honor too. And it isn't just 'one of the Barron ships.' It's the *China Dawn,* the biggest, fleetest, most luxurious clipper the tea trade has ever known. All eyes will be on it, and I'll be blasted if I like what they're going to see! It has to stop, and it has to stop *now,* before the damage is irreparable."

"But how is he going to feel?" she asked. "Your brother. If you come and just take over. Won't he hate you for it? After all, the opium trade is legal—"

"I don't give a damn if he hates me or not." Jared's face turned hard and closed, as if he were too angry even to let his feelings show. "It may be legal now, but it's evil and stupid. I don't take kindly to stupidity. Matthew made a choice, and it was the wrong one. He's going to have to take the consequences.''

Dominie sighed as one of the men came over and called him off to tend to something or other. If she had ever had any hope that she could tell him about Denis, ask for his help, it was dashed as she listened to him talk about his own brother. He could be so hard sometimes, so sure that only he knew best. Matthew was wrong—no arguments, no discussion, no difference of opinion. Matthew had been foolish, thinking he could traffic in opium. Matthew was going to have to be taken in hand.

And Dominie was young and frivolous and had no idea what she was doing. Dominie was foolish, thinking she could rescue her brother, and Dominie was going to have to be taken in hand!

He would do it too, self-righteously, smugly, absolutely certain he had her best interests in mind. And from his point of view, she had to admit he was probably right. It *would* be dangerous, especially alone. And she could hardly expect him to take time out of his schedule and jeopardize his precious ''honor'' to come with her.

Dominie spent the next few days with a wary eye on the changing weather. The repairs were proceeding, albeit slowly, and she knew she had to come up with a plan. She was reasonably certain she would find the diamonds where Aziz had secreted them. Jared had kept men posted near the little shack for some time—he hated smugglers, he had told her, especially opium smugglers, though she had the feeling that what he really wanted was to get his hands on the man who treated her so foully—but Aziz never showed. Not surprisingly, she thought. He probably assumed she had told her rescuers about the gems, or found a way to recover them herself.

Getting to shore would be more of a problem. The cutter was in clear sight almost all the way, and anyone on board would be painfully visible. But there were times when Jared was busy, when things distracted him—and she still had the gold he had given her so humiliatingly that first night. She had hated keeping it. It galled her just to think it was there. But she might need it to bribe one of men.

As the days went on, Dominie found herself turning

more and more to Jared's easygoing cousin. The monsoon seemed to be lasting much longer than usual, a fact for which she knew she ought to be grateful—her plans were far from firm—but the waiting was setting her nerves on edge. She desperately needed someone to talk to, someone who didn't make her feel she had to keep her guard up all the time, and Alex Barron with his quiet kindness and gentle gray eyes made a sympathetic listener.

"Jared is so angry when he talks about his brother," she said late one morning as they were sitting together in the chart room, watching a sprinkling of fat raindrops pelt against the window. "It seems to me, if you have a brother, you ought to love him enough to forgive him anything. Brothers are a special gift from God."

He looked amused. "I wouldn't know," he said, little crinkly lines forming around the corners of his eyes. "I don't have any myself, only sisters—but I have heard that baby brothers can be quite a nuisance. And I don't think Jared is really angry at Matthew. He's angry at the opium."

"But that seems so silly. He may not like it himself, heaven knows. He says it's 'evil,' and he has a right to his point of view. But everyone doesn't agree. Lots of companies trade in opium."

"Not Barron Shipping," Alex replied, turning suddenly rigid, like Jared at his most righteous. He even looked like Jared for a moment, Dominie thought, the way his jaw was set, the sudden hardness in his eyes.

"I believe you're as stubborn about the stuff as your cousin," she said, amazed. "Are all the Barron men so hardheaded?"

"When it comes to something they believe in, you bet! Opium *is* evil, but making money from it is worse than evil. It's the most despicable thing a man can do. Good Lord, Dominie, opium is a highly addictive drug. And don't tell me it's no worse than rum, because that doesn't hold water. There are thousands—*hundreds* of thousands—of addicts wasting away in hovels all over China, their families starving because everything they have is going for the drug. It's ruined countless lives, and it will ruin more unless it's stopped."

"But if it's so bad," Dominie ventured cautiously,

"then why aren't there laws against it? It's considered medicinal in France, I believe—and England too, and they're the ones who trade in it most. If it's so dangerous, why would they allow it in their own country?"

"Because there aren't too many addicts . . . yet." His expression was still solemn, but not quite so impassioned as before. "The Chinese emperor wrote a very touching—and naive—letter to Queen Victoria. 'Your country lies twenty thousand leagues away,' he said, 'but for all that, the Way of Heaven holds good for you as for us, and your instincts are not different from ours. . . . I am told that in your country opium smoking is forbidden under severe penalties. Why, then, do you permit it to be produced and carried to China?' A mistaken, if perfectly reasonable assumption. Who would think the English would be stupid enough to allow opium to remain legal? They will wake up one day, I suspect, and find out it's too late."

Dominie shivered in spite of herself. She didn't really believe what he was saying—it seemed too horrible—but he sounded sincere, and it wasn't like Alex to exaggerate. "Why didn't the Chinese just shut down the opium trade? Surely that would have been the most sensible solution. All they had to do was refuse to let the British bring it in."

Alex raised one eyebrow. Just like Jared again.

"They did. Of course. But regulations are only as good as the men who enforce them, and for a long time corrupt mandarins looked the other way. But recently they've been cracking down. They've not only tightened the laws, they've added death by strangulation for dealers. Including foreigners. And they seized all the supplies in the traders' warehouses in Canton. There was one heck of a party when they broke it up, mixed it with quicklime and salt, and sluiced it out to sea."

"Good for them," Dominie said, caught up in the story.

"Good, but foolhardy. There is going to be war over it, and they're going to lose. Archaic battle junks and fixed cannon on the riverbank are no match for the British Navy. Opium is going to be with us—and them—for a long time. But the tide is turning, especially in America. Public reaction has already driven more than one China trader out of the business.''

''That's what Jared's so worried about, then? Public opinion?''

''Partly,'' Alex admitted. ''He's afraid it's going to tear the company apart. That's what I'm worried about too. Barron Shipping will survive, but I'm afraid if Matthew doesn't get a chance to solve this himself, the rift with his brother will never heal.''

''I can't imagine,'' Dominie said softly, thinking about Denis and how much she loved him, and how awful it would feel if anything drove them apart, ''having a brother and quarreling with him like that . . . losing him if you didn't have to . . .''

To her embarrassment, she started to cry. Great hot tears that rolled down her cheeks and saturated Alex's shirt when he took her in his arms to comfort her. She hadn't meant to tell him—she hadn't meant to tell anyone—but suddenly the burden seemed so heavy, the loneliness so awful, and it all came spilling out.

She told him about Denis, how he had always wanted to be a Jesuit, how happy she had been for him when he was finally sent to Vietnam, and how terrified she was when she learned that priests were being executed. She told him how she had disguised herself as a nun and found her way to Singapore. She even told him how foolish she had been, taking a chance on the Arab smuggler when everyone warned her against him, though she hadn't known what else she could do.

His face was serious when she finally finished crying and he handed her a handkerchief to dry her eyes.

''Does Jared know about all this?'' he said quietly.

''No!'' Dominie gaped at him, horrified, as she realized suddenly what she had just done. ''You can't tell him, Alex. You have to promise. You have to *swear!* I only told you in confidence. Jared mustn't know.''

''But . . . why not? This is much too painful to handle alone. You've been torturing yourself, keeping it inside. Jared would want to know. He'd want to help you.''

''No,'' Dominie said again. ''He's your cousin! You know how he is. If he thought I was going to look for my brother, he'd try to stop me. He'd turn all masculine and insist on protecting me, whether I wanted it or not!

If I defied him and tried to go anyway, he'd keep me here by force.''

Alex's eyes widened. He was looking at her very intently.

"You mean you still intend to go through with it. Even after everything that's happened. I'm sorry, Dominie . . . I have to side with Jared. This is insane.''

"It's not insane!'' Dominie could feel the tears welling up again, and she was furious with herself for telling him. "I love my brother, and I'm going to find him. No one's going to get in my way!''

"Your brother is a priest, Dominie,'' he reminded her gently. "And a missionary in a very hostile land. He has chosen a path and set his feet on it. You cannot save him from that. You have to let go. You have to let him find his own destiny, whatever it is.''

"I can't,'' she said miserably. "You don't understand. I *can't!* He's my brother, the only family I have in the world. He's always been there for me, whenever I needed him. I have to go to him now.''

Alex put one hand under her chin, forcing her to look up at him.

"This is not a quest anymore, Dominie. It has become an obsession. And obsessions can only destroy.''

He watched sadly as she jerked her head away and went over to stare out the window, lost in her own tormented thoughts. It hurt to look at her, she was so young, and he found himself wishing it was his place to go over and draw her in his arms and kiss away the tears. He had been aware that his cousin was sleeping in the owner's quarters, and he had half-hoped for one brief moment that things were not as they seemed, that perhaps after all she might be receptive to another man's cautious advances.

He had loved only one woman in his life. No, not a woman, he thought, surprised at how vividly all the pain and yearning came back. A girl really, a little slip of a thing with blue eyes and the reddest hair he had ever seen. But she had not been what he thought, and he had been bitterly disappointed. He had a feeling he would not be disappointed in this lovely young woman who stood across the room staring disconsolately at the last of the raindrops.

"The Barron men have always had a weakness for red hair," he said, going over to stand beside her.

She turned slowly, and his heart skipped one quiet beat as he asked the question for which he already knew the answer.

"You love him very much, don't you?"

"Jared? I . . . I don't know. I suppose . . . No, of course not. I've only known him a little while. You can't love a man you've barely met."

"Of course you can." He smiled gently. "And you do. And for all that strong masculine act he puts on, my cousin has very much the same feelings for you. Dominie, for God's sake, tell him. Trust him enough to do what's right. You can't have love without trust. Or honesty. You'll poison it if you try. And love is a terrible thing to lose."

"I can't, Alex." Dominie felt as if her heart was breaking. He was so kind, so concerned, and she longed to be able to respond. "It may be an obsession, it may not—it may destroy my life. But it's *my* life. My decision. I have to make it myself."

He met her gaze steadily, then nodded almost imperceptibly. He didn't like it, but he knew she was right.

"Then you won't tell him?"

"I won't tell him," he agreed. "Now. But I hope you'll change your mind and tell him yourself. I've never seen Jared like this with any woman before. I wouldn't want it to end badly."

Nor would I, Dominie thought later as she sat alone in the same room and watched a fiery sunset turn the window red and gold. Nor would I. She knew now, without any doubts, that she loved this arrogant, exciting, enigmatic man who had turned her life upside down.

It was funny, she had gone back and forth with her feelings, up and down, and all it had taken was one brief talk with Alex to make everything clear. She loved Jared, and if his cousin was right, he was coming to love her too.

Trust . . . The same word Jared had used, and she knew they were both right in a way. But they were wrong too. She *could* trust him, in everything except his compulsive need to smother her and keep her safe. Love would only make him more protective. He would want to set a wall up to shield her from the rest of the world.

But she did not want a wall between herself and her brother. Or even between her and the danger she would face when she went to look for him.

Maybe she did have an obsession about Denis. But Jared had an obsession of his own, and their two obsessions set them on directly opposing courses. He had to get to Macao as quickly as possible, had to put an end to what Matthew was doing and save Barron Shipping and his own fierce honor from the taint of opium. And she had to find her brother before it was too late.

She went over to the window and laid her fingers on the glass, not hot, as she had somehow imagined, but almost cool. She loved Jared, deeply and forever, and she was going to have to leave him.

But before she went, there was one more thing she had to do.

# 16

"YOU SAID TO COME and tell you when I knew what I wanted." Dominie stood on the threshold of the owner's cabin, letting the light spill out on the shimmering red silk of the low-necked gown she had put on again. "You said, if I remember rightly, that you were particularly interested in knowing if it was you."

Just for a moment his face was impassive, and Dominie felt a pang of doubt. Had she been wrong? Was she making a terrible fool of herself? Then his eyes ran slowly down her figure, taking in the lines of the dress, appreciating, understanding, and his reaction was everything she could have hoped for.

"Dare I assume," he said, looking up rakishly, "that this means it is?"

Dominie's heart was singing as she swept past him into the room. He was glad to see her. He had wanted her to come! He had been too proud to ask, perhaps even too sensitive, but he had longed for this moment as much as she. Alex was right. His feelings for her did run deep.

"What an arrogant man you are," she said, reveling in the deliciously savory triumph of realizing that she had won, and more easily than she ever dared to dream. "That's one of the first things I noticed about you. You wear it like an emperor's ermine robe. . . . And you do have a way of making assumptions."

"But this time I'm right." He was caressing her with his voice. Caressing also, very flatteringly, with his eyes, and Dominie had a sudden exhilarating sense of power over this man who had always been able to bend her to his will before. As if she held his fate in her hands, and he knew it.

"How very sure you are," she teased.

"How sure *you* are . . . and how intriguing it makes

you. But then, you know that, don't you? Lovely, merciless Dominie. Are you going to put me out of my misery? Or are you going to keep me dangling like a little child's toy at the end of a string?''

"I think," she said, glancing up through coyly lowered lashes, "I'm going to keep you dangling." He reached out, but she was already darting back, spinning out of his grasp. "It will do you good. And where is this terrible sacrifice you're supposed to be making? You told me the owner's quarters were dreadful and cramped.''

"They are," Jared protested, enjoying the sudden new boldness he had not expected, the way her tongue flicked across her lips provocatively. Did she have any idea what kind of effect it had on him? Probably, he thought, and was amused as well as excited. She had been responsive before—she had been passionate, God knows, and he had loved it—but she had never quite had this deliciously feminine way of knowing how to manipulate a man.

"Are they indeed?" Her eyes flitted around the small outer room, taking in the rich mahogany furnishings, the plush red velvet upholstery, the half-open door to the bedchamber beyond. "Not exactly a palace, but the two rooms together look somewhat bigger than the captain's cabin. How is that a sacrifice? Or do you just miss the sound of it? *Captain's* cabin? You like feeling that you are the master over everyone.''

"Maybe I do," he admitted easily. "And maybe you don't mind." His eyes were playing with her body again, impudently, tracing every curve, reminding Dominie with a little shiver that he knew exactly how she looked without a stitch of clothing on. "I like that dress. It seems to fit a little more . . . snugly than before.''

"I gained back some of the weight I lost. You can't look down my front anymore." She lowered her gaze just for an instant, then looked up again daringly. "But I'm still not wearing anything underneath.''

Damn! Jared felt the last of his resistance weakening. The minx, she would have him begging soon. Which was precisely what she wanted.

"It's a pity it's so lovely"—his voice was husky, low in his throat—"because you won't be wearing it long.''

"Won't I?"

"Oh, Lord. . . ." She had him, the little witch. "What

do you want, Dominie? Do you want me to woo you with sweet words and pretty gestures? I will . . . . though I confess it's not exactly my inclination at the moment.''

"No . . .'' The instinct to tease was gone suddenly, and Dominie was aware of confusion mingling with the sweet, familiar yearning that swept her breath away. She loved this man so much; she did not want to play games anymore—she wanted only to be as honest as she could for the little time they had left.

"It *is* you I want,'' she said quietly. "It has always been you. And, yes—I am very, very sure.''

"Ah, Dominie . . .'' Jared felt his arms opening automatically, felt her melting into them, felt the warmth of her, the sweet perfume of her hair and skin intoxicating him until he could think of nothing else. Then her dress *was* coming off, and they were in the bedroom, and his clothes were coming off too, and suddenly they were in the bed, their bodies joining with no conscious effort on his part or hers.

The moment was as perfect as it was natural. They were familiar with each other now, the sweet rhythms already established taking over, the responses coming almost before the acts as they knew and trusted what they could expect from each other. Jared was conscious of nothing so much as his need and passion for this woman, his sense that here was something utterly new and all-consuming. This was for him the ultimate experience of love, and he knew suddenly that no other woman would ever satisfy him as she did.

Then his body was taking over again, his mind lost in a gulf of overpowering physical sensation, and he was guiding her, propelling her, traveling with her, to the peaks of ecstasy and beyond. All conscious thought was gone, nothing but the shell of instinct remaining, as he collapsed, utterly, devastatingly satisfied, onto the soft warm cushion of her bosom.

They lay for a long time in each other's arms, separate but together, so comfortable there was no need for words. When at last Jared raised himself on one elbow and gazed down at her, he was overwhelmed with a sudden irresistible urge to kiss the tip of her nose.

"Now, that,'' he said roguishly, "*was* nice.''

Dominie smiled up at him. "I think it might just qualify as something more than nice.''

He grinned and was about to respond with a slightly more colorful adjective when a noise sounded abruptly in the outer room. Like the door opening and something heavy sliding across the floor.

Dominie started to sit up, but Jared was already thrusting her back. "Damn," he muttered, grabbing the covers and hastily throwing them over her as he raced for the door. His bare back and firm bare buttocks filled the narrow space, blocking Dominie's view of whatever was beyond.

"No, just leave it there," she heard him say gruffly. "That's fine—don't worry about the buckets. I'll see to them myself. No, no—that's *fine!* I don't need anything else."

He was laughing as he turned back and saw Dominie lying on the bed, the covers up to her chin.

"I forgot I had ordered a bath. If the poor chap had come a minute sooner, we'd have had one very embarrassed cabin boy."

"To say nothing of a very embarrassed young lady." Dominie shivered as she imagined the sheer horror of that awful moment, but she couldn't help giggling too. It was so wonderfully absurd. What had she expected, coming unannounced to his room? "I think my timing left a little to be desired."

"Your timing was perfect," he said with a bawdy wink. "Ah, you mean *that.*" He caught the covers and whipped them off. "Well, your timing was perfect there too . . . and most fortunate for you. Plenty of hot water, a big bar of soap . . . It would be ungallant of me not to offer to share."

Dominie giggled again as he coaxed her into the other room and she saw the tub. It looked exactly like the one they brought to her cabin every night.

"I hardly think that was designed to share. Why, it's barely big enough for one."

"Then we'll have to take turns. And because I am always a gentleman—you did know, didn't you, that I'm a gentleman?—I will let you go first."

He was filling the tub as he spoke, pouring in the hot water, mixing in the cold, making a comical pantomime out of it. Down went one elbow, in an exaggerated test—

ah, the temperature was perfect, and he was looking up to make sure she was watching.

Dominie tried very hard to pretend she wasn't paying any attention. "I rather suspect we didn't spare that poor boy's blushes after all. The one who brought the water."

"How so, love?"

"Do you honestly think he didn't have just the slightest suspicion what was going on when you came out of the bedroom stark naked?"

"I don't see why. I've heard of women so modest they wear their chemises in the bathtub, but men usually bathe nude. How should I have come out? . . . And since you don't *have* a chemise, sweet, it looks like you'll be taking to the water the same way."

Dominie felt him easing her slowly, unresistingly, into the tub. The water was deliciously warm, sloshing up to her knees, rising almost to her breasts as she sank into it. The tub *was* small, but roomier than she had remembered, and it felt heavenly to lean back and watch him dip the soap beneath the surface, lathering it generously.

"I'm sorry it's not perfumed," he said as he lifted her hair and began, very gently, to massage the back of her neck. "Women set great store by such things. Men, too, when we're with them, but alone we're all afraid of softness. . . . Shhh, love, don't try to talk . . . just feel how smooth it is against your skin."

And it *was* smooth. Dominie closed her eyes, not minding the lack of scent at all, feeling almost sinfully decadent as the satiny bar slid over her shoulders, lingering briefly, never quite stopping. Now he was running it down her arm, toying with the soft skin of the inside of her elbow, her wrist, the little spaces between her fingers. She had never even imagined that anything so innocent could feel so wonderfully, tantalizingly sensual.

"Mmmm," she said. He was washing her back, stroking it actually, making her tingle in the strangest ways all over. Slow, every movement was excruciatingly slow, as he worked his way at last to her breasts. The soap was gliding round and round, every circle smaller, provoking and tormenting the hard little peaks in the center. Now the sudsy white foam was on his fingers and he was applying it with both hands to each engorged nipple, pinching, fondling, until she thought she would die from the desire that flooded through her.

She longed to throw her arms around him, longed to draw him down on top of her, force him to end the exquisite anguish. But the water was so warm—she felt as if she were enveloped in a suffocating languor—and she could not make herself move.

Drifting . . . she felt as if she were drifting. . . . He had found her legs, he was caressing them gently, her thighs; the tender inner flesh seemed to burn with his touch. Then, suddenly, his hand was between her legs, the soap gone, and his fingers were doing the most intimate things.

"Oh!" Her eyes popped open, shocked. "Jared, you mustn't." She wasn't ready for this; surely he understood that. It was too bold, the way he was looking at her, raking her body, and suddenly she was embarrassed, her knees tucking up to her chest.

"No, love . . ." He was easing her legs back, but gently, taking care not to move too fast, to alarm her again. She was so enchantingly passionate, he forgot sometimes how inexperienced she was. "Don't pull away from me. There's nothing to be ashamed of. You have a beautiful, very sensual body, and I love to look at it . . . and touch it." He was laughing softly as he bent to nibble her earlobe. "But you're right, I mustn't. Come, you selfish girl. Out of there. You're hogging the hot water."

Dominie felt strangely bereft as he drew her out of the tub. This was what she wanted; she had pleaded with him to give her more time, to be understanding. But now that he was drying her with a thick rough towel and her skin was tingling all over again, she couldn't bear it that he was no longer touching her in exactly the way she had told him he mustn't.

"I don't want to do this anymore, Jared," she murmured, her voice so husky she didn't recognize it. "I'm tired of this game. I want you to make love to me . . . please."

His eyes flared with desire, and just for an instant she thought she had persuaded him. But his lips were smiling and he was shaking his head.

"No fair, love . . . it's my turn now. What an impatient hussy you're turning out to be. Surely you wouldn't

want to cheat me out of my bath. We'll make love later
. . . and later . . . and later. But this is important too.
A man and woman need to get to know each other, to be
playful sometimes, teasing . . . tender.''

Dominie eyed him skeptically. ''You want me to be
. . . playful with you?''

He grinned as he climbed into the tub, soapy water
half-obscuring his lean, tanned body. ''I couldn't have
put it better myself,'' he said. Taking her hand, he closed
it around the bar of soap and guided her, nonthreaten-
ingly, to the taut muscles that rippled across his back.

Shyly at first, hesitantly, Dominie began to slide the
soap around his back and shoulders, feeling strangely
awkward even as she dared herself to move partway down
his arms. She had touched him so much more intimately,
they had shared everything in the height of passion—why
should she be timid now?

''Like this?'' she asked tentatively.

''Like that,'' he said. He leaned back, his body arching in pleasure, eyes closing as hers had before. Now
that he was no longer looking at her, Dominie found that
her hands grew bolder, almost, if not quite, as impudent
as his. The excitement of exploring a man's body was
hers for the first time, and she found herself enjoying it
wickedly.

That little scar on his shoulder—she wondered where
he had gotten it. So faint it must have happened when he
was a boy. The way his skin changed color where the sun
never touched it. The thick mat of curls on his chest. Not
nearly as coarse as it looked, tantalizing beneath her fingertips. The thin, surprising dark line of hair running
down his belly.

She faltered as her hand followed it, not knowing what
he expected . . . what he wanted. ''Is it all right?'' she
whispered, but even as she formed the words, she knew
it was, and dropping the soap, she let herself touch him,
lightly, cautiously, then more boldly. The answering
tremor that racked his body told her he was not dis-
pleased.

''I think,'' he said, opening his eyes, devouring her
with longing, ''perhaps, after all, the tub is big enough
for two.''

His arms were around her suddenly and he was pulling

her down, and somehow, amazingly, he was right—there was room for both of them. Dominie felt his tongue thrusting into her mouth even as that other, harder intrusion filled the rest of her, and she was quivering and crying, aching for release.

Afterward, when they were both wrapped in towels, sitting on the floor and looking at each other, Dominie felt a sudden need to laugh. It was the one thing she had not expected, this easy, companionable laughter following their most intense lovemaking yet. Desire, naturally, tenderness perhaps—but surely one didn't sit with one's lover, naked in a towel, giggling like a child.

"You are an animal," she said.

"Yes, thank you." He beamed. "I know, but—"

"Hush, stop that! It's not funny."

"—it's good to be noticed. And appreciated."

"A satyr, I think," she went on, determined to ignore him. "That's it. Is a satyr an animal? Yes, of course it is!"

"A satyr?" He was looking at her with something new in his eyes. Curiosity, Dominie decided, and wasn't at all sure she liked it. "Where in God's name did you pick that up?"

She frowned. "That's not the right word? And your language is atrocious. Do you always have to be so profane?"

"I'm an American. I'm supposed to be profane. And, yes . . . that's exactly the word. I'm just amazed—and envious—at your command of English. I know French, but I learned it from a book. All the pronunciations spelled out so neatly, too. It was a rude shock the first time I got to the docks at Lorient, and not a one of the blasted porters could understand a word I was saying. But you speak like a native."

"I practiced with an English governess on a neighboring estate. Then I had tutors—I was very well educated. My brother was quite modern in his thinking. About schooling for girls, at least . . ."

Her voice trailed off as she realized that she had said more than she intended. Not a bad slip—she hadn't really let anything out—but she would have to be more careful.

"I didn't know you had a brother," Jared said quietly.

She forced herself to meet his eyes. "He raised me, from

the time I was a little girl. I was very young when my parents died. I loved him very much.''

Jared heard the past tense, the sadness in her tone—though he sensed she was barely aware of it herself—and he decided wisely not to press. He had also noted that mention of a neighboring "estate," and he understood now what had been nagging at him before. She was obviously well-bred, obviously from a good family—there was nothing in her that reminded him even remotely of other women he'd encountered who traded their bodies for cash. That was why he had been so reluctant to think it of her.

Perhaps one day she would trust him enough to tell him what had driven her to such desperate measures. He hoped so. But for now, he would let it go.

"I'm sorry, pretty Dominie," he said softly. "I did not mean to bring tears to your eyes."

She smiled, the sadness leaving. Or almost leaving, replaced by a delectably impish look.

"I can think of a way you could make it up to me."

"I'll bet you can," he said admiringly.

Alex was beginning to have second thoughts about the rash promise he had made to Dominie. She had a point, of course—the decision was hers to make. It *was* her life, as she had so passionately pointed out. But standing by and letting her take risks he knew she could not fully comprehend was a little like standing by and watching some poor wretch jump from a bridge because it was, after all, *his* life.

"You might try throwing yourself on Jared's mercy," he suggested that afternoon as he sought her out on the forward deck, where she was either enjoying the sun or staring speculatively at the distant shore. It was the latter he worried about.

She seemed to sense what he was thinking, for there was an enigmatic little smile on her lips as she turned.

"His mercy?"

"He's not a brute, Dominie. And he does truly have your interests deeply at heart. If he realizes how much this means to you, he might be persuaded to help. At the very least, he might pick up the translators we shipped back to Singapore and see if they could open some negotiations in the capital.''

"And delay his departure for Macao a few more weeks? Or months? Do you really think he would consider that? Knowing how desperate he is to get there?''

Alex did not quite manage to keep his expression noncommittal. He knew only too well, none better, how anxious Jared was to catch up with his little brother. He was a damned fool—he had his priorities upside down and inside out—but Jared had always been stubborn as a mule. Set him on a path, and all the demons in hell would have trouble turning him aside.

"I think it's worth a try,'' he ventured cautiously.

"No you don't,'' Dominie said with a look of soft reproach. "You think I'd be wasting my time. You only want me to do it because you think it will be harder for me to carry out my plans if Jared knows.''

"Perhaps,'' he admitted. "But you can't carry them out by yourself. A strange country, a language that sounds like a flock of twittering birds, a woman alone . . . You have to have help. And who else but Jared?''

Dominie glanced back at the shore, at the thick green trees blocking the mystery of what lay behind. She knew what Alex did not, that she was familiar with the customs of this alien land, that she spoke the "twittering'' language. But she *would* be a woman alone.

It would be such a comfort to have Jared beside her. Her body was still aching with the sweet tenderness of their night of lovemaking, and she longed for nothing more than to be able to tell him, to throw herself on his "mercy,'' as Alex had put it. But she knew only too well what would happen if she did.

"He would never help me,'' she said sadly. "It's too important to him to get to Macao. And get there *now*. His fierce male honor is at stake. I am only his passion.''

"Don't sell passion short, Dominie. Love can be as powerful an impetus as honor. A man does strange things when he loves a woman.''

*Love.* Dominie continued to gaze at the shore, barely seeing it now. "Love'' was a word that had never come up in all the tender talk that had filled her night with Jared. "Caring'' was as close as they had come.

"I wish I could tell him. I want to—you don't know

how I want to—but I can't.'' Then, turning and catching sight of his face, that iron Barron will showing suddenly, unexpectedly, she realized she was going to have to re-assure him. And quickly, or it wouldn't matter whether she agreed to tell Jared or not.

''Don't look so alarmed,'' she added hastily, hating the lie, but knowing she had no choice. ''It will probably turn out the same in the end anyway. I may want to get to my brother, but it's hardly feasible. We're a long way from land, as you may have noticed, and I never learned to swim. It's just that I . . . I need a little more time. I can't bear—not yet—to give up all my hope.''

Alex regarded her thoughtfully. He did not trust her capitulation. It was too sudden, too easy. She had some-thing up her sleeve yet. But she was right: they *were* a long way from land, and none of the men would risk Jared's wrath to ferry her over in secret.

It would be different if she had money. He would worry if she had money; she might be able to bribe them. But where would she get it? He had seen her when they brought her in. There was no place to hide anything in that skimpy outfit.

''All right,'' he said reluctantly. ''I'll hold my tongue—awhile longer. But I'd feel better if you told him.''

''I will,'' Dominie said softly. ''In a day or two. I promise. I just need another day.''

''I hope so,'' he said fervently. ''God help us both if I'm making a mistake.''

Dominie stood for a long time on the deck after Alex had gone, and stared at the line of trees on the shore. She knew suddenly that she did not want to go, that she was desperately frightened of what lay behind that deep, impenetrable wall of green. That she would give almost anything to put it off even a day or two more.

But she also knew that she could not spend the rest of her life knowing she had come so close and not even tried to save her brother.

Tomorrow. Little fingers of fear clutched at her heart as she realized it was going to have to be tomorrow. Early. They would be down in the hold, checking to see how much damage had been done by the water that seeped in during the storm. She had heard Jared discussing it with some of the men. He would be occupied elsewhere when the boat left for what might well be the last scouting party onshore.

Dominie threw an anxious glance at the sky. Clear, not a sign of a cloud anywhere. The repairs were almost completed, the foremast up again, the spars sturdy and whole, canvas mended, new shrouds and halyards in place. If the weather held, they would be sailing soon. If she did not grab at this chance, there might not be another.

Only . . . oh, it was going to hurt to leave him. She fought back her tears, hoping no one would happen by, hoping anyone who did would think it was only a reaction to the wind. She loved him so desperately. Those last wonderful hours in his arms had been the nearest thing to heaven she would ever know on this earth. She longed to stay with him, to develop their relationship slowly, surely . . .

To have the things that could never be hers.

With a little sigh, she let the dreams go, the bittersweet love that brought such joy and pain. She had to leave him—and even if by chance they met again, he would never forgive her for that. When they parted tomorrow, it would be forever.

But she still had tonight. Dominie clung to the thought, took comfort in it, not letting herself dwell on anything else. One last sweet night to hold him close, to show him without words how much she loved him. One last sweet night to build the memories that would have to last a lifetime.

# Dare the Afternoon
## Early December

## 17

DOMINIE STOOD BENEATH the open rafters that separated the interior of the small shack from the steep thatched roof and struggled to catch her breath. She had been so frightened when she came—it was all she could do to force herself up the ladder and through the flimsy woven-palm-frond door—but without the menace of Aziz's dark eyes and evil, leering grin, it was only a simple, rather shabby room with meager furnishings and a slightly humid smell. Light streamed through the door and the single unpaned window, giving it an almost pleasant look.

It had been much easier than she expected to get there. She lingered for a moment just inside the doorway, letting her mind drift back over that surprisingly smooth half-hour or so. Most of the men had been taken off their regular chores to help in the hold, but the ship's carpenter, a surly fellow named Mackler, was apparently above such mundane labor, and Jared had reluctantly put him in charge of the group going ashore.

Dominie could not have asked for better luck. Mackler was so rapacious, it had cost her only one of the gold coins Jared had given her—she suspected he would have sold her grandmother for half that, or less—and she had salved her conscience somewhat by leaving the rest on the pillow with a hopelessly inadequate note of farewell.

Five of the men had gone with them. Two whose names Dominie did not know, though one was either Broad or Benson, for he had been left on guard that first day she was taken out to the ship; a pair of Malays who spoke only rudimentary pidgin; and the second, junior carpenter, Carmichael, he of the yellow tuft of hair and extra combs.

It was only the latter that she had really worried about. His pale eyes had bulged alarmingly when he had taken his place at the oars and seen her huddled in the bottom of the cutter in a bulky sailor's jacket with a watch cap pulled down to cover her hair. But he was clearly under Mackler's thumb—he had to work with the man, and for him—and while he had looked anxious and extremely shamefaced, he had held his tongue.

Dominie forced her thoughts back to the present as she began to look around the hut, checking it out. Nothing seemed to have been touched. Aziz's coffee cup was still where he had left it on one of the low tables, growing a thin layer of green fur on top. That meant he hadn't been back. Still . . .

Every instinct warned her to hurry. She could feel her breath catching in her throat again, and perspiration coated the palms of her hands. She didn't think there was any immediate danger. Mackler and his men had set off down the coast, heading slightly inland—she had stood and watched, pretending to readjust the small bundle of possessions she had brought with her, until she was sure they were gone.

But scouting parties could break up. Just because Mackler started out with the men didn't mean he had to stay with them. And just because he'd been going one direction didn't mean he was going that way still. Dominie had a feeling he was shrewder than he looked, and she didn't want to be around if he got curious and came back.

She would do what she had to, she reminded herself briskly. Quickly. And get out of there.

She needed only three things. The rest of her clothes from the rafters if she could manage to drag the chest over to get them down. The diamonds from their hiding place under the floorboards where Aziz had secreted them. And the gun, which she had seen him slip into one of the drawers in the chest.

The diamonds were the most important. Dominie was agonizingly aware of the beating of her heart as she hurried over and, slipping off the awkward jacket, dropped to her knees on the floor. They had to be there. They just *had* to. Anything else she could leave behind, but the diamonds were essential to her plans.

This time she had come prepared. Dipping her hand into her pocket, she took out the small knife she had removed with qualms from the crew's quarters in the forecastle, hoping it would not be too sorely missed. The space between the boards was tight, but she managed to work the blade into it.

She had just opened up the shallow niche and ascertained with a great surge of relief that the velvet pouch was still there when she heard a faint creaking sound. As if someone were mounting the ladder outside!

Terrified, she jerked her head up and listened. But the sound did not come again, and she decided she had imagined it.

Fighting back her fear, she slid the gems out on the palm of her hand—icy now, prickling with sweat. All there, she thought, and was just dropping them back into their case when something alarmed her again. She stopped abruptly, every muscle tense as she strained for a sound. More a feeling this time—she could not actually hear anything—but the hairs were standing up on the back of her neck.

Slowly, cautiously, she slipped most of the diamonds back, holding out only three, which she clutched in her hand. She tightened the drawstring and pushed the pouch as far back in the shadows as she could, praying that the lush black velvet would keep it from being too noticeable.

Imagination again? Probably. But it would be foolish to take chances. If the worst of her fears had come true—if Mackler had returned—she was going to have to outwit him.

Rising slowly, hands easing behind her back, she forced herself to turn.

Mackler was there. Dominie jumped when she saw him, even though she had known it was a possibility. He's such a big man, she thought. How could he have moved so quietly?

"Mackler!" Somehow she managed to keep her voice steady. "What are you doing here? I thought you'd be out stealing pigs from the peasants."

"They ain't no pigs left ter steal." A slow, ugly grin spread across his face. "An' the captain, 'e makes us trade fer 'em anyways. 'E's a bloody old maid, 'e is . . . we'en it comes ter pigs." His mouth gaped even wider. He was missing a tooth on one side, which gave him an oddly lopsided look. "I got ter wondering. It seemed real strange, ye know w'at I mean, ye'd give your last gold coin fer a bit of a ride didn't last 'alf an hour. Ye got plenty else ter offer . . ."

Dominie shuddered. The thought that there was anything else she might be remotely willing to share with him made her stomach turn, but she did't dare say so. All she needed now was to make him angry.

"It's a Yankee coin," she reminded him coolly. "This is Vietnam. I have no earthly use for it here. The Vietnamese aren't the least bit interested in American money."

"But I bet they's something else could tempt 'em, eh? Come on, girlie—w'at ye got be'ind yer back?"

Dominie felt a sudden stab of panic, even though this was what she had expected. What she had prepared for.

Calm down, she told herself sternly. Mackler wasn't as smart as Aziz, but he was quick enough in his own sly way. If she played her cards right, he'd jump to exactly the same conclusion.

She slid two of the diamonds into her right hand, leaving the third, alone, in the other.

"It's a diamond . . . see?" Her mouth twisted into a cunning smile as she extended her left hand, palm-up. "You can have it if you want. . . . It's yours if you let me go."

He fell for the bait. Almost at the same instant he grabbed the gem, he was reaching for her other hand. Dominie let out a little gasp of pain.

"*Hah!*" he yelped as he pried her fingers open. "Thought ye'd 'old out on me, did ye? W'at 'ave we 'ere? Two more pretty little gems. So, they be three."

"Damn you, you bastard!" Dominie cried out with a fury she did not have to feign. "There were *four!* They were mine. Aziz stole them from me. He must have made off with one of them!"

"Now, ain't that a pity." He was accepting it, as Dominie had known he would, enticed not so much by her anger, which he might have expected, as by that extra little bit of detail that strained his limited imagination. He was too stupid even to search the hole in the floorboards to see if she was telling the truth. "Well, never ye mind. Four 'ud be nice. Real nice . . . But three'll fetch a feck w'en we 'it Manila.'Course, if they was ter be a little something else . . .''

His voice slowed on the last words, almost drifting off, and he was looking at her in a way that sent shudders down Dominie's spine. She could almost see his mind working. This was the captain's fancy woman—she could only have gotten that gold coin from him. And if a man was willing to pay such a handsome sum, she must really have something to offer.

Well, if that was the way it was, she was just going to have to get the jump on him.

"We could come to some kind of . . . arrangement." She hid her distaste behind an oily seductiveness that made her voice crafty and obsequious at the same time. Fancy women didn't show distaste. "You give me one of the diamonds, you take the other two . . . I could make it worth your while."

"Well, now . . ." Dominie could see little bits of spittle frothing at the corners of his mouth. "I might be willing. Ye make it worth my w'ile, I'll give ye yer pick of the lot. Any one ye want, ye make it *real* worth my w'ile.''

You bastard! Dominie thought again. He would take what she had to give, then laugh in her face. Or maybe he wouldn't even bother to laugh!

She forced her lips into an inviting expression. Seductive, slightly parted. If she could just get him to move a little farther away.

"You'd better check to make sure no one's outside. I wouldn't want any of the others barging in. This is just for you. And of course, if word got back to the captain . . .''

The implied threat was enough. Dominie watched as he lumbered over to the door, making no effort to move quietly this time. She waited until he had just reached it, was just looking out, then raced over to the chest and pulled open the drawer.

Please, *please* be there, she thought as she groped for the gun Aziz had left. She was almost sure he hadn't moved it—she could have sworn he was nowhere near the chest that last morning—but then, she hadn't seen him take her dress down from the wall! She was panting with fear when she finally felt the hard metal beneath her fingers.

She already had it up and pointed at the bridge of his nose as he turned and gaped in shock.

"W'at the bloody 'ell . . . !"

"Don't move," she said sharply. "I mean it! One muscle twitches, an you're a dead man. This is my pistol. Aziz took it from me. I know how to use it."

"Maybe." He was eyeing her calmly. Too calmly, Dominie realized with a sudden thrill of fear. "But maybe ye're bluffing. I don't think ye ever 'eld a gun in yer life. And I sure as 'ell don't think ye could shoot a man."

"I wouldn't want to," Dominie said honestly. "I'd hate it. But I'd hate it a lot more if you put your filthy hands on me!"

His features contorted with fury, and she knew she had been right to fear his anger before. He was longing to reach out with his fist, smash it into her face. "Listen, girlie," he snarled, "ye think ye're too good fer the likes of a common tar—"

"I think anybody's too good for you," Dominie challenged boldly. If she was going to make him mad, she might as well do it right. "But that's not the point. The point is, I'm *not* bluffing. You can call me if you want. It's up to you. But either way, you lose."

"Either . . . way?" His brain was so slow, she could see him struggling to understand.

"One way, you're dead. The other way, you'll be too late getting back to the *Shadow*. Captain Barron is going to be furious when he finds out I'm gone. If you're already on board, you might get away with claiming that I batted my eyelashes and swore he'd given permission for a little jaunt onshore. But if he's waiting when they raise the cutter, if he searches you . . . How many 'common tars' have gold coins in their pockets? Or flawless diamonds? I wouldn't be surprised if he hanged you from the yardarm."

Dominie could see the color draining out of his face, and she knew he was thinking it over. His greed was so transparent. He couldn't risk burying the diamonds someplace and taking a chance on getting back, but he didn't want to let her go either. Greed and lust and anger . . .

and then suddenly there was a sound of voices below, and she knew it was over.

He wouldn't dare do anything with the others there. Broad or Benson or whoever he was might hold his tongue, and the other man, and probably the Malays. But for all his timidity, Carmichael was a decent sort. His conscience would torment him into telling the truth.

Dominie sank to her knees in sheer relief as Mackler threw one last furious glance over his shoulder and bolted out the door. She could hear his feet on the ladder, hear him calling to the men beneath, telling them there was nothing of interest in the shack—they had better be getting back to the ship.

Her fingers loosened around the gun. It fell with a little thud to the floor. She didn't know if she could have fired if she'd had to. She didn't even know if there were any bullets in it.

She knew only that she was safe. For now.

Jared was more than furious when he came into the cabin looking for Dominie and discovered the note she had left and the little handkerchief-wrapped bundle. He was beside himself, first with anxiety and confusion—he had been so sure things were finally going right between them. Then with rage as his cousin stood in front of him five minutes later, shocked and pale, and confessed what he had learned of Dominie's past and her madcap scheme to rescue her brother.

"You *knew* what she was planning?" Jared's face was black with his legendary temper, but his voice was cold and controlled. "She told you—and you kept it to yourself! You didn't think it was worth mentioning?"

"I gave my word," Alex said quietly. "A Barron man does not break his word loosely. You of all people should know that."

"Dammit, this isn't a case of gentleman's honor. To hell with your blasted word! This is a matter of Dominie's safety. She doesn't stand a chance by herself out there—and God help her if she finds her brother! They're *executing* priests. You should never have allowed her to go. How the devil could you let her talk you into keeping quiet?"

"Dominie can be very persuasive," his cousin reminded him dryly. "And I didn't allow her to go. I knew what she was planning, of course, but it never occurred to me she would pull it off. I didn't think any of the men would be fool enough to get talked into into taking the captain's lady ashore. Especially Mackler, whose heart is about as soft as a chunk of New Hampshire granite."

"He didn't do it out of tender sympathy." Jared spun around in frustration and rammed his fist against the wall at the end of the bunk. If only he had known . . . "He did it for gold hard cash."

"Where would Dominie get . . . ?" Alex broke off as his eyes drifted down to the handkerchief, now unwrapped, its burden of gold tumbling out on the dark wool blanket. "You *were* generous," he said with a faintly raised brow. "I thought you said she threw that back in your face."

"She did. But she picked it up later, and I thought . . ." He hesitated, hating the things he was remembering, unable to keep them from coming back and choking him. He had considered all the possibilities; he had gone over them carefully in his mind and come up with the one that was wrong. The one he should have known all along was wrong! "I figured she had changed her mind."

"I see." Alex was watching him thoughtfully. "I'm sorry, Jared. I wish I had handled the situation differently. But I'm not sure that would have included telling you."

Jared's eyes flashed and he started to say something, but Alex cut him off.

"She didn't want you to know. That's a fact. She didn't trust you enough to take you into her confidence. That's also a fact. Whatever she meant to you, apparently it wasn't enough to reassure her that you would be on her side, no matter what. Or she *thought* it wasn't, which is the same thing."

Jared drew in a long deep breath. Whatever she meant to him? God, she meant everything! Enough so that he would have felt a compelling need to protect her, to keep her safe. To tie her up in the cabin and hold her there by force if he had to! Surely no one could fault him for that.

And yet . . . He sensed somehow he had failed her, and he despised himself for it. God help him, if anything happened to her, he would never forgive himself.

"It's too late for recriminations," he said abruptly. "On either side, though Lord knows we both have plenty of call for it. What's important now is to find her before she gets too far. That damned s.o.b.," he muttered as he headed for the deck, his cousin directly behind him. "I counted the coins. There was only one missing. He did it for *one* lousy coin! Even Judas had his thirty pieces of silver."

They were waiting at the rail when the cutter pulled alongside and was hoisted up on the davit. Mackler was in the bow, cocky defiance belying the knot that was already hardening in his gut. The instant he had looked up and seen the captain, he had known what he was in for, but something in him, some sly instinct for self-preservation, would not let him admit it. He was rubbing his hands on his pants as he felt the boat come up. They were filthy and coated with sweat, and his eyes were shifting craftily, searching for someplace to hide the things he had taken from the woman.

But the bottom of the cutter was open and empty, and the captain was watching like a bloody vulture circling overhead. Nothing for it but to leap out of the boat, cringing and swaggering at the same time as he willed a crooked grin across his face.

"Turn out your pockets, Mackler."

Jared's voice was so soft a tremor ran through the men who had begun to gather, first out of curiosity, then mounting trepidation. They had heard their captain bellow, they had heard him rage, they had heard him threaten—but they had never heard his voice so soft they had to strain to hear.

He did not react as a grimy hand pulled out the gold coin, then, hesitantly, reluctantly, the pocket lining, and three sparkling gemstones spilled out. It was so quiet the faint pattering sound they made as they landed on the deck was audible.

Still Jared did not react. He simply stood there, as if he hadn't even seen, until someone picked them up and handed them to him.

He looked down, his face impassive, tucked them into his pocket, and said, still very quietly:

"This *is* a lashing offense, Mackler."

A collective sigh seemed to roll through the watchers,

the tension broken, as if whatever they feared, it had somehow not happened, and they were back with the familiar again. There was even some fire in the captain's voice as he turned to his cousin.

"Lash him until he loses consciousness, bring him to, then lash him again. And I don't care if you kill him! The same for the others if you strip them and find anything on them, though I doubt they'll have anything. Otherwise thirty lashes for looking the other way. For every man who was on board that boat!"

Alex nodded grimly. He felt bad about Carmichael. The boy couldn't have participated willingly, but discipline was essential on long sea voyages. A show of softness or favoritism was asking for rebellion later. And Jared was right. This was a lashing offense. Dominie could die because Carmichael had "looked the other way."

"You don't want to wield the cat yourself?" he asked.

Jared barely took time to shake his head. He was already giving orders to the men, sending some of them back for things in his cabin, others to the galley. "I'm going to have six of the crew row me in. Wait until they're back. I want all hands on deck to witness punishment. I'll be looking for Dominie. And pray God I find her in time."

He finished supervising the stowing of his gear on board and was just climbing into the cutter when a hand on his sleeve held him back.

"It's not going to work, Jared," Alex said. "She's determined to do this thing. She came all the way from France, disguised as a nun—she took terrible chances with that Arab, Aziz. You can drag her back, kicking and screaming all the way, and she'll just start scheming to do it again. He's her brother. The love between them runs deep."

"I know what I'm doing," Jared retorted, then, catching the expression on the other's face, added wryly, "even if it doesn't always look like it. You wanted command of the *Shadow*, cousin? Well, you have it. Send the men in with the smaller boat—I can handle that myself if I have to. Dougal said there's a kind of roller arrangement of logs that Aziz used to bring his vessel into the copse. You can stash it there. It should be safe enough."

Alex was studying him intently, comprehension dawning. "You want me to go off and leave you? With one small boat and no crew?" There was skepticism in his tone, but not surprise. "It's a long row to Singapore."

"I have strong arms. Give me three days. If I haven't got her back by then, go on to Manila, the way we planned. You can swing by on the way back. That island a couple of miles south ought to make a good rendezvous. Drop off some supplies before you head out—with the native fruits and whatever else I find, I should be in good shape. If I'm there when you get back, pick me up. If not . . ."

He stretched out his hand with a casual shrug, as if somehow it didn't matter anyway, as if the risk of one's life were a petty thing. They had never been a demonstrative family. No hugs, no tears, no verbal outpourings of affection. All they had was one brief handshake to express without words the feelings that had gone unspoken for years.

Jared held on a moment longer then necessary, then slowly released his grip.

"Either way, the *Shadow* is yours. Enjoy your command, Captain Barron."

Dominie took one last measure of her possessions, all arranged in a neat pile on the vividly striped madras cloth which she had spread across the bed.

The red dress—that would do for her reunion with Denis, with a white lace fichu tucked decorously into the neck, of course. Two extra pairs of harem pants, three with the ones she had on, loose-fitting and cool, the ankles gathered so they were easy to walk in. Enough undergarments to make her feel modest again. Two combs, hers and Carmichael's, a brush for her teeth, and a bar of soap. Everything else would have to be left behind. She didn't want to burden herself with extra weight.

It had taken less than half an hour to get ready. With the drawers dumped out, Dominie had found it surprisingly easy to shove the chest across the floor, and a stool on top had raised her just high enough to grasp her things where Aziz had stashed them. Five minutes to go through them and pick out what she wanted, another five minutes to search the drawers and choose several silk shirts, all in various shades of gold, all pullover style and just the right size to make long, free-flowing tunics. She had had some qualms at first, even about touching them, but then she had remembered how fastidious Aziz was. Everything would have been so thoroughly washed, not a trace of him would be left.

In fact, she had to admit, another ten minutes later, she was quite comfortable attired. The harem trousers secured with a sash at the waist, the tunic shirt coming almost to her knees above them, another sash to hold her hair back in that hot climate. If only the sea boots weren't quite so ill-fitting. She just knew they were going to cause blisters, but her own slippers were wildly impractical and she could hardly flop around in a pair of Aziz's very large sandals.

Not exactly fashionable, she thought, and was just as glad there wasn't a mirror in the shack. She knew she probably looked awful, though she couldn't bring herself to care. Looks were the last thing she had to worry about now.

Time to go, she told herself, and was surprised at the catch that came into her throat. She had been so afraid when she had first come back to the shack. Now it was familiar territory, and she was even more frightened to leave it.

But she had to. Dominie patted her waist, feeling the slight reassuring bulge that barely showed beneath the tunic. The gun, tucked into her sash. And on the other side, the small pouch safely secured in her pocket. All there, all safe. No more procrastinating.

The wind was absolutely still when she went outside. Not a leaf so much as quivered on the trees that surrounded the small clearing. The air was heavy and still, the monsoons finally ended, and heat lay like a sweltering blanket over the earth, making every move an exertion.

Dominie stood for a moment at the base of the ladder, scanning the terrain with her eyes. Green hills on every side except the ocean. Which would be the best way over? She wanted to go north, up the coast, probably two or three days' walk, and probably not straight, for she didn't want to go directly through Hué, and there was at least an equal chance that the home of Denis' contact was on the other side of the city.

Le Van Duong. She ran the name over in her mind, as if memorizing it, though it was in reality quite simple. Le was an extremely common surname in a country where there were barely more than a hundred "families." And Van was the most common copulative indicating a man. Would there be more than one Le Van Duong in the vicinity?

She was so intent on her thoughts she did not notice the sound of footsteps in the copse behind her. Only when a twig snapped sharply did she finally hear. Horrified, she whirled around. She had been so sure Mackler wouldn't dare come back. Why hadn't she taken more precautions? She was reaching for the gun, struggling desperately to pull it out, but it kept sticking in her sash.

Then the thick shrubbery between the trees was parting, and Jared Barron appeared suddenly, catching sight of her at nearly the same instant she saw him.

Their expressions were almost mirrors of each other, surprise first, then waves of sheer relief, then a sudden flash of fire—anger on his part, a terrible heart-stabbing anguish on hers.

She had lost. If this had been Mackler stepping out from behind the trees, the outcome would have been much uglier. She would have had to use the gun—if she could even get to it. But she had been willing to risk that, or worse, to search for her brother. And now here was Jared, wild with indignation and obviously determined to stop her.

And she couldn't use the gun on him.

"My God, Dominie," he was crying out. Fury gave added timbre to his voice, making it echo through the clearing. "What the hell did you think you were doing? Sneaking out while I was busy? It was crazy, coming here by yourself—"

"It was not crazy," Dominie cut in, her head tilting up, eyes blazing. "I had every right to do it if I wanted. And you had no right to stop me! But you would have thought you did. You would have thought it was just fine to lock me in the cabin and throw away the key!" They were all alike, these men who were so sure they knew it all. They ran the world and they ran their women's lives, and it never once occurred to them someone might resent it.

"You've got that right." He took a step forward, reaching out with both hands and catching her arms, as if he were afraid she might try to run again and he wouldn't be able to catch her. "Only I wouldn't just have *thought* it. I'd have done it!"

"And you wonder why I had to sneak?" she cried helplessly. "If I were a man, you'd have taken me seriously! You'd have sat down with me and discussed my plans—and asked what you could do to help. But because I'm a little fragile flower that can't exist on my own, you turn all strong and protective and come charging after me!"

"But women aren't like men," Jared protested. "And thank God." He was intensely aware of the warmth of her body only inches from his own, and he longed to draw her into his embrace. Longed for her to want him to. Why was he defending himself when he'd only done what was reasonable? "A man would have worked out some of the details first. Like bringing along a translator. Or arranging local contacts. And a man wouldn't have to worry about slime like Aziz. It's different for a woman."

"I can take care of myself."

"Like you took care of yourself with that Arab?" He gave in to temptation, drawing her closer, clinging as much as holding. He could feel her hair, soft against his cheek, teasing his lips. "Dammit, Dominie, do you have any idea how frantic I was when I found that note and wormed the truth out of Alex? I was terrified I wasn't going to get to you in time. I practically swore the ears off the oarsmen in the cutter."

"I had to come, Jared." She was squirming away, looking up at him, her eyes so earnest they hurt. "You don't understand. He's my brother—"

"Blast it, woman, don't you hear what I'm saying? I love you. I can't lose you now. It would be like cutting out my own heart."

"You . . . love me? You mean that?" Dominie felt as if she were tripping all over her tongue. It was idiotic, she had to get to her brother—she was desperate to save his life—and all she could worry about was whether this man meant it when he told her he loved her. "But . . . you never said so before."

He was laughing softly, more at himself, Dominie sensed, than at her.

"There are many things I haven't said, it seems. There are things we haven't said to each other." His face filled with aching tenderness as he looked down at her. "I make no promises, Dominie. I'm not sure what the future will bring. I'm not even sure what it means, all these new feelings I've found. But I do love you. And that's more than I've ever said to any woman."

Dominie could almost feel her heart breaking as she gazed back at him. Tears welled up in her eyes, sudden and stinging. "I love you too, Jared. I've loved you since the first time I saw you . . . and I *do* know what it means. But don't you see? This doesn't make any difference. My plans haven't changed. I came here to rescue my brother."

"How?" He released his hold on her long enough to dip into his pocket. "With these?"

The three diamonds looked small and somehow lonely on the callused expanse of his palm. So he *had* caught Mackler. Dominie found herself hoping in a most unchristian way that he had devised a really suitable punishment.

"No," she said quietly, reaching for the small velvet pouch. "With these," and she tumbled the other ten diamonds out on her hand. "You didn't seriously think I'd let that lout put anything over on me?"

Jared looked astonished, then began to laugh again, heartily this time. "I'm beginning to think I underestimated the ability of some women to handle themselves. I should have known no one would ever put anything over on you, including me. All right, love—I give up. You win."

"You mean . . ." Dominie was conscious of a pang of regret eclipsing the triumph she knew she ought to be feeling. "You're going to let me go?"

"I mean nothing of the kind." He was drawing her into his arms again. Enfolding, cherishing. "I mean I know when I'm licked. . . . I still think you're crazy. I don't think you've got a ghost of a chance of finding your brother, much less spiriting him out of the country. But if you're determined to look for him, then I'm going with you.''

## 18

JARED WAS NOT FEELING quite so strong and protective as he leaned back in the deep shadows beneath a tall silver-barked pine and watched Dominie wash the tin cups and plates from their dinner in the gently flowing ripples of a nearby stream. The moon was full, and pale blue light reflected eerily off the crystal-clear water onto her face and hair. The silk tunic and loosely gathered harem pants moved with her body, clinging just subtly, in ways that made him understand why Arab men sequestered their women.

He was also not feeling quite so sure of himself. There had been absolutely no doubt in his mind when they had started out late that afternoon that she needed him. That this sweet little creature would never be able to manage without his superior masculine brawn and expertise.

It had taken her about five minutes to give him his first dose of humility.

Jared smiled as he recalled the way he had reacted when she pulled out the gun and showed it to him. Amused, and a little condescending. How quaint it seemed, how charming—a bit like a rose showing off its fierce, sharp thorns. What was it she had called herself before? A fragile little flower?

Fragile flower, hell! She had removed the shells, showed him it was loaded, popped them in again, very expertly, and taking aim, put a bullet dead center in the trunk of a false pepper tree. She may have had only one lesson, as she had told him, but she was obviously a quick learner.

"You're deadlier than you look, lady," he had said, not altogether joking. "I'm going to have to watch my step with you."

"I do believe you are," she replied with a little half-smile that told him she had noticed the difference in the way he was beginning to look at her.

His second, considerably stronger dose of humility had come sometime later, after they had crossed the first shallow hills and come into a cultivated valley, terraced slopes of rice paddies and vegetable fields and orchards leading down to the flat below. They had both hesitated, unsure what they wanted to do, when a peasant had suddenly appeared, seemingly from nowhere, perhaps fifty yards down the winding dirt path.

There was no way they could have avoided him, even if they wanted to. He had already spotted them and was staring with frank curiosity in his glittering black eyes. Like it or not, they were going to have to be bold.

"Let me talk to him," Dominie had said. "It will be better that way."

Jared had grinned, but inwardly, at that instinctive choice of words. Talk—as if the fellow could understand English or French, or a smattering of Italian or German or whatever else she happened to have picked up. It would have to be sign language, and it would be rough going at that. The things they needed to know would be hard to put into gestures. But she was right—it would be better if she made the approach. A woman would not seem so threatening to the poor chap.

He had stood back, watching with what must have been an unbearably smug smirk as he waited for her to begin flailing her arms in big awkward motions. Instead she had opened her mouth—and started to speak.

His own mouth must have opened too, jaw dropping in utter shock. Of all the things he might have expected, this was the one that had not even crossed his mind. Tonal Asian languages—like twittering birds, as cousin Alex put it—had always been incomprehensible to him. Clearly Dominie could twitter. She twittered, in fact, quite volubly, and the peasant was twittering back. And information was obviously being exchanged.

"You didn't tell me you spoke Vietnamese," he had accused with some indignation when she joined him again and they were continuing down the path, somewhat more cautiously now that they knew they were approaching inhabited areas.

"You didn't ask," she had retorted with an impish

grin. "You just *assumed* I didn't. Like you assumed I didn't know how to handle a gun. And you still assume I can't manage without a big strong man to take care of me."

And he had thought *she* needed *him!* Humility was a new experience, and Jared wasn't at all sure he was going to like it. He rose and went over to where Dominie had begun to gather up the dishes, somehow managing to look sweetly domestic even in that unlikely setting. They would be spending the rest of the night there, and the next day as well, waiting until darkness to travel again, but he wanted to be packed and ready in case they had to leave in a hurry.

Not only did she not need him, he had to admit ruefully, he was probably a liability. A woman in a long tunic, not altogether unlike the local costume, and at least vaguely oriental trousers, would not cause any more than the usual gossip, and that because of her beauty rather than her alien origin. But six feet and two inches of broad-shouldered masculinity in sea captain's clothes with blond streaks in his hair stood out like a sore thumb.

"Here, let me help you with those," he said gruffly. The cups and utensils were balanced on top of the plates, one in each hand, and she was tilting the lot precariously as she walked. "That's a first-class mess kit, which I had the foresight to bring from the ship. I'm not going to take it kindly if you put dents in everything when you drop them."

"When I drop them indeed! I'll have you know I haven't put so much as a scratch in your precious messes, or whatever you call them! I'm very good at washing dishes."

"Liar!" He was taking the plates and stowing them in his pack, then the cups, expertly, with an economy of movement. "You've probably never done a dish in your life."

"I haven't," she admitted easily. "These are the first. I'm used to having servants for things like that. But I did them superbly, don't you think? It was really quite easy."

"Now, if we could just get you to rustle up a tasty dinner," Jared teased. In fact, it was he who had done the rustling that night. An adequate if unexciting combination of salt meat, rice, sweetened coffee, and surprisingly delicious mangoes, which seemed to grow wild on the hillsides. "And to learn how to pack properly for a journey. There wasn't a pot or a pound of rice anywhere in your gear! Aziz had a more-than-ample selection. Didn't you think it might be a good idea to purloin some of it?"

"Oh . . . I thought about it." She was grinning mischievously as she sat cross-legged on the ground and let her eyes play with him. "But it didn't seem worth the effort . . . since I don't know how to cook. I've never so much as set a pot on the stove in my life. I haven't the vaguest notion what you're supposed to do with coffee, much less rice! Except there's something about boiling water . . . ?"

Jared laughed appreciatively. She looked so pretty as he leaned back beside her, resting his weight on his elbow, watching her in the moonlight. Not reaching out, just watching, more conscious for the first time of his love for her than his desire. "At last, something I do better than you. I was beginning to think I wasn't needed on this little jaunt. Now I know I'm here to keep you from starving."

Dominie stretched out next to him, feeling the faint prickle of the pine needles as she lay on her back and stared up at a dark canopy of branches overhead. It was coming on dawn, but the air was still smoldering. With the monsoons gone, the temperature rarely dipped day or night much below the eighties, but the pungent smell of evergreens gave an illusion of coolness.

"Do you mind very much?" she said softly. "That I speak Vietnamese and you don't?"

"Do I . . . *mind?*" Jared's eyes narrowed as he looked at her. It seemed an odd question. Of course he minded. He was a man. He was supposed to take care of his lady, not the other way around. But he was finding it increasingly difficult to mind things when he was with her.

"I mind that I don't," he said truthfully. "But I think it's singularly fortunate you do. You seem to have gotten a fair bit of information out of that peasant this morning."

"Nothing very comforting," she said, turning serious for a moment. "He recognized the name Le Van Duong. That's Denis' contact—a local priest. I got the impression he's quite well-known, and not altogether safe to mention. I was told to ask instead for his grandfather. Le Van Thieu. He's the patriarch of the family, so they'll all live together anyway. Or close by.''

''And that's near Hué?''

''Unfortunately, on the other side of the city. We'll have to circle round. It will take several days longer, but I don't want to get any closer to the palace than I have to. He says, the peasant, that there are more soldiers now. All over. And better. The emperor's own private guard. They are looking very hard for someone specific . . . a priest . . .''

Jared took her hand and squeezed it comfortingly. ''It's all right, love. If they're still looking, that means they haven't found him.''

Dominie nodded. ''He was very kind. The peasant. He isn't Catholic himself, but he gave me the name of a family a day's walk away. They are Christians, he says. The whole village is Christian. That means Catholic— there aren't any other missionaries here. We'll be able to find shelter there.''

''So you'll have a roof over your head again,'' he teased gently.

''And you . . . of sorts. They are very poor. But I think you're going to find you miss the forest. We'll have to exercise a little . . . discretion, sleeping together with the family in a one-room hut. Not that anyone would mind. The Vietnamese are very earthy people. But the forest is so much more . . . private, don't you think?''

''I do.'' He was rolling toward her, his hand releasing hers with the thought of finding some more productive occupation. ''What a randy little girl you are.''

''I am not a little girl. Even in fun. I am a woman. And what makes you assume I am lusting after your body?''

''I don't assume anymore,'' he said wryly. ''I only hope.''

''Oh . . . and what are you hoping?''

''I am hoping that you want me to make love to you.''

''No . . .'' Her voice was so low in her throat he hardly recognized it. One hand was on the buttons of his shirt, and she was slipping them out, one by one, taking her time. ''You made love to me before, and I enjoyed it . . .

very much. But this time I am going to make love to you."

"Ah, sweet . . ." Jared was intensely conscious of her fingers, the way they brushed against his chest, just lightly, as if by accident. He lay for a moment, motionless, letting her do what she wanted, reveling in it, until the longing became too much. Then he was helping her, struggling to work the buttons loose himself, nearly ripping the shirt in his eagerness to get it off.

"Naughty boy—stop that!" Dominie slapped his hand back, teasing, but firm enough so he knew she meant it. "I told you, *I* am making love to you. You are not in command this time, Captain! You cannot always dominate. This time, you are mine, and I am going to do what I like with you."

She had finished the buttons and was easing his shirt off, over his shoulders, down his arms. Jared could feel himself being coaxed gently but forcefully onto his back on the soft, scratchy bed of needles. She had found the opening of his pants and was having trouble with the fastenings, but still she would not let him help. He was in an agony of anticipation when she finally got them off, and his boots somehow, and he was lying naked on the ground.

Dominie removed her own clothing slowly, almost languidly, knowing he was helpless to do anything but watch with ravenous, yearning eyes. She luxuriated in each seductive movement, savoring the sudden sense of power she felt over him. The same power he had had over her the first time—every time—they had been together and her body had tingled and throbbed while she waited for him to decide what he wanted to do with her.

This time it was he who would wait. The choice was hers. He could have everything—or nothing—as she willed. She slipped her hands between his legs, feeling exactly what she had expected.

"You *are* naughty," she said. "I wanted to fondle you and make you hard."

"Oh, God, Dominie," he groaned, and she knew he was finally truly—completely—hers. As she had always been his. She slid her body on top of him, not quite understanding the mechanics, sensing only that it would work as well this way. That somehow, amazingly, the control had passed from him to her.

She held back one last moment, instinctively prolonging the sweet agony, hers as well as his. Then, with a little gasp, as much of defeat as of triumph, she thrust her body down, and he was thrusting up, hard, brutal, satisfying, and there was no more power, no more control. Just two lovers searching for and finding each other.

Somehow, later—she could not even remember how it had happened—there was a blanket beneath them, and they were running their hands over each other's bodies, finding magic in the most mundane things. The curve of a thumb, the inside of an elbow. They were laughing softly, gently, not at anything in particular, just the sheer pleasure that came from being together.

"You exaggerate," Dominie accused when he had told her for the thousandth time how wonderfully, exquisitely, perfectly beautiful she was. He *was* exaggerating, of course, but she loved to hear him say it.

"*I* exaggerate? What about you, minx? Aren't you the one who looked at me with those devastating green eyes and said you fell in love the *instant* you saw me?"

"And it was true! I did fall in love with you. I even thought the word, though I felt an awful fool. It seemed so wildly impossible . . . but yes, I did love you. That very first instant."

"On a lurching ship? With a leering captain who clearly thought you were something you, . . . weren't? And was crass enough to mention money? Lust, yes—I can believe you fell in lust at first sight."

"But that wasn't 'first sight.' " She was smiling very mysteriously. Jared couldn't see her eyes in the shadows, but he could have sworn she was taunting him. "I had seen you before. And you had seen me."

A puzzled expression came over his face, and Dominie started to laugh. He was concentrating so hard, trying to remember—and clearly not succeeding.

"I was on the deck of a ship. A British brigantine. In Ceylon. You were on the *Shadow*—only I didn't know it was the *Shadow* then—and you looked across the water. And I realized I was in love. No reason for it, no sense at all . . . but I loved you. And, heaven help me, I suppose I always will."

He was staring at her incredulously, comprehension coming slowly.

"The . . . nun? Of course. Alex said that's how you got as far as Singapore." All the conflicting feelings were coming back, the desire, the discontent, the sense that somehow he had lost control of his own emotions; and he didn't know if he wanted to laugh or take her over his knee and spank her! "Do you have any idea, woman, the anguish you caused me? It's very embarrassing for a man to find himself having erotic daydreams about a nun."

She did not look the least bit contrite. "Only *day*-dreams?" she teased suggestively.

"The ones at night were considerably more embarrassing. You have no idea how explicit a man's dreams at night can be."

"Ummm," she said, cuddling closer, every curve of her body molded into every angle of his. "I think we still have an hour or two of night left. Why don't you show me?"

The predawn hours were quiet in the courtyard. The spacious tile-roofed home belonged to one branch of the Le family that counted among its members a black-robed priest. The entire complex sprawled over several acres, with many halls set like red and gold jewels amidst a profusion of formally arranged flowers and graceful Chinese plum trees. But the father of Le Van Duong and his wife and children, as the only Catholics, were separated from the others by a wall of bamboo stakes, set so close together that not a breeze could come between them.

It was not that the religions could not peacefully co-exist. The statues of the Virgin and her son on his bloody cross were perfectly comfortable in the niches with the ancestor tablets and the *hu'o'ng hoa,* the offerings of incense and fire. Religions had mingled easily in this same compound for many years. But there was a fear spreading over the land, like an invisible shroud; and it was this fear that had built the wall. As if somehow, when the soldiers came, the fragile spears of bamboo could separate their fates.

Denis Arielle sat on the lowest step of the short flight that led down from the large central hall with its red-lacquered pillars showing through the open front. Painted screens with images of orioles and chrysanthemums had been placed with great precision against the weather, though in reality not a breath of air was moving.

The silence was soothing. Night was always a difficult time. He could not keep the fears from coming back at night. The same terrors that had gripped him as he cowered in a clump of elephant grass and prayed ignominiously for his life—and that grew more and more insistent as he saw the time come closer.

"You are awake, Père Denis. You are restless?"

It was the boy, Tien, the younger brother of Duong. A precocious child whose French was improving by leaps and bounds. He must have been about thirteen or fourteen, but he was small and looked younger. Eager eyes blazed like pits of black fire in his narrow, intense face.

"I am always restless, Tien. You know that. I never sleep more than a few hours."

"It is not because of the soldiers? Because my father has said they are sending real men now? Not the worthless, less-than-dogmeat turtle dung like before? But naturally, no! You are not afraid of the soldiers!"

He spat contemptuously on the ground, an emphatic adult statement. Denis tried not to smile. Hero worship was such an agonizing thing. He remembered only too well how it had felt when he was young himself. He was finding it even harder to be grown up and on the other side.

"Of course I am afraid, Tien. A man is a fool if he is never afraid. But he cannot let fear rule his life."

The boy sat beside him, a companionable gesture, his elbows on his knees, his small chin resting on his hands.

"God will protect you," he said.

"God will do with me as he sees fit." He stole a glance at the boy out of the corner of his eye. So confident, so sure that the God he had been taught to trust would provide, and suddenly Denis was alarmed. What was going to happen to all that faith when his hero was caught? And executed. "We are each of us in the hand of God, Tien. We live to fill his greater design, though we cannot know what that is. Whatever his design for me, I will accept it. Humbly, I hope. And with grace."

"You are ready to die?" The boy's eyes were wide

with curiosity, and Denis knew he was looking for answers. But he didn't have any.

"Ready, perhaps—but willing? Ah, well, it is not *my* will that counts, is it? At any rate, we have a reprieve—a few days in which we do not need to worry," he added, sensing the boy's French did not quite extend to that word. "The royal funeral begins tomorrow. Who is it who died again? The emperor's aunt? The festivities and processions will go on for some time. Even the soldiers will be too occupied to think of anything else."

"The Son of Heaven hated the elderly aunt, you know," Tien said, a boyish love of gossip lightening his too-serious face for a moment. "She was a fearful old dragon. Everybody hated her. But he has to do the proper thing and pay great homage to her memory."

"And we will be able to perform our rituals openly for days. Baptisms, the celebrations of marriages, visitation of the sick. Everything will be easier until . . ."

Until the hated aunt is laid in her ostentatious marble mausoleum, he wanted to say, with all the flags and lanterns and tablets calculated to disguise a lack of affection—and then it will start again. With crack soldiers this time. The emperor's own. And this time there would be no escaping. How strange to think that the last few days of his life were a gift from an old lady nobody loved.

"Until what?" the boy asked.

"Until . . . next time. Now, come. Help me get ready for the morning mass."

The boy jumped up eagerly. He liked being asked to assist the priest. It made him feel important. He already knew the procedure by heart. First they would set up the table, in the center of the room. Some priests celebrated mass against the back wall, but Père Denis liked to face the people, the way it had been done in the old days, he said. Next came the altar stone, from the pack he always carried with him, and then the frayed white cloths with rows and rows of dainty stitches that had been made by his own devoted sister.

That was a touch Tien especially liked. He could almost see the sister, tall and frail like her brother, with red-gold hair and eyelashes that hardly showed, bending over her work, squinting when the day was done and she had to go on by candlelight. Perhaps one day he would be a priest too, he thought, and have a cloth like that, fashioned by his sister's callused fingers.

But then he remembered that his sisters were vain, silly creatures, with no thoughts for anyone else, least of all the younger of their two brothers, and he decided that, after all, he might as well do what his father wanted and study for his examinations.

"Tien?"

The priest was standing between the two central columns, smiling down, as if he knew he had caught him daydreaming. The boy straightened his shoulders and marched up the steps.

"I'm coming, Père Denis," he called out. "Can I lay out the altar cloths?"

It took seven days to reach the far side of Hué, a journey that by Jared's calculations ought to have lasted a day, a day and a half at most. But he was sensing more and more that Dominie's instinct had been right. The imperial city was a place to be avoided. Especially if the rumors they had been hearing were true and the emperor's own troops were really joining in the search for the foreign priest.

They moved mostly at night, though the moon was waning, and as travel became more difficult, they took the chance of starting out an hour or two before sunset and continuing sometime after dawn. There was, strangely, little sense of real imminent danger. In fact, they were meeting with far more curiosity than hostility, and they began to realize that the problem lay not with the people of the land, but with their ruler. And even then it was less a general distrust of foreigners than an intense and brutal hatred of the priests who were perceived as trying to impose their religion on the land.

The terrain was generally gentle, and walking was pleasant. Jared carried both of the packs, which he had combined into one, and Dominie was content to trudge beside him, her boots, tied together by the strings, dangling over her shoulder, her bare toes kicking up little flurries of dust.

Sometimes they would stop for an hour and just sit and talk. Dominie would tell him about her life in Paris, which seemed so long ago now it was almost like a

dream—about the carriage accident that had taken her
parents' lives, how alone she had felt then, how important Denis had been—and Jared began slowly to understand the attachment that bound her to her brother.

Other times they would not talk at all, but make love
in some secluded spot with the gentle splashing of a
stream nearby and only the stars above to watch and wink
down at them.

"Where did you get all that wicked passion?" Jared
said after an especially exhausting half-hour that left him
so drained he could barely drag himself up to pull on his
clothes. Dominie was still only half-dressed, clad in one
of the soft gold tunics, bare legs sticking out beneath as
she sat on the ground, her knees tucked up to her chin.
"I used to dream about a woman like you . . . who would
quiver every time I touched her. And mean it."

"And I used to dream about a man like you . . . and
it terrified me." She curled her arms around her legs,
like a little girl, innocent and somehow vulnerable. "He
was very mysterious, my dream man, and very . . . compelling. I had all these strange new sensations waking up
inside my body, and I didn't know what they were. I only
knew they frightened me. I was so sure I was going to
turn out like my mother."

"Your mother, sweet?" He was watching her curiously. "She must have been a very earthy creature to
produce a wench like you."

Dominie smiled, but her eyes were solemn. "I used to
hear the servants talking sometimes, when they thought
I wasn't around. She loved too much, they said. I remember that phrase most distinctly. She loved 'too
much.' I didn't know what they meant. I still don't, and
I'm not sure I want to. But I sensed somehow that she
had given too much of herself, and I was afraid I was
going to grow up and fall in love with a man who would
lead me astray too."

"And now?"

"Now I'm sure of it," she teased. Then her face turned
serious again. "He was not a good man, my father. I
was afraid of him. I don't remember very much about
him, but I remember that I was afraid. I used to think he
killed my mother."

"Good Lord," Jared said, shocked. "What would give you an idea like that?"

"My mother was ill for a long time. After I was born. I think he got tired of her. I would hear the servants gossiping about that too. I think there was another woman. For the longest time I had an awful feeling that somehow he had arranged the accident that killed my mother. But as he died himself, I suppose he couldn't have."

Jared did not try to speak; there were no words he could think of to respond to something like that. He simply knelt beside her, holding her for a moment, glad he could be there to comfort her. There was little open affection in his family, God knew—they had had their share of quarrels and estrangements—but he could not even imagine thinking anything so heinous about one of them.

"Come on, love," he said after a while. "It's getting late. Let's go find your brother."

Middays were spent in villages along the way. Quiet, peaceful places with men and women toiling in the rice paddies, trousers rolled up around their thighs, and little boys in funny conical hats swishing flocks of ducks ahead of them with long sticks down the dusty paths. Rangy black hogs rooted among flimsy palm-thatched huts, and dun-colored water buffalo, looking mean and lazy, wallowed in the muddy streams.

If it was a Christian village, they would be invited to take shelter in the largest home, belonging, as they soon learned, to the most important personage, who seemed to gain considerable prestige from their presence. It was almost a festive occasion. People would wander in and out all day, cutting into their precious time for sleep, and Jared and Dominie found themselves poked and prodded and peered at, with at least a hundred questions every hour.

But if there was only an isolated Christian family, the atmosphere changed subtly. The welcome would still be warm, the hospitality generous, but there was always someone standing at the door, looking out with a pinched and anxious face.

Fear. Dominie could almost feel it in the air. Nothing explicit, nothing spoken—just little hints that it was quiet now because the emperor's men were occupied with some sort of occasion in the capital. But it was always there, just beneath the surface, and she knew she would be a fool if she let herself become too complacent.

Only once did their wanderings take them inside one of the enclosures that surrounded the many affluent estates on the outskirts of the capital. Dominie was fascinated by the elaborate fortifications that had been set up to protect the privileged mandarin and his family. Stout stakes were interspersed in clumps of growing bamboo, so thick as to be virtually impenetrable, with an opening in front the only visible entrance. All around the periphery, short pointed bamboos had been driven into the ground, with sharp edges turned nastily outward.

"Better than an American fort," Jared said in an undertone as they approached. "That'll keep out the cavalry."

"More likely a herd of thundering elephants," Dominie retorted with a grin. Jared wasn't sure whether she was serious or joking, but he decided not to press the point. He had long since learned not to dispute her superior knowledge when it came to this strange and exotic land.

Inside, the house was spacious and almost cool. A broad terrace, raised about six feet off the ground to provide protection from flooding in the rainy season, formed the floor, and magnificent polished-wood pillars with huge stone pedestals held the soaring tiled roof. The vast central hall, completely open along the front and perhaps seventy or eighty feet long, was sparsely but elegantly equipped. Handsomely painted screens rested discreetly in the background on a warm day, but could be moved at will if the wind grew brittle, and varicolored silk lanterns dangled on long graceful cords from the rafters. Straw mats and brightly hued cushions provided pleasant seating without detracting from the simplicity of the setting.

"I do believe you could live here if you had to," Jared said, laughing as he watched her snuggle contentedly into the cushions and survey the abundant repast their hostess had tactfully left them alone to enjoy.

"Here? Of course. But this is heavenly!" Dominie looked over the array of dishes on several low tables that had been spread around them, selected something that looked extremely bizarre, and popped it into her mouth with apparent relish. "Not like those dreadful little hovels with pigs wallowing right outside the door and everyone crammed into one tiny room. It was a great adventure, I'm really glad I had the chance to see it—but I don't think that's how I'd like to spend the rest of my life! Here, on the other hand, I could be deliriously happy. I do adore luxury. Don't you?"

No, Jared thought, oddly, he didn't. Like the hovels, the house was a great, but brief, adventure for him. He could appreciate the openness and airy grace, the clean simple lines, and he could have lingered happily for a day, a week, even a month or two. But the thought of stuffy Boston parlors would always call him back. Redflocked wallpaper and too many furnishings crammed into too little space, the fog so thick that sometimes hardly any light came through the window, a cold wind blowing in from the harbor. Not everyone's idea of heaven, but it was home to him. He could not even imagine growing old anyplace else.

"Does it snow in Paris?" he asked suddenly.

"Sometimes." She glanced up from the little saucers she was examining and gave him a quizzical look. "But not much. Paris is not a winter city . . . it's a spring city. With sunshine and the smell of flowers. But whatever made you think of something like that?"

"I was just wondering," he said, and broke off, surprised at where his thoughts were taking him.

Wondering if a woman who adored luxury and houses in the tropics and flowery sunlit cities could be happy in cold, rainy, foggy Boston. But that was absurd! He had made no commitments to her—they had made no commitments to each other. He didn't even know how he was going to feel about her when they got to the end of their journey. He was getting way ahead of himself.

"I was wondering what you looked like with snow in your hair," he said.

"In ninety-degree heat? When I am trying so hard not to perspire indelicately? What a funny man you are."

"But not without my good points, I hope," he said, wincing as she bit down on another extremely strange-looking morsel, which made a loud crunching noise. "Do you have any idea what that was you just ate?"

"Of course not," she said sensibly. "But whatever it was, it was delicious. Here, there's some more. Have a taste." She laughed as she held out a small saucer and he recoiled with instinctive revulsion. "Don't be afraid. It won't bite. I promise, it's dead."

Jared shook his head in something between amazement and dismay. He had grown used to the Vietnamese custom of serving meals in little dishes, each at least slightly different from the others, to be eaten with the fingers or rolled in a crisp lettuce leaf. But he would never get used to the way Dominie insisted on trying everything, even though she didn't have the vaguest notion of what was in it.

"You might be a little discriminating," he persisted.

"Why?" She was licking her fingers, clearly enjoying the residue that lingered on them. "You forget. I am French. We eat everything. We're not like the Americans, who say, 'Ooooh . . . frog's legs! How *disgusting!*' Or, 'I can't eat that little bunny rabbit.' " Her mouth puckered with exaggerated distaste, as if she had just sucked on a lemon and found it unusually sour. "Anyhow, it's definitely dead, and very well cooked . . . so I don't see how it can hurt you."

Jared gave up with a laugh.

"I don't know if you're going to be a liberating influence or the death of me," he said as he took a bit of whatever it was in very cautious fingers, raised it to his mouth, and chewed tentatively, trying very hard not to let his expression mirror hers of a moment before. It was a nut of some kind. A thin shell—definitely not any sort of insect—and he had to admit it *was* delicious.

He was, Jared realized, whether he liked it or not, expanding his horizons. He was also, as the days passed and they spent more and more time together, finding that he not only loved this woman but also liked and respected her.

It was not just her enthusiasm for everything that so charmed and captivated him. It was her incredible gentleness with people. She was especially good with the women, not just the mandarin's wife and pretty giggling daughters, but peasants in the poorest villages they visited as well. She went out of her way to notice the extra little effort they made, and to compliment them for it.

They seemed to respond, understanding, as near as Jared could tell without knowing what was actually being said, that her interest and sympathy were genuine. It particularly pleased them to learn that she was the sister of a priest—*the* priest—and her presence in their homes brought a special sense of pride.

Even more, it sometimes seemed, than if the priest himself had been there. Perhaps because they had seen priests before, but never the sister of a priest who had come all these thousands of miles to find him.

"They keep telling me how much he means to them," Dominie said. It was their last afternoon, or so they hoped, and they had taken to the road early, not knowing how long they had yet to walk. "Everyone says the same thing. Over and over. How important he is. How glad they are to have him after so many years without a priest."

Jared heard the pain in her voice, and he set his pack down for a moment to take her hand. "I thought there were native priests."

"There are, but a native does not . . . inspire. He doesn't have that same mystical power to enflame the people. We French are very arrogant, you know. We always think we're closer to God than anyone else. Perhaps we have managed to convince them. . . . Oh, Jared, I'm afraid. I'm so afraid."

He did not ask what she was afraid of. He did not have to. He knew. She was afraid that her brother had sensed, as she had, the intense craving of these people for a priest from afar. She was afraid he understood the terrible void his absence would create.

She was afraid he was going to refuse to leave.

It was no more than she had been told before, than he had told her himself, than Alex had tried to tell her. No more, probably, than her own instincts had warned her, but she had not believed it then.

It's all right, Dominie, he longed to say to her. We will reach him soon, and everything will be all right. But more and more he found himself thinking that it was not going to be all right, and his heart ached for the pain that would be hers.

It was twilight. A fiery sun was just sinking beneath the horizon, sending great red streaks like dying screams across the sky. Denis Arielle shivered as he sat in the only comfortable chair in the large open hall and stared out at the beauty and the violence.

Not the blood of the martyrs this time, he thought. *His* blood. The funeral rites would end tomorrow. The elderly aunt would be laid to rest at last. And they would be coming for him.

He hated himself for the thump of fear that made his heart seem to leap out of his chest. Lord, make me worthy, he prayed. Lord, give me strength. He wanted to be brave. He wanted to be the priest the boy Tien longed for. He wanted it more than he had ever wanted anything in his life.

But like so much else, it seemed that that grace, too, had eluded him.

"I am a terrible coward," he said, turning his head slightly toward the shadows at the side of the hall where Duong was seated cross-legged on a mat on the floor. "It's a humiliating fate, but it seems to be mine. I suppose I will have to be reconciled to it."

"You are thinking of the soldiers," the younger priest said. "Of what is going to happen after tomorrow."

"Aren't you?"

Duong nodded slowly. It was different for him. With the right kind of clothing, he could blend into the landscape. And they were not looking specifically for him.

"There might still be time to get away," he said. "Perhaps a fishing boat up the coast. There are many of our people in the little villages along the shore. It would be perilous—"

"And futile," Denis cut it. "It's no good, Duong. They've circulated my description all over the place. Everyone will be looking for a tall, skinny, very pale man with reddish hair and about sixty words of extremely bad Vietnamese. I would only be risking the lives of good fishermen, and to no avail. It's too late. I couldn't leave now if I wanted to."

Duong sat for a moment in silence in the shadows and studied him thoughtfully. The French priest, he knew, did not like to speak about his feelings, but there were things he needed to ask. He was not sure why this was so, but it was.

"You could have left before," he said softly, "and yet you did not. Why? You have no deep attachment to this land. You do not even like it here. You are disgusted by the dirt and the heat and the smells. They are unbearable to you. Sometimes I think you do not even like us. And yet you have stayed. Why?"

Denis tried to smile, but he was too tired. His head fell back against the chair, his eyes half-closed.

"I wish I knew, my friend . . . I wish I knew. Sometimes I think there's no reason for it. No reason at all. This country will be no different after I'm gone than it was before I came. But here I am, and here it seems I will stay. . . . And it isn't that I don't like you. I do, very much. You and all your family. They have been generous with me, and patient—and kind enough to struggle along in French because I am so inept at their language. I like many people individually. I just don't seem to be filled with the great love for humanity that I expected to overwhelm me."

"What you are filled with," Duong reminded him gently, "is fatigue. And no wonder. There must have been five, six thousand people wanting to be baptized these last few days. Seven or eight thousand perhaps. And not a one of them would allow me to perform the rite. 'I want the French priest,' they all insisted. Your arm must be aching."

Denis finally managed the smile he was attempting. "They don't teach you that in the seminary. They teach you the words *Ego te baptizo in nomine Patris, et Filii, et Spiritus Sancti*—but they don't tell you how your arm is going to feel at the end of a very long day."

He was rising slowly, desperate for sleep suddenly, but not wanting to be alone in the darkness, afraid of the doubts that would come. Duong was rising too, standing for a brief moment beside him.

"They care, Denis," he said, not even noticing that he had used his colleague's given name for the first time. "You matter to them. You *have* made a difference here."

He turned his head abruptly, and Denis realized suddenly that the boy Tien had come into the hall. He was standing some distance away, staring at them, his eyes solemn and huge.

Denis started to go toward him. The boy had been his

shadow for the last several days, following him everywhere, making of him an idol, as he had himself once done with his mother's Jesuit confessor. He wanted to say something to him. Wanted to plan something special for the next day, the last day. Something that would strengthen his faith, prepare him for the horrors that lay ahead.

But before he could reach him, he became aware of something—someone—in the shadows of the veranda just outside. He saw the man first. A big man, roughly dressed, in clothes a seaman might wear. An American perhaps. There was something brash and arrogant about him that Denis had always associated with the new world.

Then he saw the woman. A tall, slender, very beautiful woman in a gold silk tunic over loose white pants, red hair floating to her shoulders.

"My God," he said, crossing himself against the unintentional blasphemy. "Dominie?"

# 19

THE GREAT HALL was filled with people. Dominie had no idea where they all came from; she had not seen so much as a flash of movement, but suddenly they were there, swirling colorfully in the light of dozens of gently swaying green and gold and crimson lanterns. She had barely a second to form the sketchiest impressions: several little girls with laughing black eyes, bright with curiosity, a solemn-faced boy who appeared to be a little older, a distinguished-looking man with thinning gray hair, an elderly woman, a number of servants hovering in the background . . .

Then she was hugging Denis and patting his cheeks, telling him he looked much too thin, but she loved him all the same—she had missed him dreadfully, she could not bear the thought of all that long time they had been apart! And he was hugging her back, looking dazed, as if somehow he couldn't quite take it in, and barely saying a thing.

But then, Dominie thought with a little laugh, she was hardly letting him get a word in edgewise! She was so excited to see him again, so relieved now that she knew he was all right, she couldn't think of anything else. For the first time since she had begun her perilous quest, she dared to believe—really *believe*— she was going to succeed. Denis was safe, and she would keep him safe. For always.

It took some time for everything to settle down and for Dominie to coax her brother back into the cushioned chair with its wide, comfortable arms. For some reason, he kept trying to give it to her, though he had to know she was much happier flopping down on the floor at his feet.

"I always sat on the floor," she reminded him, teasing. "And you always hated it. You told me it was very unladylike—I would be sorry if I didn't learn better manners—but you could never get me to stop. What makes you think you can change me now?''

''My dear little sister,'' Denis said, gentle hints of laughter bringing his tired eyes to life, ''sitting on the floor is the least of the things on my mind at the moment. We are on the coast of Vietnam, six thousand miles from Paris—''

''Seven and a half thousand. Nearer eight through the Gulf of Aden—''

''Eight, then. Must you always show off your superior knowledge, you sassy girl? Eight thousand miles from Paris, in a place where one is hardly likely to encounter little bunches of travelers sallying out on sightseeing excursions. Or any other Europeans, for that matter. Do you have any idea how astonished I was to look out through that portal and see you? I'm still astonished.''

Dominie smiled, but sadly. Now that the shock was wearing off, his weariness showed through, and it hurt her to see how gaunt he was. He had always been slender, but the long black cassock hung on him now, and what little flesh was left on his face sank deep between the bones like some grotesque death's-head.

''You're much too pale,'' she scolded, alarmed and trying to hide it. ''You should be brown as a chestnut from this sun. And look at all the weight you've lost! I don't think anyone has been taking care of you. Haven't you been feeding him properly?'' She surprised everybody by glancing over her shoulder and tossing off the comment in perfectly understandable Vietnamese. ''Look how scrawny he is. Nothing but skin and bones. Like an old rooster scratching in the yard. We are going to have to fatten him up.''

The last words were addressed to the elderly woman, who beamed with pleasure, clearly flattered that the priest's sister not only spoke their language but also had singled her out.

''He is a bad boy,'' she agreed. ''I try to coax. I make my best dishes. But still he will not eat.''

''Then we will have to persuade him—together. You see, Denis,'' she went on, looking at her brother, ''even this kind lady agrees with me. You have to eat better.''

"You are showing me up again, Dominie," he protested. "That is not a proper sisterly thing to do."

"I am worried about you." Her voice softened, taking on serious overtones just for an instant. "And that *is* a proper sisterly reaction. I know what a fussy eater you are. You probably haven't had a good meal since you got here and found out that the food has some flavor to it. Eggs! Do you have any eggs?"

She was turning to the woman again, exchanging knowing glances that resulted in a flurry of words and gestures as several female servants scurried out of the room.

"He'll eat an omelet if someone knows how to make it. A plain omelet. That was all I could ever coax you to take at home," she said, switching back and forth between the two languages with apparent ease. "Fresh eggs whipped to a froth and sautéed in nice sweet butter. With just the most delicate hint of *fines herbes*. I would prepare it for you myself . . . if I knew how to cook."

Denis rewarded her with a faint smile. "There are some gaps in your education, it seems. But please, don't bother. Dominie, tell them not to bother," he pleaded, knowing full well it wouldn't make any difference. An omelet was going to arrive anyway, and it was going to have at least an onion with it, or some chopped-up ground nuts and a bit of *nuoc mam* to make it taste better. "I'm much too tired to eat. We've had so many baptisms these last days . . . thousands, literally." He allowed himself another smile, ironic this time. "Perhaps ten percent have never been baptized before. And of those, one or two might actually have come out of zeal rather than curiosity. French priests *are* a source of curiosity you know."

Dominie laid a hand lightly on his arm. "It's been hard, hasn't it?"

"Not too hard," he replied, surprised to realize that it was the truth. She looked so young, and incredibly fresh and lovely—it was as if she came from another world. A world in which he no longer had any share. He had forgotten how spirited she was, how earnestly she threw herself into everything.

And how wildly impetuous she could be.

"I have missed you very much, Dominie," he said quietly, "and I am truly glad to see you. But I cannot be glad you are here. It is much too dangerous. Especially now. We've made too many converts. The emperor is growing anxious.''

"I know. We've been hearing rumors all along. He's supposed to be sending his own personal troops to scour the countryside. But we had no trouble, and it took a week to get here."

"That's because of the royal aunt," Denis said, and went on to explain, though he had a feeling she already knew about the elaborate funeral ritual. And probably had the story much better than he! He had also forgotten the incredible way she had of always finding out whatever there was to know.

"But all that is over now," he concluded. "She will be going to her tomb tomorrow, and then the troops will be free. They will not only scour the countryside, they will burn down every hut in every village if they have to. And they will not be kind to any foreigners they find."

"But they will be looking for you," Dominie reminded him quietly. "And they will only look as long as they think they can find you. What is the point of expending all that energy and burning down all those poor people's huts if you are gone?"

"Yes . . . but I won't be gone, you see. I will be right here, one step ahead of them. And it will not help me in the least if I have to worry about taking care of my little sister at the same time. . . . But where are my manners? I have not yet introduced you to the kind friends who have taken me into their home many times. And who are waiting very patiently now for me to recall myself and stop behaving like a boorish foreigner."

Jared stood at the side of the great hall, just out of the scarlet and green and gold of the lanternlight, and watched as Dominie was introduced first to the elderly couple—the senior members of the Christian branch of the family, he assumed—then the dark-robed man who had been conversing with her brother when they arrived. The native priest. Le Van Duong.

They were speaking French for the most part, with occasional asides in Vietnamese, and while he could understand most of what was being said, his lack of skill in the spoken language left him feeling clumsy and uncharacteristically ill-at-ease.

His awkwardness increased acutely when Dominie insisted on thrusting him forward and presenting him to her brother. He could feel Denis' eyes on him, probing—dammit, the man had to be wondering what he was *really* doing with his sister!—as he explained in halting fits and starts, with considerable backtracking, that he was an American sea captain on whose ship Mademoiselle d'Arielle had taken passage, and when he couldn't talk her out of her wildly impractical scheme, he had felt obligated to see to her protection.

The textbook phrases were adequate, if somewhat stilted, but his accent was atrocious, and he could see Denis' lips twitching as he struggled not to smile. Behind him, Dominie was giggling openly, the little witch, with no regard whatsoever for his punctured male ego!

At least it broke the ice. Jared gave up, laughing himself as he expressed regret for his linguistic inadequacy.

"No, no, don't apologize," Denis assured him. His gaze was still speculative, but he had relaxed enough to join in the laughter. "As a matter of fact, I am quite delighted."

"That my French is so awful?"

"I'm delighted that someone else has trouble with languages. It makes me feel less inept—though my Vietnamese, I must admit, is a thousandfold worse. And if it's any consolation to you, Captain Barron, I don't speak a word of English."

" 'How do you do?' " Dominie cut in, her beautiful green eyes dancing with little lights of love and mischief. "You know 'how do you do?' And 'please' and 'thank you.' And 'which is the way to the railway station?' "

"And that's the extent of it," he said with a faint half-smile. "A missionary who doesn't speak languages. I have heard there might be one or two somewhere else in the world, but that's probably only a rumor."

Jared was surprised to find himself liking the man. The last thing he had expected was to feel an affinity for this fanatic priest who had come halfway around the world to make himself into a martyr. But he was so wonderfully tender with Dominie. He obviously loved her as much as she loved him, teasingly, affectionately, with a quiet pride that somehow made him more human. And despite the obvious hardships he had suffered, he still had a gentle ability to poke fun at himself.

There was also, Jared realized, quiet strength beneath that fragile exterior, and he knew suddenly, as Dominie still did not, that she was not going to take her brother home with her. She was still so full of hope. Still riding on that first high crest of euphoria. She had plopped down on the floor again, in front of her brother, half-sitting, half-kneeling, hands gesturing elaborately, scolding, coaxing, cajoling.

He wanted to go to her. He wanted to take her in his arms and shield her from what was going to happen. But there was nothing he could do. He could only stand and watch.

"But, Denis," she was protesting, her voice rising slightly in exasperation, "that's silly! What on earth are you going to do if you stay here? Even if you somehow manage to escape the soldiers, you'll only spend all your time running. What use will you be to anyone then?"

"It's not silly, Dominie," he replied patiently. "It's my life. This is what I came here to do. Nor is there really any point discussing the matter, since I couldn't leave now if I wanted to. If we'd had this discussion last month, or even last week—perhaps. But they know who I am now. They know exactly what they're looking for. My description is everywhere. If I tried to come with you, I'd only get us all caught."

Well, then, let them catch us!" Her chin was up, that way she always had when she was so sure of herself, and her eyes glittered with triumph. "We'll just have to bribe them. I've heard the officials here are very corrupt. If you have a big enough bribe, you can get anything you want."

Denis smiled wanly. "Bribe them with what? The vast wealth of the church in Vietnam? We have nothing here, Dominie. Nothing. I have to borrow a robe when my cassock is being washed. Every bit of the food I put into my mouth depends on the charity of strangers."

"Not the wealth of the church—the wealth of the d'Arielle family!" She was laughing as she pulled out the black velvet pouch, utterly confident now that the diamonds were spilling into her hand. "It's very fortunate, is it not, that our grandfather was too mean to spend a *sou* more than he had to in that dreadful heathen England?''

Jared sensed a sudden change in the atmosphere. Everyone was inching closer, eager to get a better look, their gasps of admiration telling him that the stones were worth every bit as much in this part of the world. The excitement was contagious. Just for a moment he caught himself wondering if perhaps, after all, Dominie had not been right and there was cause for hope.

''It might work, Père Denis.'' The younger priest, the slim man with the curiously noncommittal face, had come over and was squatting beside Dominie, studying the stones appraisingly. ''There must be a fortune here.''

The older man nodded as he looked over his shoulder. ''It might work,'' he echoed thoughtfully. Or that's what it sounded like to Jared, though the man's accent was so thick it was hard to tell.

''And it might not,'' Denis said quietly. ''They might just take the stones and turn me over to the executioner anyway.''

''It would be worth a try,'' the young priest, Duong, persisted. ''If you wanted to leave—if you were to swear that you would never under any circumstances come back into the country—you might find a mandarin greedy enough to take a chance—''

''No!''

No one had noticed the small boy. He had been standing in the shadows, quietly watching, not calling attention to himself. But now he was there, in front of them, quivering with anger, his black eyes snapping so fiercely they seemed to be lit by fire from within.

''Only a coward would turn and run!'' he said scornfully. ''Pére Denis is not a coward!. He is not afraid. It is God's will that he stays here. He has said this many times to me. Tell them, Père Denis. You are not afraid. It is God's will.''

It was two statements actually. One he could respond to with some truth.

''It is God's will,'' he said quietly.

''There. You see!'' The boy was whirling to face them. Passion filled his small body, swelling it with pride and indignation. His hero had been challenged, and he had not failed the test! "I told you, Père Denis is no coward! He is a man of God. Men of God do not run away!"

And a little child shall lead them, Jared thought, filled suddenly with wonder and a great, weary sorrow. It was all so clear really—or it would be to the man who had already endured such sacrifice in the service of God. He knew a second before it happened that a thin, frail hand was going to reach out and touch the boy on the shoulder.

And he knew with a terrible, cold inevitability what the accompanying words would be.

"You are right, Tien. You and I understand each other, perhaps better than I thought. I am not sure that men of God are not cowards. But they do not run away."

"You are going to stay, then?"

"I am going to stay."

Dominie was shivering when Jared found her later. She was sitting at the top of the broad flight of steps, staring sightlessly into the courtyard, almost pitch dark now except for a single string of silk lanterns that flickered feebly along one of the bamboo walls. The night was warm, barely a breath of air stirred, but he could feel her shivering as he slipped an arm around her shoulders and drew her close.

"You knew this was going to happen, love," he said as kindly as he could. "You didn't want to admit it, but I think all along you knew. This is the life your brother has chosen. This is where he *wants* to be."

"But I still need him, Jared." She turned her face toward him, the faint glow of the colored lanterns picking up the moisture on her cheeks and lashes. "He was so far away—it might have been years before I saw him again—but I always knew he was there. If I were ever really, *really* frightened, or alone, he would have come to me. I can't bear to lose him now. There has to be something I can do tot make him change his mind."

Jared shook his head gently. She was so soft and trusting in his arms. He would have given everything he possessed at that moment if he could have kept her from hurting so terribly. But the choice had never been his to make.

"Do you remember what you told me once, Dominie? When you ran away from the ship and I came storming after you? You said you hadn't confided in me because I would have tried to stop you. I wouldn't even have listened to you or considered your feelings. I would just have been so blasted sure I knew what was best. And locked you up, if I had to, to keep you there."

"You would have, too," she said with a halfhearted attempt at a smile.

"Perhaps," he admitted. "Probably. If you hadn't shown me how determined you were—if I hadn't been afraid you'd sneak away again and try and do it on your own—yes, I probably would have. But I would have been wrong. It was your life, not mine, much as I love and want to protect you. You had a right to decide what was important to you, and what risks you were willing to take. And if I loved you, I had to respect you enough to support your decision."

"And if I love my brother, I have to respect him too."

She was very thoughtful, very quiet, and Jared felt a sudden great hunger to take all the pain on his own shoulders. Just as she wanted to take her brother's deadly peril, he thought ironically, and somehow wish it away.

"It's his life. His decision. And, yes . . . if you love him, you have to walk away and leave him here."

"I'm not sure I can." The tears were flowing down her cheeks again, freely, silently, but at least she was no longer trembling. "I know you're right. I know it in my head—I even know it in my heart . . . but I'm not sure I can find the courage to say good-bye forever."

"I think, love," he said gently, "you will have to."

Jared held her in his arms the rest of the night. Not making love, just holding, comforting. Reminding her with his closeness and body warmth that she was not alone in the world.

It was shortly before dawn when they finally gave up their mostly futile efforts at sleep. The house was already stirring, everybody acutely aware that the priest's sister and her American captain must be off with the first clear light. A steaming tub was waiting for Dominie, and Jared left her alone to bathe and dress, and wandered out into the courtyard.

The air was clear and almost cool. The first hints of gray had begun to seep into the sky, dulling the lanterns which still cast pale, otherworldly orbs of faintly colored light along one of the high bamboo walls. Jared thought at first that the yard was empty. Then he spotted a motionless figure, deep in the shadows beneath the gnarled black branch of an ancient banyan that protruded over the wall.

Dominie's brother.

He started to turn, not wanting to intrude on the privacy of the other man's thoughts. But Denis had already seen him. His stance changed, expectant somehow, and Jared sensed he was waiting for him to come over.

"She's just getting dressed," he volunteered, pushing his French to the limit as he approached. "Sometimes she says she's ready to leave you, if that's what you really want. And sometimes she says she doesn't think she can find the courage. This is very hard for her."

"I know. Dominie has always felt things deeply."

"She needs you," Jared said quietly. Now that he was closer, he could see that there was a bench beneath the overhanging branch. A long stone slab with graceful curving legs, like the limbs and claws of some mythical beast. "She keeps saying that over and over. It's not just a word to her. You are her rock, the only security she's ever known. The one person who has always been there for her. Lord knows, she didn't have an easy childhood."

"Nor did I, Captain." There was a dry edge to the other man's voice that made Jared glance over at him. "Nor did I. The bond between us goes both ways. She has been my rock as much as I have been hers. Taking care of her was the only thing that gave my life meaning for many years."

"Then surely you understand. It's desperately hard for her to give you up. You're the only family she has—the only family I think she's ever really had." Lord, it was a struggle, he thought, this difference of languages. He hoped he was expressing himself well, though the other man seemed to understand. "Her mother was sick for so long—Dominie barely knew her. And she told me once she was afraid of her father. She actually thought he might have murdered her mother."

Denis stiffened slightly, but not from shock. As if the

words had caught him off-guard, but not truly surprised him. Jared was acutely conscious of the way he was looking at him. Strangely speculative, with a piercing intensity that showed even in the shadows.

"Do you love her?" he said at last.

It was no more than Jared had expected, but somehow he found the question unsettling. It occurred to him that all he had to say was: "I'm very fond of her, of course. She's a great little gal, and we've had some fun together, but . . . well, you know how it is with a man"—and all of Dominie's problems would be solved. The brother whose whole life had once been "taking care of her" could never leave her in the clutches of a sex-starved scoundrel like that. What tears and pleading had failed to accomplish, a few callow words would manage in thirty seconds.

But to do that meant lying to a man he liked and had come to respect. It also meant betraying him in the cheapest possible way, and even Dominie, he sensed, would not thank him for that.

"Why are you staying here?" he said abruptly. "What do you hope to accomplish? All this 'God's-will-be-done' nonsense is fine for your sister and that little boy with the intense eyes. But I don't believe in pat phrases. I believe in actions, and I'll be damned if I can figure out what you think you're doing."

"Sometimes, Captain, I wonder the same thing myself . . . though I wouldn't have put it quite that way." The light was brighter. Jared could almost make out his face. He could have sworn there was a look of self-deprecating amusement on it. "Other times . . . Did you notice that man last night, in a robe like mine, only much less shabby? He is what they call a 'native priest.' He had almost forgotten his calling when I came. He rarely wore his cassock anymore, and it had been so long since he'd said mass, he had forgotten some of the forms. Now there is a quiet zeal about him. He doesn't like to admit it, but it's there. He has changed."

"And that's enough?"

"That and the one or two converts at the recent baptisms. If I can bring one soul to God—just *one*—if I can inspire one native priest to minister to his people, then, yes. It is enough."

"But you already have your converts," Jared argued. "There will be no more if you're dead. And you've already inspired one derelict priest. There will be no more of those either. What earthly purpose does it serve to stay?"

"What purpose?" Denis glanced up at the entrance to the hall, as if half-expecting something he did not find. "You saw the boy in there. The one with the 'intense eyes.' You heard what he said. I am an inspiration because I am a foreigner. Because I am ready to sacrifice everything—even my life—for my love of God and my compassion for these people who are not even my countrymen. If I turn my backside and run, I won't be an inspiration anymore. I'll be a hypocrite and a buffoon, and the native priest will be derelict again. And the convert will go back to his ancestor tablets."

"It's as simple as that?"

"As simple as that . . . and the fact that I wasn't exaggerating before. It *is* too late for me to leave. Even a fortune in diamonds can't save me now. They'd just end up in some mandarin's pocket, and he'd turned me over to the soldiers anyway. . . . But you didn't answer my question before. Do you love my sister?"

Jared met his gaze. It was rare when a man was tall enough to look him straight in the eye, and the experience was somehow unnerving.

"Yes," he said after a moment. "I love her very much. But we have made no promises to each other. There are no commitments on my part. I am not sure there ever will be."

Denis Arielle's pallid face lit up with an almost boyish smile in the first pink-and-golden rays of the rising sun.

"I am," he said. "I have seen the way you look at her, and she at you. The commitments are there, whether you realize it or not. And the question was unfair. I was testing, when I already knew the answer."

"Testing? Me?"

"I wanted to see if you would play on my love for Dominie to try to get me to back down. She has a very persuasive way of coaxing others to do her bidding. You are a strong man, Captain Barron—that is good. My sister needs a man she cannot wheedle into satisfying her every whim. But now I think it's time you prepared to leave. There's a boat somewhere, I assume.''

Jared was surprised at the change in his voice. The sudden crispness that took over now that details were being discussed.

He nodded brusquely. "About a day's walk south of Hué. A little longer maybe. We circled round to get here."

"You will have to go back through the city, I'm afraid. It's a risk, but not a very great one. 'Big-nosed devils' wander through occasionally—sailors and poets and other adventurers—and while the officials don't particularly like it, they look the other way. Only the priests are truly hated. Fortunately, there's an extremely thorough description of me—and expect for the height, we have nothing in common. You should be safe through the festivities today. After that, I'd feel better if you were gone."

"We will be." Jared said grimly. He had no mind himself to be here when the guards began "scouring" the countryside. And he certainly didn't want Dominie anywhere around. "Dawn tomorrow at the latest, we'll be out of here."

"Take care of my sister," Denis said quietly. "I am trusting all that is important to me on this earth into your hands. And incidentally . . ." He was starting to leave, but turned back. "She was right about our father. When they found him, his boot was caught in the carriage. He had apparently run it off the cliff and thought he could jump free at the last minute. He was so vain about his coaches. There were so many extra ornaments always on the doors . . . I thought I could protect her, but someone must have talked. Or perhaps she was just sensitive enough to guess the truth. . . . She has much to forget, Jared Barron. See that she does. The past is too weighty a burden for a beautiful young woman to carry into the future. It should be left behind."

He paused and ran his eyes around the courtyard. Plants in big ornamental pots were just beginning to show in the hazy glow, and a curving bridge in the background led to pavilions still an invisible distance away.

"You said that she needs me, but you were wrong.

She needed me once, but it is you she needs now. And you will not fail her.''

Again he started to leave, and again stopped, his eyes seeking the top of the stairs one more time, and lingering there. Turning, Jared saw Dominie in the glorious red silk gown. Her hair, catching the color of the dress and the fire of the dawn sun, floated like spun silk to her shoulders.

So she had found the courage after all.

His heart swelled with pride as he watched her drift slowly down the steps. A tremendous, possessive, utterly irrational pride came over him, as if somehow this had been his doing and not all her own.

It was amazing, he thought, how different the dress looked with that frothy bit of white tucked modestly into the neck. Elegant and lovely, and just exactly what she wanted for her final farewell to her brother. Sensing their need to be alone, he slipped unnoticed into the shadows.

Denis met her at the base of the steps.

"A crimson dress, Dominie? Didn't anyone ever tell you redheads shouldn't wear red?''

"I'm not a redhead. My hair is auburn. And anyhow, what do I care what other people think? . . . Oh, Denis, I do love you so much.''

"And I love you, darling sister, and that will never change. Wherever you are, whatever happens, you know my love will always be with you. And I will carry your love with me. All my life and beyond.''

"Denis . . .''

Her voice broke. He reached out and took her hand.

"All grown-up—and so beautiful. How did you grow so quickly, little Dominie? You were a child just yesterday, I swear. Chasing butterflies in your rose garden. Even then, you loved the roses. You didn't care if there was another flower around. You wouldn't have any of them in *your* garden. Just the pretty roses.''

"I have not been 'little Dominie' for a very long time,'' she reminded him softly.

"No, I suppose not. I just didn't notice. It's very hard for big brothers to notice things like that. I like your sea captain, Dominie. Very much. I was wrong about that, it seems.''

"Wrong? About . . . *that?*"

"About where your foolish heart would send you. I arranged the marriage with Honoré Ravaud not because I thought he'd be the perfect mate, but because I was afraid, left to your own devices, you'd make a disastrous choice. Some wastrel with a pretty face and a glib line of patter. . . . What did you do with poor Honoré, by the way? He loved you desperately, you know."

"Oh . . . well . . ." Dominie was beginning to feel a little guilty about the way she had jilted him, especially if Denis was right and he really cared. "I suppose I should at least have sent a letter of explanation . . . but I didn't love him, Denis. I couldn't have loved him . . . Ever. And what's wrong with Jared's face, anyhow?"

"Nothing." He smiled. "Or his line of patter, I suspect. But there's character behind it, and honesty. And strength. I see nothing of the wastrel I feared when I look at him. . . . I always knew you were smarter than me, Dominie. I didn't expect you to be wiser as well. At least not so soon."

He was trying to make her laugh. Dominie saw that, and she loved him for it. But it only made her want to cry all the more.

"I will never be wiser than you," she said softly. "And I will never—ever—stop missing you. Oh, Denis, it's so hard to say good-bye."

"I know. But we must." He was still holding her hand, a firm, comforting grip. "It's getting lighter every second. I want you to do one last thing for me. Will you promise?"

"Without knowing what it is?"

"Promise," he insisted.

"All right . . ." The tremor was in her voice again, but she was trying to control it. "I promise."

"I want you to smile—that devastatingly pretty smile that always twisted me around your little finger." He slipped his hand out of hers, easing slowly away. "I don't want you to say a word. I just want you to smile one more time and turn around and walk away. Without looking back."

"Denis, I . . ."

"Shhh. You promised. Where is that smile? There, that's better. Now, turn around—see, there's your handsome captain waiting for you. And don't look back."

She faltered, lips trying but trembling, and he thought for an instant she was going to fail him. But he had underestimated her. She managed the smile he asked for, warm and wonderfully full of love, and turned toward the gate, where her American was standing. The man stepped wordlessly forward to join her, a tall, quiet figure, half-merging with the shadows.

He would be her rock now, Denis thought—her security. The one person who would always be there for her.

God, how he loved her. There was no blasphemy in the thought, only a prayer of thanksgiving that she had been a part of his life, and that he had had one last chance to say farewell. He had made so many mistakes with her. He had doted, he had overprotected, he had tried too desperately to shield her from the horrors of the past— but somehow it had come out all right in the end. She was the best of him, the one thing he had done truly and perfectly in his life.

He had thought his love for her was his great weakness. His one irredeemable sin. But he knew now how foolish that was. She was his one comfort, and he could not believe God in his infinite compassion would not forgive him for that.

She cheated when she reached the wall. He had known she would, but she smiled as she turned back, a sudden dazzling, heart-wrenching smile, and then she was walking through the gate, the man beside her. Not touching, just together. The strength of his body seemed to flow into her, and the purity of her heart into him.

It was not going to be so bad after all. The things that were yet to come. He was still afraid of dying. He could almost hear the bloodthirsty chanting of the crowd in his ears, smell the dust and the heat, feel the silken cord tightening around his neck. But it would last only a few minutes, and he could bear a few minutes' pain and fear as long as he knew that she was safe.

And she would be with her American captain.

A sudden peace and the only contentment he had

known for months flooded over him. The warmth of the morning sun felt good, like the warmth of the sun in Paris as it peeked over the garden wall, and he could almost see her again, little Dominie playing in her roses. Little Dominie all grown up and safe with the man she loved.

It was enough.

## 20

DOMINIE WAS QUIET for the first half-hour of the trip into town, and Jared, sensing her need to retreat into herself for a time, did not intrude on her pain. They were riding in an elaborate palanquin, a kind of enclosed sedan chair hoisted on the shoulders of eight sturdy bearers, which, rather to their surprise, had been lent to them by the patriarch of the Le family.

"This will be safer for you," Duong had told them as he slipped through the gates for a brief moment to see them off. "The curtains offer some shelter from inquisitive eyes, and, of course, the vehicle is well-known. . . . My grandfather is a kind man, mademoiselle. It grieved him that he did not receive you last night. He did not wish to be rude. You must understand—he is afraid. Everyone here is afraid."

"But he's not afraid to have us seen in his palanquin?"

Duong's bland features had broken out in an amiable grin. "He is also a very shrewd old man. He's sending the bearers to offer their services to his brother, who lives nearer the festivities. If they hire out for money to a pair of curiosity-seekers along the way . . . well, how is he to know about such a thing?"

Shrewd indeed. Dominie had tried to smile, but there had been a sudden catch in her heart. "What about you, Duong?" she had asked. "They know who you are. We were told that several times when we tried to make inquiries. They know where you live . . . who your family is . . ."

"There are rumors," he had admitted with an easy shrug. "But no proof. And of course, I will not be here. I will be off in the countryside—dressed in baggy pants and an ill-fitting shirt, which, I regret to say, will not have seen soap and water for some time—leading an ox to market. But I am only a native. They do not fear the native priests. They should . . . but they do not. They will not be looking for me.''

No, Dominie thought sadly, they would not be looking for Le Van Duong, beyond perhaps a cursory search. But they would be looking for a man with hair the color of the sun at dawn and a lanky body that couldn't have been hidden in peasant's rags even if he weren't too proud to take off his cassock. She was aware of tears in her eyes as she turned away from the shimmering light that filtered through the curtained windows.

''Oh, Jared,'' she whispered softly. ''I did do the right thing, didn't I?''

His hand was on hers, as she had known it would be, and he was clasping it tightly. ''You did the *only* thing, love. If he's going to have any chance at all, he has to move fast and free. And alone.''

''You think he does have a chance, then?''

Her eyes were searching his face, and Jared hesitated, but only for a second. He longed to lie to her, to offer at least a small shred of comfort. But lies would damage the trust they had built up between them.

''No . . . but I am not God, Dominie. I cannot *know* what will happen. All I know is that we have to put as much distance as we can between ourselves and this blasted city by nightfall. That was what your brother wanted. The only thing you can do for him now is honor his wishes and take care of yourself.''

Dominie nodded. He was right, of course, but it was desperately hard, leaving someone she loved behind. What was it Alex had said? *Your brother has chosen a path and set his feet on it . . . you cannot save him from that*. A bitter lesson, but she had to learn to let go of yesterday and move forward.

Denis had his path . . . and she had hers. And she would have to follow it.

She forced her eyes back to the sheer silk curtains, and inching them apart, peered out onto the road. Duong had told them that they could keep the palanquin only until they reached the Perfumed River, which divided the imperial capital of Hué in two. Perhaps not even that far, he had warned, if the crowds grew too thick.

And judging from the number of people who were already flocking toward the city, though they were still barely on the outskirts, Dominie had the feeling they would be getting out soon.

In spite of herself, she could not help being curious and fascinated by the assortment of people who had turned out to see the royal aunt off on her final journey. Many were peasants, dressed in the manner of those they had already encountered on farms and in the small villages they had passed. The same dark loose-fitting trousers dangled anywhere from knee to ankle, topped by the same bulky shirts with their small round collars, and sleeves that never seemed to come quite to the wrist.

But there was a sprinkling of the upper classes too, and here the Oriental love of color burst out in a riot of gaudy finery that made her think of great flocks of tropical birds flitting from branch to branch in lush green rain forests. Gia Long had shortened the traditional Chinese robes when he reunified the country nearly a half-century before, and trousers now peeked from beneath the gracefully flowing upper garments of people of rank. Ladies especially defied the heat and sported layer after layer in varying colors, the undermost coming nearly to the ground, the ones on top shorter and shorter, making a dizzying rainbow of color as they walked.

The sense of festivity seemed to touch everyone. A young man with a slender, drooping mustache swaggered self-importantly down the center of the road. A junior mandarin probably, Dominie thought—no stinting on the fabric of *his* sleeves, which extended well over his hands, but the nails that stuck out beneath had been trimmed to a scant three or four inches, humiliating evidence that he was still forced to toil for his keep. Whole families had spread out vividly tinted cloths—patches of saffron and azure and green dotted across the dust-brown earth—and were picnicking on cold steamed buns and great mouth-watering arrays of mangoes and melons, bananas and berries and jackfruit. Children seemed to be everywhere, running around and shrieking with delight, miniatures of their parents: a boy dressed exactly like a mandarin, a pretty sloe-eyed girl in multicolor layers made even more striking by a gold crescent necklace, another in a floating gossamer tunic of pale lime and silver.

Dominie noticed an old woman, dressed simply but

very elegantly in black, walking along the side of the road with only a single *mu-tsai* slave girl to hold the long-handled silk parasol over her head. Her feet must have been bound once in the Chinese fashion, perhaps before the time of Gia Long, when she was barely more than a girl herself, for they were very small and she hobbled with extreme slowness. The ceremony would be nearly over by the time she got there—no doubt the last funeral she would attend before her own—but she plodded on patiently, determined to share in this one small part of the life that went on behind the high red walls of the forbidden section of the city.

The crowds were becoming denser with each passing minute, and the bearers seemed to be stopping almost constantly, shouting out gruffly to clear the way ahead, and not always succeeding. Dominie could see a number of other palanquins now, not broad and curtained like theirs, which was quite unusual, but completely open and incapable of accommodating more than one person. In fact, they looked like nothing so much as hammocks slung down from a long central pole and topped with a kind of awning or pinjaree of fine matting and decoratively painted paper. Occasionally a servant would trot alongside with a parasol for added shade, or perhaps a huge palm fan.

"What the devil is that?" a voice said in her ear. Dominie was surprised to find Jared with his head next to hers, peering out almost as curiously as she. "A poor man's version of the contraption we're traveling in?"

"Actually, it's quite upper-class. Even the emperor himself would ride in one like that. Unless there's some need for secrecy, it's much more practical. That hammock arrangement is made of silk net, so it's cooler and naturally absorbs the bumps and jostling of the road better. It can also be managed by only two bearers, who go as far as fifteen miles a day without changing. . . . I have all these little gems of information because the old retired fathers of the *missions étrangères* loved to tell stories when they came to visit."

"Well, I will have to take their word for it . . . and yours. The way I always do when we stop for information and you tell me what someone has said. For all I know, you're just trying to impress me—pretending you understand all that babble and twitter that comes out of their mouths. I've been listening for a week now, and I haven't been able to pick out a single word.''

"It's a different language," Dominie conceded generously. "There are only a limited number of basic sounds, so the way you say each one is extremely important. Whether the tone is high-rising or high-level, falling—or rising-and-falling! There are definitely pitfalls. If you're falling when you're supposed to be high-rising, or high-rising when you're supposed to be rising-and-falling, you can think you're saying, 'How do you do, I'm so pleased to meet you,' and end up with something more like: 'Come into my bedroom, my dear, so I can do strange, depraved things to you all night long.' ''

Jared was surprised to find himself chuckling. He hadn't expected laughter to be a part of their day. "Are the two expressions really so close?"

"I wouldn't know," she admitted with a puckish grin. "There were certain things the good fathers didn't teach me how to say. But embarrassment is always just a tone away in a language where inflection is so important."

"Like Mandarin Chinese?" Jared said. "Or Cantonese?" He was already familiar enough with the Orient to know the answer, but he sensed it was important for her to talk.

"Exactly." She saw what he was doing, but she loved him for it, and in fact the distraction was welcome. "There are many similarities in the languages. Don't forget, Vietnam was under Chinese domination for more than a thousand years. Much of their culture remains to this day, including, unfortunately, enough vocabulary so there are two words for nearly everything."

"*Two* words? In a language with limited sounds? That must be confusing."

"More than confusing," Dominie said. "Take 'red' for instance. The Chinese word they use here is *hong*—England is *Nuoc hong mao*, or the Red-haired Country—but the local word is *do*. And sometimes the meanings are different. Say *hoang*, the Chinese word for 'yellow,' and you're referring to the imperial color. But talk about a man with jaundice, and he is *vang*, which is the native word."

"I begin to see the difficulties."

" 'Blue' is even worse. *Thanh* is Chinese, as in *thanh-thien*—blue sky—but the Vietnamese have a nasty habit of using it for 'green' as well. Then there is *bich*, also 'blue,' which, when combined with the word *luc*, means 'sky blue'—as opposed to 'blue sky.' Or *bich luc* can be something luminously blue, like maybe a sapphire. But you can also use *ngoc xanh* for a sapphire—though that can mean 'jade' as well.''

"You've convinced me!'' Jared gave her hand a squeeze, glad to see that she could think of something else, if only for a few minutes. The pain of her brother's loss was easing, and she had not yet begun to worry about the perils that still lay ahead. "I don't think I'll try to pick up any Vietnamese my last afternoon here. I have enough trouble with French.''

"Actually, you did very well—after you got over your initial self-consciousness. You're like all Americans. You're so insulated, you don't see any reason to bother with other languages. You think all the world should speak English.''

"Oh . . . and the French aren't like that. They don't think the whole world should speak French.''

"That's different,'' she retorted with a twinkle. "French is a *civilized* language.''

They were laughing easily as they approached the interior of the city, still holding hands, so engrossed in each other they had not even noticed that the palanquin was stopping more and more frequently and sounds from the distance were intruding on the laughter and good-natured grumbling of the crowd around them.

Only as they felt the vehicle being lowered with a rather startling thud to the ground did either of them realize that they had reached the end of this stage of their journey and were going to have to rely on their own resources from now on.

Dominie parted the curtains and peered out, a little surprised at herself for having forgotten to keep track of their progress. She was even more surprised when she saw how close they had gotten—no more than half a mile surely, perhaps only a quarter—to the imposing red walls of the imperial city.

It was so much bigger than she had imagined. Dominie could not take her eyes off it as Jared helped her from

the palanquin and she felt the ground beneath her feet
again. The elderly *pères* had always referred to it as the
"Citadel," and she could understand why. It seemed to
rise out of the earth itself, sheer and massive, like a great
fortress, as imposing as the medieval walled cities of
Europe, and every bit as arrogant and impregnable.

She racked her brains trying to remember what they
had told her about it. A new city when they had been
young themselves and still in favor with the court—Gia
Long had razed everything on the spot sometime around
the turn of the century to erect his new capital—though
is was so sturdy, it looked as if it had already survived
the ages. How exciting to have been privy to those first
grand plans, Dominie thought with a twinge of envy.
Never a modest ruler, this emperor of reunified Vietnam
had patterned his stronghold after the great Forbidden
City in Peking, deliberately throwing down a gauntlet to
the dazzling splendor of the northern dynasties that had
occupied them for centuries.

Inside the high red walls, she knew, were three separate sections. The outer part, or *Kinh-thanh,* was the capital city, where many of the court officials were housed,
together with a myriad of lesser dignitaries. Next came
the *Hoang-thanh,* or imperial city, with the palaces and
gardens and temples of the emperor's court. And finally,
the *Tu-cam-thanh*—the Great Purple Forbidden City—the
residence of the Son of Heaven himself, into which no
strangers, not even the gentle fathers, had been permitted
to enter.

It must be so wonderfully grand. Dominie stared with
longing at the sheer, impenetrable walls. It seemed bitterly unfair, being so close and having to leave before
she could get even a peek at all those magnificent things
she had heard about since she was a little girl. She would
have loved to walk along the great esplanade of the capital city and pass through the three-doored Bull Gate, the
*Ngo-Mon,* with its yellow-tiled roof, into the *Hoang-
thanh.* She would have loved to see the way the Three
Bridges crossed the Great Water, and admire the Temple
of the Generations and the Nine Dynastic Urns, which
were said to range in size from barely a few feet to over
two thousand tons. She would have loved to step into the
*Thai-hoa,* the only room in which the emperor held pub-

lic audiences, and stare in awe at the eighty carved wood columns, splendidly lacquered in red and gold, and the great gilded throne raised on a platform eye level from the floor.

"Dominie?"

Jared's voice called her back with a start. He was standing at her elbow, looking patient and serious, and she realized unsettlingly that the bearers were already gone. Obviously they hadn't wanted to be seen a moment longer than necessary with the turtle-dung foreigners.

"It's all so foolish," she said softly. "We only want to be friends."

Jared, who had seen all too clearly what similar offers of friendship had gotten the Chinese, was tactful enough to hold his tongue. "They don't want to be friends, Dominie," he reminded her. "And right now there's not much we can do about it."

"Except get out as fast as we can?" she replied with a wavering smile.

Jared had already taken her arm and was steering her toward the center of the road, where the crowd was somewhat thinner. "I think the river is over there. We'll work our way as close as we can, but I'm afraid we're not going to be able to get through."

Dominie was inclined to agree, though she didn't like to think about it. The sounds in the distance were growing more insistent. She could have sworn she picked out the long, sweet note of a horn of some sort—surely a sign that the ceremony had begun. Over the heads of the people in front of her, she caught sight of something vivid and colorful. Plumes, she thought, gaudy pink and azure and a bilious shade of yellow-green, bobbing on top of some gray, moving mass.

Elephants! There were elephants ahead. They would be at the vanguard of the procession, clearing onlookers out of the broad avenue along the riverbank. It *had* started, then! And it might go on for hours.

And as long as it continued, no one could get to the other side.

Dominie was intensely conscious now of the milling of the crowd around her. Heads turned to watch as they shoved their way through; eyes took them in, dark and speculative. This was not the gentle countryside anymore, where people were friendly and they could be passed from family to sheltering family. And they were not under cover of darkness. This was the city, and it was broad daylight. And everyone they passed had to be wondering who they were and what they were doing there.

"Perhaps we ought to go around," she said, throwing a dubious glance at the long, massive walls. "It might be faster."

"I doubt it. It looks to be several miles, and God knows what's on the other side. Besides, we're supposed to be adventurers, love. We came to see this curious spectacle, remember? Adventurers don't slink round the back, looking for an easy way out, when all the action is in front."

"I suppose not," she admitted. "But all the same, I don't like it, Jared. I'm frightened."

"So am I, but you know what they say. The best place to hide is in plain sight." He saw her startled expression and added, with a slightly grimmer laugh than he had intended, "If we cower around, trying to slither through the shadows, people are going to start asking themselves what we have to hide. But if we're bold and make a joke out of everything—and look like we're having the most marvelous time—they're just think we're a couple of boorish fools and forget after a while that we're even here."

Dominie sensed he was right, but somehow it didn't make her feel any better. They might not have been any safer in the shadows—they wouldn't have been *as* safe— but it would have seemed safer, and she found herself looking back on long nights of traipsing through the hills and rice fields almost with nostalgia. Every time someone turned to peer at them, she imagined what he had to be thinking: Is this man the priest they are searching for? Is he another priest? Do they have women priests, these strange, unnatural Christians? And she wondered if there was a reward.

No, not *if,* she thought with a shiver. How much?

"I'm glad you don't have red-gold hair," she hissed in an undertone, though there was no one nearby who looked remotely capable of understanding another language.

"So am I," he hissed back. "And I'm glad you're wearing such an . . . interesting dress. Though I think it could use some adjustments."

He was pulling her out of the crowd and off the road, beneath the gnarled branches of a squat, thick-trunked tree that twisted almost to the ground in places. Before Dominie even realized what he was doing, he had grabbed the pretty lace finchu, plucked it loose, and was stuffing it in his pocket.

"There, that's better. Just a little more abandon, I think . . ." He plunged one hand into her neckline, boldly pushing her breasts up until they popped almost completely out of the dress. "Sorry, gorgeous, but you have to look the part. Now, a little more tousle to the hair—yes, that's it."

"Jared . . ." Dominie had recovered enough to gasp a halfhearted protest. "What on earth are you doing?"

"Making you into what I once thought you were—and with great apologies this time. But if we want to get out of this with our skins, we're going to have to allay some very ugly suspicions. Rumors will be flying around about a ship off the coast—and they'll probably be none too hostile since I had the men barter with tools and nails and all those little chiming clocks I'd brought for high officials. What could be more natural than that the bawdy captain, or maybe a mate, should be out for a bit of a lark? And if he'd picked up a little sweetie in Singapore— well, wouldn't he bring her along?"

Dominie saw the merits of the plan instantly. Not only did it give them a reason for being there, but everyone who knew anything at all about priests knew there were certain things they didn't do with women.

"Well, I suppose I could pull it off." She smiled shakily. "After all . . . I did fool you once."

"That's my girl. Now, come on—back on the road. Let's find that blasted procession before we've missed all the fun!"

Dominie laughed a little brittlely, as if he'd just said something wildly funny, and tried not to think about he way her breasts were hanging out. She had to admit it seemed to be working. There was a difference almost immediately in the way people were looking at them. With curiosity still—and a certain degree of disapproval—but none of that awful, eerie speculation she had seen before. Here was something familiar, something in the realm of their own experience. A loud, rather lewd man, and the woman he had bought, who clearly was not averse to pleasing him.

Just for good measure, every time he saw someone looking their way with an expression he didn't like, Jared put on an extra show. His hands were all over her, and he stopped—right in the middle of the road—and planted a great moist kiss on her mouth.

"There," he said, doing impudent and quite obvious things to her ear with his tongue, "let them think I'm a priest now!"

"You really *are* an animal."

"A satyr," he agreed. "And you love it—but I'd feel a lot better if I could get my hands on a bottle of cheap rum. It's hard to play the part of a drunken lout with not a hint of liquor on my breath."

"I can help you with that," Dominie said unexpectedly. "Not rum, but that woman over there is selling jugs of rotgut rice wine, which ought to give you just as fragrant an odor. If you live long enough to breathe again!" Lifting her skirt with little regard for modesty, she unknotted the handkerchief she had tied like a garter below her knee. "Duong's mother gave me a few coins before we left. Not enough to arouse suspicion—just so we'd have it if we needed something. . . . People always seem to be giving me money in handkerchiefs."

She straightened up with an impish look. "Brown jug or gray? That seems to be the only choice. I expect what's inside is the same."

"Brown will do fine," he replied, shaking his head in mock bemusement. "You never cease to amaze me."

Dominie was a little amazed herself as she went over to the woman and held out one of the coins in a hand that was so steady it might have belonged to someone else. She was not feeling quite so confident a few seconds later when her fluent Vietnamese met with an angry, suspicious stare.

Just for an instant she thought the woman was going to refuse her. But a second coin on top of the first thawed some of her reluctance, and a much-chastened Dominie brought the bottle—gray, as it turned out—back to Jared.

"I think I might forget most of my Vietnamese for the rest of this trek," she said soberly.

"That's a good idea," he agreed. "It is, as you pointed out, a difficult language. Foreigners wouldn't be expected to speak it."

"But surely, if I'm a working girl in Singapore, I might have picked up a little."

"Not that much," he reminded her, and she had to agree.

The elephants had already passed by the time they reached the wide avenue that led along the river toward the undulating countryside where the royal tombs were located. Dominie, still nervous, was very grateful for the elaborate charade Jared had created, which allowed her little time to think of anything else. Her hands were slippery on the bottle he handed her, but she managed a pretty good imitation of pleasure as she raised it to her lips and smacked a swig. Not enough to burn her stomach or dull her senses—just enough to give her mouth the same ripe aroma as his. Jared, she noticed, had managed to spill a considerable part of it on his clothes.

"You smell awful," she said with what she hoped was a drunken grin.

"So do you," he replied, and slipped an arm around her waist to press her forward through the crowd. "Isn't it wonderful?"

The noise, which had been subtle from a distance, barely an undertone to the laughter and conversation of the crowds, was almost deafening here. Drums and rattles joined the long, drawn-out wails of the horn Dominie had heard before, and an occasional loud protest from a nervous elephant trumpeted above the keening of the mourners.

Almost in spite of herself, Dominie felt her eyes being drawn toward the center of the broad thoroughfare. The procession was exclusively women now, the stark white of their robes contrasting dramatically with the almost violently brilliant colors of the banners and lanterns. Their arms were overflowing with profusions of gloriously scented flowers that spilled out occasionally along the dusty avenue. Behind came a group of musicians, then dancers drawing murmurs of admiration from the crowd, and then at last the Chariot of the Silken Soul.

Dominie stared in frank fascination, trying to recall what she had learned of the predominantly Chinese funerary rituals of this ancient land. The chariot, she knew, would be carrying the Tablet of the Soul, a tapering slab of wood five times wider than it was high, containing the name of the deceased and the date of her death. Over it would be draped the white silken sash that had been knotted around the breast of the royal corpse at the beginning of the hundred days of mourning when the tablet had been placed on a table beside her. It was then that the body had been washed in the Water of the Five Herbs, and embalmed, and the nine grains of rice and nine pearls placed in her mouth.

Which would have been nine cowrie shells, Dominie thought wryly, if the royal aunt had been a commoner. Considerably less buying power! Rank had its privileges, it seemed, even in the afterlife. The chariot was followed by the Eight Lanterns, each hoisted aloft on a long pole, and then, walking backward, a solitary man in white.

Dominie could feel Jared behind her, craning to see, almost as curious as she, despite his own anxiety.

"That's the chief mourner," she told him, trying to speak as quietly as she could, but having almost to yell sometimes to be heard over the din. "That man in white, walking backward. That means the bier is coming. If the corpse had been someone more important—the emperor's mother perhaps, or one of his senior wives—he would have been the chief mourner, and you would have had the rare opportunity to catch a glimpse of the Son of Heaven himself. Or as much as you could, lying flat on your belly, not daring to raise your head—which probably would have been the hem of his robe! But since no one is falling prostrate, I think it's safe to assume he sent a substitute."

"White is the color of mourning here too, then—as in China?" Jared half-shouted in her ear.

"Not white, actually, but the absence of color. The purest expression of grief. And because he's the chief mourner, his is the deepest mourning, meaning that his garments are made of the coarsest cloth."

While they were waiting for the arrival of the catafalque, which seemed to be approaching with excruciating slowness, Dominie went on to describe what she could remember of the Ceremony of the Great Dressing. The ritual, as it had been explained to her by one of the slightly scandalized fathers, would have begun when the coffin was brought in on a kind of heathen sleigh, known as the Dragon Sledge, and the body removed and laid in the sarcophagus.

With it went the six objects of jade which would fortify the deceased in her new existence. Jade was also used to plug all the orifices of the body: oval pieces laid on the eyes, a cicada set in the mouth, octagonal wedges in the nostrils, with larger pieces reserved for the navel and other, more private openings. No way the restless spirit was going to get out and haunt those who had cared little enough for her in life!

Dominie was just going on to explain the lengthy period of mourning and the elaborate procedures the imperial astrologers went through to pick auspicious dates for each of the rituals, when the bier finally appeared.

She understood at once why it had taken so long. She had expected a large sarcophagus, but this was almost incredibly massive. Dominie had never been good at judging size, but she couldn't imagine it weighed less than two or three tons, and she counted at least fifty bearers on their side alone, which meant more than a hundred in all. They were moving at an agonizingly slow pace, feet dragging on the ground, slender, straining figures, all alike in their black tunics and trousers and trim white turbans. Each was biting down on a piece of bamboo to keep from crying out with the exertion.

It took the better part of an hour for the catafalque to pass, and Jared, having long since overcome his initial awe at the magnitude of the procession, was beginning to have serious qualms. He was tall enough to see well into the distance, which did nothing to reassure him. Endless columns of soldiers in varicolored uniforms seemed to stretch on forever, alternating with black-and-white clumps of what looked to be pallbearers—replacements for the men who dropped in their tracks, he supposed—and groups of musicians and dancers. And in between, bamboo poles with brightly colored lanterns dangling from crosspieces, and masses of banners stretched taut on rigid frames.

At that rate, he thought glumly, it would be dark before

the road was cleared. It was already well into the afternoon. The sun had long since passed its zenith and was dipping alarmingly into the west.

A contingent of troops paused almost directly in front of where they were standing, and Jared, trying not to appear too obvious, studied them apprehensively. Imperial Guards, he thought. Their uniforms were smartly tailored, yellow and green and blue, the fabric finer than the common soldiers', the sleeves longer, and they carried themselves with the military bearing of crack troops.

They had just started to move again when one of them turned, his eyes flickering briefly over Dominie, dismissing her, then settling on Jared. Dark, shrewd, intensely searching eyes that sent shudders of apprehension down his spine.

He's asking himself who I am, Jared realized with a terrible cold sense of helplessness. There was no way to wriggle out from under that excruciating gaze. He knows I'm not the priest they're looking for, but he's asking himself if other priests might have entered the country. He knows priests wear long black robes—but would they take them off to make themselves less conspicuous? He knows that priests aren't supposed to have anything to do with women—but what humiliations might a priest be willing to suffer in order to save his life?

Those were questions he was going to want to have answered. Jared could feel the man memorizing his face, measuring the length of his nose, the width of his mouth, picking the Chinese and native words to describe the blue-gray color of his eyes, and he knew that by morning there was going to be an extremely thorough description of him.

And having some knowledge of Oriental subtleties of torture, he knew the questioning would not be gentle if he were caught.

"I think we've overstayed our welcome, love," he said, trying out make his expression vacuous as he bent down and nibbled her ear again. "The best of the party seems to be over anyway. Yonder lies the river, methinks—shall we?"

Dominie tried to respond with a little erotic giggle, but he could tell from the tepidity of her reaction that she, too, had noticed the man.

"We can't cross the road, Jared. Haven't you seen . . . not a soul has so much as set foot on it. I think it must be sacrilegious or something."

"But we are only ignorant foreign turtle-dung pigs, my little lotus flower. What do we know? Look, there's an old man over there selling sugarcane. Have we enough to buy some? Good. I don't see any on this side. What better excuse?"

"Dogmeat," Dominie replied distractedly. "Turtle-dung *dogmeat* foreigners. Or less-than-dogmeat if you really want to get it right." She was scanning the road with her eyes, both sides, checking out the crowd. "It might work. . . . Let's just wait till that guard goes by. I don't like the looks of him. He's too sharp."

"No—now! While he's still here. I don't want him to think he's got us scared. And I sure as hell don't want him peeking over his shoulder somewhere down the road and seeing us sneaking across."

Dominie nodded. She was desperately frightened now—her heart was beating so fast, it felt as if it were pounding against the wall of her chest—and she had all she could do to concentrate on looking carefree and just a little drunk. It was a chance, but not a really bad one, and they did have to get across.

She held back one brief moment, waiting until there was a slight gap in the formation of guards. Then, grabbing Jared by the hand, she pulled him behind her, giggling and pointing at the vendor all the way, and babbling on about how she just *adored* sugarcane.

The reaction was instantaneous. People came at them from all sides, shouting and shaking their fists, and the guards broke pace to glower fiercely, though mercifully they made no threatening moves.

Dominie and Jared feigned the greatest surprise. With overelaborate gestures—and sheepish, none-too-sober grins—they managed to convey that they had just wanted to get a stalk of sugarcane. They had no idea they weren't supposed to cross the path of the procession. They were very sorry, but as they were already here . . . well, what could they do? It wouldn't happen again.

And it wouldn't, Jared thought grimly. Nothing on this earth could get him back to the other side of that road!

This time Dominie was wise enough to negotiate by

pointing at the sugarcane and extending the smallest coin she possessed on the open palm of her hand. Even at that, they were badly cheated, paying at least twenty times what they should. But as she could hardly admit she knew the going price—and she certainly couldn't argue in Vietnamese—she meekly accepted the sticky length of cane and popped the end of it with a great show of relish into her mouth.

They turned back to the road with only desultory interest now. An occasional lantern or banner seemed to catch their eye, or a particularly agile group of dancers, but they were obviously growing bored now that the most dramatic part of the procession was over. The guards had moved ahead, but Jared, running his eye nonchalantly up the street, saw that the one man had stopped and was looking back one last time with the same dark, strangely piercing gaze.

It occurred to him it was just as well they were going to be down the coast by daybreak, and preferably off the mainland. If they tried to stay longer, he at least would be a dead man. And God knew what would happen to Dominie.

He drew her closer, nuzzling her again, making no effort to hide his lecherous intentions. He had begun to ease her away, coaxing her toward the riverbank, where the crowds were noticeably sparser, and Dominie, playing along, kept throwing little glances at the road, pretending she wanted to stay just a bit longer, but letting herself be persuaded as his advances grew more and more blatantly amorous.

She was teasing him now, licking the tip of the cane pointedly with her tongue, pressing it to his lips, and Jared, for all his tension, felt his body beginning to respond. Soon they were sucking alternately on it and each other, and there could be no doubt to anyone watching that they were extremely anxious to culminate what they had clearly been aiming at all afternoon.

There were several idle sampans when they reached the bank. The sarcophagus might have passed, but the excitement of the day continued, and most of the revelers would not be leaving until well after dark. Several boatmen converged on them, greed for a fare overwhelming their innate suspicion of the strange-looking foreigners.

Dominie, spotting one who looked familiar, hustled Jared over to the small, dirty vessel he was indicating.

It was one of the bearers who had brought them into the city. He was dressed differently now, in rags that were a far cry from the handsome livery of the Le family, and there was a servile, groveling air about him, but she recognized him instantly. He wheedled and whined and demanded an inordinate number of coins, but she found them tucked into a corner of the rickety seat when she climbed on board and lifted her skirt out of the filthy water sloshing around the bottom.

As she slipped them into Jared's pocket and snuggled closer, she realized the lengths Denis' friends had gone to to make sure his sister got safely out of the country. And the terrible risks they were willing to take.

They reached the other side without incident, and by dusk were far enough along the coast that they dared to stop and enjoy some of the steamed buns and cold bean and eggplant pastes that had been slipped into their bag. No one was in sight now; the road had been almost eerily empty for the last two or three miles, but they decided to leave it anyway, following instead the slightly more rugged hills and embankments of the shore. The light was getting scant—a faint quarter-moon had just begun to rise—but the way was clear, and they knew they would be able to walk all night.

"We're going to make it, love." Jared grinned as he shifted the small pack to his shoulder and pulled himself to his feet—a great wide grin, spreading across a face so dusty it almost looked brown. "I didn't think we were going to for a while . . . but we are."

"I do believe, love," Dominie replied, mimicking the lightness of his tone, "you may be right."

They burst out laughing, feeling suddenly, incredibly, like little children who had just pulled off a prank. All the tension, all the fear of that last agonizing afternoon seemed to tumble away from them, and the world was right-side-up again.

They were safe. They had had to leave everything behind. All they had were the clothes on their backs, a few scant toilet articles in their pack, and another bun and a mango apiece—they hadn't dared run the risk of being caught with anything more—but they were going to make it.

They were safe, and they were together—and that was all that mattered.

## 21

THE ISLAND TO WHICH Jared brought his lady was as pretty a place as she had ever seen, a tiny gem of lush verdant slopes and shallow white-sand beaches set in the placid luminosity of an almost glassy emerald sea. Now that the churning monsoons were over, the sky seemed to stretch endless and azure-clear across translucent expanses of water, and sultry breezes were heavy with the perfume of flowers that dangled in vinelike clusters from the trees and spilled down hillsides almost onto the beaches.

There was a slight breeze the morning they arrived, and Jared was able to rig the fore-and-aft sails on the small cutter so they skimmed with ease into the half-hidden cove etched by time and the waves in the craggy coastline. The sand ran back only a few feet, but it was soft and almost powder fine, and they had no difficulty dragging the boat up and into a convenient niche in the rocks. A few minutes later it was covered with branches, so well concealed even a sharp-eyed mariner with a glass would not notice if a ship passed too near, and their private paradise belonged exclusively to them.

They spent the rest of the morning and most of the afternoon exploring the island. It was extremely small—no more than a mile, perhaps a mile and a half at the widest point—but the variety was dazzling. In some places the tropical vegetation grew so thick it would have required a machete just to get through, and insects buzzed in the deep green shadows. In other places natural stone paths led to tiers of pools, sparkling in the sunlight, with little streams cascading from one to the next, frothing like miniature waterfalls as they cast a glittering spray into the breeze.

Birds of every imaginable color flitted through the

trees, blue and green and the most vivid yellow Dominie
had ever seen in her life. A flock of ravens might rise
from a grove of mangoes as they approached, a sudden,
unexpected cloud of black soaring into the sky, or a pure
white false egret take wing to float feather-light and incredibly graceful across the horizon.

"I think this is what the Garden of Eden must have
been like," Dominie said. They had returned to the cove
and were sprawling on the sand while dusk drew the
mainland off into the distance. "I used to love to hear
stories about it when I was a little girl. I imagined sultry
breezes, just like this . . . perfume in the air . . . flowers
all around. Only in my Eden the flowers were all roses.
They were always my favorite . . . I don't suppose there'd
be roses on a tropical island."

Jared was smiling as he stretched out on the still-warm
sand beside her. It was dark enough now so they could
not be seen from the mainland, even if someone were
watching. Purple hills receded into the distance, layer
after ever-paler layer, like the Chinese paintings he had
admired so much when he first came to the Orient, and
the faintest dusting of feathery palms was just visible on
the shore.

"No," he agreed. "Roses seem unlikely, but there are
profusions of everything else. Those pretty white things
seem to grow wild all over the place. They have the
sweetest fragrance, just like your hair . . . which ought
to smell dusty, but it doesn't. . . . Then there are those
pink and red things . . . and bits of mauve floating on
the water . . ."

"That's because I washed it when we bathed in the
pond, which you well know, since you insisted on helping . . . and were no help at all! You kept distracting
me . . ." He was distracting her again, teasing her hair
with his nostrils, pretending to breathe in the scent, but
in fact it was just an excuse to trail the most tantalizing
little kisses down her neck. Dominie was trying with an
increasing lack of success to pretend she didn't notice.
"Those 'things' are frangipani, I suspect . . . and azaleas, and maybe water hyacinths, though I'm not very
good at flowers when they aren't roses. But I saw plenty
of mangoes on the hillsides, and clusters of bananas and

papaya too, so maybe someone lived here once. Did Adam and Even have mangoes and papayas, I wonder.''

"They had figs,'' he said wickedly. He had rolled closer, almost touching, and was gazing down at her with an unmistakable expression. "Adam wore a fig leaf. And Eve too, silly thing . . . it must have been dreadfully scratchy. Did you picture Eve in your Garden of Eden, love, wearing nothing but a little green leaf and her long, glorious red hair? And Adam looking at her the way I'm looking at you now . . . and thinking the same thing?''

"Of course not. I was just a child. I didn't know about evil things like that.''

"Well, then, I'm glad you're all grown-up. And your mind—and your body—are not quite so innocent.''

"Ummm, not innocent at all,'' she said as his lips came down on hers—or were her lips rising to his?—and all thoughts of scratchy fig leaves and purple blossoms half-hiding inland pools vanished from her mind.

Her body was hungry for him, and his for her, as eager as they had been that afternoon with the cooling waters of a gentle stream rippling over them, and the sweetness of their swift, overwhelming fulfillment was every bit as complete. This might not be the first Eden, but it was the first for her, and he was the first man—the *only* man— she had ever loved or ever would.

The hours turned into days, and the days into weeks, as they waited for the *Shadow Dawn* to complete the long voyage to the Philippines and return to pick them up. Dominie had, in truth, little more to wear than the fig leaf Jared had joked about, but she was finding that she needed little, except perhaps at midday, when the sun turned brutally strong. They had paused just long enough at Aziz's hideout for her to discover another assortment of shirts, this time in various shades of red—he was as compulsively fastidious about his drawers as about his personal hygiene, it seemed—and these, together with the crimson dress, only slightly worse for its one day's wear, now comprised her total wardrobe.

There was also the drab gray outfit with the rose-pink collar and cuffs, but that had been salvaged only "for an emergency,'' and only under the greatest protest. Jared had taken one look at it and pronounced it utterly unfit for a woman of her beauty and sensuality to be seen in, and as she had never cared much for it herself, she had graciously given in and let him have his way.

He himself had only the clothes he was wearing, which, as Dominie reminded him with a faint ladylike puckering of the nostrils, had not been cleaned for some days now. He was going to be quite ripe by the time they were finally rescued! He responded with mock horror that he was shocked to learn she hadn't even *heard* of laundering garments in a convenient stream. Since she was presumably ignorant of such feminine duties, apparently he was going to have to do it himself.

Dominie feigned even greater shock, first that he thought someone of her breeding and background would consider soiling her hands with such disgusting labor, and second, that he—a man!—even knew about such things.

"You forget, my adorable Eve," he responded with a chuckle. "You have fallen in love with a seaman. Ships don't exactly carry a full contingent of servants."

"But you're the captain! Surely captains don't do their own laundry."

The chuckle turned into a full-fledged laugh, warm and full of affection. "No, but I didn't start out as a captain. I started as a cabin boy. And cabin boys do all sorts of things I wouldn't care to mention."

Jared not only knew how to do laundry—and quite efficiently too, Dominie thought as she watched him prance around in not even a fig leaf, searching for a clean rock to plaster his trousers against so they would dry smooth—but also had other hidden talents. He managed to build a quite acceptable shelter by tying lengths of branch together with vines and draping the windward side with one of the blankets they had brought from the Arab's well-stocked shack. He was also an excellent fisherman, which proved fortunate, for their supplies were extremely limited.

True to his word, Alex had dropped off several crates, whose contents, together with the coffee and sugar they had raided from Aziz, were ample to stave off starvation. But rice and beans and salt meat made blandly unappetizing fare, and they desperately needed the fish and fresh fruit to add savor to their diet.

Jared's hidden talents did not, however, rather to Dominie's surprise, extend to cooking. He could make quite passable coffee and boil edible, if rather soggy rice, but subtleties were utterly beyond him. Salt beef and pork were chopped into bits and added with no other seasonings to a woefully unpalatable pilaf, or sliced and served either cold or fried in olive oil, which was only slightly better. Alex had provided an ample supply of the spices for which the Orient was famous—anise and fennel, Szechuan pepper and cinnamon, five-spice powder and big jars of soy and fermented bean paste—but it was clear that Jared didn't have the vaguest notion what to do with them.

"It looks like I'm going to have to take over," Dominie said after the fourth dinner, which was only slightly more monotonous than the third and the second. "I've been watching, and I think I can manage the rice. Which, since that's all you know how to do, means I ought to be at least as good."

In fact, after the first couple of tries, she proved considerably better. She had a natural flair for cooking, and was much less reluctant to experiment with things she had never tried before. The rice and beans were mixed together—no reason, just that she thought it might be more interesting that way—and flavored with a little bacon, and fish was wrapped in banana leaves to keep it from drying out as it roasted slowly on the coals. The olive oil was reserved for pungent dressings, flavored with dried herbs and sprinkled over cold rice and fruit for the noonday meal, and bacon fat was used to sauté the meat, just lightly, before turning it into delicious stews with plantains and big chunks of jackfruit, which they had found growing on the other side of the island. All the spices were opened and sniffed, and combined with various peppers to create quite creditable approximations of an Indian curry.

"I think you were lying to me, love," Jared said as he scooped up the last bit of roasted garoupa fish and mangoes with just a hint of cinnamon and clove, which had sounded awful, but definitely wasn't. "You said you'd never set foot in a kitchen in your life."

"I did not! I was in the kitchen all the time, trying to coax extra sweets out of the cook. It usually worked too.

Little girls with big hungry eyes can have almost anything they want. I said I'd never set a pot on the stove—and I haven't.''

"Where did you learn to cook, then?"

"I didn't. I'm French. Frenchwomen are born knowing how to cook. It's in the blood, I think . . . and isn't it lucky for you?'' She took an appreciative sip of the cool amber liquid in a cut-crystal glass in her hand. "And lucky for me, being French, that your cousin had the good sense to include wine among the supplies.''

Jared grinned as he tossed another stick on the fire. They had found a sheltered hollow among the rocks, almost completely enclosed on three sides and invisible from the shore, and he did not have to worry about the orange-gold glow. A typically wry note from Alex had been waiting when they opened the first crate of food-stuffs.

"Sorry I couldn't leave chickens for fresh eggs,'' it read, "but I didn't know when you'd be back to feed them. But if Mademoiselle Dominie will follow the path to the south, she'll find something that should make up for her precious omelets.''

How like Alex, Jared thought, to cover his concern with a touch of humor. And how like him to remember that his cousin's lady had a passion for omelets. Mademoiselle Dominie had indeed followed the path—to discover several bottles of wine chilling in a deep pool. And a pair of crystal stem glasses under a broad-leafed shrub.

"Alex was always the romantic in the family,'' he said. "He knew I'd want something to court you properly . . . and he knew I wouldn't have had the foresight to think of it myself.''

Firelight mingled with the last deep red of the dying sun, and Dominie, watching the warm colors play on his face—on the rugged bone structure that made him look so aloof sometimes, the craggy strength of his jaw and chin, the full, almost startlingly sensual mouth—thought again, as she had so many times before, how alike they could be, these Barron men. And yet how different. Unexpectedly she found herself recalling Alex, the way she caught him looking at her sometimes, the strange, aching loneliness in his soft gray eyes.

"Has he ever been in love?" she asked curiously. "Your cousin?"

"Alex? Not that I know of . . but then, I wouldn't be likely to know. Alex has always been one to keep his own counsel. We're all a little like that. We don't wear our hearts on our sleeves, except Matthew perhaps—and he changes his with the seasons."

Dominie's eyes were still on his face, and Jared sensed the question in their depths an instant before she uttered it.

"What about you?" she asked quietly. "You said once that you had never told any other woman you loved her. But it seems to me that's the kind of thing men say sometimes."

"No. At least not this one. I haven't exactly led a monastic existence, God knows, but I've never been in love. I've *cared* sometimes . . ." He thought briefly of Mei-ling and considered mentioning her, but talking about his Chinese mistress meant talking about his Chinese sons, and that was a subject he was not ready to bring up. A subject that might never need to be brought up unless things progressed further between them. "I've cared very deeply. I hoped sometimes it might turn into more . . . but it never did. Until you."

He was holding out his arms, making Dominie forget that slight catch she had detected in his voice, and she slipped willingly into them. The warmth of the fire was welcome with a brisk breeze blowing in from the ocean.

"I'm glad you've never loved before," she said huskily. "But I'm glad you weren't a monk either. I like the things you're teaching me." She flickered her tongue across his lips, light, teasing, evoking just the response she knew she was going to get.

"Shameless hussy." He was touching her tongue with his own, half-licking, half-caressing. "You're full of questions tonight. . . . And what about *you*? Are you going to tell me you've never been in love? No man has ever kissed you like this before?"

"Not like this. There was Honoré, of course—my fiancé . . ." She felt him stiffen with surprise and regretted instantly having mentioned the man she had almost forgotten. Honoré *had* kissed her, of course, and she had most definitely responded, but he had never made her feel anything like this.

"Your . . . *fiancé?* Are you still engaged to him?"

"I don't think so—he's probably broken it off by now. He's an old man. I never loved him, or even *liked* him awfully much. It was an arranged marriage . . ." She was beginning to feel uncomfortable again, guilty, thinking about the man she had left behind, and she shoved him out of her mind. The last thing she wanted now was old memories intruding on the very cozy tenderness that was building up between them. "But that was a long time ago . . . and this is now. And I am very interested in all those things you were going to teach me. I think it might be time for another lesson."

Her hand slid boldly between his legs to the place where she knew she would find ample evidence of his feelings for her.

"Ah, Dominie . . ." He surrendered with a little moan of pleasure. "It isn't only *little* girls with hungry eyes who get everything they want."

## 22

THE WEEKS DRIFTED BY, so slowly sometimes it felt as if they had been in their secret paradise forever, and Dominie could not even remember any other kind of existence. Other times everything seemed to be happening so quickly—a day was gone before she knew it, sunset lapping with the gentle waves upon the shore—and she ached to think that they would be leaving soon.

Christmas came and went, noted only by the calendar that Jared scratched out every day in the sand. Her birthday was in early December, and Dominie was a little surprised to realize that somehow it had passed and she was nineteen. If she had remained in Paris, she would have been Madame Honoré Ravaud by now.

But she had not remained, she thought with a heartfelt sigh of gratitude. She was not trapped in a terrible, empty marriage with an old man for whom she had only the mildest affection. She was on a tropical island with a young, virile, handsome man she loved with all her heart, and she could not imagine anything more perfect.

It was a lazy, languid idyll. Mornings, very early, when the sun was barely rising and shadows were still long and deep, they would stroll along the beach, hand in hand, collecting pretty seashells and not worrying about prying eyes from shore. Afternoons were spent safely inland. They might lie beside one of the deep crystalline pools, listening to the murmur of the streams that tumbled into them, and make love alternately with tenderness and such passion it took Dominie's breath away. Or Jared might try to teach her how to swim, but as that involved holding his hands reassuringly beneath her while she floated on her stomach, and as those hands had a tendency to stray to her breasts or the smooth inner skin of her thighs, or the moist downy patch of dark red between them, it usually amounted to the same thing.

Or they might sprawl in some cool glen, Jared with only his trousers on, Dominie's bare browned legs peeking scandalously out from under one of the red silk shirts, and just talk for hours. They were so new to each other, they had so much yet to learn, it was like a special voyage of discovery with new delights on either side.

Jared heard all about the house in Paris—the statues in the garden that used to frighten her when she was a little girl and fountains spurted suddenly all around, her secret hiding place in the vault with the diamonds where no one had ever been able to find her, the faithful maid who had come with her mother from London and taught her English when she was still just a toddler. And Dominie listened enthralled while he told her what it was like to be a cabin boy at sixteen and go to sea for the first time, and how mysterious and enveloping the cobbled streets of Boston could be in a quiet, heavy fog.

She learned about his grandfather, the indomitable Gareth Barron with the wild white hair and even wilder temper, who had built a vast shipping empire out of one leaky old tub and a convenient knack of turning a blind eye to law and honor in the early days of the struggle for American independence. And his grandmother Judith, stately and gracious, a reserved woman, but strong as steel underneath; the true foundation of the family, Dominie sensed, and certainly its moral core.

She learned about the lengendary Dawn, for whom all the ships of the line had been named, and the beautiful daughter who married the son of the man who had once courted *her*. Jared's face changed subtly when he spoke of Aurora, and Dominie was surprised somehow, without truly knowing why, to realize he had been deeply attached to his mother. Perhaps because he had never talked about her, or indeed any of his family—except his brother, and that with a notable lack of *tendresse*.

"How old were you when your mother died?" she asked one lazy afternoon as they lay side by side on soft tufts of grass under a gnarled old mango that no longer bore any fruit.

"Fifteen when we buried her," he replied with an oddly cryptic look. "But she started dying long before that, bit by bit, the day my father was thrown from his horse and killed. I was just eight then. Matthew was a baby.''

''She loved him that much?''

''She adored him . . . and he doted on her. It was hard for others to understand sometimes—my grandfather in particular could never bring himself to acknowledge it. She was a silly, frivolous, exceedingly vain woman, but she was fun and loving . . . and they were happy together. She never recovered from his death. She just turned into a shadow, growing a little more insubstantial with each passing year.''

Dominie raised herself on one elbow to look down at him. ''That must have been very hard for you,'' she said softly.

He reached up and, taking her hand, touched it to his lips.

''That was a long time ago, sweet. I managed to recover.''

''It must have been even harder for your brother. He was so much younger. Growing up without a mother can be very painful. Perhaps it's hard for him still.''

Jared saw what she was doing and tried to be annoyed, but it was difficult when the sun was so warm . . . and she was looking so particularly seductive.

''Perhaps, like Alex, you think I ought to be gentler when I catch up with my brother?''

''Perhaps.'' She traced a finger around his lips, lightly, intentionally provocative.

''And perhaps we're so far behind schedule,'' he reminded her, ''it doesn't matter anymore.'' She was making it exceedingly difficult to form his arguments, and she knew it, the minx! ''By the time we arrive, it will probably all be over—one way or the other. If Matthew has managed to get things straightened out, I'll do you and Alex proud and clap him on the back and tell him what a fine job he's done—and he'd sure as hell better not try anything like that again!''

''And if he hasn't gotten things straightened out?''

''Then I'll sort through the rubble and salvage what I can. Dammit, I'm not being hard-hearted about this!'' He caught both her arms and pulled her down, almost on top of him, wanting urgently to make her understand—

and wanting to forget it all and kiss her protests into oblivion. "I care about Matt. Matt's the charmer in the family. He's always been able make me laugh. He was such a damned funny little fellow, with all the Barron pride and a wonderfully droll sense of the ridiculous. I *like* Matt. I even love him—but I want him to stand on his own two feet and make something of himself for a change!"

"But how can he do that, my dearest"—her voice was teasing, but her eyes were serious—"if you keep fighting his battles for him? And against him?"

How indeed? The urge for oblivion was rapidly winning. He was very much aware of the absolute nakedness of her supple body beneath that flimsy silk shirt. Her nipples were hard little peaks, tormenting his mouth and tongue.

"Why are we talking about things that can't be settled now anyhow," he said, his voice husky and low in his throat, "when there are much more . . . interesting things to discuss?"

As always, she was equal to the occasion.

*"Discuss?"* she said with a wicked sultriness that told him she knew exactly what he had in mind.

"Perhaps," he admitted, "that might not be quite the right word."

Jared eased her body full-length out beside him, slowly, tenderly, aching for more, but not wanting to rush the moment that was so fulfilling in itself. They had been together for weeks now, every day and every long, bewitching, sensuous night, barely apart for more than a few minutes, and he had waited to grow tired of her. To find the routine wearying, as he had with all the other women he had ever known.

But every day, he seemed to find something new about her. And about himself. Every day brought new pleasures, not merely in the fervor of their physical joinings—which continued to make him burn and throb at the mere thought of coming to her—but in the depth of their feelings for each other. In the companionship that continued to grow, the contentment that allowed them to sit together for hours, not speaking, not even needing to touch, just finding it enough to be close. The deep sustaining love that made a man think it might not be so bad to grow old if he had a woman like this at his side.

"You are so beautiful," he said softly. "Not just your face . . . which is exquisite." He was kissing the tip of her nose, not altogether playfully, savoring the slight salt taste of her skin with his tongue. "Or your body . . ." His hand was sliding to her breast, cupping it, massaging through the sheer silk, "which is magnificent. But your heart as well, and your spirit . . . and your character."

"My *character*?" Dominie pulled back just slightly to look half-teasingly into his eyes. Deep gray eyes, all the blue lost somehow in shadow—smoky eyes, dark with longing. "I didn't think men desired women for their character."

"Neither did I, love . . . neither did I"

His tongue was seeking her mouth now, lightly, as before, half-playing, striving to tantalize more than satisfy, though his body swelled with the desperation of his aching need for her, and every virile male instinct urged him to drive that hard, engorged, thoroughly aroused shaft into the accommodating warmth between her thighs and make her groan with agony and yearning. Willing himself to hold back, ignoring the sweat that glistened over his naked chest and shoulders, plastering dark blond hair onto his forehead, he forced his lips to be gentle, his hands patient as they had never been patient before.

No sudden urgency this time. None of the violent, almost savage abruptness that thrust them to such excruciating peaks when they were both excited—and pleased them both—but left no time for the sweet, lingering love he longed to be part of their lovemaking.

He had never felt like this before, even with her. Never wanted a woman so devastatingly, and wanted at the same time to do nothing but give.

This was what he had been looking for—thirsting for all his life, like a man trapped in the great arid expanses of an endless desert—only he hadn't known what he was seeking. This was why no other woman had ever been able to hold him for long. His mouth was soft as he opened it over hers, ravaging, but gently, a humble suppliant pleading for entry. It was not lust he sought, not satisfaction merely of that hard, male part of him which had always been so easily placated . . . but love. Honest, genuine, sometimes even unselfish love.

Dominie felt the slight pressure of his lips, different somehow, not like any way he had ever kissed her before. Hardly a kiss at all, she thought—it shouldn't have been so thrilling, but suddenly she couldn't bear the longing that seemed to be surging inside her until she thought she would die from the sublime, exquisite pressure. Without even being aware of it, instinctively her mouth was opening, wanton and hungry; she could feel the hard, sinewy length of him beside her on the ground, the heat and closeness almost unbearably intimate.

She was intensely conscious of the man-smell of him in her nostrils, the powerful muscles that rippled across his back and shoulders and down his naked arms, the slightly rough matting of chest hair teasing her neck and bosom in the low V of her shirt, the taut urgency that seemed to emanate from his body into hers as his mouth grew forceful, demanding now, calling for the familiar feverish responses she was eager to give.

As many times as they had been together, as often as they would lie together in the future, Dominie did not think she would ever fail to be surprised by the wonder and excitement of his body, and the confusing, agonizing, deliciously exhilarating sensations it always evoked in her.

His mouth still fastened hard on hers, his tongue still searching the moist inner depths, claiming everything it encountered, Jared allowed himself the luxury of exploring the soft, quivering body that fitted so perfectly into the enclosure of his arms, his legs, his rock-strong chest and lean hard hips. The flimsy fabric was only a partial barrier between them; his hands knew and recognized every delectable curve they encountered, just as each part of her knew and reacted to his touch, and throbbed desperately for more.

The silk felt incredibly smooth against her skin, not cool, but hot, burning every place he touched. Dominie sighed as his caresses ran down her back, along her hips, toying with her buttocks, insolently, teasing the deep hollow between them.

Suddenly her own hands were just as brazen, slipping beneath the waistband of his trousers, no longer shy, as they once had been, but bold, finding the muscular hardness of his own buttocks, pushing him against her, so tight she could feel the shaft of his manhood pressing into her belly.

The sighs turned to whimpers, little soft sounds of longing and encouragement as he found her breasts at last, fondling, provoking, making her nipples stand out so erect even the sheer silk was painful against them. She wanted him so much—she longed to grab hold of him *there*, where the satisfaction of all her desires was centered, and force him to plunge it into her and put an end to the exquisite torment that threatened to tear her apart.

And yet . . . she did not want it to end. She wanted it to go on forever and ever, a timeless eternity trapped in one moment of intense, unquenchable sensation.

Then his hands were under the shirt, touching her at last, making her tremble with the sudden, only half-anticipated intimacy, and he was slipping it over her head . . . and it no longer mattered what she wanted, or didn't want. Her body had taken over now, and she could no more control it than she could control the painful little gasps coming out of her mouth.

The firelight was warm on her naked limbs and torso, intensifying the feverish flush of her skin, giving her a glow that seemed to match the glow that burned from deep within. Jared, looking down from where he had pulled himself up, half-kneeling, half-crouching above her, was struck all over again with the miracle of her body, and how it seemed to have been created just to please his strong male tastes.

He drank in the perfection of her lips, ripe and sensually curving, slightly parted . . . the provocative fullness of swollen young breasts, creamy-pale mounds crowned by dark, impudent nipples . . . the slender perfection of her waist rounding into womanly hips and thighs . . . the dark red triangle between them, open to his view, waiting to receive him. An intense jolt of desire shuddered through her body, and he was suddenly, ridiculously afraid he wasn't going to be able to hold off even long enough to thrust his throbbing member deep inside her.

Lord, he hadn't suffered that humiliation since he was

an overeager adolescent, just learning about the mysterious delights of a beautiful woman's body.

"You make me want you too much, Dominie," he
murmured, his voice muffled with passion. "You make
me lose myself in you."

"I want you to lose yourself . . . and I want you in
me."

"Oh, God . . ." He could feel the sweat pouring off
him now. He ached for her, his body was pulsating and
screaming with anguish, but he wanted to give this time,
not take—to possess her in a way he never had before.

His tongue was finding her again, not her mouth now,
but her breasts, and he was licking first one taut, engorged nipple, then the other, little darting motions like
tongues of flame that seemed to sear through her and
kindle the fire burning deep within. Dominie was writhing with pleasure and sheer, unbearable agony as he
moved downward, a slow, sensual passage that made her
want to shriek with longing. Her hands were tangling in
his hair, and she was drawing him closer, holding him
hard against her, craving something more and not knowing what it was.

Sensing her need, Jared thrust one hand boldly between
her legs. The spasm that shuddered almost convulsively
through her entire body told him she was ready for what
he had in mind.

And he was ready too. His hand was wet with her; his
mouth longed suddenly for the taste of her, and he hurried his progress down her belly, lips and tongue torturing and enflaming each bit of flesh they touched, playing
for a second with the perfect roundness of her navel before sinking into the slight depression where her hips met
her thighs. Her body seemed to sense what he was doing;
she was pressing his head down, instinctively, not even
aware of what she was doing, urging him lower, and the
sounds coming out of her mouth now were little animal
moans of anguish and arousal.

Her legs were spreading for him even before he reached
them. He found the silken skin on the inside of her thighs
first, moist with her desire for him, quivering beneath his
skillful kisses. Then the damp dark-red curls that were
the only fragile shield against his passion . . . then at
last the sweet object of his quest.

No cries of shock or protest greeted him as he parted those soft, smooth lips and ventured, gently at first, inside. No maidenly flinching at the impudence of his assault. She had long since ceased to be embarrassed by anything he did, or ashamed of the passionate intensity of her own reactions. She simply accepted—and enjoyed—as he accepted and enjoyed every deliriously ecstactic moment he spent with his body coupled to hers.

His tongue grew bolder, flicking, darting, creating all sorts of bewildering and absolutely overpowering sensations, and Dominie was no longer master of her own body. No longer even wanted to be. He was scouring that intimate cavern, ravishing it as thoroughly as ever he had ravished her mouth, and with even more devastating results.

Her legs were twining around his neck suddenly, her hands still twisted in his hair, and his hands were beneath her, thrusting her up, bringing her so hard against his mouth and wildly darting tongue she thought she would die from the delicious torment. Then, just as she was sure she could bear it no longer, just as the pressure in her body, the terrible swelling and burning between her thighs, threatened to consume her, she caught a glimpse of that peak she could now recognize, and she realized with a little groan of anticipated rapture that relief was in sight.

Jared felt the change in her responses, the culmination that was so close, and while it was exactly what he had planned, he felt suddenly, inexplicably bereft. He wanted to give this to her. He *would* give it to her, often and freely if she liked, and he would teach her to do the same for him. But now, with all the new emotions that seemed to be swirling through him, the new feelings he had only begun to sort out, he could not bear to be alone.

This was a special moment, a perfect moment, and he needed desperately to share it with her.

Dominie gave a little murmur of protest as he eased his head from between her legs, and he half-expected to find a well-deserved pout of reproach on those pretty pink lips. But when he looked up, he could have sworn he saw a faint smile melting into the desire that was still clearly unsatiated.

"I wondered what he meant," she said, and started unexpectedly to giggle.

"He?"

"That awful Arab. He said he didn't think the Sultan had the eunuchs' tongues cut out so they couldn't *talk* to his wives. . . . I didn't know what he meant."

"Blast it, woman!" Jared muttered with mock severity. "Don't you know you're not supposed to make a man laugh at a time like this?"

"Why not? I like to laugh."

"So do I, my angel . . . so do I."

A great wave of tenderness overwhelmed him as he sank down on her, no longer fighting his own urges, needing only to be with her, inside her, to feel the nurturing warmth of her body welcoming and enclosing him. He did not even notice that for the first time it was she who grasped his turgid manhood, guiding him into her, she whose hips rose up, initiating the first sweet stab of their union. He knew only that he loved her with all the passion in his being, and he understood at last why this moment had seemed so important. Why he needed to share it with her. Because it was the moment of his final and complete surrender.

He would not grow tired of her. He realized that now, as he should have realized it long ago had he not been so busy comparing her to everyone else—waiting for what happened with her to duplicate the things that had happened in the past. She was not everyone else, and this was not the past. She was unique and beautiful, and he did not love her because she filled some empty space in his life, or even because she brought laughter and excitement and a new savor to each day.

He loved her because she was his heart, his spirit, the best of him and the best he would ever be.

It was his surrender . . . and his greatest triumph. He felt the deep downward thrusts of his body into her, the slow sensual withdrawals, as he had never felt them before. It was almost as if he were innocent again, experiencing the act of love for the first time . . . and in a way, he was. He had known the physical gratification often enough—his was a virile body, quick to arouse—even the tenderness sometimes, and the great, compelling need to protect. But there had never been a sense of permanence before, a deep, abiding commitment to something beyond and outside of himself. He had never known that the woman beneath him, so warm and receptive, was his. Now and forever.

And she *was* his. He felt the ache in his groin intensify, frenzied and consuming; he held on a moment longer, then let go, spilling the vitality of his body into her, drained in a way he had never been drained before. Loving and needing, and not ashamed to admit it. She was his, and he would never let her go.

Dominie woke feeling strangely restless. It was the hour before dawn, an almost eerie time, with not even a hint of color seeping into the gray luminosity of the atmosphere. The air was balmier than usual. No wind broke the stillness, and a faint warming glow rose from the coals of last night's fire, but she found herself shivering. Almost uncontrollably, as if she had taken a chill.

Jared was still asleep—reasonably so, considering the exertion that had gone on most of the night—and she slipped quietly from beneath the blanket, taking care not to disturb him. The moonlight was ebbing, day had not yet begun to filter over the horizon, and she could barely make out the shimmering white expanse of sand along the shore.

She stood for a moment in the small hollow where their camp was sited, staring at the elusive arc of the beach, and tried to analyze what she was feeling. It took her a moment to realize, with a little jolt of surprise, that she was afraid.

Nothing tangible had alarmed her—there were no subtle noises in the background, no sense that she and her lover were not alone on their private island—but still, there it was. She was afraid. The palms of her hands were cold with sweat, and she was shaking again.

She slipped on the red silk dress, feeling an impulse to cover herself—belated modesty perhaps, or maybe just the longing for a comfortably familiar garment—and wandered out onto the beach.

Everything was even quieter here. Only the soft, barely audible murmur of waves caressing the shore sounded at rhythmic intervals, but she was more afraid than ever. Darkness seemed to be closing in, the ghosts of every nightmare she had ever had, and suddenly she knew what it was that had frightened her.

"Denis?"

She barely whispered the word, not daring to say it aloud. No answer came back. She had not expected an answer—but she *had* expected a feeling, and there was nothing. Nothing but the vast void of night that seemed to catch and magnify her panic and hurl it back at her.

She tried desperately to picture him. To bring his face into her mind. That last evening, the thinness and deep weary lines that had wrenched her heart as she sat on the floor and gazed up at him—why couldn't she see it again? Where were the tenderness and love in his eyes when they stood in the first clear light of dawn and said good-bye for what they both knew would be the last time?

*Little Dominie, chasing butterflies in your rose garden. . . . How did you grow so quickly?*

Tears rose to her eyes, bitter and stinging. She could remember the words so clearly. *I want you to smile. . . . Don't say a word. Just smile one more time and turn around and walk away. . . . See, there's your handsome captain waiting.* Oh, God, it hurt so much.

*No looking back, Dominie. . . . My love will always be with you.*

She could remember the words. She could even see his features if she worked at it hard enough, the way the light struck them, the terrible pallor of his skin. But she could not bring back the essence behind them. The feeling.

Always before, when she had thought of him, he had been there with her. No matter what the distance, she had had a strong sense of him, the reality of his existence, a spiritual presence in the shadows beside her. Now for the first time he was gone.

She had lost him.

The tears fell silent and unnoticed down her cheeks. For the first time, he was completely out of her heart. For the first time, she did not know if he was lonely or at peace, frightened or comfortable, safe or hurt—or no longer even alive. For the first time, there was a great empty world out there and she could not feel him in it.

She did not know what it meant. She did not know if he was dead, or if she had simply moved on with her life and left him behind. She only knew that the almost mystical bond between them was severed at last.

She had lost him, and she felt unutterably sad.

"Dominie, love?"

Jared's voice, soft and unusually hesitant, drew her out of her reverie, and she turned to find him standing some distance behind her. His face was concerned, but reserved, as if he weren't sure whether she wanted him there.

As if he didn't know there was nothing too private, too painful, to share with him!

Dominie longed to tell him—she *tried* to tell him—but the tears were coming again and somehow she couldn't manage all those words.

"I was thinking of *him*," she said, hoping he would understand. "Denis."

He did not fail her.

"I know," he replied quietly. "I was too. I don't know why, but I was."

"Oh, Jared, I'm frightened . . ."

His hands were on her cheeks, touching her softly, no desire in them now, just a tremendous need to comfort. He would have taken the pain if he could, gladly—but there was no way. All he could do was remind her of the things she already knew.

"Your brother was a very brave man, Dominie." He was not even aware of his instinctive use of the past tense. "He would want you to be brave too. He would want you to go on with your life. No regrets . . . no hankering about the past. That's what he was telling you that last morning. *No looking back. . . .*"

"I know, but—"

"No, love . . . no arguments." He was wiping the tears away, but they kept coming back, spilling warm and wet on his hands. "It's over now, and you have to let go. No matter how it comes out—no matter what happens to your brother—he's no longer part of your life. . . . Do you know what he said to me, almost the last thing? He said you thought you needed him, but you were wrong. It isn't him you need anymore—but me. I think he was being tactful."

"Tactful?" She was trying to smile, but finding it hard. The sun was coming up at last, a magnificent red dawn that reflected on her tears and seemed to turn them to flame.

"I think what he really meant was that *I* need you . . . and I think he was right."

Her expression changed, questioning for a moment, then softening, and Jared realized that she was coming to terms with her grief, leaving it painfully, reluctantly, behind.

" 'Want' maybe—but *need*?" She was teasing a little, managing it better, he sensed, than she had expected. "A big strong Barron man. I wouldn't have thought you *needed* anyone."

"I wouldn't have thought so myself, love, but it seems we both have lessons to learn from each other. Though yours are more fun," he added with a rakish wink, then changed, looking suddenly, uncharacteristically awkward. "No, that's not true. Mine have been extremely pleasurable too. Damned pleasurable. You're everything I want, Dominie. Everything I'm ever going to want."

He paused, waiting for a reaction, but there was none. She just looked at him silently, expectantly, not making it easy at all. He couldn't even guess what she was thinking.

"Blast it, Dominie," he burst out, "I'm trying to propose to you! I'm not doing a very good job of it—I'm making a hell of a mess, as a matter of fact!—but I'm asking you to marry me."

The corners of her mouth turned up, just the faintest hint of what might have been the smile she was trying for before. "I know," she said softly.

"You know? You *know*? That's all you have to say?" He tried to look bluff, but he wasn't quite making it, and he realized uncomfortably that for the first time in his life he had absolutely no control over his fate. "Not . . . 'Oooh, Jared, how thrilling. Jared, I'm positively swooning with delight! Darling Jared, I never guessed you were going to ask me anything like that.' "

"Oh," she said with a sudden unexpected glint in her eye, "but I did."

"Of course you did, woman!" He longed to clasp her in his arms, to hold her tight, get the thing settled and accepted once and for all. Dammit, she wasn't going to make him go down on his knees, was she? "You probably knew it long before I did. But that isn't an answer."

"You mean you need an answer? . . . But you've always been so sure of yourself. And of me. Surely you've already *assumed* what the answer is going to be."

"I have . . . and I've assumed it's going to be yes. I have, if you want me to be completely and humiliatingly honest about it, been *praying* that it's yes. But I'd like to hear the words."

Her eyes turned solemn, melting and beautiful in the hazy glow. And suddenly he didn't need the words anymore, but she was giving them to him anyway.

"Yes, Jared, it *is* thrilling. Yes, Jared, I *am* swooning with delight. And yes, my darling Jared, I would be proud to be your wife."

Proud? He drew her close at last, feeling the warmth of her next to his body, as he knew he would feel her every day for the rest of his life. It was he who was proud that this strong, beautiful, generous, incredibly loving woman had consented to be his wife.

"I think," he said humbly, "we might seal the bargain with a kiss."

It was sealed with somewhat more than a kiss. The sun was just erupting over the horizon, streaking the sky with great joyous bursts of color as they retired into the shadows of a grassy glade just beyond the fringes of the sand. Neither of them noticed that the *Shadow Dawn* had sailed into the bay and lay quietly at anchor, waiting for the first pure light to send in the cutter.

It was over, though they did not know it yet, and would not have grieved if they had. Many things were ending in their life. The perfect idyll in their tropical paradise, the great adventure that had brought them so close together, the strengthening hardship of their last days on the mainland—the laughter and the fear, the hope and ecstasy and sorrow they had shared.

But every ending meant a new beginning, and the fiery dawn that warmed the earth and splashed the heavens with sheer untamed exuberance was a symbol of the laughter and fear, the hope and ecstasy and sorrow they would share in the future.

The dawn of their great love for each other and the promise of two lives magically, miraculously blended into one.

# Evenings on Troubled Waters

## Mid-March 1841

## 23

DOMINIE AND JARED were to find a new city waiting for
them when the *Shadow Dawn* sailed into the deep,
sweeping bay that opened out of the mouth of the Pearl
River. No longer was Macao the queen of the China trade;
she had been replaced by a brash younger sister whose
character was yet to be determined. The building of this
bawdy upstart had barely begun, only slightly more than
a month before, but already half-erected structures were
rising on either side of bustling streets, bamboo scaffold-
ing seemed to be everywhere, piles of bricks clogged the
waterfront, and the sound of hammering continued well
into the darkness. Long after midnight, the view from
ships in the harbor included broad patches of gleaming
lanternlight against a backdrop of deep green-black hills.

The first phase of the war Alex had predicted had come
and gone, with devastating swiftness for the Chinese. On
the morning of January 7, while the lovers were still
basking in the sunlight of their secluded island, fifteen
hundred British marines, infantry, and sepoys had gone
ashore under cover of their ships' guns to lay siege to the
outermost of the Bogue Forts which guarded the water
entrance to Canton. Beyond lay the proud, disdainful city
where foreigners were tolerated only during the trading
season, and then only in the narrow confines of their own
small settlement.

Meeting the land troops had been three thousand en-
trenched Chinese, their flanks supported by field battal-
ions. On the water, a flotilla of massive war junks—great
crimson-and-black hulls with bamboo-battened lug sails
dyed red-brown in pigs' blood and bark—had sailed out
with supreme arrogance, backing up heavy chains that
had been drawn across the channels. Around and between them had darted the fire rafts with their deadly

projectiles of niter and sulfur, pitch and willow charcoal, which had struck terror into the hearts of enemies for centuries.

The Emperor of the Chinese Heaven had made his preparations and was ready for the presumptuous invaders.

It did not last three hours. The war junks, for all their haughty grandeur, were no match for the more maneuverable British vessels, especially the squat new steamers that did not rely on the wind, and the forts were hopelessly obsolete. Too far apart to be mutually supportive, their rear walls without bulwarks or embrasures to defend against landward attack, their guns lashed to solid blocks, rendering them incapable of being turned—their powder so inferior that shots fell short even if by coincidence the antique muzzle-loading cannon happened to be pointed in the right direction—they did not stand a chance. The first marines landed sometime after eight; at eleven o'clock, blue-jackets on board the great British ships of the line saw the Union Jack rising over Fort Chuenpi.

The Chinese paid dearly for their overconfidence. Six hundred Tartars dead, with only a hundred wounded— they had fought ferociously if not wisely—and the core of their navy broken by the loss of numerous junks. The terms of the treaty that followed were humiliating: trade to be reopened on the victor's terms; official and direct communication between the two nations; no more seizure of foreign property; an indemnity of six million dollars to be paid for the opium that had been destroyed. And on January 26, 1841, a barren, virtually uninhabited rock less than a mile off the mainland was formally turned over in perpetuity to the empire on which the sun would never set.

The British suffered thirty wounded, most of those in an accidental explosion.

The rock was called Hong Kong. Fragrant Harbor, as it was translated. A pretty, romantic-sounding name, Dominie thought, though as she stood on the deck of the junk Jared had procured for their living quarters and studied the shoreline in the waning light of a rapidly sinking sun, she could not detect anything particularly pretty or romantic about it. Or fragrant, for that matter. There was a distinct aroma, ever present, of all manner

of things she didn't even like to imagine floating with the
refuse on the water.

The ocean was crowded, dotted with vessels of every
description. Troop ships hugged the shore, all flying the
distinctive red-and-white flag of the East India Company,
and farther out, fleet rake-masted clippers represented
the great trading houses: Jardine, Matheson; Russell and
Company; Dent; Olyphant; J. P. Cushing; Barron Shipping. Clusters of sampans connected by planked walkways formed floating villages, mail packets came and
went, and longboats and cutters were constantly crossing
back and forth, carrying officers and traders and their
families from boat to boat or for excursions onshore.

The land was even more crowded. Tents for the soldiers of the expeditionary force sprawled along the waterfront—four thousand men, Dominie had been told, and
she could well believe it—and makeshift shanties already
formed a nearly solid mass on the hillsides behind them.
The Chinese were settling in even before their British
masters, ingeniously finding ways to turn defeat into
monetary victory, and laundries and gin shops and shoe-
shine stands were sprouting up everywhere, brothels and
opium dens, tailors and toolmakers, restaurants under
canvas with rough-board floors, and even rougher taverns
near the vast tent city.

At least she had a comfortable place to live, Dominie
thought as she waited for the cutter that would bring Jared
back from the *Shadow Dawn*, where he had gone to
change for the dinner ball that was to be held that evening. Colored lights were already twinkling on the shore,
hundreds of silk lanterns marking the spot, and the sound
of music had begun to drift temptingly across the water.

Most of the traders and their staffs had to make do with
shipboard accommodations, whole families crammed like
tinned sardines into cabins smaller than the one she and
Jared shared on the *Shadow*. Fresh fruit and vegetables,
even drinking water, had to be brought in daily at great
expense by sampan, laundry flapped all over the deck,
bored and whining children had no place to play, and
sanitary conditions were truly awful. Fortunately, Jared,
with his usual resourcefulness, had managed to purchase
a surprisingly luxurious junk, which, he said, somewhat

tongue-in-cheek—she wasn't sure whether he was joking or not—had belonged to a notorious pirate.

Whoever the previous owner was, he had clearly known how to live. The boat was what they called a "longliner," well over a hundred feet, and as she glanced back over her shoulder, the dark, polished decking seemed to glow like mahogany in the illumination of glass-shaded oil lamps. Beyond, a shimmer of red showed through an open doorway, like the deep rich luster of a candlelit ruby.

The cabin had come as a complete surprise to Dominie. Red like the roses in her garden, and sumptuously elegant, silk and velvet everywhere, even draped across the ceiling, with huge, magnificent chests lined up against the walls and mirrors above catching and reflecting the fiery-warm light. She could still remember her astonishment when she first saw it. A raised platform like a dais on one side held a low, absolutely exquisite lacquered red table, and a matching platform on the other the most massive bed she had ever seen in her life.

"I bought it for the bed," Jared had whispered wickedly in her ear. "I thought we might find a use for it."

And they had. Dominie felt the heat rising to her cheeks, and she was grateful that there was no one around to see. The best thing about their somewhat unconventional quarters, she had quickly discovered, was the fact that servants scurried across the boardwalks that connected them to one of the sampan villages only twice a day. An hour or so in the morning to clean up, an hour again to prepare their evening meal. The rest of the time they were wonderfully, completely, and very happily alone.

A slight jolting drew her out of her thoughts—which were becoming quite shameless—and she looked around to see that Jared had arrived. He was in the cutter from the *Shadow*. Ordinarily they walked across the planking to one of the smaller sampans, but tonight he had wanted her to arrive in style.

Jared . . . but not Jared. Dominie stared in utter fascination as a man she had never seen before stepped onto the deck.

A tall, very elegant man, strong, muscular shoulders stretching the black broadcloth of an extremely fashionable tailcoat, legs looking long and tantalizingly lean in well-cut trousers of a somewhat lighter fabric. A patterned white satin waistcoat, no color to it, just a subtle design embroidered into the cloth, settled snugly over a torso that was hard and firm without the assistance of the stays or corsets stockier men affected, and shiny black pumps looked as if they had been made for dancing. Which, in fact, they probably had.

It intrigued her to think that beneath this stranger's debonair facade was a body she knew right down to the last mole and hair.

"I had no idea you were going to look like this," she said, then laughed as she realized he was staring at her with much the same expression. Just as she had never seen him in anything but tight-fitting trousers and shirts will full, casual sleeves, this was his first glimpse of a stylish young lady with her hair piled on top of her head and a brand-new gown copied from sketches of the latest fashions in Paris. "I didn't know they had such excellent tailors in the colonies," she said with a teasingly skeptical look. "You did bring that outfit with you, I presume?"

"I did . . . and we aren't the 'colonies' anymore. We haven't been for more than half a century. Though I must admit, while our tailors are superb, our seamstresses definitely look colonial next to the woman you found to whip up that bit of fluff for you."

"She is clever, isn't she?" Dominie said. She had been delighted, among the steady stream of workers who flooded in from the mainland and Macao, to find several with quite useful skills, especially among the dressmakers and milliners. "In just a week, I've already gotten four dresses, so you won't have to be ashamed of me. But this is absolutely the best."

She spun around, enjoying the effect she knew she was creating. The gown was silk, sheer and full-skirted, drifting down from a deep pointed waist, with softly bouffant sleeves dropping slightly off her shoulders and an echoing V in the daringly low neck. Not her usual red this time, but a deep emerald green, which her mirror told her brought out the color in her eyes and made her sun-bronzed skin look not unfashionable, but exotic and glowing.

Her hair she had done herself, if not skillfully, nonetheless prettily, in a kind of modified topknot with wispy tendrils curling onto her brow and cheeks and little clusters of wild myrtle strategically pinned to hide her mistakes.

The expression on Jared's face as she spun back to face him was everything she could have hoped for. Nor would his thoughts have disappointed her as he raked her body slowly with his eyes, taking in the smooth, slim lines of her bodice—she had no more need than he of stays—the way her skirt floated with her when she moved, the deep, quite spectacular cleavage that reminded him with uncomfortable physical manifestations of how plump and tempting her breasts were and how much he loved to fondle them. He had been feeling somewhat guilty before, that he hadn't found time to arrange for proper jewelry, but now he was almost glad. With her fresh, clean, absolutely unadorned beauty, she was going to put every other woman to shame.

"You're looking like a satyr again, Jared," she accused.

"Am I? . . . I was just thinking what a lovely gown that is. My second favorite of the outfits I've seen you in. I liked best what you wore on the island."

"But I didn't usually wear . . . *Oh!*" She was blushing again, ridiculously. There was no reason for it, but she was, and she knew he had to have seen.

"I miss my beautiful Eve." He laughed, with just enough huskiness to deepen the color in her cheeks. "With her long red hair and no fig leaf. . . . Perhaps, after all, we ought to skip the party and stay here."

She glanced up through lowered lashes, a devastatingly seductive look—and she had to know it, the little witch!

"As you wish, love. I am quite willing to do anything you want."

And she was, too, he thought, amused and suddenly overflowing with tenderness. She had been so excited all day; the glow in her eyes had rivaled the lantern on the cutter as he drew up, and her toes had already been tapping to the music. But she would remove the pretty dress—and those absurd little flowers that looked so charming in her hair—and go with him into the bedroom if he asked. And they were so new to each other, she wouldn't even mind.

"Not on your life," he said, laughing as he offered his arm and helped her gallantly into the cutter. "I have no intention of spoiling your fun this evening. Or my own. I can hardly wait to show up with you on my arm. I'm going to be the envy of every man there."

Only a few last stragglers had yet to arrive when the cutter left them off, and the bank was nearly deserted. Dominie wondered, just vaguely, if perhaps Jared hadn't timed their arrival deliberately to make an entrance. She had a feeling it was a slight understatement to say that he hadn't exactly lived like a monk. There were probably going to be quite a lot of surprised faces when people found out who the lady on his arm was. And Jared was just the sort to enjoy their consternation.

Lighted torches had been rammed into the soil every couple of feet on both sides of the path that led from the landing to the great outdoor ballroom. The flickering warmth was welcome, for nights in Hong Kong could be cool, and Dominie, conscious of the beauty of her new dress, had steadfastly refused the shawl that Jared was carrying for her over his arm. Music and laughter floated toward them—her feet were tapping again even as she walked—and colored lanterns could be glimpsed just ahead, vividly clashing red and orange and green and purple giving a whimsically festive air to the scene.

Jared, looking down at the excitement on her face, felt a pang of something almost like sadness. He had wanted to give her so much more tonight. There would be more later, of course, and she didn't seem to mind. But he forgot sometimes how very young she was. And how easily the young could be hurt.

Catching her arm, he held her back for a moment.

"Do you mind very much," he said, "that I will not be presenting you as my wife tonight?"

*"Mind?"* To his relief, she looked genuinely surprised. "Why should I mind?"

"Gossip travels in a small community," he reminded her. "In my heart, you're already my wife. I know that . . . and I hope you know it. But there are some who are going to say you're my mistress."

"Really? How very silly of them." She smiled, or almost smiled. Just a flicker of something on her face. "And yes, my darling, I do know I am your wife. As you are my husband, in every way that counts. Except perhaps *one*."

"I know," Jared said gruffly. "The priest." He had ridden uncomfortably in the owner's cabin all the last leg of the voyage on the *Shadow,* not even attempting to challenge his cousin's command, with his only consolation the fact that Captain Alexander Barron had the authority to marry them at sea. But Dominie, as always, had surprised him, insisting on a religious service. And because he loved her to distraction—and because he firmly believed that feminine whims should be taken into account at such times—he had agreed.

It had come as a rude shock when the only priest who happened to be in Hong Kong had flatly refused to perform the ceremony. Jared, who had been willing to put up with the incense and Latin mumbling that always made him uncomfortable, had been more than a little nonplussed to find that he, as a staunchly upright Protestant, was counted unworthy.

The man had been horrified to think of a good Catholic girl living in sin—he had had quite a few choice words to say on the subject—but he hadn't been willing to do anything to change her status.

"There'll be other priests," Dominie assured him, laughing a little as she sensed his thoughts, and tucking her hand tighter under his arm. "We could have been married by my brother, you know . . . if you hadn't been so slow to figure out what you wanted. He would have liked that. But there's always my guardian, the Bishop of Paris."

"Your . . . guardian?" Jared arched one brow, giving his face an almost devilish look in the torchlight. "He won't mind that I'm a Protestant?"

"Of course he will," Dominie said sensibly. "He'll mind terribly. But he'll like you, as Denis did . . . and he'll know you're right for me. He's really very nice," she added cryptically, following some thought of her own, "for a bishop."

She had not, Jared noticed, mentioned the proximity of Macao, which, as a Portuguese enclave, had more than its share of priests. The omission both relieved and made him uncomfortable. It would have been the easiest thing in the world to take her there—half a day's sail if the wind was right. But the entire colony would know about her ten minutes after they stepped off the boat, and there was a beautiful lady who had once meant something in his life who had the right to hear it first from his lips.

Only he could hardly go by himself without explaining why. And explaining meant telling Dominie about Meiling and the two Chinese boys he had fathered.

He didn't think it would matter. He was sure—almost sure—after seeing her with the people of Vietnam that there was no prejudice in her nature. But he was making assumptions again, and keeping secrets, which was not only wrong but also foolish. He would hate like hell to have someone blurt it out before he'd had a chance to tell her himself.

Maybe tonight, he thought, when they got home from the ball, if they weren't too tired. Or tomorrow morning, when they'd have all the time in the world to lounge on the deck and talk.

# 24

THE BALL WAS ALREADY alive with light and music and the warm tinkling sound of laughter when they arrived. People seemed to be everywhere, gathered in little clusters or pausing to greet old friends on flower-lined paths that led off in several directions. Dominie stood for a moment just looking, intrigued with how pretty everything was and how cleverly it had been arranged.

The "ballroom" was not a room at all, though oddly enough it almost looked like one. Dancers were weaving in and out of elaborate cotillions on a slightly raised wooden platform, wide planking sanded shiny smooth so no slivers would penetrate the thin soles of ladies' dancing slippers. Railings ran all around, with openings to provide access to the various paths; and tall posts, placed at intervals, supported crosspieces strung with ropes that zigzagged back and forth from one side to the other. Wild myrtle from the hillsides had been twined through them, dotted here and there with camellias or vivid red and pink azaleas to form a kind of ceiling, and clumps of colored lanterns hung down like great gaudy chandeliers. More myrtle, interspersed with wild orchids this time, swung in graceful festoons between the posts.

A number of tents, whimsically painted in various shades of blue and white, with stripes and triangles and crosses that looked almost like the flags Dominie saw flying on some of the traders' vessels, sprawled around the dance floor on three sides. In the largest, open along the front, more planking had been set up to form tables, covered with lengths of silk instead of cloths and decorated with flowers and flickering candles. The first shift of diners was already helping themselves from several buffets groaning with a surprising variety of food: smoked ham and great haunches of pork, cold chicken, pickled pigs' feet in sweet jelly, fresh and salted fish, fat pink prawns and huge bowls of sticky white rice, oranges from Macao and melons and enormous bowls of Canton bananas, and sweet honey cakes speckled with almonds.

Other tents seemed to have been set up as resting places for the ladies—no doubt with fainting couches, Dominie thought, for those unrealistic members of the fair sex who insisted on lacing their waists down to twenty-two inches!—and still others provided refuges for the gentlemen to enjoy postprandial cigars or perhaps to refill their tankards from the vast kegs of chilled beer without having to walk too far. Slender Chinese waiters, dark and unobtrusive in neat black trousers and tops, circulated among the guests carrying trays of champagne and cherry brandy and a rather violently colored punch in little glass cups for the ladies, sack and ale and considerably stronger substances for the men.

Dominie threw an amused look at the great splashes of wild myrtle and nudged Jared with her elbow. "I think they must have known I was coming," she said, pointing to the blossoms in her hair.

"If they didn't," he replied with an indulgent smile, "they'll notice soon enough."

In fact, they already seemed to be noticing. A tallish man with dark brown hair, bushy brows, and a distinguished touch of gray at the temples was detaching himself from a group of acquaintances and coming their way. Not exactly young, Dominie decided—he looked to be somewhere in his mid- to late forties—but he kept himself in good shape and was quite handsome in a debauched sort of way. A fact of which she sensed he was very much aware.

"Rawlings." Jared greeted him with restrained warmth. "I didn't think you'd miss a bash like this."

"Barron." He accepted the hand Jared offered and shook it heartily, but his eyes were on Dominie, making no effort not to notice the depth of her décolletage or the slim waist that could easily have been spanned by both his strong-looking hands. "I heard there was a new lady in your life . . . and I heard she was lovely. But 'lovely' is not a word, my dear—if an old salt may be permitted to say so—that does justice to your very delightful attributes."

Dominie felt Jared stiffen just slightly beside her. "You can put your eyes back in their sockets, Rawlings. This is Mademoiselle Dominie d'Arielle . . . and before you look at her like that again, I suggest you remind yourself that she belongs to the man who will one day own the company which employs you."

*Belongs?* Dominie was only mildly amused, and a little surprised. Rawlings raised one shaggy brow, apparently contemplating the wisdom of a bawdy retort, and she sensed that this was a good-humored game they had played over other women in the past. Fortunately Alex stepped up behind his cousin just in time to hear the last comment.

"*One* of the men who will own the company," he reminded him with an easy grin. "There are three Barron grandsons, remember? Captain Rawlings." He was extending his hand, which the other man grasped. "I saw the *Eliza Dawn* in the harbor, but I'm afraid I haven't had time to pay my respects. I had thought you'd be halfway to Manila by now."

"It's this damned war," Rawlings grumbled. A pretty black-haired girl with stunning violet eyes had appeared at his side and was clinging possessively to his arm. "The Chinese keep making treaties and breaking them—and we just shilly-shally around. We ought to take Canton once and for all and drive the little yellow bastards out."

There was a murmur of assent from several men who had gathered around to greet Jared and throw curious glances at his lady. For all of Alex's protestations, it was clear that they considered him the driving force of the mighty Barron empire, and the obvious heir when the old tyrant finally gave up the reins.

"Hear, hear," one of them was saying. "You tell 'em, Rawlings."

"Damn right I will! Two weeks late already, and I can't get as far as Whampoa to load up. Fighting all around, they say. Newcombe's giving it a try with the *Scarlet*. He's a pushy bastard, he just might make it—but I decided to hang around for a couple of days to see how the wind was blowing."

"And have yourself a good old time at the ball," someone chimed in, and was rewarded with a burst of laughter. There was an easy camaraderie as Dominie was introduced to everyone, traders for the most part, with a sprinkling of officers who strolled over to see what was going on, but she noticed a sense of tension too, as if they were all waiting for something that didn't quite happen. The black-haired girl, whose name was Camilla Crale—the niece, apparently, or ward, of someone at Russell and Company—was hanging all over Rawlings, but Dominie noticed that her fluttering eyelashes were aimed at Jared.

"We've been hearing rumors," a man the others called Dent interjected after a few minutes of bluffly jovial chit-chat.

The conversation stopped abruptly, and Jared's posture went rigid. Dominie could almost feel the vibrations emanating from him, and she knew suddenly what everyone had been waiting for. And what the conversation was going to be about.

"What kind of rumors?" Jared said with deceptive quiet.

"The wrong kind, I fear," Rawlings broke in, all the bawdiness gone from his expression now. He shook the girl off his arm and stepped closer.

"As well the gentleman knows," Dent growled in an undertone.

Rawlings ignored him. "It's being said that Barron Shipping is into opium now. Only rumors, as our friend Lancelot here made a point of mentioning, but they were circulating pretty freely a few months ago when the *China Dawn* pulled into Macao. I haven't heard much of them recently. But then, I haven't seen the *China* for a few weeks either."

"We're not afraid of the competition," Lancelot Dent was saying. "There's plenty of action for everyone. But you want a piece of the cake, you've got to help make it. You don't play holy with the Zion's Corner crowd and undermine us officially—and then jump in and grab what you can get. Let me make myself clear, Barron. You've got two choices. You're either with us or against us."

"Against," Jared said tersely. "Let me make *myself* clear. Barron Shipping has never handled opium. It does not handle opium now. And it will not handle opium in the future. Anyone caught trafficking in the drug on any of our vessels is subject to dismissal on the spot."

"*Anyone?*"

The taunt was unmistakable. Dominie turned in alarm to look at Jared. He had been extremely frustrated when they arrived in Hong Kong and had found no sign of Matthew—he'd been even more upset to learn that no one knew where the *China* was—and she was afraid he was going to let himself get backed into a corner.

"I think you know the answer to that, Dent," he said.

"Do I, now? And does that mean . . . yes?"

Once again it was Alex who stepped into the breach. "It means we've already said as much on the subject as we intend to. Barron Shipping does not deal in opium. Period. But I'm shocked, gentlemen. Where is your gallantry? Here you are, gossiping about rumors which you admit yourself haven't been substantiated, and not a one of you has offered his congratulations. . . . You did tell them, didn't you, cousin?"

You know damn well I didn't, Jared's glower seemed to say. But the barely suppressed laughter in Alex's eyes brought back his sense of humor.

"No, as it happens, I hadn't gotten around to that. I was waiting for an audience."

"Well, you have one now." Alex threw out his hand with a broad wave which took in quite a number of people, more of whom seemed to be coming over every minute. The ploy had worked. Opium and the whereabouts of young Matthew were forgotten as everyone turned toward Jared Barron with frank curiosity.

"Um, yes . . ." He looked uncomfortable just for a moment—rather, Dominie thought to her amusement, as if his collar had grown too tight. She had the feeling he was wishing now he had broken the news quietly to individuals. "I will spare you the speech, my friends, which I am sure you can all do without. And I trust you will spare me some of the biting 'wit' I can see coming my way. I was not quite forthright with my introductions before. I presented you all to Mademoiselle d'Arielle, but I failed to mention that she is the woman who has done me the honor of agreeing to become my wife."

Your . . . *wife?*

Not a person uttered the words aloud, but Dominie could see them thinking it. And so could Jared, whose collar appeared to be getting tighter and tighter every second. There was absolute silence for a moment, as if everyone were in a state of shock; then the air was filled with bursts of laughter and congratulations, and much backslapping and calling over of friends and acquaintances with great broad sweeps of the arm.

Almost too much, Dominie thought, and she sensed that her instincts had been right before. Jared's bachelor days *had* been a little wilder than he was letting on. Quite clearly his friends were surprised—and perhaps a little disbelieving—to see them coming to such an abrupt end.

She didn't know whether it was thrilling or disconcerting to have captured the most notorious womanizer in town.

A little of both, she decided.

Jared put up with the good-natured gibes for a while; he even put up with the mock sympathy that was being offered in large doses to his bride-to-be. But when the reminiscences started getting a little too explicit, he threw in the towel and called a halt.

"Enough, enough!" he protested, only half-joking. "You'll destroy my marriage before it's begun. Leave my future wife a few *small* illusions about the man she's going to spend the rest of her life with. Here, Lieutenant!" He tossed a couple of coins to a young man in an immaculate scarlet coat with a grin that was spreading from ear to ear across his homely face. "See if you can persuade the band to play a waltz. Not too tinny, if they've got it in them! I think, on an occasion like this, a gentleman has a right to a dance with his lady."

Amidst the smiles and laughter that accompanied them as Jared led her onto the dance floor, Dominie noticed one pair of very pretty cupid-bow lips fixed in a definite pout. Plainly Captain Rawlings' black-haired companion for the evening was not thrilled with the news. And she probably wasn't the only one!

"I had no idea you were leaving such a string of broken hearts behind," she said as he settled one hand lightly on her waist, the other clasped in hers while they waited for the band to begin.

"I did warn you I hadn't exactly been celibate . . . and no, I don't think there are that many broken hearts. Much as it pains my ego to admit, most of the ladies with whom

I've had my celebrated flings have moved on rather easily to the next grand romance."

"Is that why you hurried me onto the dance floor so quickly?" she said with a glint of mischief. "Because you were afraid somebody was going to start talking about one of those 'celebrated' flings?"

It was a bit too close to the truth, and Jared was grateful to hear the music begin. More than a little tinny, but the melody was pretty enough, and he whirled her gracefully out into the center of the floor. The other couples pulled aside just slightly, drawing back to watch their progress, and even without turning to look, he was aware of the curiosity and amusement and sometimes envy in their eyes.

She was as light as a feather in his arms, soft and very beautiful, and he allowed himself the pleasure of enjoying most of the dance in silence. Only as he sensed the music drawing to a close did he slow down, easing her just a little farther away so he could see her face and she could see his.

"I have had many flings, Dominie," he said. "I won't pretend I haven't. But there's only one that has ever been worth celebrating . . . and that will last me the rest of my life."

The music stopped and they stood for a second alone in the center of the floor, not even noticing that people were watching again as they stared into each other's eyes and longed for the same sweet rhythm to come back again. It seemed an idle hope—waltzes were rarely played twice in a row—but they were looking for an excuse to be close again, to hold and touch each other.

Glancing toward the stand where the musicians were riffling through their music, Dominie caught a glimpse of black curls and eyes that were shooting violet daggers in her direction.

"I don't think she likes me very much," she said with a slight tilt of her head. "Do you suppose she's jealous?"

Jared followed her gaze. "Ah . . . Camilla. She was born jealous, poor child. If there's anything she hates more than a beautiful woman, it's an exceptionally beautiful woman. You must be the bane of her existence right now."

The band was beginning again, another waltz, a little

softer this time, more romantic. Dominie might almost have thought it was a pleasant coincidence had she not seen Jared's cousin slipping away from the shadows at the side of the stand.

So . . . Alex was also anxious to keep her from being regaled with more tales of her fiancé's exploits. Just for a second, she wondered if perhaps Jared was hiding something, but she dismissed the thought as unworthy. This was the man she loved. The man who was going to be her husband. She owed him her trust.

Still, there was the girl with the fire-and-ice eyes . . .

"I thought there might be another reason she was jealous," she ventured, trying to sound teasing. "She wasn't one of your . . . uncelebrated flings, was she?"

"Cammie? Good God, no!" He was so startled he missed a step, and Dominie had to move quickly to keep her toes from being trodden on. "She's barely seventeen now . . . and it's over a year since I saw her last! That would make her about fifteen and a half. I may be a satyr, love, but I'm not a pervert—at least not that kind. I don't molest little children."

"I doubt she was *ever* a little child," Dominie said, feeling a sudden urge to be catty and not quite knowing why. "And I can't imagine at fifteen and a half you would have been the first."

He laughed easily. "Or the last. Cammie's a piranha. She eats men alive."

"Oh . . ." She arched her head back, eyebrows rising just a fraction of an inch as she gave him a playfully challenging look. "And you don't like being devoured?"

"You can have me for breakfast anytime you want, my dear," he said with an obligingly lecherous leer. "Or lunch, or dinner . . . or snacks in between. But Camilla collects men. She strings them up like little beads, just so she can have them, not because there's any feeling there." He ignored the beat of the music for a moment, slowing just slightly. "I have done many things in my life—not all of which I'm proud of—but I've never taken a woman to my bed, even for pay, for any other reason than because I liked her and I wanted to be with her."

"And did the amount you paid," she asked with a hint of something he couldn't quite identify in her voice, "have anything to do with the degree to which you liked them?"

"Only once," he replied, catching on, "and then all the gold in the world wouldn't have been enough to measure her value. She was insulted and threw it back in my face."

"Perhaps she wanted your heart instead."

"Perhaps," he said, "she has it."

He drew her scandalously close, her bosom nearly touching the patterned satin of his waistcoat, and swept her around, past the other dancers, between them, almost but not quite touching. Much *too* close, Dominie thought. People had to be talking—but as they undoubtedly knew she and Jared were living together on the junk, they were probably talking anyway, so it didn't seem worth worrying about. Besides, the music was so compelling, the rhythm seemed to pull her out of herself, carrying her like a leaf on the wind, and it was just such heaven to float in his arms.

It wasn't until the band had stopped again and Jared was leading her back toward a shadowy spot beside one of the paths that Dominie recalled how adroitly he had maneuvered the conversation away from Camilla Crale, and it occurred to her that the girl had almost certainly thrown herself at him. And perhaps come a bit closer than he cared to admit.

There was so much she didn't know, so much she supposed she would never know, and just for a moment, until she brushed it aside, she realized that the thought of his past made her somehow uneasy.

A little glass cup appeared suddenly in her hands—she hadn't even noticed Jared taking it from one of the trays—and she looked down to see an almost savagely orange liquid coming halfway to the brim. On the assumption that things aren't always as bad as they appear, and that everything ought to be tasted at least once, she took a tentative sip.

Jared laughed at the grimace that came almost immediately to her face. "I keep forgetting about the famous French palate." He was signaling for the waiter, who had moved a few feet away. "The champagne will probably be cloying—it's not usually the finest on these occasions—but if you can tolerate a touch of sweetness, there's an excellent Madeira.''

He was just selecting a glass when his expression changed. He did not stop what he was doing. He continued to raise the glass and held it out in one fluid movement, but his eyes were fixed on something over her shoulder.

Tightening her fingers around the stem, Dominie turned. There were perhaps a dozen people near the end of the dance floor where the torchlit path from the waterfront came in, but she spotted him instantly.

She would have known him anywhere, she thought, even without Jared's reaction to cue her.

He was not a particularly tall man, or powerfully built. Just under six feet, Dominie estimated, and slender, but there was an inherent grace in the way he was standing, and his body gave the impression of being hard and sinewy. Fair hair, almost silver in the colored light, was echoed in a neatly clipped mustache and small trim beard. Even from that distance she could see that his eyes were an incredibly piercing blue.

He was not dressed for evening. His shirt was loose and white, almost defiantly casual, with elegant flowing sleeves and an open neck, his trousers tight and superbly tailored to show off a pair of extremely well-shaped legs. But it was not the inappropriateness of his garb that caught and held her gaze. It was the strong, angular Barron nose, the high Barron cheekbones, the wide, arrogant Barron brow. And she would have been willing to bet that underneath that beard was a stubborn Barron jaw.

So Matthew had turned up. It struck Dominie as disturbingly peculiar somehow that not even the latecomers had made any mention of the *China Dawn* pulling into the harbor.

She watched as the younger Barron spotted his brother and very slowly, with the faintest, almost imperceptible movement of his head, gave a slight nod. She did not know what she had expected. Anger perhaps, rebellion— something to match the tension she could feel building up in Jared beside her. Certainly not the broad grin that spread across his features: challenging, insouciant, a little reckless, but also brimming over with genuine affection.

He did a little dance step, bobbing up and down as he worked his way through the intricately patterned cotillions, oddly comical and very reliably calculated to ease the atmosphere.

*Matt was always the charmer of the family.* Jared's words, coming back with vivid clarity. *Such a damned funny little fellow, with a droll sense of the ridiculous.* He had also said that Matt could always make him laugh, and she hoped suddenly it was true. For absolutely no reason she could account for, she found herself liking this youngest member of the Barron clan, and she wanted things to be all right between him and his brother.

He was laughing as he approached them.

"Now, how did I know I was going to find you here? Or more to the point, how did I know you'd be coming to this part of the world?" He stuck out his hand—it seemed a strange way for brothers to greet—but Dominie noticed that Jared took it with no apparent reluctance. "Actually I expected you much sooner. What kept you so long?"

"I was delayed," Jared replied dryly. Dominie noticed that he was watching the younger man intently, but there was no hint of the violent flare of temper she had expected. For the first time, she saw that Matthew had brought a Chinese servant with him, a rather tall young woman in a bulky black jacket, with loose black pants rolled halfway up to her knees and a conical straw hat completely covering her hair. Hakka apparently, for her large, bare, very dirty feet showed no evidence of having been bound.

Matthew seemed to remember her at the same moment, for he put a hand on her arm, a strangely familiar gesture, and drew her forward. "This is Chin-Chin," he said, with something in his voice that sent a little shiver of apprehension down Dominie's spine.

"Werry plenty happy meet big brother," the girl piped up in the singsong pidgin that was already becoming cloyingly familiar after two weeks in Hong Kong. "This piece cow-chillo hear plenty good-good big brother. Wantshee meet long time." She squatted on the ground directly in front of him and beamed up with a distinctly unservile expression on her soot-covered face.

Dominie was very much aware that all conversation in the vicinity had stopped. Even the nearest cotillion had come to a premature end, and people were inching closer. Alex had slipped up beside them, protective of Matthew, she sensed. But when she threw a nervous glance in his direction, he appeared more curious than wary.

Jared, too, seemed curious as he looked down at the girl. No, more than curious—amused.

"Werry plenty glad-glad meet cow-chillo too," he was saying. The right words—but there was no attempt at the lilting tone she had heard him use so often with the servants. It was almost as if he and Matthew were playing a game. Baiting each other somehow through the girl.

Dominie was conscious suddenly of feeling terribly left out. It was as if this man, who had been so proud of her all evening, had completely forgotten her the instant his brother appeared.

"Jared . . ." she said hesitantly.

He turned distractedly, as if he were still just vaguely recalling her existence. "I'm sorry, my dear. This, of course, is my brother, Matthew. And, uh . . . Chin-Chin. This is Mademoiselle Dominie d'Arielle."

"Mademoiselle?" Matthew Barron's smile was infectious and just slightly impudent as he responded to the introduction. "That means 'miss,' if I recall my French correctly . . . and I don't see a ring on your finger, so I assume it would be premature to welcome you to the family—now. But I trust it won't be long."

"Now, how the devil did you know that?" Jared burst out, startled.

"Easy. I know *you*, big brother. I knew the instant I saw the lady—even before you got around to acknowledging her—that this was it for you. And about time, I might add." He took a long, slow pause, then continued, so quietly that all the eavesdroppers around the fringes had to strain to hear: "And you know me, though you won't let yourself trust your instincts. I am impulsive, I am foolish, I can be a downright ass at times, but I am not a complete son of a bitch. I did pick up a shipload of opium in Calcutta, as you have no doubt heard, and I did think I was going to make my fortune selling it in

China. But I have long since changed my mind. I destroyed some of it, as much as I could. And when I get my hands on the rest, I'll destroy that too.''

He smiled again suddenly, a boyish, entrancing smile that lit up his whole face.

"So you see," he said, "I have learned my lesson . . . even without my big brother to spank some sense into me.''

Dominie could tell that Jared wanted to smile back—his mouth at least was trying—but he was not quite ready. She understood suddenly what it had meant, that slight nod Matthew had given before, and why there had been no burst of temper as he approached.

He had been telling his brother that everything was all right, and Jared had been saying in response that he wanted to believe. There was, after all, a bond between these brothers that she and even Alex, who had moved closer to lay a reassuring hand on her arm, had not sensed.

"You give me your word," Jared said at last, "that there is no opium on any of the Barron vessels?"

"Of course not! That's a preposterous question. There is undoubtedly opium somewhere, in *somebody's* possession, on at least seven Barron ships! But I can give you my word that there is none in my possession. I do not stand to make a profit from the sale of any drug. Now or ever.''

"Little brother plenty good man," Chin-Chin said softly. She had risen sometime when no one had been paying attention and was now looking Jared directly in the eye. "Plenty stupid sometimes. Brain like miserable good-for-nothing turtle, but heart first-chop. Werry plenty good-good man.''

"And this werry plenty good-good woman," Matthew said, like Jared, using the words but not the inflection. "No, better than good," he added. "She is the best." He put an arm around her waist, very obviously, very pointedly, and Dominie realized with a jolt what it was that had made her so apprehensive before.

This was not some saucy servant girl who had traipsed after him into a fancy ball. This was his mistress!

She did not even dare look at Jared. Her eyes were still on Matthew, but she knew how the one of the three Barron grandsons who cared most for the family "reputation" had to be taking it.

He might have turned a blind eye to a back-alley affair. She supposed he would; men had a tendency to be like that. He might even have accepted an open liaison with some silken-pretty creature in a perfumed love nest somewhere. She had heard that sort of thing was common in the Orient. But to take up with a barefoot peasant? And flaunt her in front of everyone?

She watched, sick with dread, as Matthew drew the girl in front of him, his hands possessively on her shoulders. With the hat, she was only an inch or two shorter than he, and he had to crane his neck to look around her.

"Brother Jared," he said, "I'd like you to meet your new sister-in-law."

# 25

EVERY EYE TURNED, not toward the man who had just spoken, but toward his brother, and Dominie knew that they all had to be thinking exactly what she was. If she'd been worried before that Jared would be furious at Matthew for taking up with a Hakka peasant, how was he going to react to the announcement that the youngest Barron had actually *married* her?

She waited apprehensively for the dark rage she was sure would flare out at any moment. But Jared only looked the girl over, up and down, very thoroughly, then threw back his head—and laughed!

"By God, Matt, you were always one for surprises. She looks like she'll wash up quite nicely. I congratulate you, brother. You seem to have beaten me to the altar."

Matthew was grinning easily. "I've been waiting for years to do something better than you. Though," he added with apologies to Dominie, "perhaps 'better' is not the word. Equal, but first—for a change." He had a natural, very charming smile that took in his whole face. "Being seven years younger, I've always had to watch my brother do everything first. And do it so well I never measure up. It can be a strain."

Is he joking? Dominie wondered. Pulling some prank that his brother had caught onto? He had to be, though he didn't look like it. Nor did Jared, she had to admit.

Then she looked at the girl, whose eyes were positively glowing with love and pride as she gazed at Matthew, and she knew suddenly that this was no joke.

They really *were* married. She must have given a little start, for Alex's hand tightened reassuringly on her arm. She glanced up, a little surprised not to see concern written across his handsome features. If anything, he looked almost amused.

And, in fact, Jared seemed to be accepting things with amazing good grace. There was more than formal courtesy in his smile as he turned to the girl; there was kindness and what appeared to be genuine warmth.

"Now it is I who must welcome my brother's wife to our family," he was saying. "I'm not sure congratulations are in order—we're a most difficult family to put up with. But I expect you'll learn that as you go along, uh . . . Chin-Chin?"

The question mark seemed to hang in the air, and Dominie could have sworn she saw laughter in the girl's dark brown eyes. "Wat for big brother no like 'Chin-Chin'? Werry plenty good name Chinee cow-chillo, heya?"

"Plenty good," Jared agreed. "For a Chinee cow-chillo. But I think it might be easier all around if I had your real name. . . . And I am most curious to know what color hair is hiding under that enormous hat. I'm betting on red. Barron men have always had a weakness for women with red hair."

The girl tilted her head to one side, as if trying to make out what he was saying. Then, with a little laugh, she gave up.

"That's very unfair, Captain Barron," she replied in flawless English, her accent distinctly American. "Jared, if I may. And most unkind. I thought I was going to have at least a little fun with you. What gave me away?"

"Two things." Jared's laughter was echoed in chuckles that seemed to come from all around as everyone picked up on what was happening and began to enjoy the situation. "In the first place, as my brother said, I *do* know him. He has always had an eye for lovely ladies. He's been looking them over quite expertly since he was twelve—"

"Eleven," Matthew cut in indignantly.

"Eleven. And his taste has grown ever more discriminating. I knew that the lady he finally picked would be the loveliest of all."

"And you didn't think he was capable of finding a yellow-skinned woman lovely?" There was just a hint of defiance in the way the girl tipped up her chin.

"Quite the contrary. I wouldn't have been the least surprised if he'd shown up with a Chinese beauty—and I would have approved. But I did say there were *two* things." He touched the middle finger of his right hand just lightly to his lashes. "Next time, you might want to take a little more care with that stuff around your eyes. It's smudging—quite charmingly—and there's something lighter showing through. Yes, definitely red, I'd say."

She was laughing. "I confess. You've caught me out. My real name is Rachel Todd." Then, catching a faint cluck of disapproval from her new husband, she corrected herself: "Rachel Barron now, of course. My parents run the American Protestant Mission outside the Macao Gate. And actually, my hair is more blond, though it has a definite reddish cast. Strawberry blond, you might say."

"I'm glad to hear it. You can't have too many redheads in the family. Especially pretty ones whose parents do good works. I've met your father, incidentally. Several times. He's a fine man. One of the few in his profession I respect." He was drawing Dominie to his side as he spoke. "My fiancée's brother is another."

"Your brother is a missionary?" Rachel turned to Dominie.

"In Vietnam. Cochin China, some people call it." Dominie was conscious of feeling a little left out again, and somehow awkward. There was so much rivalry between the Catholics and Protestants, especially among men of the cloth who ought to know better, and she hastened to put things straight. "My brother was—is—a Jesuit."

Rachel nodded knowingly. "We've had many of them pass through over the years. Ours is primarily a medical mission. I've always admired the Jesuits greatly. They are men of dedication and self-sacrifice. You must be very proud of him."

"I am," Dominie said, and knew that from that moment on she was going to love this new sister of hers.

"Rae . . . ?"

Matthew barely raised his voice, but his wife turned immediately, grinning as she caught sight of his expression.

"You're right," she said. "And very foolish of me not to remember." She was looking back at Jared and Dominie. "I'm afraid we're not exactly attired for a fancy ball. We came in such a hurry, the minute we got into the harbor and heard the music. Matt was sure he'd find you here . . . but now he's getting embarrassed because he thinks he doesn't look as stylish as he rest of you.''

"I don't *think,*'' Matthew said. "I know. And as darling as you look in trousers, my love, I suspect you'd be more comfortable on the dance floor in something just a bit more graceful.''

"If we get to dance,'' Rachel said with a strange look, then shrugged off what seemed to have been a dark moment. "Never mind—I have a dress in my luggage that ought to do. It's not very elegant for evening wear, but I suppose everyone will forgive me. I packed rather hastily. . . . Matthew, of course, never travels without a tailcoat and silk cravat. I think if we went to the jungles of deepest Africa, he'd tote along a full case of formal wear.''

"You never know when a good party will come up,'' her husband protested.

"That's true, dear heart—you never do.'' Her face turned serious as she looked back at Jared, drawing him just a little aside, so no one but their immediate group would hear. "You know my father, so you must know that no daughter of his would ever lie. Nor would she marry any man, no matter how she loved him, who would have anything to do with drugs. There is no more opium.''

"I'm not worried about your father's daughter,'' Jared said a little stiffly, "but my father's son.'' His eyes were on his brother, hard and questioning. "Matt?''

Matthew hesitated just for a split second. There's something more, Dominie thought with a sudden skip of her heart. Something he hasn't said yet—and he's afraid for Jared to hear.

She could feel Jared thinking it too, but he didn't press, waiting instead with remarkable patience for his brother to reply.

"There is no more opium,'' he said at last. "I've made a couple of mistakes here and there—we've still got a few little matters to discuss—but I can swear to that at least. There is no more opium, and there never will be again. Now, unless you want to be humiliated by a brother who looks like a beggar, I suggest you give us an hour or so to put on some fancier duds. You're looking like a fashion plate yourself.''

''We Barron men have a reputation to uphold—don't we, Alex?'' Jared's voice was cautious, but apparently he had decided to hold back. ''What do you say? Should we let them go get changed?''

''If we don't,'' his cousin reminded him, ''we'll never see how much red is under that hat. Being a Barron man myself, I'm waiting with great anticipation.''

It took about forty-five minutes for the party to get back to normal. Two Barron bachelors surrendering to Cupid in one evening—the first announcing his engagement, the other actually showing up with a wife!—was enough to compete with the band and even the bars that had been set up in some of the tents for the gentlemen. And the third bachelor, Alex, was in for a considerable amount of good-natured ribbing, being the one Barron left unstung by Cupid's arrow.

''Someone has to maintain sanity in the family,'' he protested with a grin as champagne was passed and belated toasts made over and over to the brides and grooms, one pair of which was no longer present, though that didn't make much difference to the celebrants. ''Besides, we seem to be doing this in reverse order. Matthew is the youngest and he went first, then Jared. I, as eldest, naturally have had the sense to hold out longest.''

Laughing, he evaded further jokes by asking Dominie with a courtly, rather old-fashioned bow and a distinctly new-fashioned twinkle in his eye if she would do him the honor of being his partner in the next dance. As Jared had been drawn into conversation with some of the other traders, she was only too happy to accept. She wasn't feeling quite comfortable with the others yet. And a little nagging voice in the back of her mind kept reminding her of that slight hesitation in Matthew's manner before . . . and her sense that something unpleasant was still to come.

Alex was as good a dancer as his cousin, and ordinarily Dominie would have loved to match step for skillful step with him, but tonight her heart wasn't in it. Everything was turning out so differently from what she had expected. It was almost as if Jared were not the same man she had fallen in love with. Ever since his brother showed up, his manner toward her had completely changed.

No, even before that, she thought uncomfortably. There had been something oddly strained in the way he had introduced her to his friends. Not that he had seemed ashamed of her exactly, but he had been in an awful hurry to get her away from them. As if somehow he felt awkward bringing the two parts of his life together.

"You're looking very solemn," Alex said as he maneuvered her gracefully between two pairs of dancers into a slightly more open space on the floor.

"I was just thinking," she said. "It's so easy to fall in love . . . and so hard to get to know someone. There's so much about Jared I'm only beginning to learn."

"And much about you," Alex reminded her gently, "that he has yet to learn. Love takes time, Dominie. It doesn't just happen. It has to grow and be nurtured. Tropical islands are easy—the real world is a little harder."

He was right, Dominie thought as the dance ended and they wandered over toward the dining tent. The real world was harder . . . and there *were* many things Jared still didn't know about her. She hadn't even told him, really, about Honoré—the man she was supposed to marry—but somehow that was different. Honoré wasn't important anymore. She hadn't talked about him because he didn't matter; and she sensed again, more troubling this time, that there was something Jared was holding back. A part of himself he was not willing to share and perhaps never would be.

The musicians had just paused for another break, and the dining tent was crowded when they reached it. The band had been borrowed from the army, a splendid-looking group in shiny-buttoned crimson coats, but without much soldierly stamina, Dominie thought, for they seemed to be stopping more often than playing. The air was stuffy, the noise almost deafening, and they changed their minds and sauntered back to the edge of the dance floor. Jared had drifted off somewhere with his friends, and Alex stayed close by her side, seeming to appoint himself as her temporary protector.

"You're looking solemn again," he said. They were

standing by the railing that ran around the slightly raised platform.

"I'm not feeling solemn . . . at least I don't think so. 'Bewildered' would be more like it."

"That's not surprising," Alex said, and wished again, as he had several times that evening, that his cousin had found a more appropriate way to introduce his future wife to the community. He should have let her meet people slowly, a few here, a few there, choosing the ones who liked him most and would be kindest to his bride. There was too much rivalry between the traders of the Orient, friendly enough most of the time—but it was a rare man who would pass up an opportunity to score points against one of the others if the occasion arose. "I'm afraid we're rather a raucous crowd. It must be confusing to be plunked down in the middle of us."

"Mademoiselle Dominie . . ."

Camilla Crale had slipped up from behind while they weren't looking. Alex, who had been leaning against the rail, sat back on it, stretching his long legs out in front of him.

"Why, Cammie," he drawled dryly, "what a surprise."

She ignored him. "I was just *thrilled* to hear about your engagement, Dominie," she purred in a tone that made no effort to disguise just how "thrilled" she really was. "I may call you Dominie, mayn't I? We're all so close here. I just had to come over and get to know you a little better. Tell me, is this your first engagement?"

"As a matter of fact," Dominie replied, knowing full well there was only one reason the girl had really come, and that was to try to twist the knife, "it isn't. I was engaged once before. In Paris."

The violet eyes seemed to enjoy the admission. "Really? Isn't that too interesting! I do think women tend to be more experienced in these things, don't you? Though men, poor souls, can't bring themselves to admit it. This is Jared's *first* engagement." There was just subtle emphasis on the word, which Dominie did not fail to catch.

"And his last," she said quietly.

The girl laughed, a surprisingly light, very natural sound that reminded Dominie a little disconcertingly of how pretty she was. "What an optimist . . . and so deliciously naive. Here I thought Frenchwomen were *born* jaded and knowing. The 'last' engagement comes just before the marriage. And, of course, if Jared were really planning on marrying you, he would have done so already. You *are* living without benefit of clergy on some old junk, aren't you? Or is that just a nasty rumor?''

Alex stood up, ready to intervene. Even for Camilla, this was going too far. The little cat could be amusing sometimes, but her claws were sharp. Then he got a look at Dominie, cool and very dignified, and decided she could handle it by herself.

"It's not some old junk," she was saying. "It's really quite luxurious. And the only clergy whose benefits I'm interested in are those of my own faith. Jared understands that I want to be married by a priest. He has been kind enough to respect that."

"Oh?" The beautiful eyes opened wide. "But aren't there lots of priests in Macao? I thought the place was just *crawling* with them. And it's only a few hours away."

Dominie winced inwardly—the one taunt she couldn't answer truthfully—but she wasn't going to give the girl the satisfaction of letting her see it. "There are priests all over the world," she said as sweetly as she could manage. "The problem is finding the right one. I don't want just any priest officiating at my wedding. As a matter of fact, we were thinking of being married by my guardian." She took a brief pause, just enough to alert Camilla that something was coming. It was very petty, name-dropping, and very childish, but it was also very satisfying. "My guardian happens to be the Bishop of Paris."

"The *Bishop*? Of *Paris*?" Pretty pink lips tightened with a little twinge of pique, then suddenly, unexpectedly, they were laughing again, warm and surprisingly good-humored, and she almost looked friendly. "Score one for the pretty fiancée," she said softly. "Ah, there you are, darling . . . where have you been? We were just talking about engagements, and Mademoiselle Dominie has put me down, quite cuttingly. But I'll find a way to get back at her."

"Camilla knows all about engagements." Captain Rawlings stepped over to her side, giving her arm a squeeze as she tucked it under his. "How many times have you been engaged now? Four? Five?"

"Three . . . but it feels like *eight!* It's all so tedious. My uncle keeps trying to arrange these things for me," she explained to Dominie. "And I keep trying to disarrange them. The first two weren't so bad. I just had to be spiteful enough, and they decided after all they didn't want to spend the rest of their lives with me. But this last one was a dreadful old man. Really, he must have been *sixty!* All he wanted was someone young and pretty—disposition didn't matter in the least. *Nothing* discouraged him!" She gave a delicate shudder. "I was terrified I was going to be forced to the altar."

"But surely your uncle couldn't actually force you to marry the man," Dominie said. "He might make things very unpleasant, of course, but all you'd have to do is put your foot down." A talent which she suspected young Camilla had developed to perfection.

The girl shrugged carelessly. "Unfortunately, he can. As I'm not twenty-one yet, and as he's my legal guardian, he can force me to do anything he wants. I have absolutely no rights, even when it comes to getting married . . . which is very tiresome. I don't know about priests, naturally—they may have some qualms—but there are plenty of ministers and a sea captain or two who wouldn't hesitate to perform the nasty little ritual on his authority."

"I must have been away when all this happened," Rawlings said, amused. "How *did* you get out of it?"

"Oh, that was easy. I just reminded him that if he married me on Friday, he would be a cuckold on Saturday. And I think he knew me well enough to know I wouldn't be discreet about it. Old men do hate being made to look like fools, especially when it comes to romance. Their egos are so fragile."

Old men—like Honoré?

Dominie was startled by the thought, and she turned away, staring down the torchlit path toward the harbor, where dots of ships' lights glittered like golden stars on the water. He had loved her, Denis said—and his ego must have been desperately wounded when she left him. This was the second time that night he had come into her mind, and she found herself wishing fervently that she could be more like Camilla Crale and just brush him off, as if his feelings didn't matter.

The conversation drifted into other channels, man-talk for the most part, about the hostilities that continued to drag on with the Chinese and the controversy that raged over the barren, uninhabited, fever-infested rock the British had claimed as their prize of war. Rawlings clearly considered the acquisition of Hong Kong a mistake. They should have held out for a chunk of the mainland, he said. Camilla hung on Rawlings' arm, looking bored while Alex argued that a superb natural harbor and the lack of potentially hostile population more than made up for any other failings. And Dominie was left to follow her own thoughts, which were growing more and more disturbing.

*If Jared really wanted marry you,* Camilla had said, or words to that effect, *he would just have taken you to Macao. There are lots of priests in Macao.*

And of course, there were. It would have been the simplest matter in the world. Dominie had wondered about it herself once or twice, but she hadn't wanted to dwell on it. Hadn't wanted to consider the very unpleasant possibilities.

*Was* he having second thoughts about getting married? She felt cold suddenly—there were goose bumps on her bare arms—and she looked around, trying to locate Jared, needing to be reassured. Or if he wasn't having second thoughts exactly, was he finding excuses to put off giving up his precious male freedom? And if he put it off long enough . . .

She forced herself to turn back to the men, concentrating on their conversation. They were talking about the *Scarlet Dawn* now, and a Captain Newcombe, who had gone up to someplace called Whampoa on the Pearl River.

"Damned fool insisted on pushing through before the fighting was even over," Rawlings was saying, with broad gestures that threatened to throw Camilla off his arm. "Said he wanted to get loaded up and aimed at the Sandwich Islands—Hawaii, they're calling them now—while the weather held. Hell, the weather'll hold till June! I think he just wants to be rid of the Frenchman."

He caught Dominie's quizzical look and grinned.

"Pardon my language, ma'am. One of your country-men, an old dandy from Paris, caught the *Aurora Dawn* to Boston and transferred to the *Scarlet* with about ten minutes to spare. Seems he thought he'd get to the Orient faster that direction. He's heading for Calcutta or Singapore, someplace like that, chasing after a girl—and at his age, too!" He winked broadly. "Must be right up there with Camilla's last suitor. An intolerable prig—he's used to better things—but with no hotel in town, he's been staying on board till he can find an East Indiaman going his way."

A Frenchman? From Paris? Dominie must have shivered, for Alex was offering to fetch her shawl and she was refusing. It was wildly improbable, what she was imagining. Just because the man was chasing some girl to the East didn't mean it was Honoré Ravaud. Men chased women all the time. He'd popped into her head only because she'd been thinking about him before.

"I wonder if I know him," she said, trying to keep her voice casual. "The Frenchman. What does he look like? Do you remember his name?"

"Kind of tired-looking. Sort of gray, if you know what I mean, though he was probably a dapper devil once. Looks ill, as if maybe his health was broken by the voyage. And, no, I don't think I caught his name, though I don't suppose it's likely you'd know him anyway. Paris is a big city."

"No, I don't suppose I would," Dominie agreed, and tried to smile attentively as they went on with their discussion.

In fact it was extremely unlikely that this man was her former fiancé, but she found herself wishing all the same that she had taken him just a little more seriously. She began to scan the paths again, searching for Jared. Fortunately, she still had plenty of time. Even if, by the most awful chance, the Frenchman turned out to be Honoré, he was still off with Newcombe and the *Scarlet* at Whampoa, wherever that was. Surely he couldn't be back for days.

She had just spotted Jared, almost directly opposite, on the other side of the dance floor, engrossed in what seemed an intensely earnest conversation with several other traders, when she heard Rawlings stop abruptly in

mid-sentence and begin to chuckle. Alex was rising,
brows arching up—just like Jared's did sometimes—and
Dominie glanced around to see what they were looking
at.

Rachel Barron had indeed washed up very nicely.

She was standing just under one of the lanterns, which
spilled pale yellow light down on creamy skin and a simple white cotton dress. It was not, as she had said, an
elegant gown, or even fashionable, but it was pretty and
it became her fragile softness. The high waist and slightly
flaring skirt, which barely brushed her insteps, the loose-
fitting round-necked bodice, and the little puffed sleeves
emphasized an almost childlike slenderness, making her
look as ethereal as a Christmas angel.

She was not beautiful, but it took Dominie a moment
to realize it. Her hair, halfway between the blond she
had claimed and the red that reputedly fascinated the
Barron men, had been cropped quite short and brushed
into loose curls, cascading in a burst of color just to the
curve of her shoulders. Enormous brown eyes peered out
of a heart-shaped face, more piquant than pretty, and her
nose was a little too slim for the fashion of the day, her
mouth too small, but well-proportioned.

Then she was smiling, suddenly, radiantly, and it didn't
matter if she was beautiful or not. She was captivating,
and utterly feminine, and Dominie sensed that not a man
there was unaware of her charm.

Or a woman either, she thought, amused. If she herself
had not already decided that she liked this devastatingly
enchanting creature, she would probably be feeling more
than just the slightest twinge of jealousy right now.

It was a moment before she even noticed Matthew lingering a little to one side, looking very dashing in immaculate evening dress and obviously enjoying the
sensation his wife was creating. Then his face changed,
tightening just slightly, and Dominie saw that Jared had
noticed too, and was approaching to greet them.

She made a move to go over, but Alex put a hand on
her arm, holding her back.

"He needs some time with his brother," Alex said
quietly. "There are things they still have to talk about."

Dominie felt her heart stop just for a second, and she

remembered again the uneasy feeling that had come over her before.

"I understand . . . but I want to be there, Alex."

"You'd only be in the way," he said rather more curtly than usual. "The friction between those two goes way back, and they need to thrash it out. By themselves. It will be better—for everyone concerned—if you stay here."

"But *she* seems to be going," Dominie protested. "Rachel." Jared was gesturing toward one of the smaller tents, and Matthew, nodding, had placed a hand on her slender waist and was guiding her in that direction.

"She's his wife, Dominie," Alex reminded her gently. "It's appropriate that she be there. She *should* be there. For him."

Appropriate? Dominie bit her lip to hold back the sudden tears that stung her eyes. Rachel was his wife. It was appropriate for Rachel to be there. But *she* was just the woman who was living on "some old junk" with Jared, so all she could so was stand around on the sidelines and wait.

she tried to pretend it didn't matter as Alex left her in Captain Rawlings' care and head off to join the others in the tent. To protect Matthew again, she sensed, not to support Jared, and the nagging uneasiness grew more persistent.

A waiter passed with a tray of refreshments, and Rawlings selected two cups of the bilious orange punch, handing one to her, the other to Camilla. Dominie accepted without comment, not because she wanted it but because she was afraid her voice would break if she tried to refuse, and because her hands were trembling and she needed something to hold on to.

It was silly. She was being childish, and she knew it. Jared had come all the way to the Orient to come to terms with his brother, as she had done in a way with her own brother. He had given her all the time and support she needed. She had to give him time too. Alone, if that was the way it had to be.

But, oh, it hurt that he didn't *want* her there.

She looked up from the punch to find Camilla Crale's unpleasantly shrewd violet eyes fixed on her face. The Cupid's-bow mouth was twisting quite smugly, and Dominie was reminded suddenly of the girl's vow to get back at her.

"Quite a transformation, isn't it?" she was saying in a sly amused tone. "The new Mrs. Barron. Much better than that dreadful Chinee cow-chillo, don't you think?"

"Cow-chillo?" Dominie said automatically.

"Person of the female persuasion, for those of us who wallow in pidgin now and then. She really *is* quite lovely. I don't wonder Jared was so ready to welcome her to the family if he guessed she was going to look like that . . . and of course, being Caucasian is a definite plus. Though he did say he'd have approved, didn't he, even if she were Chinese? But then, Jared's hardly in a position to say much of anything else, now, is he?"

Dominie set her cup on the edge of the dance floor, beneath the railing where it wouldn't get kicked over. Suddenly she felt very tired, and not up to playing games.

"What are you getting at, Camilla?"

"Oh . . . I was just thinking of Jared's fondness for Chinese, uh . . . *ladies*." She was having fun now, watching Dominie, anticipating her reaction. Rawlings had moved closer, looking a little uncomfortable, but she ignored his obvious attempts to divert her. "He was with his mistress for so many years. The beautiful Mei-ling was becoming quite famous. Or should I say infamous? Everyone was terrified he was going to marry her—which simply isn't *done*. I do think it's wonderful of you to be so . . . understanding about it."

Dominie was beginning to wish she hadn't put down her cup. Her hands were trying to tremble again, and she was struggling not to let them.

"I thought such arrangements were common in this part of the world," she said, surprised at how cool her voice sounded. If Camilla was trying to find out how much Jared had told her, she was going to be very disappointed. "Surely some of your lovers have also had Chinese mistresses. Or are you going to tell me you're really an innocent little lamb and you've never taken a man to bed in your life."

She heard Rawlings chuckle softly. "Score two for the pretty fiancée?"

"Of course I'm not," Camilla replied, unruffled. "How dull. . . . And we'll make it one and a half." She flashed a smile at Rawlings that looked almost real. "But of course in Jared's case the affair was so much more . . . intense. And he does still seem very attached to his boys. He takes quite good care of them, I've heard." She turned wide, absolutely guileless eyes on Dominie's face. "You did know, didn't you, that Jared has two half-caste sons?"

Dominie felt suddenly as if the world were falling apart. Sons? Jared had two sons—and he'd never even mentioned them to her? She took a deep breath, trying desperately to steady herself.

"Naturally Jared sees to their care," she replied with as much dignity as she could muster. She could not bear to let this hateful little cat see how deeply she had been wounded. "Surely you would expect no less of him. He is a decent man—nor would I love him so much if he weren't. Now, if you'll excuse me, it's been a long evening. I'd like to freshen up." She started toward one of the tents that had been set up for the ladies, then glanced back over her shoulder. "And that, I think," she said quietly, "*is* two for the pretty fiancée."

She was shaking badly when she finally found an empty table behind one of the screens in the tent and sank down to stare at herself in the mirror that had been propped up on top of it. I look awful, she thought. Even the flattering light of a pale pink lantern couldn't disguise how drawn and ill she seemed, and for the first time in her life she didn't even care.

He hadn't told her he had sons. There had been many other omissions, heaven knows, but none like that! She could understand why he hadn't wanted to tell her about his rakish reputation. Or even about the many other women he had been involved with. That was hardly the sort of topic one brought up casually at the breakfast table.

But not to tell her about his *sons!* That was shutting her out of a huge part of his life.

Her head dropped down onto her hands, and she was suddenly so weary she couldn't even cry. What had she expected? She *belonged* to him. The word came back, bitter and brutal, as sharp as a knife stab in her heart. She belonged to him, like a piece of property he owned and managed and did with as he chose. He adored being with her, he loved having her in his bed, he was perfectly ready to pamper her when it was convenient . . . but stay out of the way when something important came up!

When it was time to deal with his brother—when they were going to fight out whatever dark things still lay between them—he didn't want her around. Rachel was there. Matthew didn't push *her* away. But Jared had completely forgotten the woman he was supposed to want to marry!

Sick at heart, she sat for a long time alone behind the cheap flower-painted screen, trying to sort through the events. But the longer she thought about it, the worse it seemed. It was not just that Jared had failed to mention the boys: he had failed to mention their mother, who must have had a significant place in his life, and for a long time. She had a name, Mei-ling—which apparently everyone knew. He couldn't have married her, of course. It simply wasn't ''done.'' But had he wanted to?

He had said once that he'd never *told* any other woman he loved her. But that was not quite the same thing as saying he had never loved. Had this woman meant more to him than he cared to admit?

Did she mean more still?

There was a commotion at the far end of the dance floor when Dominie finally pulled herself together enough to go back. The band had stopped playing—a break again? she wondered—and everyone was craning his neck to see what was going on.

She was just in time to catch a last glimpse of Jared striding onto the torchlit path that angled down to the harbor. Matthew was beside him, his face visibly crimson above the neatly trimmed lines of his beard. She could not hear what they were saying, but the sound of their voices carried, and she knew they were raised in anger.

It was a minute before she saw Alex standing in the center of the platform, looking around anxiously. He spotted her at almost the same time and came hurrying over.

''We have to be leaving, Dominie. I'm sorry.'' He had taken her arm and was already leading her toward the sputtering line of torches. She saw that he had retrieved her shawl and had it flung carelessly over one shoulder. "This is what I've been worried about, though I hoped I was wrong. . . . But I couldn't think of any other reason for the *China*'s not being in the harbor. Matthew has lost her, I'm afraid."

"Lost her? The *China Dawn?*" She stopped for an instant, forcing him to break stride. "But she's a huge ship, the biggest of the line, Jared said. How could anyone *lose* something like that?"

"He left her where he shouldn't have," Alex replied grimly, urging her forward again, "and she was taken. Pirated by a man he had no business trusting. But that's a long story, and I don't have all the details myself. Jared's convinced he can get her back—"

"You mean that's where he was going in such a hurry? To wherever he thinks the ship is now?"

"With a quick stop at the *Shadow* to pick up the things we'll be needing." He was gripping her arm, forcing her to walk faster. "I wish he wouldn't take this on himself. I'd like Matt to have a chance to undo the mess he's made—he's got a good plan—but I can't argue this time. The *China Dawn* is Barron's finest. The flagship of the line. I don't blame Jared for not wanting to leave her rescue to a young man whose judgment so far has been none too sound."

The flagship of the line? Dominie felt a stab of helpless frustration. These Barron men were so wrapped up in their arrogant pretensions. As if the whole world revolved around them. Even Alex. It was only a boat, after all!

"So he has to go himself? And he has to go *now?* Without talking it over with me? Without . . ." Her voice quivered as she realized the full implication of what was happening. "Without even saying good-bye?"

"I'm sorry, Dominie. We tried to find you, but you weren't around. There's no time to be wasted. Jared's the only one who knows where some of the maps are. He's getting them from the *Shadow* while I see you settled in. We're going to meet at the sampans Matt has hired. We have to be up the coast before daybreak."

"But . . . what about *me?*" she asked miserably. She could hear her voice getting shrill, and she hated it, but she couldn't stop herself.

"You'll be all right," Alex promised her. "I'm going to arrange for some of the servants to sleep on the junk, and Dougal will keep an eye out. As first mate, he's the acting captain of the *Shadow* while I'm gone. He's a good man. He won't let anything happen to you."

"All . . . *right?*" She stopped again, staring at him in dismay. The thought of the man who might be Honoré Ravaud came into her mind, and just for an instant she was tempted to tell him. But that was silly. The man was almost certainly someone else. And anyway, he was the least of her problems now. "How can I be all right when Jared doesn't even care enough to discuss this with me? He just decides what he wants—and goes ahead and does it! He doesn't care what *I* think. Or how *I* feel!"

Alex paused for a second, hearing the pain in her voice she made no effort to conceal. He took the shawl from his shoulder and wrapped it very tenderly, protectively, around her. She looked so terribly, vulnerably young.

"This has nothing to do with you, Dominie," he said gently. "Or the way he feels about you. It has to do with Matt. There is a bond between those two that goes deeper than I realized—I sensed it for the first time tonight—but there is a passionate rivalry too. Jared has always been first, and Jared has always been best. And Matt has always tried to catch up. They have to find some way to settle things between them, and they have to do it now, or it's going to tear the family apart."

The family! They were almost to the shore now. Dominie could see the cutter waiting through a glittering blur of tears. That was all they cared about, any of them. The Barron family, the Barron ships, the precious Barron name. Whether the Barrons survived intact or not.

It had nothing to do with her?

Dominie could have screamed with fury and frustration. It had everything to do with her, but there was no point trying to say so. Even Alex, kind, compassionate, thoughtful Alex, didn't have the vaguest notion what she was suffering. Maybe only another woman could understand.

He had left without saying a word. He hadn't even cared enough to kiss her good-bye!

But then, she thought bitterly, she belonged to him. She was a possession, nothing more . . . nothing less. And one didn't say good-bye to a chair or a settle or a writing desk when one set off on a jaunt.

# 26

DOMINIE WAS UTTERLY MISERABLE for the next three days. Everywhere she looked in the large main room of the luxurious junk, she saw reminders of Jared. His shirt hanging on a peg on the wall, his pants sprawled across one of the cushions on the dais that held the red-lacquered table, his toiletries on a chest beneath his shaving mirror. She refused to let the servants touch them when they cleaned, as if somehow by not allowing any changes, she could make everything back into the way it had been that last afternoon when the pants were thrown aside so hastily and they lay on the wide, soft bed and made love.

Only it wasn't that same sweet afternoon anymore, and she wasn't the same naive young woman who had cuddled up in his arms. Dominie sighed as she got up and wandered over to the window, looking out on the seaward side. The doubts were there; she couldn't just ignore them. The feelings Jared had for his former mistress . . . the reason he hadn't told her about his sons . . . why he hadn't seemed to want to share his friends with her . . . why he kept shutting her out where his brother was concerned . . .

Any one of them, individually, could be explained away. But all together they were frightening and oppressive, and she longed desperately for the easy, carefree days on their isolated island again.

Alex was right. It was a lot harder in the real world. And she wasn't at all sure she was going to like it.

She rested her forehead on the glass and stared idly through the window. The sky was gray, not threatening exactly, but it had been drizzling that morning and looked as if it might again. She didn't even know where Jared was. Everything had happened so quickly, she hadn't thought to ask where he was going to be. If there would be any danger. She didn't even know if the early rains would make things easier or more hazardous for him.

She turned back into the room, feeling fretful and out of sorts. She had to admit she had been reasonably comfortable since Jared had left. The servants spent most of the day there now, especially the kitchen amah—a wizened old woman with a marvelous three-toothed grin who spent much of her time trying to teach Dominie Cantonese—and one of the boatmen, Chan, and his two teenage sons slept on the deck every night.

But comfortable was not the same thing as happy. The days were long, the nights even longer, and her body and heart ached for the man she was missing. She wanted him to come back and clasp her in his arms and tell her what a silly little girl she had been—and somehow, miraculously make everything right again.

But that wasn't going to happen, she reminded herself firmly. At least not for several days—and perhaps never. In the meantime, she could sit around moping or she could get her life straightened out and do something constructive. Like getting Jared's pants folded up, for one thing, and his shirt off the peg and neatly put away in one of the chests. Yes, and his toiletries could be packed up too, until he came back. No point torturing herself with constant reminders.

She had just started toward the peg with the shirt when she heard footsteps on the deck. Soft, like a child's sandals.

Or someone moving stealthily?

Tensing automatically, she cocked her head and listened. Surely she was imagining things. Chan had taken the kitchen amah out to a boat that had just arrived with supplies from Macao, and the two boys were off fishing. No one else should have been there.

Then the steps came again, unmistakable this time. Quick like a cat, Dominie slipped over to the chest where she kept the pistol she had picked up in Singapore.

She was doubtless being foolish. It was probably just Chan, back earlier than she had expected, or maybe one of the servants had forgotten something. The laundry amah, no doubt—she was the most forgetful thing alive. But it was better to be safe.

She had barely gotten the drawer open and pulled out

the pistol when a figure appeared in the doorway. Very small, a slender black silhouette against the stark glare of the sky behind, and Dominie let the gun drop back on the top of the chest with a low, unconscious moan.

She had forgotten. With the things that had happened, she had completely forgotten. She had not prepared herself for this.

The world seemed to stop in the brief moment it took that dark figure to come through the small antechamber and into the light of the large main room. Even before she could see him properly, Dominie knew he would be carrying a bundle in his hands. And she knew it would be wrapped in old rags that had gotten extremely dirty over the journey.

"Hello, Tien," she said softly. "*Bonjours, petit. Viens ici.* Come here. . . . I see you have brought me my brother's things."

The boy's face underwent several changes of expression. He had been thinking about how he was going to tell her; he had been rehearsing the words over and over in his mind, steeling himself for the terrible screams of anguish and sorrow that would come out of her mouth. But there had been only that one soft little sound, and it seemed that the words weren't going to be necessary after all.

He had also been afraid he was going to cry, and he was fighting the impulse manfully.

"He was very brave, mademoiselle," he said earnestly. "I have never seen a man so brave. The soldiers were all around. They were beating the bushes with great long sticks. My brother and I could only watch. We were in a wagon with chickens and things for the market. We wanted to help him. *I* wanted to help, but Duong said we could not. There were so many soldiers, and they were so good. The emperor's own guard, mademoiselle. But even then, I would have tried . . ."

His voice was cracking and he had to push himself to go on. Dominie wanted to tell him not to bother, that she knew the end of the story already, that she had known since that last gray hour before daybreak on an island off the coast, but she was too numb to speak.

"I *would* have tried. In truth, mademoiselle! I almost did . . . but just then he stepped out from the clump of elephant grass where he had concealed himself. He put the stole around his neck he used to say mass—and just stepped out. Very straight, mademoiselle. Very proud. My brother says it is better that way. A man does not want to be dragged like some trembling animal out of the shadows of his hiding place. It makes a man feel like a coward to tremble in the shadows, he says. It is important to face your fate. I don't quite understand, but perhaps one day I will.''

"Perhaps you will." He was so solemn, Dominie thought—only a child yet, but with such intensity burning out of his eyes. Had Denis' eyes ever looked like that? "I think you will, Tien. I think you will understand much.''

He had set the bundle down on the edge of the dais, near the place where Jared's pants were carelessly spread out, and was starting to unwrap it. Dominie tried to tell him to stop, tried to tell him she didn't want to see, but she couldn't make her mouth work, and anyhow, the bundle was almost open.

"They were afraid to kill him in the daylight," the boy said disdainfully, his voice louder, as if to drive away his own horror as he struggled with the last knot. "He died honorably. By strangulation," he added, as if somehow that would be a comfort. "It was in the place of public execution, but before the sun came up, when almost no one would be there to see. He made too many believers, mademoiselle. They were afraid we would rise up and fight. And we would have!''

He spat on the ground for emphasis, a grown-up gesture that made him feel better.

"I was not there," he went on. "But my brother was. He went to the execution place disguised as a peasant. He said that Père Denis should have a priest with him when he died. It seems strange that a priest would need a priest, but I suppose it must be so.'' He took a deep breath and gulped, hard. "Duong said he was very brave. He was not afraid, mademoiselle.''

It was not quite true. Duong had said that the priest was terribly afraid. He had said that his hands were shaking at the end when he raised them to make one last sign of the cross, and his voice was shaking too as he forgave his persecutors. But Duong had said that he was smiling faintly, inwardly, almost as if he were laughing at himself, and the guards had been very much frightened. The story was already spreading. People would not soon forget the priest who had died.

"He was very brave, mademoiselle," he said again. That, at least, was true; the boy had learned the difference now between fear and cowardice. "He was a man of much courage."

"Yes," Dominie agreed. "He did not always know it himself, but he was." She watched, horrified, but unable to tear her eyes away, as the last knot came undone and the filthy rags were falling loose.

"These are the clothes he was wearing," the boy said unnecessarily. "Duong told me to try to find you first, and if I could not, then to bring them to the holy fathers in Macao."

Dominie shuddered as a length of black fabric came into view, dust-smudged and stiff in places with dark, clotted stains. Like the relics of martyrs she had heard about as a little girl. They had seemed so sadly romantic. But even then she had wondered why there was blood when someone was strangled.

"They must be taken to Paris," the boy was saying, but she was having trouble concentrating on his words. For the first time the grim reality of her brother's death was sinking in. "Père Denis has talked many times of the great house in Paris where the Jesuits keep the clothes of all their martyrs in Christ."

He was getting the story mixed up. In fact it was the Lazarist mother house on the Rue de Sèvres where Denis had first seen the relics of Pierre Clet that set his feet on the path that would bring him to his own death many years later. But he was right, Dominie knew, in saying that the garments must go back to France. The Society of Jesus would want to display them as a holy example of courage and selfless dedication.

Denis would have been horribly embarrassed. He would not have wanted the martyr's crown laid so openly on his head, would not have wanted the adoration and awe fixated on his cassock, as if, in death, somehow he had become a kind of god himself. And he would absolutely have hated it if they attributed miracles to him and started talking about canonization or beatification.

But he would have endured it all, gladly, if he thought his humble example would inspire one young man to the service of Christ, as he himself had been inspired long ago.

But perhaps, she thought, conscious once again of the fire in the boy's eyes, he already had.

"Thank you, Tien, for bringing me these." She threw out her hand, gesturing toward the crumpled heap on the edge of the dais, unable to force herself to look at it again. "His sacrifice will be remembered. My brother did not die in vain."

He seemed to sense what she was thinking, or perhaps it was just that he had been thinking the same thing himself.

"I am going to be a priest, mademoiselle. There is no more school in Vietnam, but I will find a place. They do not want me to go. My father is very angry, my mother weeps—even my brother is unhappy. There is much pain and fear in his eyes when he looks at me. But I have told them I must. . . . I will be a good priest, mademoiselle. I will not be as good as Père Denis. But I will try to be worthy of him."

"I am sure you will be a very good priest, Tien." Dominie wanted to lay her hand on his shoulder, but she knew the gesture would seem patronizing, and he longed passionately to be treated as a man. "But you must try to be worthy of our Savior, and not another mortal, no matter how you may admire him. That is what Père Denis would have wanted."

And he *would* be a good priest, she thought, too numb yet for tears as she sat alone after the boy had crossed over the walkways through the sampan village and disappeared out of her life. He had zeal and courage and a faith that would not die. Denis would have been proud.

The clothes were still where the boy had left them, the cassock, the stole, the sandals—would they have included the cord that strangled him? she wondered—and she knew she ought to bundle them up again, but she couldn't bring herself to touch them. It was too painful yet, and she took the shawl she had been wearing the night of the dance and threw it down on top. She would deal with them later. She was not ready now.

She remembered a story that one of the fathers of the

*missions étrangères* had told her when she could not have been much older than the boy Tien. The Emperor Minh Mang had been very frightened of the priests, the elderly *père* had said, and very superstitious of this foreign God he could not understand. When he had had the first priest executed seven years ago, he had remembered Christ's resurrection and had the body exhumed after three days to make sure he was still dead.

They did not do such things anymore. Bodies were abandoned now and allowed to be spirited away under cover of darkness. Dominie had at least the small comfort of knowing that Le Van Duong would have made sure her brother had a decent burial. No longer did that mystical "three days" hold any terror for them. They would be sure that the dead priest would not rise again.

But they would be wrong.

Denis Arielle would be resurrected, not in his own body, but in the body of the boy Tien. It would be more like ten years than three days, but he would be back from the seminary and preaching the same passionate message that had infused her brother's heart. And after Tien, there would be another and then another . . . and another.

*They do not fear the native priests*, Duong had told her once, *but they should.*

They should.

The faith would never die in Vietnam. Dominie understood that now, as her brother had before her. It would burn as a torch, carried from generation to generation, ever brighter with each passing. This was what Denis had given his life for. This was his legacy to the future.

It still hurt, and she knew that in a way, it always would. Nothing would ever truly assuage the pain that left her stunned and heartsick, but at least she could take comfort in the fact that her brother had done what he wanted with his life. How many men could say that?

She stared at the little pile on the dais—only a dark corner of the cassock peeking out, none of the blood visible, though she knew it was there—and thought that she ought to be crying. But still there were no tears.

She thought she had said good-bye that last dawn on the island. She thought she had accepted the inevitable, thought she had come to terms with the pain and the loss, but she had not. She had still hoped—foolishly, illogically.

Now the hope was gone, and she couldn't even cry.

## 27

DOMINIE WAS SO INVOLVED in her thoughts, she did not hear footsteps for the second time on the deck, nor did she notice a faint darkening of the room as something blocked the doorway. She was not on the luxurious junk Jared had procured for her in Hong Kong harbor anymore. She was at home, in Paris, in her pretty red rose garden. Little Dominie again, five years old and terribly frightened. The servants kept whispering all around, sneaking the funniest looks in her direction, and she didn't know what they were talking about. . . . Then Denis was there, Denis was lifting her up in his arms and hugging her . . . telling her everything was going to be fine. He was home now, and he would take care of her.

He would always take care of her. Forever and ever. . . . Only, oh, God, forever had turned out to be so short a time.

*"Dominique . . . ?"*

The voice was harsh enough to call her back. She had been sitting on the edge of the dais, next to all that was left of her brother's effects, and she felt so drained suddenly it was all she could do to raise her head.

An old man was standing just inside the doorway. European, by the look of him, and very thin, with ashen skin drawn taut across sunken cheeks and dark hollows around his eyes, as if he suffered from chronic pain. His hair was almost completely gray, much too wispy for the dandified style he had brushed it into, and she wondered vaguely what he was doing there.

Then she knew.

Honoré Ravaud.

She had forgotten about him too, it seemed. He looked so much older than she remembered, and not at all handsome anymore. *Probably a dapper devil once*, Rawlings had said of the Frenchman on the *Scarlet Dawn*. So it *had* been Honoré. And the long, arduous sea voyage had broken his health.

Dimly Dominie was aware that she had done this to him. He had come halfway around the world searching for her, and he had given a good part of himself in the process. *Poor Honoré,* Denis had once said, *he loves you desperately.* She should at least have had the decency to break off the engagement before she left. Any other time, she would have been sick with guilt, but she was too engrossed in her own overwhelming unhappiness to think of anything else.

"I'm sorry, Honoré. Truly I am . . . but I can't explain anything right now." She tried to gesture him away with a wave of her hand, but all that came out was a helpless little flutter. "I'm so tired . . . and everything's such an awful mess."

"Good Lord, Dominique!" Honoré Ravaud stared at her, horrified and somewhat taken aback. This was not at all how he had imagined their tender reunion. He had expected her to throw herself into his arms, weeping with gratitude now that she had no doubt learned the folly of coming all by herself to search for her brother. And she looked absolutely ghastly. "You don't have to do anything. I'll see to it all. You must be in shock. My dear, dear child, what has been done to you? I have never seen your beautiful spirit so terribly broken."

"Oh, Honoré, I told you . . ." Dominie looked at him wearily. Why was he being so dense? "I'm sorry. I know what I did was wrong, but I can't go back and change it now. I'm just so very tired. I want to be alone. I *need* to be alone. You're not part of my life anymore. Please go away and let me be."

"It's all right, Dominique," he said soothingly, deliberately ignoring her protests. "It's all right. Honoré is here now. He'll see to everything. It's going to be all right."

But even as the platitudes slipped out of his mouth, he had an awful feeling they weren't true. She knew she had done wrong, she said. She had done *wrong* . . . and he found himself scanning the very sumptuous lush red room with a cold sense of dread.

He took in the shirt on the peg, the man's pants, carelessly rumpled—something disgusting beneath that shawl on the floor. A filthy, untidy, decadent place . . . he could not keep his eyes from drifting toward the massive bed. The rumors had been wild and vague; he had heard them just that morning. A stunning woman with auburn hair living on a junk that belonged to a notorious pirate . . . a seaman with a debauched reputation . . .

Quite a love nest, they had said, but he hadn't wanted to believe it. He didn't want to believe it now. Surely she had been taken against her will. *Wrong* meant only that she had been defiled. Not that her ripe young body had enjoyed it.

A new, extremely unpleasant thought crept into his mind. If she cared for him . . . if he cared for her, this man with the pants and the shirt . . . but that would ruin everything! He was already reaching for her hand, drawing it up.

No ring. He breathed a sigh of relief. That was good . . . but women didn't always wear their jewels. And she seemed to be in a state of some dishabille. He ran a practiced eye down her figure, taking in the little silk concoction she was wearing, a reddish color—he had never cared for her in red—and very flimsy, clinging. More a peignoir, really, than a dress. Probably *he* kept her that way so he could have easy access.

He was a little surprised that the thought excited as much as repelled him, and he found himself very conscious of the huge, soft bed again. If she had already been defiled . . .

"He did not marry you, I presume," he said coldly. "The man who brought you to this place. He took what he wanted and did not have the decency to make your position honorable."

Dominie looked up numbly. Her heart was still so heavy with grief; perhaps she *was* in shock, as he had said before. There was no way she could find the energy to explain her relationship with Jared. She wasn't even sure herself what it was.

"No," she said quietly. She drew her hand back, clasping it with the other in her lap. "I am not married to him. Things are just as you have imagined. So you see, Honoré, I have nothing left to give you. It's over now. All over."

The tears were coming at last, not flowing, but touching her eyes and lashes. It was indeed all over. So much of her life. She was not even sure yet how much . . . but at least she was going to be able to cry.

Honoré felt desire melting into pity at that first sign of feminine distress, which he dared to hope also meant she was ashamed and ready to be rehabilitated. Pity and a terrible, impotent rage as he thought of what this nameless monster had done to her. What he had done to *him*.

He had wanted to be first with her. He had wanted to undress her tenderly, to caress away her natural anxiety, coax her legs gently apart. He had wanted to break that virginal membrane with the hard thrust of his own aroused manhood. He had wanted the first cry of female satisfaction to come in response to *his* passion, and this bastard had taken it from him!

He hated what he had lost. He could taste it like bile in his mouth. He would hate and resent it until the day he died. But he knew as he stood and looked down at her, helpless and forlorn, with her hands folded in her lap, that it was not just his lust that hungered after her body. Not vanity merely that thirsted for her youth and beauty. He loved her with his heart as well.

"It's all right, my dear," he said again, and meant it truly. "I can forgive this. You're tarnished, of course, but it's not really your fault. I'm sure you fought as hard as you could. He was probably too strong. Some men might not be able to live with this, but I love you enough to forgive you."

But I don't *want* you to forgive me, Dominie thought, only she was too exhausted and desolate to argue anymore. Besides, he wouldn't believe her. She had already been brutally frank.

And what did he mean, *forgive?* If she had really been taken by force and raped repeatedly, as he seemed to believe, then what was there to forgive *her* for? Why couldn't he just go away and leave her alone? Couldn't he see that she didn't want him?

All she wanted was Jared. She had had the seamstress make up the red silk gown as a joke for him, but it had come too late and he had never seen it. Very sheer, draped so it would cling, with fastenings that fell away at the slightest touch. And nothing underneath. Jared hadn't liked her to wear chemises and stays. He liked to put his hand on her breast, he said, and feel her nipple through the fabric. He liked other things too, and suddenly she wanted him desperately, urgently.

It didn't matter what had happened that last evening, how hurt she had been when he left her, how angry that he seemed to forget her very existence. All of that was forgotten now. She was in pain, and she wanted him to take her in his arms and kiss away the sorrow . . . and tell her once again how much he loved her.

Then at last the tears were coming, hot and healing, down her face. She was only dimly aware that Honoré was crouching beside her, half-kneeling, half-bending over her.

She was weeping for her brother and the terrible empty space he had left in her life. She was weeping for the man she loved and the doubts and questions that had shaken her trust in him. She was weeping for herself because she was lonely and frightened and she wanted the world to go back to the way it was before.

But Honoré, misunderstanding, thought she was weeping with humiliation and shame, and there was at least as much relief as pity in his heart as he coaxed her up and began to ease her toward the door. She was going to be his again; he was sure of that now. It would not be the same, of course. It could never be the same. But even a damaged Dominique was better than no Dominique at all.

Dominie did not even notice what he was doing until they had nearly reached the door to the small antechamber. Balking for a moment, she started to resist, then realized that it wasn't such a bad idea. If she wanted to get rid of him, she could accomplish it much more easily when they were already out on deck.

Besides, obsessed as he was with getting her back, she wasn't at all sure she wanted to be alone with him. Better to be in the open and in sight of passing vessels.

He seemed to hesitate briefly. Dominie could not feel him behind her as she stepped into the anteroom. But then he was there again, gripping her arm, and they were going out on deck.

She did not realize her mistake immediately. The rain had started again, heavier than before. More than a drizzle now, cold, oozing through the shoulders of her dress even in that first brief second, and the deck was dangerously slippery. She thought only that she wanted to go back, but Honoré was behind her, blocking the way. Then she saw the men in the cutter next to the rail.

Three strong, very rough-looking men. And they were already reaching out, as if by prearrangement, to grab her when Honoré thrust her over the side.

Of course he would have brought hired thugs with him! Her mind snapped into focus, all the shock and cloudiness gone now. Honoré was not a man of action—and he had no way of knowing he'd find her alone. He would never have come without someone to take care of the pirate he had doubtless heard owned the junk.

She turned abruptly, trying to throw him off-guard, desperate to get back into the cabin. All she could think of was the loaded pistol lying on top of the chest of drawers. If she could just get to it . . .

But he was faster than she thought. He had both her arms and was dragging her forward, toward the rail.

"The poor child is distraught," he was calling out, gasping for breath, but managing to keep his grip. It had not occurred to her he would be so strong. "She's been through a dreadful ordeal. Worse than I feared. Naturally she's horribly embarrassed. She can't bear to face anyone."

He was *explaining* to the men! Dominie felt a stab of fear. Not ruffians at all, then. Decent seamen who thought they were rescuing some sweet, unfortunate damsel from a fate worse than death. Which would make them even more eager to do the job well.

And all her protests would be put down to feminine modesty!

She was struggling as hard as she could now. She had almost gotten away—all he had was one wrist, and she was at arm's length and they were skidding together along the deck. But one of the men was scrambling over the rail. She could see him out of the corner of her eye, and another was following.

A shout came from the far end of the deck. Looking up with a great surge of relief, Dominie saw the boatman, Chan, coming toward them with an enormous cleaver in his hand.

The kitchen amah! He must just have brought her back, a little early because of the rain. Thank God the woman was too possessive of her utensils to go anywhere without them!

It was going to be all right after all. She was going to be safe! Surely Chan would be able to hold them off for a few seconds while she went for the gun.

She had just jerked her arm free and started to turn when an explosion sounded in her ear. An awful deafening noise, and the acrid aroma of burning powder singed her nostrils. As she watched in horror, the cleaver clattered to the deck and Chan gripped his arm. Something red was seeping between his fingers.

Terrified, she looked around to see little wisps of smoke coming from the pistol Honoré was lowering to his side. His face was chalky, his hands shaking, but his aim had been hideously accurate. And the pistol was *hers!*

That was why he had paused for a second when they left the cabin. Why hadn't she paid more attention?

With a cry of anguish she leapt forward. All she wanted was to see how Chan was, to make sure the bullet hadn't gone too deep. She wasn't trying to escape—there was no hope of that now—but he was grabbing her anyway, the gun tucked back in his belt, and the men were hurrying to help him.

Dominie managed to wrench free, but her feet slid on the treacherous deck, and suddenly she was falling. A helpless, sickening sensation, and she felt her head smash against the railing with an awful cracking sound.

She had only the vaguest sense of what happened after that. She had not struck her head enough to lose consciousness, but she was weak and dizzy, and her hand came back with blood on it, so she knew she was hurt. Not badly hurt, she heard someone say. There was a jacket over her shoulders, and one of the men was examining her with surprisingly gentle hands. It would not leave a scar. As if something like that mattered now!

She remembered casting one last helpless look at the junk and seeing Chan, shouting and waving his arms. Both arms. At least nothing was broken, and there was only the slightest trace of red on his sleeve, so he was going to be all right.

The next thing she knew, she was on the deck of a

ship, her mind still groggy and her head throbbing horribly as she looked around, trying to form some hasty impressions. The rain had stopped, but the smell of wet wood and canvas was heavy in the air, and she spotted the familiar Barron banner fluttering next to an American flag.

The *Scarlet Dawn,* then—back from Whampoa or whatever that place was called. The sails were flapping fiercely in a rising wind, like claps of thunder, so loud the men had to shout at each other to make themselves heard. But why would it be carrying all that canvas? she wondered. They must just have gotten in minutes ago.

Then a man coming toward her. The captain, he said he was. Newcombe. Dominie remembered the name, and she started to tell him that she knew Jared Barron, and Alex and Matthew. But he was looking at her very strangely, and she realized with a rush of horror that Honoré had told him exactly the same things he had told the other men. He thought she had been held captive by a maniacal, sex-crazed beast who had used her over and over in unspeakable ways.

She could almost see him wondering what the man had done, pitying her for it, sympathizing, but also curious.

Her face must have reddened, for there was only sympathy now, and he was suggesting that she might like a nice bracing cup of tea. In his quarters. She would be more comfortable there.

It sounded heavenly—hot, sweet, soothing tea—and Dominie accepted gratefully. The explanations could come later. She would tell him what had happened and ask for his help. But right now she needed to sit down and do something about her aching head.

She noticed that Honoré remained behind, signaling to the captain that he wanted a word with him, which was just fine with her. She needed time to compose herself. She was feeling dizzy again, and it was getting harder and harder to think.

But she had to. She had to come up with the right things to say, or her former fiancé was going to drag her back to Paris with him. And she couldn't leave Hong Kong. Not now! Jared would be coming back, looking for her. She had to be there.

The *Scarlet* might have been the least imposing of the

Barron vessels, but the captain's quarters were extremely comfortable. A good-size sitting room opened into a narrower chamber beyond, which Dominie supposed contained the bunk. Against the wall next to the window she spotted a high-backed bench, tastefully upholstered in a rich brown fabric and surprisingly soft as she sank into it. And a table in front, just the right height to prop up her feet.

She leaned back just for a second, and thought how nice the tea was going to taste—her head was finally starting to feel better—and promptly fell asleep.

There were voices in the room when she woke up. She could hear Honoré speaking softly, and someone else was answering. Newcombe? She tried to stand up, but everything seemed to be swaying in a strangely rhythmic motion. Her head was pounding horribly, and shimmering rings of light seemed to be dancing up and down around the lanterns.

Odd that the lanterns should be lit, she thought. It hadn't been that dark.

They were looking at her now, smiling and saying they hoped she'd enjoyed her little nap and they were glad she was awake. Newcombe, as she had guessed—and Honoré, of course. She started to say something about the lanterns, when she noticed through the window that everything was black outside. And suddenly she understood why the swaying motion had seemed familiar.

"We're moving," she said. That was why the sails had been raised. She managed to struggle to her feet. "You were just waiting for Honoré to bring me back! We're leaving the harbor."

Newcombe gave her a kind, fatherly look. "We left some time ago, as a matter of fact." He had a twinkle in his eye, as if he were amused or secretly pleased about something. "We should be far enough out by now. Perhaps even a little farther than necessary. The law is very strict about such things, but I think it would be safe to begin."

Dominie noticed for the first time that he was carrying a black book, and little tendrils of apprehension squeezed around her heart. She didn't know why—it was just a book after all.

"Begin what?" she heard herself saying in a voice that was not altogether steady.

"I told you it was going to be all right, Dominique." Honoré had come up and was standing at her side. "I promised I would see to everything, and I have. Under the circumstances, I'm sure you'll agree that it would be better not to wait. You are safe now, my dear. You will always be safe. With me."

He had changed his clothes, she saw, and thought how strange it was that he had taken time to be so formal. He was looking a little more like himself in a fashionable suit with a black velvet collar and smart black waistcoat, but he still seemed terribly old and frail. In spite of all that had happened, Dominie couldn't help feeling a little sorry for him.

"I do truly regret everything, Honoré," she said softly. "*Everything*. I know how desperately worried you must have been when I left. I put you through a great deal of suffering. It was very kind of you to come after me, but—"

"No apologies, Dominique. You don't need to say this. I cannot truly blame you, though you were very foolish. Naturally, it was a terrible blow, finding you like that . . . but, there, I am willing to forget everything. We will never speak of it again. We are just going to set the calendar back and begin all over. As if these awful things had never occurred."

"You're a very lucky girl," Captain Newcombe said with what he probably intended as a kindly smile. "Not all men would be so understanding after . . . well, after what you have endured. They should be perhaps—they *definitely* should be—but alas, too many are not. Now . . . shall we get on with things? I must say this is one of the happiest duties a captain can perform, though I'm afraid it's all too rare."

"Marriage?" Dominie's mouth went dry as she looked from one to the other.

"Of course, my dear," Honoré was saying. "Did you think I meant any less? I know you are feeling very unworthy now, but I will never hold this against you, I promise. You should have been my bride three months ago had you stayed home where you belonged. I intend to marry you tonight and restore your reputation."

Dominie could only stare dumbly as he went over to the table at the side of the room and started shifting through some papers, spreading them out. Her head hurt terribly, and she was feeling dizzy again, and nauseous. He wanted to *marry* her! Tonight. She had been so afraid he was going to try to take her back home—and that had been the least of her problems!

He really thought she was going to fall down on her knees in gratitude because he still wanted her! As, no doubt, did the fatherly-looking captain. And if she tried to protest, they were just going to think she was feeling "unworthy" and not pay any attention!

She forced herself to concentrate again just in time to hear Newcombe say something about "documents," and Honoré was answering:

"Yes, yes, as you see, everything is in order. This is the paper her brother signed, naming Honoré Ravaud as one of her guardians. And here is the bishop's release, turning over her care solely to me."

Guardianship papers?

Dominie was becoming truly alarmed. She could feel herself getting sicker every second, from dread as much as the painful blow to her head. What was it that silly Camilla Crale had said at the ball? Something about how her guardian—her uncle—could make her do whatever he said because she was under twenty-one.

A priest might have some qualms, she had said, but she knew several ministers who would perform the rite. And a sea captain or two.

Especially a sea captain who thought someone was a "lucky girl" because an old man was still willing to marry her after she had been debauched?

She must have made a sound, for the captain turned to look at her, and Dominie thought for a moment he seemed vaguely troubled. But then he was smiling, a benign, encouraging smile, and she had the awful feeling that he was ready to go through with the service—no matter what she said—for her own good!

What was it with these men? she thought helplessly. Why did they always think they knew so much better than she what she really needed? What was right for her? Even Jared, whom she dearly loved, kept making decisions on his own. Never asking, just going ahead and doing things—and assuming it was what she wanted.

"These do seem to be in order," she heard Newcombe say, and then the papers were rustling and he was picking up the book, opening it.

Dominie felt a sudden rush of blind panic. What could she say to convince him not to do this? That she knew several members of the Barron family, and they would be most distressed to hear how she had been treated? But that was absurd. The time to have said that was when she first came on board.

That she was actually *engaged* to Jared Barron? Who would believe her? Certainly not the captain of one of his own vessels. She had seen the incredulous way everyone at the ball reacted when he announced his impending marriage. And they had heard it from his own mouth!

She had to buy time. Her head hurt so badly, she couldn't think. Just a little more time . . . at least until morning. By morning she could figure out what to do.

There was only one thing she could think of. Newcombe was already moving to the end of the table, the papers were being collected and set aside—Honoré would be coming for her in a second. She felt a little foolish, but she had to stop this somehow.

"*Oh!*"

She gave a little gasp, drawing their eyes toward her. Then, as gracefully as she could manage, she collapsed in a swoon on the floor.

## 28

THE BOATMAN Chan was tense with anxiety and lack of sleep as he squatted on the ground in front of Jared Barron and tried haltingly, with extremely awkward English, to relate what had happened. He had traveled continuously for a day and a half—it was already well into the following night—without even taking time to tend to his wound, which Rachel was now dressing efficiently and very disapprovingly.

"It wouldn't have taken an hour to stop and clean this properly," she scolded in fluent Cantonese as she finished swabbing with strong soap and boiled water and began to tear what had previously been her petticoat into long thin strips. "It's foolish to take such chances. An untended wound can become infected very easily."

"I didn't have time," Chan protested, shaking his head distractedly. "All I could do was find my sons where they were fishing, and then we had to leave. It was my fault, this awful thing. I was supposed to take care of her." His face was solemn, his eyes full of the pain of his failed responsibility. "I only left for long enough to take the kitchen amah to get supplies—I didn't know she would be in danger. I did what I could when I got back . . . but it was not enough."

Rachel heard the strain in his voice, and she sensed it was not only his own failure that was tormenting him but also fear of the famous Barron temper. Her hands still occupied with the deft winding of the bandages, she threw a curious glance at her brother-in-law out of the corner of her eye.

Half his face was black with shadow, the other half almost garishly yellow in the light of the single flickering lantern that illuminated their camp. Both halves were utterly impassive, as if they had been chipped from the granite of his native New England, and she could not even guess what he was thinking.

In fact, Jared Barron's first reaction had been a great howl of rage, but it had ended up somewhere deep inside him, and he had stood in absolute stony silence ever since the news reached him. He had been tempted to berate Chan, using his temper as an outlet for his fear and terrible sense of helplessness, but the man's wound was clear evidence that he had done everything he could. It would not be reasonable to blame him.

If anyone was to blame, he thought with a grimace, it was he himself, and his almost fanatical need to defend Barron Shipping against every possible threat. And to do it himself.

And if Dominie had paid the cost of his self-absorption . . .

He drove the thought to the back of his mind. No point worrying about what had already happened. What was important now was what he was going to do about it. He made Chan go back over the story again, probing for details, pressing Rachel into service as translator when the clumsy combination of English and pidgin became too difficult.

Several things were emerging about the man who had abducted her. He had been accompanied by three other men, who Chan was relatively sure were Americans. He had been very old and appeared to be in frail health. And he had the same accent as Mademoiselle, only more so, which meant he was probably French.

"The fiancé." A few brief words leapt into Jared's mind, uttered by Dominie on their island paradise before she had abruptly changed the conversation. "It has to be," he said emphatically. "I'm almost sure of it."

"The fiancé?" Alex, who had been standing quietly to one side, took a step closer. His face, catching the light full-on, seemed to float like a mask out of the night. "*Dominie*'s fiancé? I didn't know she'd been engaged."

"There was some man in France. She barely mentioned him once. Very old, she said he was. I meant to ask her about him later, but I never got around to it. It didn't seem important."

"You two didn't spend a lot of time *talking*, did you?" Alex said dryly. "Not that I blame you . . . but a little conversation might have been in order. I hope to God you got around to mentioning Mei-ling. And the fact that you have two sons—of whom you are justifiably proud.''

Jared's reaction was all too clear an answer.

"Oh, Lord,'' Alex went on. "I hope I'm wrong . . . but I had to leave her with that little puss Camilla when I went off to referee between you and Matthew. She was looking very pale when I got back. I had a nasty feeling . . . but, as I said, I may be wrong.''

Jared groaned. He wandered restlessly over to the edge of the circle of light and stared broodingly out into the darkness. He could well imagine the kinds of things Cammie Crale had been filling Dominie's head with, and how she must have felt when she heard them.

"I'm a damn fool, Alex. A damn fool! I had everything I wanted. Everything I've *ever* wanted, and I risked it all for . . . What? To show how rugged and forceful I am? To prove that Barron Shipping can't do without me?''

Alex walked over to stand beside him. They were alone except for Chan and Rachel, who was still binding his wounds. Matthew had gone almost immediately to transfer Jared's things to the sampan that had brought the boatman and his sons up the coast and to restock it for the return journey.

"She's going to be all right, Jared,'' he said quietly. "The man who took her is almost certainly the fiancé. An older man, French—it's too much to be coincidence. And didn't Rawlings say something about an elderly Frenchman on the *Scarlet Dawn* who was chasing after some girl?'' He turned his head abruptly, verifying in a few terse words with Chan that Dominie's abductors had last been seen heading in the direction of the *Scarlet*. "There, you see—it has to be him. If he's come all this way, he must love her very much. He'll see that she's taken care of.''

"He used a gun, Alex,'' Jared reminded him grimly. "That's not the act of a loving, caring man.''

"He was probably frightened out of his wits. He may have thought she'd been kidnapped—you would have to put her on a notorious pirate's junk!—and he was going to her rescue. Then along comes a Chinese waving a cleaver at him! Chan did say the other men were some distance away. He might have been acting in self-defense.''

Jared nodded reluctantly. ''It could have happened that way. But Chan also said it looked like she was trying to get away and he was holding her forcibly. It isn't always love when older men fancy pretty young women. It becomes a kind of sick compulsion sometimes. If he wants her that much—if he feels driven to possess her—what's he going to do when she refuses him?''

Alex was silent for a moment, and Jared knew he was thinking the same thing. Had perhaps been thinking it even a moment before he had.

''She's a fighter, cousin,'' he said at last. ''She's feisty and she's strong—a man would have to go some to put anything over on her. Besides, you're forgetting, he took her back to the *Scarlet*. Newcombe is one of our best captains. And one of the most honorable. He won't let anything happen to her.''

''Not if he knows what's going on,'' Jared replied darkly. ''But if he believes the man is her legitimate fiancé . . . ?''

Again Alex did not answer, and again Jared knew they were sharing the same concerns. Newcombe *was* an honorable man. He would do everything he could to help an unprotected woman. But he wouldn't be likely to get in the middle of a lawfully prearranged marriage. There were no doubt papers, signed by her brother, the Jesuit. And her guardian, the Bishop of Paris! The word of a bishop carried a great deal of weight with most honorable men.

Oh, God, if he was too late . . . He stared out into the darkness, seeing nothing but the terrible empty black spaces in his own heart. He could not even imagine the indignities she might be suffering—might *already* have suffered—the wounds to that lovely, unquenchable spirit. All he could think about was the way she had looked when they stopped briefly on the torchlit path leading up to the ball. The glow in her eyes, the toes that kept tapping on the ground, even when the band was awful. She had been so eager for the evening that lay ahead. She had expected so much from it—and he had made such a blasted mess of everything!

*His* needs. That was all he had thought about. His

interests. His own compulsions. Barron Shipping had lost its biggest vessel—and there was Sir Jared, off on his white charger to save the family business!

Well, where the hell was Sir Jared when Dominie was alone and no doubt feeling neglected? Where was Sir Jared when she had been taken from the junk by force? Where was Sir Jared now that she must be terrified and facing God-knows-what?

"I *am* a fool," he said again. "Barron Shipping could survive very nicely without me."

"Not necessarily," Alex said calmly. "But you're not the sole reason for the line's existence. You don't have to do everything all by yourself. It's a bitter way to learn a lesson, *younger* cousin, but there are some quite capable shoulders more than ready to share the burden."

"Meaning, elder cousin," Jared replied with a faint but dark touch of humor, "I would have done better to leave this little task to you?"

"Considering the fact that you have a very beautiful young fiancée who could use some attention, and considering the fact that I can handle this as effectively and perhaps a bit more tactfully, yes, I think you should have left it to me."

"And considering the fact that you have a younger brother," Rachel put in unexpectedly, "who needs a chance to prove himself—and that Alex would be fairer— yes, you should have left it to him!" She had finished bandaging Chan's arm and moved closer when the two men were not watching. The lanternlight, so harsh on their faces, was gentler to her, muting her striking coloring and giving her an almost unearthly fragility. "It's just a ship, Jared," she said softly. "If it's lost, it's lost. I don't think it is—but does it matter so much?"

"It isn't 'just a ship,' " he replied stiffly. He was a little surprised by the sudden attack, even more surprised that it didn't seem to take him aback. Perhaps these months with Dominie had accustomed him to outspoken females. "It's the *China Dawn*. The largest, finest clipper the tea trade has ever seen. And the most expensive, I might add."

"It's still just a ship." Her eyes were flashing as she faced him. "Just wood and brass and canvas and rope. All you have at jeopardy is an economic investment, and maybe some family arrogance, of which there seems to be an abundant supply. Matthew is a living, breathing person, and the only brother you'll ever have. If you don't know which is more important, I think you need some basic lessons in the realities of life.''

Alex's silence was eloquent beside him. Jared knew he was laughing inwardly—gently, as Alex always laughed.

''I know Matt is more important than a ship,'' he said gruffly. ''I never claimed he wasn't.''

''Didn't you? But you implied it . . . Matthew has always looked up to you. You were more than his big brother—you were his idol. All he ever wanted was to please you. And he always failed because you set exactly the same standards for him that you had for yourself. You wanted him to have the same aspirations, the same values, the same talents. Just like old Gareth. Only he was trying to make his grandson into the son he had lost . . . and you were trying to make him into a little image of Jared Barron! Why is it that no one ever wanted Matthew to be himself?''

''I can fight my own battles, tiger.''

Matthew's voice was quietly reproachful as he stepped into the light. But as Jared turned to look at him, he saw pride in the younger man's eyes and a gentle humor that reminded him for an instant almost uncannily of Alex. He realized that his brother loved this woman, as he loved Dominie, and enjoyed her and was ready to indulge her. And perhaps respected her too.

''Are we battling, Matt?'' he said.

''We are if you're going to try to pass judgment on me.'' He was looking him straight in the eye, as he never had before, standing his ground, and Jared had the oddest feeling suddenly that his baby brother was all grownup and he hadn't been around to see it happen. ''I made the right decision. I could either take care of the *China Dawn* or I could get rid of the opium I had brought into the country. Or as much of it as possible. Opium destroys lives. I didn't think there was really a decision. And I can't believe you would have wanted me to do anything else.''

''I would have preferred you not to put yourself in the position where you had to make that kind of decision.''

''Ah, well . . .'' Matthew's face was crinkling up, his

good nature getting the better of him. "I would have preferred that myself. What do you want me to say, Jared? That I was stupid? I was. I've never had any difficulty admitting my mistakes, unlike some people I could mention. But the young man who got himself into that predicament wasn't the same man who came to grips with it later. The opium was my responsibility. I decided to do something about it—and the devil take the wood and brass and canvas and rope!"

Jared felt the corners of his mouth twitch involuntarily. Damn, Matthew had always been able to do that to him. "You were listening a little longer than you let on."

Matthew grinned. "I may not need anyone to fight my battles, but I do like hearing a lovely lady stick up for me. . . . I have a great deal of affection for you, big brother, though that may surprise you. And you have a great deal of affection for me, which may surprise you even more. If you tried trusting me for a change, you might not be disappointed. I *will* get the *China* back. Or die trying."

"It seems I have no choice . . . though I'd prefer you didn't go to such drastic extremes," Jared said, smiling wearily. He had a long night ahead, and an even longer day. Matthew had made mistakes, God knew, but he wasn't the only one who desperately needed a chance to set things straight. And the very lovely young wife had been right. It was just a ship.

He finally understood what was really important, and it occurred to him that it had taken a damn long time to get to that point. Dominie was important, the love they shared . . . the future that was theirs. The children they would have were important . . . the house filled with laughter and sorrow and dreams .. the joyous moments, the volatile quarrels . . . the quiet years of growing old beside each other, feeling comfortable together, always knowing someone was there.

Unless he'd ruined everything with his blasted stupidity!

"I'll commandeer the *Eliza Dawn* when I get to Hong Kong," he said, grabbing up the last of his packs from the ground beside him and swinging it over his shoulder. "I'll be about three days behind Newcombe, maybe four, but he should be some time in port at Lahaina. I ought to catch him there.''

"The *Shadow* is faster," Alex said. "And in better shape. You could at least pull into Hawaii even.''

Jared shook his head. "The *Shadow Dawn* is yours. I took her once before, and I was wrong. I will not do it again.''

"You're not taking her. I wouldn't let you. I'm offering this time. Dammit, Jared, your pride wouldn't let you ride as a passenger before when you should have. Now you're too stubborn to take command when it makes good sense. Haven't you got your priorities figured out yet?''

Jared managed a brittle laugh. He had as a matter of fact gotten his priorities straight about an hour ago when Chan had come stumbling into the camp. It was accepting generosity he was having a little trouble with, or expressing his gratitude gracefully. Or perhaps letting go of his pride . . . though he seemed to be learning.

"Thank you, cousin. I'll take good care of her. You can have her back when you sail into Lahaina.'' He turned to his brother with a crooked half-grin, aware suddenly of all the things that had never been said between them and that he didn't have time for now. "When you and Matt sail in on the *China Dawn*.''

When and if, he thought as he followed the twisting path down to the shore where one of Chan's sons was waiting with a lantern. So many ifs. If only he was in time. If only he hadn't messed things up so thoroughly they couldn't be put right again.

If only Dominie hadn't been so badly hurt she would never be able to forgive him.

Damn, it was hard, finally learning what mattered in his life—what he really wanted—just when he might be about to lose it.

## 29

DOMINIE HAD BOUGHT herself only a brief respite with her fainting act.

She had known she was in trouble when they carried her, still limp and unresponsive, through a very comfortable-looking sitting room into a darkened chamber with a wide bunk, clearly capable of accommodating two. Through cautiously fluttering lashes she recognized an almost exact duplicate of the owner's quarters on the *Shadow Dawn,* and her heart sank. With no owners on board, the suite would have been rented out to whichever passenger had the most money to pay for it.

And Dominie had not doubt who that was.

Her fears were confirmed a few minutes later when she heard Honoré through the half-open door telling the captain that he would make up the bench in the sitting room as a bunk for himself until the wedding could be re-scheduled, tomorrow or the next day at the latest. New-combe, to his credit, sounded hesitant, but as there were apparently no other suitable quarters, and as the couple were, after all, to be married imminently, he reluctantly agreed.

Honoré kept his bargain well into the night. In fact, the little scuffling noises from the outer chamber died away quite quickly, replaced by rhythmic and rather annoying snores, and as Dominie finally became confident enough to drift asleep, she vowed that she would have a long, serious talk with the captain in the morning. Obviously this intolerable state of affairs could not be allowed to continue.

Sometime in the middle of the night she woke abruptly. At first she thought it was the heavy lurching of the boat that had disturbed her. The storm was much worse now, and the small room seemed to be rocking treacherously back and forth. But then she felt hands all over her, slipping inside the red silk gown she was still wearing, for she had no other garments, trying to force her legs apart, and she had jerked upright with a jolt of shock.

Mercifully the struggle that followed was brief. For all his months at sea, Honoré Ravaud was not much of a sailor. His body had not yet learned to adjust to the violently churning movements of a rough ocean, and it was a matter of minutes before he was sprawled out on the bed, groaning not from passion but seasickness.

It was ironic, Dominie thought as she scrambled out and managed to fasten the gown around her again, that she had twice been saved from similar situations by a weak stomach. First hers, and now Honoré's.

She spent a miserable night, sleeping on the bench in the sitting room, which had in fact actually been made up with pillow and blankets and even a glass of water on a table at the side. Apparently Honoré's intentions had at least started out to be honorable, she thought grimly. Perhaps the storm had awakened him, and the temptation of her so near in the next room had been too much to resist.

Still, she was more determined than ever to have that little talk with the captain in the morning. Honoré might be groaning in misery behind the closed door, but he would not remain ill forever. And she never wanted to endure anything like that again in her life.

As it turned out, Captain Newcombe proved to be extremely understanding. Dominie was as honest with him as she dared, withholding only the name of the man to whom she assured him she was officially engaged. He would almost certainly think she was deluding herself if she told him she expected a man like Jared Barron to meet her at the altar.

Not, she had to admit, that he seemed the type who would force her into an unwanted marriage with Honoré Ravaud even if he did.

In fact, he listened attentively and very sympathetically while she told him all about her brother and the quest that had brought her to the Orient in search of him. And how, with the help of the man she was now planning on marrying, she had finally managed to find him. He was also the first person she told of Denis' death and how devastated she had been on receiving the news.

"But . . . why didn't you tell me all this, Dominique?" he said at last when she had finished.

"Dominie," she insisted. "I hate Dominique. No one ever called me that—except Honoré, who doesn't care what I think. . . . And darling Sister Jean-Luc, who took care of me when I was little . . ." Her voice trailed off. She could hear the tears threatening to break through—talking about Denis had been more painful than she expected—and it was a struggle to contain them. "I put up with a great deal from her."

"And she from you, I suspect," replied the kindly captain, who had eight children of his own, five of them girls. "But you really *should* have told me . . . Dominie. I would have stopped the marriage immediately if I had realized it was against your will."

"I wasn't thinking clearly," she admitted. "I was still stunned—I had just learned of Denis' death. And . . . well, I didn't know you, and I couldn't be sure . . ." She went on to explain about Camilla Crale and the story of the guardian who had tried to pressure her into a marriage she didn't want. And nearly got away with it because she wasn't twenty-one.

Newcombe, who seemed to know the young lady very well, chuckled appreciatively, especially when Dominie got to the part about the gentleman's being a cuckold on Saturday.

Rather to her surprise, he was inclined to agree with her.

"You were wise to be cautious. As you said, you didn't know me. And considering what had happened to you—what *appeared* to have happened—well, I think many guardians would have been grateful for any husband that could have been found for you. And many a well-meaning sea captain might have been persuaded to sign his name to a paper when he really shouldn't. You were, as you put it yourself, too distraught to 'think clearly.' It did seem like the best solution."

Dominie shook her head. "Even if things were exactly as they appeared," she said quietly but firmly, "it still wouldn't have been right. There has to be more than necessity to make a marriage. I couldn't be the wife of a man I don't love. Or have *any* feelings for really. Especially when there's someone else who holds my heart.''

Newcombe was watching her closely. The same fatherly expression she had noticed before, only now she knew it was genuine.

''Are you really sure this man is planning to marry you?'' he asked not unkindly, but not quite comfortingly either. ''He's not just saying the things he knows you want to hear?''

Dominie was not sure at all. In fact, she was relatively sure that Jared *was* having second thoughts. Or third. Or fourth! But she couldn't bring herself to utter her doubts aloud.

''He did try to marry me when we left Vietnam. After my brother had given his blessing. He wanted us to be married by the ship's captain, but . . .'' She almost smiled, remembering Newcombe's own words as he had opened up his small black book the evening before. ''I'm sure it would have been very romantic, a wedding at sea, but somehow it didn't seem right. A marriage just isn't a marriage to me unless it's performed by a priest.''

''It might not be a marriage in the most sacred sense of the word,'' he remarked reasonably, ''but it would be a legal union. I can't help thinking how much simpler everything would have been yesterday if you could have produced a document that said you were another man's wife.''

And how much simpler it would be now, Dominie thought that afternoon as she sat alone in the captain's sitting room and listened to the rain drumming against the window, if she had a document that guaranteed that Jared would come back to her.

He might be having second thoughts—or twenty-second thoughts—but if they were married now, if theirs were a *legal* union, then he couldn't be able to change his mind. He would have to take the time to work things out with her.

She had had her chance, she reminded herself miserably. He had tried to marry her once, and she, like a fool, had let the moment slip through her fingers. What if the chance never came again? What if she had lost him?

* * *

The days passed drearily as the *Scarlet Dawn* moved slowly through a succession of storms, ever increasing in severity, toward the islands of Hawaii. Captain Newcombe had insisted that Dominie take his quarters, and while she had been extremely uncomfortable about it, knowing that he and the first mate, who were now sharing a single hammock, would have to sleep in shifts, there was nothing else available, and all she could do was accept gratefully and apologize for being so much trouble.

He had also given her some of his wife's clothing, and Dominie now had a wardrobe of two outfits: a rather ugly gray-green dress and something in navy blue that almost made it look chic. Marjorie Newcombe, who occasionally traveled with her husband and had left some of her wardrobe on board, was a good five inches shorter than Dominie, and about as broad as she was tall. Fortunately several of the crew were quite handy with a needle, and if Dominie didn't look exactly fashionable with the bodices nipped in and dark red ruffles made from an old bed throw on the bottoms of both the skirts, she was at least presentable enough for a stroll on deck.

Not that she was likely to do much strolling in the open air, she thought glumly. The way the storms kept blowing in, it looked like she was going to be confined belowdecks for the duration.

The foul weather did have the advantage of keeping Honoré too incapacitated to cause any further trouble. Dominie, swallowing her horror at the memory of that brief degrading struggle, insisted on taking over his care herself. The captain, who had gone out of his way to be kind to her, was short enough on crew as it was, and with the gale winds, all hands were needed topside. No one could be spared to heat up endless cups of tea and bowls of steamy soup to cater to a demanding patient.

Besides, it salved her conscience somewhat. Honoré had behaved abominably, and she was more and more grateful with each passing day for the good fortune that had spared her the awful fate of becoming his wife, but she was still guiltily aware that he wouldn't have been there in the first place if it weren't for her. All it would have taken was one brief letter from Lyons or Geneva or Marseilles, and he would have known once and for all that no matter what happened, she was never going to consent to be his wife.

But that was so brutal, so cruel, she hadn't been able to bring herself to do it. It seemed so much easier to just let him get used to the idea gradually. To stop missing her bit by bit as time went on.

Now she was realizing how much crueler it had been to let him keep on hoping. And how much aggravation she had caused for herself in the bargain.

She balanced the tray she was carrying on one arm and shoved open the door to the pleasantly furnished sitting room. A fetid odor greeted her and she was tempted to leave the door open, but remembering the way Honoré always complained about drafts, she decided against it. Setting the soup, reheated for the third time, and a pot of fresh tea on the table, she tapped on the bedroom door.

Ordinarily Captain Newcombe preferred that she bring one of the men with her whenever she actually entered Honoré's room, and she sensed that the idea of her being alone with her former suitor made him somehow uneasy. The poor man was a threat to no one in his present weakened condition. But when she had mentioned that to the captain, he had replied rather cryptically that Monsieur Ravaud had been ill once or twice during previous storms, and it had never lasted quite so long before.

This time, however, the burly carpenter's assistant who usually came with her had been needed to tend to a broken spar, and when Honoré's voice called out in response to her knock, she entered alone.

She was surprised to see him sitting up, for the first time in days. There was actually a little color in his cheeks.

"Hello, Honoré," she said, trying to sound cheerful and aloof. "You're looking better."

"I'm not feeling better," he replied peevishly. "I'm feeling much worse. You never come near me anymore, Dominique. You keep bringing that man with you. Anything that needs to be done, you have him do it. That's not a very wifely way to behave."

"Perhaps that's because I'm not your wife, Honoré."

"You soon will be," he persisted. "It's almost the same thing."

"No, I won't." Dominie took a deep breath as she struggled to retain her composure. No matter how many times they went over this, he always came back to the same thing. "My brother agreed when I saw him, and so will the bishop as soon as I have a chance to write. And 'that man' isn't here now, so tell me what you want and I'll do it for you. A nice cup of tea maybe? I have some just outside."

"I don't like tea. I don't want any. Get me my pillow—I've dropped it. See, it's there. On the floor."

It was indeed "there," right next to the bed, where he could easily have reached down to get it himself. Sighing, Dominie went over and bent to pick it up. He was punishing her, of course, because she didn't love him, but she supposed it would have been even more unpleasant if he'd been sweet and forgiving and looked at her with pained puppy-dog eyes.

She had just picked up the pillow and was starting to tuck it behind him when his hands shot out, grabbing her by the arms, pulling her down on the bed beside him. She was so stunned, she didn't even have time to react as he rolled her against the wall, wedging her in suddenly and very forcefully.

Too late she remembered Newcombe's veiled warning, and she wished she had paid more attention. He had been faking all along, biding his time, lying in the bed moaning every time she came in with one of the men—waiting until he could her alone.

And she had walked right into the trap.

"Let me go, Honoré," she said, trying to make her voice stern and forceful, almost succeeding. He was rocking over against her now, pressing her into the wall with his horrible gaunt body. She could feel his bones through the thin nightshirt he was wearing. "I don't want to scream, but I will if I have to. It will be more embarrassing for you than for me."

"No one will hear you. They're all up on deck, and the storm is so loud. The sails and the ropes and the wind . . ." He was grinding himself against her, sickeningly, grotesquely. It was not just his bones she could feel now. His erection was huge and embarrassing, and he was trying to hold on to her and pull her skirt up at the same time. "No one will come anyway. They know you're my wife. Almost my wife. You would have been my wife if you'd stayed home like you should. I have a right to this.''

''You don't have any rights at all with me.'' Terrified, she tried to push him away, but her hands were trapped, helpless, and she knew with an awful rush of fear that he was right. No one *would* hear. The noise on the deck of a sailing vessel in a storm could be deafening. ''I don't want you, Honoré. Don't you understand? I don't *want* you! I can't bear the thought of your touching me!''

''You liked it all right when *he* touched you.'' His voice was so hoarse she didn't even recognize it, his face so close she could feel the heat of his breath on her lips. He was trying to kiss her and she was wrenching her head to the side, clinging frantically to the wall. She could not believe he was so strong. No matter how she fought, she couldn't budge him an inch. ''He put his filthy hands all over you. On your breasts . . . between your legs . . . like this!''

He still hadn't managed to work her skirt up, but he was feeling her through the fabric, thrusting his hands between her thighs, pushing them apart. And she was struggling desperately to hold them together.

''No, don't . . . please, Honoré . . . *please* . . .'' She was begging now, nearly crying with fright, but he didn't even seem to hear. He was too wrapped up in his lust and anger.

''He forced you the first time. I know he forced you. You would never have gone with a man like that.'' Her skirt was sliding up now. Dominie could feel his hands groping her bare skin, but the more she squirmed, the more it seemed to excite him. ''You fought him, like you're fighting me now . . . but you loved it in the end. He drove his hard shaft into you, and you writhed and screamed for more. And he gave it to you, didn't he?''

He was sweating now. Dominie could feel it pouring off him, hot and sticky and absolutely terrifying. His fingers were almost *there*, where she felt like she would die if he touched her.

''I'll give it to you too, Dominique . . . better than he ever did. You used to get hot all over when I kissed you. I could feel the desire coursing through your body. You loved it . . . I know you did . . . and you'll love it even more now!''

I won't love it, Dominie thought helplessly. I'll hate it! But she would never get him to believe that. He was totally lost in a world where rules of logic and compassion were suspended. Because she had been "defiled" once, it was all right to defile her again. And if she had responded to one man, then she would respond to any man with an erection and the power to drive it into her body.

She was not strong enough to get away from him. Dominie fought back the fear that threatened to engulf her. She would be lost if she gave in to it now. She could not save herself with force or persuasion. But she could still use guile.

"Oh . . . *yes,* Honoré . . ." She willed her body to go limp, as if he had touched her in some magical way that reached a deep inner core of passion. "Yes, you're right . . . I *do* want you . . . I always did, but I was ashamed to admit it.''

"I knew it, Dominique," he responded, weakening somewhat, but still holding her much too tightly. "I knew you did, my dear . . . all along . . . you were just so innocent. But now you're not innocent anymore.''

"Kiss me, Honoré," she murmured, forcing her voice deep into her throat. "Don't talk anymore . . . just kiss me . . . the way you used to.''

His mouth was on hers suddenly, horribly. His hand had found the place it was seeking; his fingers were doing the most awful, intimate things, and she struggled to keep herself from gagging. She could almost have thrown up again, but she didn't think it would make any difference. He was so far gone in his need to possess her, to punish her for having hurt him, she wasn't sure he would even notice.

But at least he was caressing now, not holding her in an iron-hard vise. If she could just get him to back off a little.

"No . . . not so fast, Honoré." He was trying to roll on top of her, alarming and nauseating. She had to get some space. "I don't like it that way. I want . . . I want to touch you too.''

It was working. He was pulling back, so excited he

couldn't even wait to get his nightshirt off. He was just tugging it up above his waist. In spite of herself, Dominie could not tear her eyes off him. No wonder he'd had such a reputation with the ladies when he was younger.

"You're so . . . big, Honoré." She was playing to his ego, and he was lapping it up. "I didn't know." She opened her lips, darting her tongue over them, as if unconsciously. "You didn't tell me."

He was staring in rapt fascination at her mouth, speechless now, and Dominie knew he was imagining all the things she had done with the man who had had to "force" her at first. Things that, in fact, were not yet part of their lovemaking—but she had an imagination too, and she saw that it was exciting him enough to get careless.

She flicked her tongue one more time over her lips, obviously, all the way around, then eased her knee back— and rammed it into his groin!

He responded with a grunt of pain. She drew her knee back and jabbed him again, and then again. There was a chamber pot next to the bed, and she picked it up by the handle and began hitting him with it, over and over in the chest. He was deathly pale now; his body was jerking back convulsively, but he did not make a sound.

"You don't understand!" she cried, anger and frustration mounting almost to hysteria. "You don't understand! You don't *understand!* I hate it when you touch me—it makes me cringe! I loathe you! And *he* never had to force me. I went with him willingly. Because I wanted him. As I will never want you!"

"Ah, Dominique . . ." he moaned as he doubled over on the bed. She could not tell if it was a cry of pain or disappointment or rage. Or perhaps a combination of all three. "I just wanted to love you. I love you so much . . ."

*Love?* She collapsed in the hallway just outside his door, too weak and horrified to move another step. Her legs would not hold her up anymore. She could still feel the way he had touched her. She was shivering suddenly, unable to stop. She could still feel the terrifying helplessness of being pinned again the wall.

And he called that *love*?

Love was not the lust and possessiveness she had been

subjected to in that stifling little room. Love was what she had shared with Jared—and prayed she would one day be able to share again—and suddenly she felt very alone and frightened.

She needed him so much now. She needed the warmth and comfort of his arms around them. And she didn't even know where he was.

This time Dominie had learned her lesson. She went right to Captain Newcombe and, choking back her embarrassment, told him exactly what had happened.

He was immediately solicitous. A few fatherly but very explicit questions elicited the fact that she had not actually been harmed, but his face was grim as he sent a couple of men to Honoré's cabin.

He relaxed somewhat after they came back and he had had a chance to speak with them.

"They say your old boyfriend has several very nasty bruises, though I gather he's going to keep everything he was born with. He also seems to have a couple of cracked ribs."

Dominie managed a weak smile. "You don't think I was *too* rough on him?"

He didn't seem to find the attempt at humor amusing. "I think you had every right to shoot him . . . though I'm glad it didn't happen on my vessel. I blame myself for this. I should have been more alert to what was going on, but .. he's not a *bad* man. He just crossed the border sometime in the last few days to the other side of sanity. You had become an obsession to him apparently. He had to have you—no matter what. He could no longer look at things and see them rationally."

An *obsession*.

Dominie was to think of that word often in the days that followed. As if to compensate for what she had been through, the sun came out, the sea was almost glass-smooth for the rest of the voyage, and as Honoré was now being kept under lock and key, she was free to wander around the decks and enjoy the balmy weather.

An obsession. That was what Alex had accused her of having, all those long months ago when she had insisted on finding her brother and bringing him home—whether he wanted to come or not. And Alex had been right.

Denis *had* been her obsession, as Jared's brother was his. It was not just Barron Shipping that mattered, she sensed now, or the loss of an individual ship—it was Matthew, who was somehow supposed to live up to everything Jared had dreamed for him. Jared had been so busy trying to make Matthew behave the way *he* wanted, he had lost track somewhere along the way—as she herself had for a while—of the fact that brothers were individuals with lives and dreams of their own.

They had all had their obsessions, she thought sadly—she and Jared and poor, pathetic Honoré. And none of their obsessions had brought them anything but grief.

She found herself dwelling more and more on Jared as they approached the Hawaiian Islands. Wondering where he was, if he was all right . . . whether he was thinking of her. By now he surely knew that she had been taken off the junk—Chan would have sent someone with the news, or at least given it to him on his return—and he had probably figured out by whom.

How had he reacted?

The thought troubled her more than she cared to admit. He would have been worried, of course. Even if he *had* been having second thoughts about getting married, she knew that he did truly love her and cared about her safety. But had he, somewhere deep inside, had a little twinge of relief that someone might be bringing her back to Paris and immersing her once again in the life she had left behind?

The air took on a sultry feel as they neared their destination, reminding her poignantly of the small island off the coast of Vietnam, and she longed more than ever to be back there again. Not to have to worry about anything more than how to prepare the fish Jared had caught for their dinner. Not ever to have to doubt the man who held her in his arms and made sweet, passionate, turbulent, tender love to her all night long.

But she did have doubts, she thought sadly, and they would have to be resolved. And she did have a number of things to worry about, not the least of which was how she was going to manage once they got to port at Lahaina. She didn't have so much as a penny to her name, the diamonds that were her family legacy were safely locked away on the *Shadow Dawn*, and the only possessions she had were one red silk dress of her own and two rather oddly thrown-together outfits courtesy of the captain's wife.

It seemed strangely ironic. Here she was, one of the wealthiest women in France, and she couldn't buy a night's lodging, much less purchase passage back to Hong Kong. She was going to have to rely on her own glib tongue and the generosity of strangers. Or casual friends like Captain Newcombe.

She decided that the only thing to do was level with him, totally and without reservations this time. It was the afternoon before they were due to dock—they would be arriving in Lahaina sometime around noon the next day—and she knew she couldn't put it off any longer.

It would mean bringing up the name Jared Barron, of course; he would almost certainly think she was extremely naive. But if she wanted his help, she was going to have to be completely honest.

She was just coming out on deck when she became aware of a sudden startling commotion. Men seemed to be running everywhere, scrambling past her in a frantic hurry, some still pulling on their shirts and trousers, heading for the other side. "Pirates," someone shouted, and she craned her neck, but one of the lifeboats was blocking her view. "She's not flying any flag," came from somewhere else, and, "Damn, she's trying to broadside us."

Pirates?

Instinct prompted Dominie to do the one thing she shouldn't. The shouts and clatter of booted feet mingled with a sound of heavy equipment being dragged along the deck, and she hurried with the others, out into the open on the starboard side. She was just in time to see an even larger vessel coming at them, and to feel the awful, reverberating shudder as the two ships crashed.

Dominie had never encountered a pirate before—she had only heard stories about them—and she was wild with curiosity to see one.

What she saw was a tall man, dark blond hair blowing in the wind, standing on the rail of the ship that had just rammed them once and was about to come into them again.

In that one brief second, as the two vessels touched,

before the men with grappling hooks had time to secure them to each other, Jared Barron was leaping through the air, landing on the deck of the *Scarlet Dawn* with a resounding thud.

"Newcombe," he bellowed, "you have something on board that belongs to me!"

## 30

*BELONGS.* THERE IT WAS, that word again—and Dominie was just so grateful to see him, so happy when he held out his arms and she raced into them, that she couldn't even be properly indignant.

It was only later, when they were sitting together in the owner's suite on the *Shadow Dawn,* trying to catch up on everything that had happened, that she finally remembered to protest. And then it was only between kisses as they reassured themselves that they were both there, and both safe, and somehow the world had come right-side-up again.

"But of course you belong to me, Dominie," he said with mock consternation when she finally managed to voice her objections. "*I* belong to you. Isn't it only fair that you should also belong to me?"

Dominie was embarrassed to feel two tears running down her cheeks. It was so silly—everything was working out at last—and here she was crying.

"*Do* you belong to me, Jared?" She was even more embarrassed to hear a quiver in her voice. "Truly?"

He seemed to understand, for he raised his hand and brushed away the tears, which were promptly replaced by two more of the same. "I am very sorry, Dominie. I should never have left you alone. I would give a great deal if I could go back and spare you these past weeks. And yes, I do belong to you. Truly."

"I thought . . . When you left without even saying good-bye, I . . . I thought you were getting tired of me. I thought you were beginning to regret giving up your freedom."

"My freedom?" He looked genuinely puzzled. "What in heaven's name would I do with my freedom, love—except search for someone exactly like you? . . . And I didn't want to leave without saying good-bye. There were things I had to get from the *Shadow*—no one else knew where they were—and we were in a hurry. We had to get as far as we could under cover of darkness.''

"It would have taken only a few minutes," Dominie protested, but gently. It was so good being with him again. He was holding her hand and looking into her eyes, and she didn't want anything to cause them to quarrel.

"I spent more than a few minutes looking for you," he reminded her. "You were off somewhere. I couldn't find you. And I was only going to be gone a week or so, for God's sake. It wasn't like I'd be spending months at sea. . . . I seem to remember, my sweet, an occasion when you left me even more abruptly. To go to your brother.''

He did have a point, Dominie thought uncomfortably, though she wasn't quite ready to admit it. "That was different, Jared. I was afraid you'd try to stop me. And anyway, I left you a note.''

"Yes," he said wryly, "and a bundle of gold coins which you'd already thrown in my face once. You can imagine how that made me feel! At least I sent Alex to make sure you were properly informed. And to see that you were taken care of . . . or I tried to. I seem to have made a mess of that.''

"It wasn't just your leaving without saying good-bye," she went on, feeling suddenly troubled again. She hated the way things kept coming between them, but if they didn't start talking to each other now, when were they ever going to? "I kept having this awful feeling you're holding something back. There was so much I didn't know about you . . . Why didn't you tell me about that woman, Jared? Mei-ling?''

"Ah," he said softly, "Cammie the cat strikes again. No, that's not fair. This isn't Camilla's fault. It's mine. There just never seemed to be a right time—we *were* quite frequently occupied with much more interesting things, my pretty temptress. Though I did mention that there had been one serious relationship in my life. I just didn't happen to mention the lady's name. Or," he added, studying her intently, "the fact that she was Chinese.''

She did not seem to flinch. She was looking him directly, very probingly, in the eye.

"Or the fact that she bore you two sons."

Jared got up and went across the room toward the window that was now bathed in deep warm light. The afternoon had latened. The sun was nearly down, and the glassy surface of the water shimmered like molten gold.

"I did you an injustice," he said at last. "I was afraid you would mind that their skin is more the color of their mother's than mine. There is, even here, a certain stigma. I wasn't planning on keeping you in the dark forever, incidentally." He was looking back at her again. "I realized, that last night when we were walking up the path to the ball, that I had let it go too long, and I thought: Tomorrow I'll tell her. Perhaps she'll want to go there with me. To Macao. Perhaps we might find that priest. But tomorrow never came."

He was watching her closely, but her face was half turned away, and he couldn't tell what she was thinking. For one brief agonizing second he was afraid she was not going to be able to forgive him, and God help him, he couldn't blame her.

"Dominie . . ."

Then she was turning back, and he saw that her eyes were full of tears again. And suddenly he knew that Meiling had been forgotten and there was something more.

"I needed you so much, Jared," she said. "I was all alone . . . and it was so awful. I *needed* you."

He was beside her in an instant, one knee on the narrow settee, drawing her up to him. "What, Dominie? What is it, love?"

"Oh, Jared . . . my brother's dead. That boy, Tien, came all the way to tell me. He brought Denis' clothes. The things he was wearing when they . . . they strangled him."

"Oh, God."

All he could do was close his arms around her, holding her now, as he should have held her then. Cursing himself for not having been there.

He couldn't have known. There was no way he could have guessed that they would send someone to notify her directly. But he *had* known how vulnerable she was just then. He should have been there for her.

She had needed him, she said—she had needed him so much. And where had he been? Out chasing his own personal demons!

"I'm sorry, love," he said again. "I am so, so sorry." He took a handkerchief out of his pocket and handed it to her, a blasted ineffectual gesture, but he couldn't think of anything else. "I could tell you I was a damned fool, but I've been telling myself that for days. And if it isn't any comfort to me, I can't imagine it will comfort you."

"It all happened the same day." She had taken the handkerchief, but she was just holding it in her hands, making no effort even to dab at her cheeks. "I had just heard about Denis when he—Honoré—found me. He'd never have been able to take me like that if I'd had my wits about me. I was just so shocked, I didn't realize what was happening. Then Chan came—" She stopped abruptly, remembering. "He was shot, Jared! He was trying to protect me, and Honoré shot him!"

"He's fine, love. It wasn't much of a wound, and Rachel dressed it for him. She's an excellent nurse. He came to tell me himself, up the China coast. Immediately. That's how I managed to catch the *Scarlet* before she could dock in Lahaina."

"Honoré was crazy, Jared. I don't know what happened to him. He was just . . . crazy! It was like I wasn't a person anymore, but some . . . some *thing* he had to possess. And he didn't care what he had to do to get me!"

A shudder ran through her. Jared felt his whole body turn to ice. He had been so sure she was all right. She looked all right, and she hadn't said anything . . .

"If he hurt you, by God, I swear I'll kill him! If he abused you in any—"

"No . . . no." Now it was she who took his hand, comforting him. "He tried to . . . to . . . well, he tried. But I hurt him more than he hurt me. It's going to be a long time before he uses that part of his body again. Where I kicked him. And it will probably take his broken ribs a while to heal. I hit him with the chamber pot."

"You hit him with . . . the chamber pot?" He could only stare at her for a moment, not sure whether to be amused or aghast. She was gazing at him so earnestly. Then her eyes were sparkling, her natural high spirits coming back, and he dared to roar with laughter. "By God, I wouldn't like to be the man who tried to force his attentions on you! The first one you threw up all over. This one you beat to a bloody pulp. With a *chamber pot*."

"It was the only thing handy." The corners of her mouth were turning up, all the sadness and horror gone, at least for now. And when it came back, Jared reminded himself, he would be there to comfort her. "And I didn't beat him to a bloody pulp. There was no blood at all, actually. Just a few living bruises . . . though I suppose he'll be walking kind of funny for a while."

She was laughing now, a light, childlike sound that did his heart good to hear. Damn him for twice the fool if he ever let her down again!

"What's this, heartless wench? Emasculating the wretch is one thing. He deserved all of that and more. But to enjoy it so much?"

She shook her head. "I didn't emasculate him. Only temporarily . . . and I was just imagining the expression on Captain Newcombe's face when you rammed his ship broadside and came flying onto the deck. You're lucky he didn't shoot you for a pirate. I heard the men say you weren't showing your colors."

"We'd had trouble with the flag line. We were just seeing to it when the lookout spotted the *Scarlet* in the distance. And Newcombe's one of the best captains I know. He runs a tight ship. He wouldn't let any of his men fire without provocation."

Without provocation? "No flags flying, no signals or 'ahoys'—you just pull alongside and get out the grappling hooks? Some men might consider that 'provocation.' "

"Not Newcombe. He knows the Dawns inside out and upside down. He would have recognized the ship the minute he picked it up in his glass. And as I happened to be standing forward, he would have known who the captain was too. What *I* liked was the look on his face when you came up and flung yourself at me. I take it you hadn't told him about us."

"I was afraid to." She was snuggling in his arms, feeling safe at last. It was beginning to occur to her that he hadn't kissed her for several minutes at least, and her mouth was definitely missing him. "He knew there was *someone*, but I didn't dare name names. You seem to have quite a reputation, Jared. I figured if I told him I expected to marry you, he would think I was some deluded little ninny.''

He was smiling. ''I doubt it. Newcombe is a very clever man. I suspect he knew I was susceptible . . . and exactly what kind of woman it would take to entice me. But I understand your dilemma.'' He could feel the change in her body, the way she was molding it supply against his, and everything in him ached to respond. He didn't think he had ever wanted her so much . . . or wanted so much to show some restraint.

''Did I tell you, love,'' he said lightly, ''that's the ugliest dress I've ever seen?''

Dominie looked down, startled, then began to giggle. She was wearing the grayish-green outfit, with a dark red ruffle, of course, and little frills around the neck and bodice that made it especially unbecoming. ''You should see the other one! Captain Newcombe gave me two of his wife's dresses since the outfit I had on was rather unsuitable. I suppose I ought to be grateful.''

''Marjorie Newcombe is one of the finest women I know,'' Jared agreed, ''but she's never been known as a dapper dresser. However, as you said, gratitude is in order. I'll see that she has a dozen new ones to make up for her loss. No, I'll see that she has something for her children or her house. She'd like that better. In the meantime, I had your clothing put on board before we left Hong Kong. It's in the captain's cabin. You might like to change.''

She was smiling slowly, a very sure, beguilingly sensual look coming over her face. A look he had never quite seen before.

''I . . . might,'' she said softly.

''I vote for the red dress. The one you were wearing the night we . . . met. Without that little bit of froth in the neck.''

''You might want to help me change.''

As he stood there staring at her, so warm and beautiful and utterly feminine, Jared could feel his resolve weakening. It would be so easy just to take her into the other room. The bed was waiting . . . their bodies were ready for each other . . .

But there was something else that had to be settled first.

"Not this time, love," he said, and saw the look turn questioning and just a little frightened.

"You don't . . . *want* to be with me?"

" 'Want' has nothing to do with it. I wanted you the minute I swung down on that deck and grabbed you in my arms. You're lucky I didn't do something indecent right then and there. But there's more than wanting involved here. I made you a promise once, and I'm not going to be able to keep it."

Dominie felt her heart stop beating. She had been so certain everything was right between them again. The way he had acted . . . the things he had said . . .

Then she looked at his eyes and saw that they were smiling. And his mouth was smiling too.

"What promise was that?"

"I promised I'd wait patiently until we could find a priest to marry us. But I'm not a patient man, love. I want you now. Tonight. We'll have a religious service later, if you still want it—that much of the promise I *can* keep—but we're going to be on the high seas for a few hours yet. And all you need to get married at sea is a ship's captain."

Dominie laughed softly and very happily. It was, in fact, exactly what she had been thinking for some time now, though she didn't mind letting him believe the idea was all his own.

"There's only one problem. You're the captain of this ship. Can a captain marry himself?"

"Actually, I turned command over to Angus Dougal when I boarded the *Scarlet,* so we'll have someone to perform the rite after all. And much as I'm looking forward to the honeymoon, my darling, I think it ought to take place *after* the ceremony. I asked you once before to be my wife, and you said you would be proud. Considering all that's transpired in the meantime, I'd be content with a 'pleased' now."

Dominie was conscious of him next to her. Very close, but not touching, and suddenly she didn't want to reach out and touch him either. The next time their hands met would be as they exchanged their vows.

"Pleased and proud both," she said. "If you would be pleased and proud to marry me."

"More than pleased . . . and more than proud. You are my heart and soul, and I want you . . ." He paused, his lips twisting wryly. "*I* want to belong to *you* officially."

# A New Dawn

## 31

THEY WERE MARRIED an hour later in a quiet ceremony in the small sitting room of the owner's suite, Dominie in the red dress Jared had requested, though with the white lace fichu tucked modestly into her neck. She had had some qualms about wearing scarlet for her wedding, but it was a pretty gown and becoming, and the color glowed rich and ruby-deep in the light of candles that had been set around the room to give it a romantic aura.

Angus Dougal read the words of the ritual slowly and painstakingly out of a large black book, his Scottish accent dour but his tone mellifluous and laced with considerable pride. He had been with Barron Shipping since he was barely more than a boy himself, and each of the Barron lads had passed at one time or another through his keeping. Each had known his kindness and his generosity—and, on occasion, his sharp tongue—and it gave him great pleasure to officiate at such an important milestone in the life of one of them. Especially since, in a manner of speaking, he was the one who had brought them together.

The honeymoon began where their love had blossomed a few short months before, in the hard, narrow bunk in the captain's cabin. It was both a reunion and a beginning as they shared old feelings, old passions, and explored the new tenderness that came from knowing that they did at last truly "belong" to each other.

The winds were brisk, and the *Shadow Dawn* came within sight of the Hawaiian shore just before daybreak. Jared, sensing the change in the ship's rhythm—and ever the captain, no matter what his official status—grew visibly restless, though he made an effort to hide his feelings; and Dominie, knowing she would never get the smell of salt out of an old seaman's nostrils, suggested they go up on deck and watch the approach. Their tender lovemaking would resume soon enough anyway, if she knew this new husband of hers and his nearly insatiable appetite. Besides, she was eager herself for a first glimpse of this new land she had not yet seen.

Jared had told her a little about it during brief respites in their night together. It was almost as beautiful as their own special island, he had said. Bigger, of course, with more people on it, but if you headed north from the town of Lahaina, you could walk for hours and hours along a broad sandy beach with absolutely no one on it.

"I think I'm going to like this new island," she said as she stood at the rail, the breeze blowing her long loose hair back from her face. She was wearing the red dress again, no fichu this time, but a colorful Chinese shawl was draped around her shoulders and strategically covered her front.

"It's not new," he said, smiling over at her. "It's very old, in fact . . . and very beautiful. At least it was before the whalers and merchants and tavern keepers set up their raucous waterfront town and the missionaries put Mother Hubbard outfits on the ladies, as if God and nature are somehow incompatible. I hope we won't spoil it too much."

Dominie smiled back, but she sensed she had lost him for the moment. His eyes were drifting toward the horizon. He seemed to be staring beyond the almost phosphorescent green-white of their wake at things she could not see.

"You're looking for the *China Dawn*," she accused him softly. "You are hoping to see great white billows of canvas, swollen in the wind, and the red-and-white Barron flag symbolizing the rising of dawn. You want Matthew to have rescued her already and be sailing toward us even now."

"You know me very well." He put an arm around her waist and drew her close, and Dominie was content to stare with him out over the ocean. The sun was beginning to rise across the bow of the ship, staining the water a deep luminous red, like old glass that had mellowed but not lost its luster. "*Too* well. But this time you're wrong. Matthew will either get the *China* back, or he won't. And if he doesn't . . . well, we'll build another. It's just wood and brass and canvas and rope.''

*It?* Not she? Dominie turned to look at him with quizzically raised brows. "Wood and brass and canvas . . . and *rope?*"

"I admit the expression isn't original, but it's apt. The *China Dawn* is only a ship after all, and ships are replaceable. It's time I let Matthew make his own decisions and learn from his own mistakes. I've spent so much time trying to make a man out of him, I forgot that only Matthew can do that himself. Or fail to do it. I don't pretend I'll be quite so calm in two or three weeks when we can reasonably expect to get word. You'll probably find me on the waterfront quite frequently pacing back and forth. But not because I'm worried about the ship. Because I care about Matt. I don't want him to fail.''

Dominie nestled closer in his arms, trying to figure out if this was really the same Jared Barron she had come to know and love, and deciding that miraculously it was.

"If you weren't imagining the *China* skimming across the Pacific, then what were you seeing? Off there in the distance?''

"All the places we've been, love. The harbor in Ceylon. Do you remember the color of the water? And the lady in the prim black-and-white outfit with the wild, lusty eyes? . . . The coast of Vietnam, the ship battered in the storm—and one very arrogant captain who thought he could go down and tell a certain young mademoiselle to get the hell out of his cabin! . . . Lush green forests and rice paddies—and tanned legs sticking out from under a gold tunic, which made it very hard to think about what we were supposed to be doing. . . . My beautiful, beautiful Eve in her long red hair in a paradise that has never been before and will never be again. . . . So many memories . . .''

So many memories, Dominie thought, and just for an instant, it was another dawn. Red like this one, and as glorious. The air was warm and sultry, and Jared's arm was around her waist . . . and she was turning to look at her brother one last time.

*My love will always be with you, Dominie.*

It had made her a little sad, the night before, when she had gone through her things in the captain's cabin and seen that his effects were not there. She had not really expected to find them. The servants would have thought they were rags and thrown them away. And, in a way, she knew that was right.

Denis would not have wanted his clothes to be worshiped. He would have hated the notoriety, the idolization from people who had no idea what he was really like, the canonization that would surely have followed. Saint Denis of Vietnam—or even the Blessed Denis. How he would have disliked that! And if some callow youth might have been drawn to the priesthood by gaping at the ghoulish remnants of his death . . . well, he would probably have been drawn anyway.

Denis would have been prouder to know that he had touched a noble young man like Le Van Duong. Or the boy Tien, who was the future of his country. It was through them and their kind that his spirit would live. Forever.

"I wonder what it will be like," she said softly. "Vietnam. In a decade, or a generation. I wonder if we will ever be able to go there again. If our friends will be all right. Duong and his family. The people who took us in along the way."

"Duong will be fine. He's a survivor. Tien too . . . though I suspect that boy is going to cause his rulers a great deal of trouble." He tightened his arm, pulling her even closer. "You're missing him, aren't you?"

There was no question who the *him* was.

"No," she said truthfully. "It hurts sometimes when I think of him. A part of me will always feel sad that he's gone . . . but I can understand and accept. And move on. There's a whole new life out there, just waiting—so full of exciting new possibilities. That's the difference between you and me, love. You look across the ocean and it reminds you of the past. I am seeing the future."

He laughed gently. "And what is this future you see on the waves?"

"I see the *China Dawn,* whole and safe and very arrogant, like all the Barron ships, flying the red-and-white flag until she's so old she looks funny and antique and she's even slower than the tugboats. I see Matthew and Rachel, and Alex and whatever lady he chooses, and Dominie and Jared, with the children and grandchildren all around, talking about the days when they were young and what is was like that time in Hong Kong when Matthew 'lost' the *China*. I see a city called Boston, and I wonder what it's like when the fog is so thick you can almost hear the silence, and how it feels to have snow all the way up to your waist.''

Jared was watching her, fascinated at the way she always seemed to find some new enthusiasm for everything, and feeling guilty because he knew he had forced at least part of it on her.

''I've been thinking,'' he said clumsily. ''If Boston is too cold for you, if you don't like it . . .''

''Of course I'll like it.'' Dominie recognized the sacrifice he was about to offer, and she was almost as amused as touched. The sky was so bright now, it almost seemed to be on fire. Breathtaking and beautiful. ''How could I not like it if we're there together? Besides, it's a new city, Jared. I've never even seen it! That's what I love about looking to the future. It's so exciting! There are wonderful new things everywhere if you only let yourself look at them.''

Yes, he thought, coaxing her head back on his shoulder. There were wonderful new things . . . and wonderful old ones too, and he had the best of both. The shore was so close now, he could see the buildings along the waterfront. The sun behind was a blaze of color, warm and vibrant, touching the earth with promises of new beginnings, new hopes. The future *was* exciting. And he was glad he was going to share it with her.

# There's an epidemic with 27 million victims. And no visible symptoms.

It's an epidemic of people who can't read.

Believe it or not, 27 million Americans are functionally illiterate, about one adult in five.

The solution to this problem is you... when you join the fight against illiteracy. So call the Coalition for Literacy at toll-free **1-800-228-8813** and volunteer.

## Volunteer Against Illiteracy. The only degree you need is a degree of caring.